Graham Lang was born in Bulawayo, Zimbabwe. He is the author of *Clouds Like Black Dogs* and *Place of Birth*, which was longlisted for the *Sunday Times* Prize, South Africa's premier literary award. An accomplished artist, he has exhibited widely and taught art in both Australia and South Africa. Graham has lived in Australia since 1990.

www.grahamlang-author.com

GRAHAM LANG

LETTAH'S GIFT

UQP

First published 2011 by University of Queensland Press
PO Box 6042, St Lucia, Queensland 4067 Australia

www.uqp.com.au

Cover design by Nada Backovic Designs
Cover illustrations by Friedrich von Hörsten/Alamy and iStockphoto
Typeset in 12.5/16 pt Spectrum MT Regular by Post Pre-press Group, Brisbane
Printed in Australia by McPherson's Printing Group

Twenty-three words from *Memories of My Melancholy Whores*
by Gabriel Garcia Márquez, published by Jonathan Cape.
Reprinted by permission of The Random House Group Ltd.

National Library of Australia Cataloguing-in-Publication Data
Lettah's Gift / Graham Lang
ISBN: 9780702238994 (pbk)
            9780702246562 (epub)
            9780702246579 (kindle)
            9780702246555 (pdf)

University of Queensland Press uses papers that are natural, renewable
and recyclable products made from wood grown in sustainable
forests. The logging and manufacturing processes conform to
the environmental regulations of the country of origin.

For Allen, Nabeel and Shaynne

My world nothing but this. Wrapped in a blanket on her back, my head pressed against her soft breathing bulk. Her slow, rolling gait. Her soulful voice. Songs sweet and lilting. Strange clicks of her tongue as she sings of a tree called uxhakhuxhaku. The way she sings its name is the way it sounds to eat its fruit. Feeling her move, taking me with her. Nothing but this. Nothing but this and her voice to fill the world.

I

On the face of it, not much has changed. The same small mining town straddling the railway line halfway between Harare and Bulawayo. A scabrous cluster of shops and houses huddled together against the encroaching bush, red roofs baking under the sun, walls the colour of old bone. The reek of iron and melting bitumen. Thirsty jacaranda trees with white-painted trunks lining the roads. Everything covered with a fine layer of dust whipped up by passing traffic. People wander about the streets. Drifting like leaves, like chaff. Serenaded by the endless tenor of insects.

Turning off the main road, I head towards a ridge of hills on Kwekwe's northern outskirts, passing forgotten places, suddenly familiar: the post office with its squat clock tower, the Phoenix Hotel, rows of shabby storefronts with stepped gables and awnings. I'm surprised by the accuracy of my memory, that it guides me so well. I was a boy when my family left this place, the first of many moves. After all this time there's a strange nostalgia in coming back to this small oasis of the past — an awakening of sorts, but no sense of belonging. I know that nothing is as it was. This is not the place of my boyhood. Everything has changed. Even Kwekwe's name, derived from the sound of croaking frogs, is different. The town I knew was spelled Que Que. The country I knew — Rhodesia — is not this country. Rhodesia had a war and became Zimbabwe. Another place.

Approaching a sports field on the left, I pull over and climb out

3

of the car. The field is empty, sun scorched; yellow grass and thorns survive in patches, stark against the bare ground. Dusty trees and a row of corrugated iron huts along the far periphery, shimmering in the heat. A cloudless sky. The air filled with the whirr of insects and the chatter of people teeming along the road.

I lean on the roof of the car and aim my camera at the field. The light has a glittering, metallic quality; I'm facing into the sun and must shield the lens with my hand. I take just one photograph before a group of men passing by interrupts my view. Their loud talk ceases abruptly as they walk past. They glance at me with strange expressions. Angry, unintelligible mutterings in Shona. A man wearing the frayed remains of a peaked khaki cap peers into the camera lens. Brandishing a knobkerrie, eyes wide beneath the black plastic visor of his cap, he feints at me, grunting, 'Heeyah!' I lower the camera, smiling uneasily. The man walks on, mouthing indignant words, slapping the ball of the club against his palm. I'm puzzled, taken aback. Why are these men angry? What does the sight of a lone white man with a camera evoke? I carry with me media images of beaten people. Dazed stares from swollen faces. A man with his back pocked with cigarette burns.

I climb back into the car and drive away.

I should take more care. This is not the place to be giving wrong signals. There is no ulterior motive for my being here, other than to deliver a gift of money — a mission that compels me to seek out the places of my childhood.

This talk of belonging. I'm an Australian of African origin — white colonial African, that is. But I'd be quite happy to declare myself Australian and be done with it. I don't pine for the past, for a mother country. The umbilical cord that tied me to Africa was cut long ago. My recollection of my Rhodesian childhood is mostly vague and fragmentary, bits and pieces that somehow comprise a whole, of sorts. Of my time in Que Que, there is no clear sequence; memories emerge and retreat, arbitrarily, as though through a dense mist. Some, very few, have an almost luminous clarity. Like shooting stars they burst into my mind, burn brightly for a few seconds, then fade. Among the most persistent of these is being carried on Lettah's back. Her slow, rolling gait – the texture of her neck, the mournful lilt of her singing. Her raw soap smell. I like to believe that what I remember is true, I take comfort in it, yet also suspect that such old memories often rely more on the workings of my imagination than fact.

Lettah is the reason I'm here. She is the one to whom the money must be given, on behalf of my mother. A complex tale of post-colonial guilt. By finding her, by delivering the gift, I will mend the past and in the process rise from my rut of failure. Such was my mother's reasoning. I pass ragged processions heading to and from town – women balancing absurdly heavy burdens on their heads; men sporting axes and knobkerries as Englishmen might sport brollies. Again I wonder what prompted the anger from those men at the sports field. My motive was entirely innocent. I stopped to photograph the sports field because of something I'd suddenly remembered.

Every year the Boswell Wilkie Circus came to Que Que. It would appear miraculously on that same sports field for a few days, and then just as suddenly it would be gone. I remember the spectacle of the night-time shows: the laager of trailers and caravans pulsing with coloured lights, the huge glowing tent beneath the starry sky. Jammed with my brother between our parents on the packed stands. The smell of sawdust and canvas. Howls of laughter at the clowns' antics. Tatty-looking lions jumping through flaming hoops. The crack of the lion tamer's whip. Contortionists and acrobats in glittering costumes. Drum rolls before amazing feats. The human cannonball. He wore a silver helmet and an electric blue suit with a yellow lightning bolt across his chest. The cannon made a sharp bang and he shot out across the arena into a net. We heard later that he missed the net in Bulawayo and was killed. One year we saw the Strongest Man in the World lift a horse clean off the ground. He was a burly white man who sported a leopard skin costume and Brylcreemed hair with

5

a cowlick, like Elvis Presley. He straddled two twenty-foot vertical ladders and climbed up, one rung at a time, with the horse hanging from a harness between his legs like a gigantic, whinnying scrotum. I'm convinced this started my older brother, Max, on his life-long quest for superhuman strength.

We lived on an eleven-acre smallholding in an area called Hillendale, just outside Que Que. The road to Hillendale went past the sports field. When the circus was there we could see the animals out on the field during the day. There were elephants, palomino horses and Shetland ponies. Once there was a bear shackled to an iron stake in the hot sun. Lions and tigers paced back and forth in trailer cages that stank of their excrement. Max and I would pester our mother, Lydia, to stop when she was driving past, and one day she did. Max was sitting in the front of our green Opel station wagon with her. I was in the back. A loaf of bread, some carrots and a newspaper Lydia had just bought at the shops were on the front seat between her and Max.

She parked the car near where the elephants were hobbled together in twos in the far corner of the field. It was hot and the car's windows were wound down. Benny King's 'Spanish Harlem' was playing on the radio. Lydia explained that they were Indian elephants because of their smaller ears. The elephants, a dozen or so, observed us curiously and then came sauntering up and surrounded the car. Lydia commenced to wax lyrical about what sweet, gentle animals they were, compared to their more savage African cousins who, she said, could *never* be tamed. At that point, a jumble of bristly trunks burst through the windows from all sides, grabbing at things. The bread, carrots and newspaper vanished before our eyes. The little Rhodesian flag I'd been waving out the window disappeared into a gaping mouth, dowel rod and all. Max and I thought it was all great fun. We liked the feel of the bristly trunks. But then Lydia, perhaps imagining her boys or even her large self disappearing into those gaping mouths, lost her nerve and began to shriek. Her fear was contagious; Max and I joined in with ear-splitting screams, although later on Max would deny any part in it.

Spurred on by this commotion, the stupid beasts began to bump the car with their foreheads and rumps until it was almost rocking off its wheels. Our screams rose to a crescendo. At no time did Lydia do the sensible thing and just turn on the engine and drive away. She just put her head back and shrieked as the car rocked. Benny King sang away, unperturbed.

Help finally arrived in the diminutive form of Ticky the clown. About my height at the time, give or take. He ran up, slashing at the air with the lion tamer's whip, mouthing words Max and I had never heard before, and which my mother forbade us ever to repeat. He was wearing little rugby shorts and a grubby vest. He didn't have any paint on his face and had a half-smoked cigarette clamped in one corner of his mouth. The elephants dispersed, trumpeting rudely.

Ticky apologised profusely. Clasping her bosom, Lydia looked as though she was about to have a heart attack. Her pretty, brooding face was flushed, beads of sweat had formed above her upper lip. She tried to say something but her eyes closed and her jaw dropped – later we got used to these mild bouts of cataplexy. She started the car and stalled as she took off because her legs were shaking so much. Finally we got going. It took us a little while to regain our composure. I wondered why it was Ticky who came to save us. What was the Strongest Man in the World doing? Pretty poor show on his part, it seemed.

I leave town down a long straight road through thickening bush, past ramshackle dwellings strewn about like meteor debris. A widow bird with long black tail feathers flies a bobbing course beside the car for a while, before veering off. It surprises me that some long-forgotten names of African birds and trees are suddenly poised for expression on my tongue. A lost language suddenly remembered. My father was a botanist and amateur ornithologist, driven to giving things their correct name. A smidgen of his knowledge must have rubbed off, I guess.

I ascend the ridge of hills that guided me through Kwekwe to

Hillendale. Just over the crest, on the left, is Sunnyside, my first home. The entrance is how I remember it: a stony road winding through tall stands of msasa and mukwa trees. Ahead stands the house built of red jasper stone, a corrugated iron garage, some sheds and a chicken run. Down a path through the bush is a compound consisting of a few rooms in a single block – the old servants' quarters. Despite its original acreage it was never, by any stretch of the imagination, a grand property. The grounds still consist mostly of undeveloped bush. Even when my parents owned it, it had a slightly derelict air. Like so much about Rhodesia, it was imbued with a doomed potential. The grounds around the house were partially landscaped into a garden of stone-walled terraces and Christ-thorn hedges. There was a summerhouse, an obelisk-like fountain on the front lawn and a large aviary in which my mother used to keep canaries and budgies. A place sadly falling short of its English pretensions, constantly battling to keep the heathen bush at bay.

The house is now completely dilapidated. The corrugated iron roof sags and is rusted through in places, broken windows are patched with cardboard, a door hangs askew. Detritus lies everywhere, mostly old car parts, within the perimeter of a high security fence. The backyard is strewn with old cars, hulks in various stages of disembowelment. Outside the fence, the stone terraces have been overwhelmed by bush. The summerhouse stands in ruin, just a few rotting wooden rafters left precariously on the stone pillars enmeshed in bougainvillea creepers. A small crop of withered maize now occupies what used to be the front lawn.

A woman is sweeping the back porch outside the former kitchen with a straw broom. Some children appear in the doorway behind her, alerted by the sound of my car. There are two men working on a battered pick-up in the backyard. They peer out from under the bonnet as I pull up at the locked gate. One of them, a thin young man in ragged blue overalls comes over to the gate. I get out of the car to greet him. We shake hands through the gate. The man has a nervous air; when he is not speaking his jaws clench incessantly. I explain that the house was once my family's home.

The man looks at me blankly. 'Who are you?'

'Frank Cole. I lived here long ago. In the sixties.'

The man gives a short laugh and shakes his head. 'I wasn't even born then.' He turns and calls across in Shona to his companion still working under the pick-up's bonnet. The other man, older, with grey hair, straightens up. He looks at the sky pensively and shakes his head.

'My father doesn't remember any Coles,' the man says.

I shrug. 'We were only here a few years.'

I ask to take a few photographs of the property. To show my family in Australia, I explain. The man inspects me carefully. He glances at my hire car, a Nissan with Harare numberplates. He sniffs the air and clenches his jaws.

'Your father was owner here?'

'Yes, he owned this house.'

'But now you are from Australia?'

'Yes.'

The man nods slowly, eyeing the camera around my neck. The older man comes sauntering up to the gate. The kids who had been watching from the house run across the yard, a naked toddler bringing up the rear. They lean against the fence, poking their fingers through the wire, staring at me silently. Thin-legged, pot-bellied, a sheen of snot under their noses. The two men converse in Shona. Of Zimbabwe's two native languages – Shona and IsiNdebele – I know only a smattering of the latter, courtesy of being half-mothered by Lettah.

'You can pay for photographs?' the older man asks.

'How much?'

The two men deliberate. A sum is decided. When I left Rhodesia you could buy ten thousand houses for what these men are asking for; now it's barely enough for a loaf of bread. I go back to the car and rummage in the boot, returning with a few 'bricks' – the local term for the wads of banknotes necessary for simple transactions. The children watch, wide-eyed, as I count the money; the younger man unlocks the gate and lets me inside.

I walk slowly around the house, taking photographs. I'd hoped to be left alone, to be able to quietly contemplate this moment where I tread again the soil that I once felt under small bare feet. But other small bare feet have dominion of this ground now. The children, who seem to have grown in number, follow me around like little fish behind a diver, scattering when I turn around. A few have found their voices; they ask, please, sir, give me money. I part with the loose change in my pocket – the few banknotes left over from paying the men. The begging becomes more persistent, almost hostile. I try to make light of it, to joke with them. I pull out my pockets. 'Look – all gone,' I say. The two men are watching me from the veranda at the front of the house. They are joined by three women. I feel uneasy with their eyes on me. I take a final shot of the old fountain poking surreally out from the miserable maize crop. Then I nod and wave at the men on the veranda.

As I make my way back to the car, the kids clamour around me. I'm almost overwhelmed as I near the gate. Tiny arms grasp at me, cling to me, a shrill chorus of voices beseeches me. I panic and run the last few metres. There is a wild frenzy as the kids scramble after me. The naked toddler is bumped over; he starts bawling. Breathing heavily, I slam the gate closed behind me, filled with self-loathing at having created such a wretched scene.

On my way back to town I turn into the overgrown driveway of another house. Brak Malan's place. Once we were like brothers, inseparable. We roamed the bush around Que Que, acting out heroic fantasies spawned by the westerns and war movies we saw at the local bioscope. Masters of our domain. I walk around the Malans' house, also derelict. The roof is gone, just weathered brick walls remain, festooned with cacti and creepers. A dense grove of mukwa trees has encroached upon the house from the property's rear boundary. Another victory for the unruly bush.

Back in Kwekwe I stop for a Coke at a grocery store in the main street. Since I don't have an empty bottle to exchange, I'm asked to drink it on the premises – Zimbabwe has a bottle shortage. I stand next to the counter while the shopkeeper, an old Indian with a white beard, cuts up some meat on a wooden block. On the wall above his head is a large framed photograph of Robert Mugabe. The same dour visage that, by law, presides in every public building or business premises in Zimbabwe. Mugabe's face seems made up of squares. A square skull, square jaw, square glasses, even a square sliver of a moustache nestling in the philtrum under his nose. He gleams like a block of black granite hewn by a totalitarian sculptor. This analogy surprises me. He's never impressed me before as someone to whom the word 'solid' might apply – I've always seen Mugabe as an absurd caricature, all head and no body, a dainty puppet. Laughable for his pompous voice and convoluted parodies of etiquette. But gazing into his blank eyes behind the big square glasses, I realise there must be precious little about him to laugh about for Zimbabweans. He *is* solid. Hard.

The store is empty of people. Only a few items remain on the shelves. Some spices, a few tins of condensed milk, half a dozen bags of mielie meal. A single packet of Lobels biscuits. Some straw brooms, sisal rope, paraffin. I finish the drink and push the empty bottle across the counter.

'How's business these days?' I ask the shopkeeper.

It's a question that needs no reply. The shopkeeper gestures at the sparse shelves with his knife, gives a small grunt, and continues cutting the meat.

'In the old days this used to be a cycle shop,' I say. 'Phoenix Cycles.'

The old man pauses. He rests a gnarled hand on the haunch of meat. 'I remember. Mr Malan owned it. It's been sold twice since he left.'

'My family were friends of the Malans. We lost touch with them years ago. Do you know where they've gone?'

The old man rubs his beard with the back of his hand. 'I can't say for sure. I think Mr and Mrs Malan went down south. After the war.'

'I was hoping to find Brak Malan. Their son.'

'The wild one.' The old man taps his temple with his finger. 'Not right in the head. Always in trouble. The last I heard he was working on the Baldwin farm.'

'Vic Baldwin?'

'Yes. But that farm has been occupied by war veterans. Mr Baldwin moved to Bulawayo. What has happened to your friend, I have no idea. I'm sorry, that's all I can tell you.'

I return to the car. A beggar emerges from the shade of a nearby tree and quickly relieves me of the change I got from the shopkeeper. Driving out of town, I wonder if it's possible to live here without a heart hardened to poverty.

Just beyond the Kwekwe River I'm waved down at a police road-block. Officers in blue combat fatigues carrying rifles ask the purpose of my visit. They are mildly intrigued by my claim to be a tourist, but wave me through – tourists are rare birds these days, it seems. I drive on towards Bulawayo. I turn on the radio and twist the station dial, but find only static. Finding out so little about the Malans is disappointing; I'd hoped Brak might still be around, but knew it was a long shot.

The last image I have of him is in a photograph which came with a letter – the last letter – he sent during the war, long after my family had left Rhodesia. It's not an easy image. Brak is standing with a group of soldiers in a bush clearing. Two helicopters wait in the background, their blades spinning, the air thick with dust. Beyond the helicopters are some big granite kopjes. Brak and the other men are laughing. They look like savages, like wild men – filthy and unkempt; sweat streaks their faces; one has a bleeding hand. Brak's pale blue eyes shine vacantly. He is wearing the non-restrictive gear that Rhodesian soldiers preferred – a short-sleeved camouflage shirt, shorts and running shoes, no socks. Ammunition pouches around his waist. No headgear. He leans on his rifle as casually as those cowboys and soldiers did in the movies we watched long ago. And there, poking into the picture in the background near one of the helicopters, are the sprawled-out legs of a corpse. No face, no body – just bloodstained khaki trousers and bare black feet.

What did Brak intend by sending that photograph? Was it to shock? Or did he not even notice the corpse in the background? Were corpses just part of the landscape, like rocks and trees? He never explained it in the letter.

II

The shock of being back is such that I'm not quite *here*. And yet the bush and open grasslands that flash by seem so utterly familiar it's as though my entire life away from Africa was lived in the blink of an eye. As my head gropes for terra firma, I feel her watching me. Lydia. The one who has brought me here to find Lettah.

I remember how they used to chat away in the kitchen at Sunnyside. Lydia, a farmer's daughter, spoke fluent IsiNdebele. Lettah was a rural Ndebele, raw and uneducated. A plump woman, always cheerful, given to bouts of infectious laughter. Listening to them prattling on in the kitchen, you'd have thought they were on equal terms – friends, even. They gossiped and laughed; carefree, unrestrained. Their relationship seemed devoid of the complex protocol that separated white women from their servants. They had much in common. Both had grown up on Whitestone, a fifteen-thousand-hectare farm near Fort Rixon owned by Lydia's parents, Cyril and Betty Metcalf. Lettah was the daughter of Whitestone's headman, Solomon Ndlovu. The farm was their common ground, the place where their different worlds intersected. They had known each other since childhood and their familiarity was such that they could tease one another about intimate things, such as their tendency to put on weight – for Lettah, an attribute of beauty; for Lydia, a curse.

But there was a line that Lettah could not cross. My mother was a complex, emotional woman, at the mercy of a heart that in an instant could melt like butter or turn to stone. Any familiarity between them was at her discretion. Perhaps Lettah enjoyed more privileges than most domestic servants, but in the end that's all she was — a black servant in colonial Rhodesia. She was secure as long as she knew her place.

And so it was during our time in Rhodesia. Lettah's happy presence. Part of the family, almost. She followed us when we moved to Salisbury and Bulawayo. The memory of her becomes slightly clearer in these other places. Her face acquires a sharper focus: beautiful almond eyes, like an Egyptian queen; the straight ridge of her nose, flared nostrils; her curling lips. Always neat and clean in her pale blue servant's uniform and headscarf. Always laughing. Her lilting songs as she went about washing and ironing clothes, making beds and cleaning the many rooms of the increasingly up-market homes we rented. She lived in the servants' quarters of these properties, the khaya — usually a bare unpainted room with an adjoining toilet and shower. The toilet was just a hole in the floor and smelled of bleach. The discrepancy in living conditions never struck me as odd. This is what Africans were used to, I was told. This was luxury for her. After all, had Lettah not come from a hut in the bush?

Then it all changed. The friendly chatter in the kitchen suddenly ceased. Lettah became reserved and tearful, subject to relentless reproach from Lydia. One day she was gone.

It was so unexpected even my father, Errol, was caught unawares. He had no idea what had caused the rift, and no say in the matter. Lydia would not brook any interference in domestic affairs, including the hiring and firing of servants. Max and I were heartbroken at Lettah's sudden absence. We missed her cheerful company, her infectious laughter. We were made suddenly aware of how closely we had bonded with her — it was no exaggeration to say she was a second mother to us. And we had no idea of the intractable politics lurking between whites and their servants, or of any line that could not be crossed — that *must* have been crossed. But if anyone mentioned the matter, Lydia would withdraw into a fortress of stubborn silence. Even when Max and I were grown up the issue remained out of bounds.

My father got a job with a fertiliser company in South Africa and we moved down to Pietermaritzburg. There was a new home, a new town, a new country. Lydia employed new servants. As I grew into my teens, Lettah began to fade from my memory. For a while we heard odd bits about her from my grandparents. We heard that she'd planned to marry, but a bad miscarriage had left her infertile and her suitor discarded her for someone else who could bear his offspring. Devastated, she had taken refuge back on Whitestone with her father, Solomon. Cyril and Betty took pity on her and employed her three days a week.

Max and I wrote to her but she was illiterate and could not respond, except through sparsely worded messages relayed through occasional letters from Cyril and Betty. *Lettah says it's good that you have a nice new home. She says work hard at school.* We soon grew bored with this second-hand contact and our letters petered out.

The war in Rhodesia erupted and quickly began to escalate. The news was full of grim stories of attacks on lonely farmsteads in the dead of night, of atrocities inflicted on defenceless innocents. Farmers we knew were killed. A boy Max knew in junior school died in a landmine explosion. Isolated farms like Whitestone were the sort of soft targets favoured by the guerrillas — terrorists in the eyes of Rhodesians — infiltrating from Mozambique and Zambia. Errol and Lydia thought it too risky to visit the farm so they paid for Cyril and Betty to come down to South Africa once a year, usually over Christmas.

Cyril and Betty doted on their daughter. Lydia's brother, Maxwell, was killed in North Africa in the Second World War. Since we were their only grandchildren, they also doted on Max and me. Each year we hired the same beachside cottage at Port Edward on the south coast for their visits. The old people would sit on the veranda all day gazing out at the Indian Ocean and listening to the waves breaking on the rocks close by. They never tired of the sight of all that water. An early riser, Cyril would get up before dawn, make himself a cup of coffee and go outside to watch the sunrise. Betty found him there one morning, dead from a heart attack. He was seated in his chair as though sound asleep. I remember Betty and Lydia's voices raised in alarm, their crying; my father steering me and Max away from the scene. Just a glimpse of the old man in his dressing-gown hunched forward in his chair, his back to us. A broken cup on the floor.

Lydia accompanied her mother back to Rhodesia. The funeral was held at the Daisyfield church near Shangani. Cyril was laid to rest in the graveyard near the church, next to his son, Maxwell. Betty had to sell up and move into a flat in Bulawayo. She had offered the farm to my parents, but Errol knew that to take on the debt-ridden place would be an uphill battle, especially with the war raging. Betty died two years later and was also buried in the cemetery at Daisyfield. Lydia organised the funeral. She said that Lettah attended with her father and some other workers from Whitestone. She didn't get the chance to talk to her, or so she said.

My thoughts are interrupted by a sudden realisation. I've been cross-ing the vast grassland plains near the town of Gweru. On both sides of the road fields of grass stretch to the horizons. Yet there are no cat-tle. The fields are empty, except for the odd squatter's kraal, three or four mud huts in each, amid meagre plots of dying maize.

Islands of poverty in seas of grass . . .

After Betty died we heard no more about Lettah. We got on with our new lives. We liked Pietermaritzburg. A nice, friendly town, far from the troubles in Rhodesia – a good place for Max and me to grow up in. Max started pushing weights in his adolescent years and quickly developed into a massive, acne-ridden slab of muscle. At Maritzburg College, he captained the First XV and was opening batsman for the First XI. He held the school record for discus throwing and shot-put. A ferocious water polo player, a deputy head prefect, a conscientious student with an aptitude for science and mathematics. In his spare time, he joined a canoeing club and each year competed in the singles of the Dusi Marathon, always finishing in the top twenty.

Unlike Max, I found it hard to embrace Maritzburg College's antiquated ethos, fastidiously modelled on British public schools of the Victorian era. Apathy and a fierce aversion to team sports ensured my permanent billing among the school's no-hopers. Athletically, I wasn't entirely without talent. Being of lanky build, I showed promise as a swimmer, but never reached my full potential due principally to a smoking habit I picked up at age fifteen. Academically, I inclined to the Arts. My best subject was English, for which I always received good marks. I read avidly and began to write short stories, rather slavishly in the style of Ernest Hemingway, which my English teachers praised inordinately, literary pretensions being something of a rarity among my sports-mad peers. I was vaguely interested in history and geography. The rest was a torment. I scraped through each year by the skin of my teeth. My father fumed at report cards that labelled me 'scatterbrained' and 'bone idle'. He despaired at my low marks; he castigated me for my laziness.

Lydia never closed ranks with him on this. She believed I would yet prove myself. She had faith that my creative bent would one day flower and dazzle everyone. As any psychologist knows, the belief of mothers in their sons often verges on the chronically delusional, yet I did vindicate her faith to some extent when I matriculated with a university pass.

After school Max did his compulsory national service in the Parabats, an elite parachute battalion based in Bloemfontein, where he attained the rank of second lieutenant. He emerged from the army with his mental faculties reasonably intact and immediately breezed through a BCom at the University of Natal. During this time he became a Springbok canoeist and won the Dusi Marathon twice. For some 'pocket money' he started making fibreglass canoes and surf skis. Much to his surprise, this backyard business suddenly burgeoned; soon he was renting a factory, employing people and exporting overseas. The Australian market proved particularly lucrative; Max established outlets in Perth and Sydney. In 1976, just when the townships in South Africa began to erupt, he moved to Australia permanently. He went with Errol and Lydia's blessing, though Lydia was depressed and tearful for months after.

Nothing elite about my national service. The plain old infantry battalion in Middelburg did its best to mould me into the killing machine it needed to defend South Africa, but ultimately decided it could function more efficiently if I was restricted to 'maintenance duties'. And so I whiled away my time painting the camp's diamond-mesh perimeter fences silver – a task I rather enjoyed, since it allowed my mind to wander.

After discharge, I began a BA at the University of Natal, majoring in English and History. For the first time in my life I was enthused by the prospect of study and achieved consistently high results. During this time, I began to write again. I had a short story included in an anthology of new writing published by the university, and several others found their way into minor literary journals. When I graduated with a Distinction in Modern English Literature I couldn't help noticing Lydia's *I-told-you-so* expression in the presence of Errol. Never suspecting, of course, that this would be the high point, my life's modest summit. Ahead, just the slow descent . . .

Because I had no idea what to do after graduating I reluctantly undertook a teaching diploma, at my father's urging. For two years I was a relief English teacher in various high schools around Pietermaritzburg. I liked teaching about as much as I liked being taught, which fell well short of painting diamond-mesh fences. A long period of inertia followed. I flitted between jobs. At twenty-seven I was still living with my parents. Then I received a letter from Max, extolling the virtues of Australia, urging me to emigrate. He had since married and had two children, a girl and boy. They lived in a big house in up-market Dalkeith. Max missed his family, but business was too good to think of returning to South Africa. His canoe and surf-ski enterprise had expanded into other products; he was making a killing manufacturing fibreglass guttering and fascia boards for the building industry. He hoped that by my leaving, Errol and Lydia would soon follow. If you come over, he wrote, the folks will be on the next plane, guaranteed.

I decided that greener fields lay in Australia. I talked it over with Errol and Lydia. They agreed the move would do me no harm, since my life seemed in limbo anyway. I applied to emigrate and was accepted on the basis of my teaching qualification.

And so I found myself in Perth. At first I stayed with Max and his Aussie wife, Michaela, in Dalkeith while looking for work. Admittedly, I might not have given the impression of looking very hard. I steadfastly refused to teach, yet nothing else seemed up to scratch. Max offered me a job as a floor manager in one of his factories; it took just one visit to the factory to realise that the smell of resin and the cacophony of sanding machines did not agree with me, so I declined. This irked Max no end. More than once he called me a bludger to my face.

I now had big brother glowering over my shoulder, not to mention that powerful telescope Lydia kept trained on me from across the Indian Ocean. The only way to get the two of them off my back was to compromise on the issue of teaching. I soon got a post at St Xavier's College, a Catholic high school in the northern suburb of Scarborough. I took out a loan and bought a small flat with a glimpse of the ocean not far from the school. And so I commenced a bland professional life teaching English to teenagers whose only purpose appeared to be to remind me of my own indolent adolescence. In fairness, I should say that I wasn't a bad teacher; I performed my duties with due diligence and even sporadic bursts of enthusiasm. And some of the brighter kids did provide a measure of satisfaction, but never enough to alter my view of teaching as a thankless and servile calling.

Outside the classroom, though, life was generally good. I liked Australia. I felt at home in my new country and barely missed Africa. Australia offered a safe future, along with social and political freedoms hitherto unknown to me. It seemed to cut people like me, whose minds wander, a bit of slack. I started writing again. Living on my own enabled me to establish a productive routine, notwith-standing weekends which were set aside for some serious sampling of Australia's beer and wine. Perth's sunny skies also rekindled in me a love for swimming. Each weekday I rose before dawn to put in at least two hours at the typewriter before heading off to school. After knocking off, I'd go down to Scarborough Beach and complete a two-kilometre surf swim, weather permitting. I even contemplated joining a lifesaving club, but my loathing of team culture quickly nipped that in the bud. I began a novel tentatively called *The Wastrel*, a meandering tale about a young South African migrant in Perth who wins the lotto and proceeds to squander the money through riotous living. It took me two years to finish. I began the slow death of send-ing samples to agents and publishers and having them returned. A sense of failure grew. Naiveté is perhaps my worst character defect. It took a while to twig that a book about a debauched white South African émigré might not be a sure-fire success at a time when people of conscience were sickened by the horrors of apartheid.

Contrary to Max's expectations, Errol and Lydia didn't immedi-ately follow me to Australia. Their move came ten years later, once Errol reached retirement age. They were installed in a granny flat Max had built especially, adjoining his house. They were happy to have their sons around them again. They were besotted by their grand-children and got on well with Michaela, a bubbly, gregarious soul. Naturally, they missed Africa but were never ones to mope around pining for the past. Recognising the pitfalls of nostalgia, they avoided expatriate cliques, occupying themselves with local church activities, gardening, playing bowls and watching the grandchildren grow up. Lydia liked a flutter on the horseraces now and then.

Fretting about me took up a fair bit of their time, I'm ashamed to say. Unable to find a publisher for my novel, I became mired in it. Its countless transformations produced a torrid mess of a book. The more time I invested in it — in the end a decade, at least — the more frightening was the prospect of failure. The long silences writ-ing demanded of me became increasingly debilitating. Inevitably there came that terrible moment where I knew, unequivocally, it was hopeless. I experienced a mental breakdown. Not the wild hysterical type; just a slow slide into despair. I was finished, washed up. A writer needs to be read for the demands of his craft to find full purpose. I could no longer face the silences. And the prospect of teaching for the rest of my life was too much to bear.

The upshot was that at the age of forty I resigned my job at St Xavier's and became a bus driver, ferrying tourists around Rottnest Island. My mother's horrified expression remains forever etched in my memory. She believed that I'd fallen from an already modest professional perch. This, to Lydia, was a major cop-out, an excuse to drift aimlessly. The reality was, I was quite happy as a bus driver. It allowed my mind to wander. The work was stress-free: just an easy twenty-kilometre circuit around that barren island until my shift was up; lying in the sun on Scarborough Beach on my free days, reading or sleeping off the odd hangover. Just one bad experience: one Australia Day a drunken yobbo punched me in the face when I tried to evict him from the bus, badly breaking my nose. The only thing that gives me character, Max still opines. The injury, in fact, permanently restricted my breathing, forcing me to inhale mostly through my mouth, giving me a dog-like demeanour. This aside, being a bus driver beat being a teacher. Or a writer. But to convince my parents that I remained engaged in loftier pursuits, I told them I was still writing; there were countless old dog-eared *Wastrel* drafts that I could trot out to give the impression of productivity.

Lydia's faith in me had long begun to falter, and she made her disappointment plain. A few published short stories in the distant past was hardly her idea of a flowering creative talent. Not that she doubted my potential — no, she now questioned whether I had the *fibre* to reach my potential. She began referring to me as 'our gay bachelor', seemingly oblivious to the connotations of such a label nowadays. She chided me for my unhealthy habits; criticised my general laziness and unwillingness to exercise — by this time, those long surf swims had become few and far between. She always hoped that a 'decent girl' would come into my life and point me in the right direction, but noted, grimly, that I seemed forever attracted to hippy types – scrawny women draped in sarongs with starved, spaced-out expressions, fingers yellowed from smoking. Drifters whose lives would briefly, aimlessly, intersect with mine (mercifully without progeny), then move on.

But then Lydia began to feel unwell. She seemed always sapped of energy, out of breath. When her condition deteriorated and she finally consulted a doctor an enlarged thyroid was diagnosed. Tests showed the swelling was benign; the operation to remove the goitre was meant to be routine. Enter human error. During surgery a clumsy hand paralysed her larynx. For the next three years she was forced to breathe through a stent protruding from her lower neck. She could only speak in a laboured, bubbling whisper. Countless operations ensued. She was passed from one specialist to another. We watched helplessly as her health steadily declined. Nothing the doctors did made any noticeable improvement, yet Lydia was convinced she was making progress. She died believing the impossible.

A bug smacks into the windscreen. Its smashed thorax and flimsy wings flicker for an instant, then break loose in the wind and vanish, leaving just a whitish smear spreading upwards over the glass. I overtake a spluttering truck, its open back crammed with people, the rear numberplate nearly scraping the road. The passengers are covered in dust, their eyes liquid behind ochre masks. Voices like leaves in the wind.

I accelerate into the empty road ahead, as if speed might help me elude the past. A futile impulse . . .

Her death shook us to the core. None of us were prepared for it. In our grief we harboured bitter thoughts. We were convinced that negligence had killed Lydia well short of her time – she was seventy-three. Max's grief turned to anger; he threatened to sue. But Errol would have none of it; he would not allow money to measure Lydia's life.

The funeral was a quiet affair, just the family and a few friends. We buried her ashes in Max's garden, which she and Errol had nurtured so well. Max was inconsolable. He turned his house into a virtual shrine to Lydia. There were ornately framed photographs of her in every room.

And now the will. Lydia had inherited the proceeds from the sale of her mother's flat in Bulawayo – not a great deal of money, since the sale occurred during the property market collapse in war-torn Rhodesia. But Lydia had invested her inheritance wisely and this little nest egg now amounted to $94,000. Her will was read to us – Errol, Max and Michaela, and me – by the lawyer who settled the estate. Of the family, only Errol had been privy to the will's contents prior to this moment. It was quite simple and specific: $20,000 was to be invested on behalf of each of her grandchildren – Max's kids – and given to them when they turned twenty-one. Nothing out of the ordinary about that. What was out of the ordinary came next. The remaining $54,000 was left to Lettah Ndlovu, minus the costs incurred in finding her. In the will Lydia persistently referred to this money as 'Lettah's gift'. She further stipulated that I alone be entrusted with the job of finding Lettah, addressing her rationale directly to me:

> It is my hope that you, Frank, will embrace this task in a sincere and genuine spirit. That you will do your utmost to find Lettah and deliver this gift to her, always bearing in mind that this is my wish. I sincerely hope that by setting you this challenge the talents you undoubtedly possess will at last be given purpose. It is time for you to do something worthwhile.

For all of my life, criticism of my inertia had been like water off a duck's back. Now, for the first time, I was stung by it – it was as though that last sentence was delivered at the end of a whip. I was ashamed, mortified. And then came Lydia's last surprise – a strange appendix, written almost as though it were an afterthought:

> If all attempts by Frank to find Lettah Ndlovu prove futile, the money set aside for her will become Frank's to dispose of as he sees fit.

'Might as well write out the cheque now,' Max muttered.

It was simple incredulity, not envy or avarice, that prompted Max's remark. He was grateful that his children had been thought of — indeed, he saw their inheritances as an indirect gesture of love to him by a mother he adored. But how could his mother have placed such absurd trust in me? How could she have given me — irresponsible Frank — such a mission, with such open-endedness as to my commitment or accountability? It is my *hope* that you, Frank . . . It was a foregone conclusion that I would fail.

My shortcomings aside, what possessed her, after all this time, to bring Lettah back into our lives? A person we had all forgotten. A person she had made us forget.

I stop off at the tiny settlement of Daisyfield near Shangani. The small Dutch Reformed Church, with its belltower and plain exterior, is easy to find. I walk around amid the late afternoon shadows, searching for the graveyard. The place is deserted and silent save for the gentle calling of doves. The graveyard does not adjoin the church, as I expected. I'm about to give up looking when an old man walks by, pushing a bicycle with a flat tyre. In my crude IsiNdebele I ask him where the graveyard is; he points to an overgrown track leading off down along a row of gum trees into some bush.

I follow the track for a hundred metres, the tops of the gum trees rustling in the warm breeze. The graveyard is hidden beneath chest-high elephant grass; just the tops of fence posts mark its perimeter. I wade across and enter through an iron gate. I follow each row of graves, bending the grass aside to read the names on the headstones, mostly Afrikaner names. I locate my grandparents' graves, next to that of Maxwell Metcalf, the uncle I never met. After clearing away the grass from around their headstones, I stand, head bowed, in the long shadows of the late afternoon, paying my respects.

III

Milton Ogilvy is the only one of my small circle of university friends that I've kept in touch with since leaving South Africa, and my only contact in Zimbabwe. He has a double-storey house in faux Tudor style in Kumalo, once an up-market suburb on Bulawayo's eastern outskirts. Despite the pitfalls of living in Zimbabwe, Milton has done well for himself. A senior partner in a property law firm, *Braithwaite, Ogilvy & Hall*. Married; his wife, Ruby, is a magistrate. Their adopted son, Vernon, is fourteen. It's hard to imagine Milton as an upstanding citizen, given what I remember of him as a student in Pietermaritzburg – a chubby, hirsute anarchist drunkenly exuding disdain for convention of any sort. In those days Milton inhabited no grey spaces.

The drive from Kwekwe has taken the best part of four hours, given my stop in Daisyfield and another two police roadblocks at Gweru and Shangani. I arrive at the Kumalo address at nightfall. As I pull into the gravel driveway, Milton comes out to open the gate. His round spectacles glint in the headlights; he is short, rotund, his beard and thinning hair grey. I'm mildly shocked to see how he has aged – my surprise stemming more, I suspect, from the realisation that I'm of the same vintage. I drive in and park under a carport next to the house. Joints creaking, I climb out of the car and shake hands with Milton. He is exuberant as we exchange pleasantries; he has been looking forward to my visit. He lugs my suitcase around the house to a small guest cottage next to a swimming pool. The cottage is comfortable and compact. A bedroom with an en suite and a combined kitchen and living room; terracotta-tiled floors with rugs.

We return to the house where I'm introduced to Ruby and Vernon. Ruby is slightly taller than Milton, an attractive, convivial woman in her mid-forties. A full build, as they say these days. Dark eyes and hair. At fourteen, Vernon is the tallest in the family. Confident, polite. Black. As a baby he was found abandoned on a roadside, covered with ants, a shallow breath away from dying.

We sit in the lounge. Milton brings out a choice of drinks: Coke, Fanta or cordial. I'm dying for a beer but have been warned alcohol is forbidden in the house. Ruby's father was a violent alcoholic; Milton's emails described her phobia for alcohol as 'pathological zealotry'. It must have been, to pull him into line. We catch up on lost time. Milton has a skilful way of keeping the conversation focused on me. How was the flight from Perth? How are my father and jock-strap brother getting on? What happened to my nose? My head starts to spin – it seems an eternity since I arrived in Harare this morning. Foolish not to have flown to Bulawayo instead but I convinced myself the drive from Harare would be a worthwhile wander down memory lane. I have trouble focusing on the colourful flower paintings that adorn the walls, alongside large photographic composites of both sides of the family. A delicious aroma of curry emanates from the kitchen. I haven't eaten all day.

As though reading my mind, Ruby asks: 'Are you hungry, Frank? Dinner is ready if you want to eat.'

'I'm bloody starving!' Milton responds.

'You're always starving – I wasn't asking you.'

'I'm famished, to be honest,' I reply.

Ruby smiles. 'Well, then, you boys better sit down.'

We go through to the dining room and sit at the table. Ruby goes to the kitchen and brings in the food. She sits next to Milton and dishes up the curry. For a while there is just the scrape of cutlery as we eat. I struggle against a desire to wolf down my food. The beef curry is superb — nice and thick, not too hot. My restraint is fostered, in part, by the spectacle of Milton. He eats with the fevered relish of a hungry boy. Smacking his lips, eyes gleaming, ruddy jowls chomping furiously.

Pausing momentarily, he asks: 'If we can put aside the thrills and spills of your life as a bus driver for a moment, how's the writing going?'

The dreaded question, though I knew it was coming. In the correspondence that has passed between us over the years, I've fibbed a bit about my writing, at times even suggesting that publishers were banging on my door. Now I face the grim choice: continue the lie, or tell the truth.

'Pretty good,' I reply.

'Pretty good? When will I have the privilege of reading this masterpiece? Hell, it must be the size of *War and Peace* by now!'

I heave a long sigh. 'I can't really say.'

Milton laughs. 'Maybe you're too much of a perfectionist. But at least you're still writing. That's the main thing. At least you never gave up.'

'Maybe I should.'

'What do you write about, Mr Cole?' Vernon asks.

'I'm sure Mr Cole doesn't mind being called Frank,' Milton says.

I flounder. 'Oh, I don't know, Vernon. How to squander life, I suppose — according to an expert.'

Vernon smiles uncertainly.

Milton looks at me, one eyebrow raised. 'Don't listen to him, Vernon. I'm sure he's writing a great book.'

I change the subject by describing the small incident in Kwekwe, how the man with the khaki cap had threatened me while I was photographing the sports field.

'All I was doing was taking a damn photo!' I conclude plaintively.

Milton gives a wry grin, dimples creasing beneath his grey beard. 'Strange white men photographing obscure sports fields in obscure towns do not bring smiles to the faces of Mugabe's faithful these days. Probably thought you were a journalist.'

'Could be there was a police station or something in the background,' Ruby says, matter-of-fact. 'You know, of course, that it's illegal to photograph police or military installations? It could land you in jail.'

I look at her dumbly.

Milton chuckles, his mouth full. 'You're probably right, Ruby. Good one, Franco! If the fine townsfolk of Kwekwe had decided to make a citizen's arrest, you'd have been in a bloody pickle. And I can just imagine the cockamamie explanation you'd have offered your police interrogators. Please, sirs, I was just photographing the sports field. Where the circus used to be when I was a little boy.' He strikes his forehead with the heel of his palm.

They all laugh at my abashed expression.

'Don't worry,' Ruby says. 'Tomorrow's another day.'

We finish eating and go back to the lounge. Ruby brings in some tea. I ask Vernon about his school and learn that he attends a private school, St Aidan's. He is embarrassed when Ruby proceeds to extol his virtues. A model student, an excellent cricket and soccer player. Ruby points to his trophies on the mantelpiece.

'Needless to say, Vernon's sporting prowess didn't find its inspiration in me,' Milton says, patting an ample belly. 'So tell me, Franco. You're here to find some lost servant you last saw forty years ago.'

'That's right.'

'What on earth possessed your mother, after all this time?'

'Trying to right a past wrong, I think. I was hoping you and Ruby might point me in the right direction. You would know the legal avenues. There must be a population register or something. There must be records.'

Milton scoffs: 'Records? This country's in a state of chaos, boyo. You'll battle to find registers of any sort that are up to date. Depends on where this person was living. Depends on a lot of things. Any idea of her last whereabouts?'

'Last we heard she was on my grandparents' farm in the Fort Rixon area.'

29

'When was that?'

'Back in the war years. Mid-seventies.'

'If she's still alive, she'll have certainly defied Zim's life expectancy rate which is around thirty-four these days. I wouldn't get my hopes up too high, if I were you.'

Ruby nods. 'Ja, but you may be lucky – she might still be on the farm. Or at least someone may know what happened to her. Fort Rixon, hey? Years ago I was the Insiza District magistrate. I used to drive out to Fort Rixon once a week to hear the local cases and got to know the police inspector there quite well – I believe he's still there. If you want to go on any of the farms in that area, it's important you see him first. Most of those farms have been taken over by war veterans.'

I rub my brow. 'I was hoping to avoid the police.'

Milton gives me a sober stare. 'Some things you can't do in this place, Franco. Like photographing obscure sports fields. Your grand-folks' old farm will almost certainly be occupied by vets. Ruby's right. Go see the cop in Fort Rixon first. You can't just walk onto farms and start asking questions.'

'His name is Julius Chombo,' Ruby says. 'As far as policemen go, he's reasonably friendly and cooperative. I'll give him a ring tomor-row. And don't look so worried! There're just some ways of doing things here in Zim that you'll have to get used to. While you're in Bulawayo you might as well drop in at the Births and Deaths Registry. I have a colleague who can run a check, for what it's worth. Come to my office tomorrow and we'll get the ball rolling.'

My eyes begin to droop.

'We better let this boy get some sleep,' Milton says. 'Weird, isn't it? We last saw each other thirty years ago, and here we sit talking like it was yesterday.'

I lie in bed, exhausted, yet unable to sleep. Outside, a bird (a night-jar?) calls in the dark – a series of abrupt *a-wok* sounds, then a long *krrrr* – evoking my father as a younger man. The pleasure he took in identifying birdcalls. Dogs bark – the incessant night-time chorus of African towns. A truck with grating gears slows as it nears Bulawayo along the Harare road, not far from the house.

The brief talk with Milton about writing plays on my mind. A rekindled sense of failure scratches at my conscience, like a dog at a door. Milton's opinion matters to me and his charitable (patronising?) words rankle. But then hasn't Milton also fallen short of the ideals we had? Judging by the decor in his house, all Sturm und Drang has been expunged from his taste; I well remember the walls of his room at his ramshackle student digs in Pietermaritzburg festooned with German Expressionist posters. I suspect Ruby has demanded a more comprehensive abstinence.

My disquiet, I know, stems from debt. I *owe* Milton. I owe him for the only time I ever truly felt a sense of purpose – the only time I ever felt engaged with the world. That halcyon time at university when the heavens seemed to smile down at me, when Lydia imagined future triumphs after my stories were published. How much of it would have happened had I not encountered Milton? I recall how he was then: the oddball law student with bad asthma, who loathed conformity and any form of physical exertion in equal measure – the only sport he appeared to enjoy was drinking and aimless discussion. A man after my own heart. At our favourite haunt in the Emmeline Pankhurst Bar at the Imperial Hotel in Pietermaritzburg we'd booze and bullshit the nights away with our small coterie. Milton had a sharp, provocative intellect. Exasperating, the way he vacillated, always the contrarian, as though divorced from belief or principle. A postmodern cynic ahead of his time. God, how he loved drinking! Many were the times that I was forced to heave his half-comatose bulk back to his digs after closing time.

Yet he had one passion that remained curiously untouched by cynicism: a pure and idealistic yearning to be a writer – strange, in that it belonged more to a redundant romanticism than the fickle pessimism of his age. He believed in writing as a heroic quest for immaculate truth. Truth lay in the silences of solitary creative toil;

allegiance to art was the only fidelity that mattered. His passion was infectious; it carried me in its wake. He foisted on me the authors that are still my favourites – Joyce, Beckett, Faulkner, Márquez. We wrote short stories, showing a preference for stream-of-consciousness prose and magic realism. We drove each other, eyes aflame. And when he read my stories I saw something else in his eyes that had never glowed at me before – envy. That look gave me more of a sense of worth than anything else. Before or since.

Now he is different. What does he feel about writing now? It's hard for me to come to terms with the new Milton. Perhaps I miss that special look of envy. But a light must be absent from my eyes too. Of the two alternatives Milton once proposed – allegiance to art or going with the flow – my choice, no matter how I might dress it up, brings me no honour.

I wake from a dead sleep to the sound of a burglar alarm going off next door. The sun is casting a faint strip of yellow light across the bed through a gap in the curtains. I lie in bed, semi-conscious, listening to the commotion. After an interminable few minutes the alarm is switched off. There is a terse exchange in IsiNdebele between two people; the owner of the house admonishing the gardener, apparently. I vaguely follow the conversation. It seems the gardener has accidentally set off the alarm, not for the first time.

Peace is restored at last. Birds begin their morning songs. Long-forgotten songs that awake in me an obscure longing. I sit up and begin writing in my diary, filling in the events of yesterday. One of the few writer's habits I've kept up. I don't know why. There is a gentle knock on the door.

A maid with a tea tray.

'Good morning, baas,' she says cheerily. She is young with a big buck-toothed smile. 'Missus says breakfast is ready.'

'Thank you. What's your name?'

'My name is Precious.'

'Thank you, Precious. I'll be ready in a few minutes.'

After the tea, I quickly shower and shave. I see my father in the mirror before I recognise myself. The same jut of the jaw, the same frown. Hair grey and receding, close-cropped. That same blue stare. Something of his distinguished though irascible air. Time has moulded us alike, my flattened nose and nascent beer gut notwithstanding. Then the noble visage implodes, as always; a sudden glimpse of the lurking reprobate hastens my ablutions. Sessions in front of mirrors are never lengthy. I dress in long trousers and a short-sleeved shirt and amble across the lawn to the house. A light dew on the patchy grass. Already it's hot. The rising sun burns through the frilly leaves of a syringa tree near the swimming pool. I notice a tennis court at the far end of the yard has been converted into a flourishing vegetable garden. The city traffic grumbles in the distance.

The family has finished breakfast. Ruby is fussing around getting Vernon ready for school. Milton is still seated at the dining table, going through some documents in a clip folder. All very formal: Milton and Ruby in their dark business suits, Vernon in a bright red school blazer and tie.

Milton looks up as I come in and gestures at a seat next to him. 'Take a pew. How did you sleep?'

'Like a log. Until that racket started up next door.'

He laughs. 'Burglar alarms have become one of the definitive sounds of postcolonial Africa, unfortunately. Precious! Bring baas Frank's porridge!'

'Yebo, nkosi,' Precious calls back from the kitchen.

'While some definitive colonial sounds remain unchanged,' I say.

Milton gives me a wry look. 'She's got a job and a place to stay. That's more than most Zimbabweans can claim these days.'

I'm given a short lecture: Precious is a widow. Her husband was killed in a bus accident shortly before her home in Killarney, one of Bulawayo's shantytowns, was destroyed by bulldozers in Operation Murambatsvina. She arrived at the house one day, destitute, with two small children in tow, asking for work. Milton houses them in the servants' quarters next to the kitchen and also covers the cost of the children's education at the same private school Vernon attends. 'So don't get too sanctimonious about servants, boyo,' he says, tersely.

I make light of it: 'I was only kidding, Milton.'

'Turned out to be a blessing in more ways than one. She teaches Vernon IsiNedebele. It always bothered me that adopting Vernon might separate him from his people – especially if he lost the language.'

Precious comes in and places a steaming bowl of mielie meal porridge in front of me. I mix a lump of butter into the porridge and begin eating.

'Tell me,' I say between mouthfuls. 'Does the name Brak Malan ring a bell?'

'Can't say that it does. Someone I should know?'

'No, just an old acquaintance from the distant past. And Vic Baldwin? Ever heard of him?'

'Everyone in Bulawayo knows Vic Baldwin. Farmer from Kwekwe. Booted off his land a while ago. My firm handled his case. Not me personally – one of my partners. You'd always know when Vic arrived to do business. Voice like a bloody foghorn. Why do you ask?'

'He was a friend of my folks. I'm hoping he may shed some light on Brak's whereabouts.'

'He lives in Hillside, I think. Easy enough to look up his number.'

Milton gets up and goes through to the adjoining hall. He returns with a telephone directory and flips through some pages.

'Here it is. Under Kent.'

He underlines the number in the directory and pushes it across.

'I'll need my glasses to read that. Did you say Kent?'

'Ja, he lives with a woman called Kent.'

'As in Hazel Kent?'

'You know her?'

'If it's the same Hazel Kent. Another one of my parents' crowd. Are they married or what?'

34

Milton shrugs. 'Don't ask me. I don't fraternise with Vic. They strike me as a bit of an odd couple. Vic's a tiresome bloody boor, Hazel's an aging hippy. Runs what's left of a craft centre in town. Slim pickings these days with no tourists around. How she puts up with a bigot like Vic, I don't know.' He gestures towards the hall. 'Phone's through there. Give them a ring. I should warn you, though: you'll need to exercise patience – the landline system's a bloody shambles. That's why everyone's got cell phones.'

I finish the porridge. Ruby comes in and sits at the end of the table. 'Sorry to get you up so early, Frank, but I didn't want you to wake up and find everyone gone.' She turns to the kitchen. 'Precious! Bring baas Frank's food!'

'Okay, missus.'

I hold my stomach in protest. 'That porridge was plenty for me, Ruby. I'm not used to big breakfasts.'

Ruby waves her finger at me. 'You can't go the whole day on one plate of porridge.' She eyes Milton. '*He* can't, anyway.'

Precious comes through with a plate of scrambled eggs on toast. With a deft flourish she places it in front of me and removes the porridge plate.

'You really shouldn't go to such trouble,' I say.

'It's no trouble,' Ruby replies. She turns and calls, 'Vernon! Come on, it's not holidays already!'

Vernon enters the room. 'Don't shout, Mom – I'm not deaf!'

'Precious! Are Rosie and Geldof ready?'

'Yebo, missus, they are waiting.'

Milton gets up. 'Okay, we're on our way, Franco. See you later. Let me know if there's anything I can do for you.'

'Don't forget to come by my office,' Ruby says.

Through the window, I watch the family, now joined by Precious's shy children, immaculate in their school uniforms, climb into Milton's beige early model Ford Cortina and drive off. Precious waves and shuts the gate after them. She is waiting patiently next to the sink when I take my plate through to the kitchen. She frowns as I put

35

the plate down next to the sink. 'You must call me when you finish,' she says.

I fetch my glasses from the cottage and try Vic Baldwin's number. A woman answers. After all these years, I recognise her voice.

'Is that Hazel? It's Frank Cole speaking. Errol and Lydia's son.'

An intake of breath.

'Frank Cole? My goodness! What on earth are you doing in this God-forsaken place? Someone told me you were all in Australia.'

'It's a long story. I was hoping to speak to Vic.'

A brief silence.

'Vic's still asleep. Why don't you come for lunch. You can talk to him then.'

'It's just a couple of questions I need to ask. If he's not well —'

'Oh, he's fine. He just stayed up a bit late last night. I'm sure he'd like to see you. We'd both like to see you.'

'Okay, if it's not too much trouble.'

Hazel gives directions to her address in Hillside; I write them down and hang up.

I make my way through the traffic up Leopold Takawira Drive into the city centre. Bulawayo was never a city to wax lyrical about, even in Rhodesia's heyday. Its drab outward sprawl across the thorn-scrub plains of Matabeleland resembles a crude virus: a hiccup of office blocks against a grimy row of cooling towers; far suburbs floating on heat waves. Never a pretty face, but then don't towns, like people, lack character when they rely only on looks to get by?

As in Kwekwe, I'm led unerringly by memory. Only the signs of neglect suggest that time has not stood still. Verges and traffic circles are overgrown with grass and weeds, parks unkempt. Razor wire sprouts everywhere like vigorous creepers. Piles of rubbish lie rotting on the kerbs. Also new to my eye are the different street names. Gone the colonial stalwarts. In their place, and difficult to my tongue, the names of liberation heroes.

It's hot and windless, the air blue with exhaust fumes. Weaving through a slow tide of people that has spilled from the pavements into the street, I park near the High Court and walk around the block to Tredgold House, a three-storey government building with an ochre and red colonial façade. A security guard directs me upstairs along musty corridors to Ruby's office. Her door is ajar; she sits at her desk with a pile of folders in front of her. She looks up and waves me in. Glancing at the pile of folders, she shrugs. 'I was hoping to have the morning free,' she says.

'If it's a problem —'

'No, no. My work just seems to come in deluges. It's the same with Milton. He wanted so much to take a week off while you're here, but he's also been inundated. By the way, I tried to get hold of Inspector Chombo at Fort Rixon but the lines are busy. I'll keep trying. When can I tell him you'll be coming?'

'Tomorrow, if that's possible.'

Ruby gets up. 'Okay. In the meantime let me introduce you to someone else who may be able to help you.'

I follow her downstairs and along a labyrinth of corridors to the Births and Deaths Registry section of the Passport Office. We enter a room with high ceilings, barred windows facing the street outside and a long wooden counter. Two female officials are working at the counter, on the public side of which a queue zigzags out the door. A middle-aged man is seated at a desk in the corner, slowly typing at a computer. A spinning fan on the ceiling is reflected in Mugabe's portrait on the wall, lending him a strangely energised appearance.

Approaching the man at the computer, Ruby introduces me: 'Good morning, Geoffrey. This is a friend from Australia, Frank Cole. Frank, this is Geoffrey Dlamini.'

We shake hands. Dlamini has large black-rimmed glasses and a patient air. His old suit looks several sizes too big for his skeletal body. His handshake is gentle, his greeting polite; he gestures at two chairs next to the desk.

'I can't stay,' Ruby says. 'I've just had a dozen cases dumped on my desk. Frank's trying to locate a missing person, Geoffrey. I thought you'd be the best person to talk to.' She pats my shoulder. 'See you later, Frank.'

As I sit down there are two loud bangs from directly outside. A sudden hush in the office. All eyes turn nervously towards the door. More bangs further down the street – a car backfiring. Someone laughs, and the hubbub resumes. Dlamini grins and shakes his head; he swivels in his chair to face me. 'How can I help you, Mr Cole?'

I explain. Dlamini taps a pen on a notepad as he listens. He writes down Lettah's name followed by a full stop. He writes nothing else, just twirls the pen around on the full stop until it grows to a big black dot. I show him the only clear photograph I have of her, plundered from the family albums: a close-up depicting a smiling Lettah in her servant's uniform and headscarf, her head averted slightly. As he scrutinises it, I feel a vague sense of shame that I have so little to substantiate the existence of someone once so intimately enmeshed in our lives.

When I finish, he asks: 'You have no national ID number?'

'No.'

'No date or place of birth? No employment record or official documents of any sort? No other details, other than her name and this photograph?'

'No.'

'Mmm . . . this is very difficult. Hopefully we will have her birth records. If she is alive this woman would be old. Excuse me for saying so, but you should accept the strong possibility that she has passed away. If she died in the Fort Rixon area we may have a record of it. But a lot of people die and go unreported, Mr Cole. Especially in the Fort Rixon area during Gukurahundi. Many just disappeared. It's very difficult. We are short-staffed, as you can see.'

'Gukurahundi? What do mean by that?'

Dlamini gives me a level stare. He jerks his head towards Mugabe's portrait on the wall. 'In the eighties our president sent the army into Matabeleland to kill dissidents. The 5th Brigade. Let me just say, they killed more than just dissidents. Those worst affected were the ordinary people in the bush. People like the one you are looking for. This operation was called Gukurahundi, a Shona word for the cleansing wind that blows the chaff from the ground before the spring rains. The army was very active in the Fort Rixon area, from what I remember. Who knows if this has anything to do with this Ndlovu woman. In a normal country it's a straightforward business finding out if a person is alive or dead. It's a straightforward business finding out where a person lives. But this is not a normal country, Mr Cole. Documents are not up to date. Documents are missing. People are missing. The police take documents from this office as they please and never return them. You have just given me a name – Ndlovu is a very common name. You know only her English first name – most of us have an African first name too. No ID number. You should prepare yourself for disappointment.'

'I can only do what I can.'

Dlamini smiles. 'Eh-ja, it's best that you remain positive, but realistic.' He gets up. 'Excuse me while I go through our records. It may take a few minutes. You can wait here.'

In a rustle of loose clothes, Dlamini leaves the room. I sit and watch the slow movement of the queue as people are processed by the two officials. Most appear to be applying for passports. Some chat with each other, others stare into space with resigned expressions. Among them, a women with a baby on her back. For an instant, I feel Lettah's rolling gait, and hear the strange clicks of her tongue as she sings. Nothing else to fill the world.

After an hour the two officials break for tea. Everyone just stands waiting for them to return. Half an hour later, just one official returns. The queue grinds slowly forward again.

At last, Dlamini comes back. He sits at his desk and shakes his head.

'I'm sorry, Mr Cole. We have no records of Lettah Ndlovu – not even a birth certificate. I've gone through everything. That's not to say she has disappeared, or that she is dead – we can make no presumptions. We just have no records of the existence of this person.

I think that you should look for her in the Fort Rixon area first. If that fails, my advice is to put an advertisement in the newspaper – *The Chronicle*. That is often a successful way of finding missing persons. It wouldn't do any harm to put up some notices here in the townships. It's common for poor country people to come to the towns and cities to find work. You can also check with the churches and missions. But as far as our records are concerned, she doesn't exist. I'm very sorry.'

'I appreciate your efforts, Mr Dlamini. Fort Rixon seems to be shaping up as my only realistic chance.'

Dlamini hesitates. He drums his fingers on his desk. 'Look, I have the name of this woman. If I can find a spare moment I'll make some enquiries. I know a few people in government departments around the country. My counterpart in Harare, for example, could be persuaded to conduct a search. I'll make some phone calls. You never know, she might be listed in a Welfare Department branch in some corner of the country.'

'I'll be happy to pay you for your trouble.'

Dlamini gives me a tired stare. 'I won't pretend to quibble about your offer, Mr Cole. What you are prepared to pay me to do my job is up to you. Life has become such that few Zimbabweans will do anything without some additional incentive. This is how we survive.'

He walks me to the door. We shake hands again.

'Good luck, Mr Cole,' he says.

Leaving Tredgold House I'm imbued with a strange confidence that I know is unfounded. It's simply a reaction to the way I've been received so far. Here, my foibles and failures lie safely concealed on another continent. I bask in the queer realisation that people like Ruby and Dlamini appear to see me as someone who carries an aura of competence.

With time to kill, I cruise around the city, astonished at just how familiar everything is – the wide streets lined with jacaranda or flamboyant trees harking back to a time when a wagon and team of oxen could be turned around in one manoeuvre; the old landmarks – Charter House, Bulawayo Club, City Hall with its classical columns and Art Deco clock tower. One after the other, these colonial relics make forty years seem a day. But the familiarity fades as I drive up past the railway station and cooling towers towards the townships. Past bustling taxi ranks, squalid with refuse. Healthy kids smile from billboards advertising Mazoe orange juice and Bata shoes, a far cry from the ragged barefoot urchins below. The part of Bulawayo whites avoided in the old days. Foreign to me then, as it is now. The streets choked with people. Women trudging along as though in slow motion, babies on their backs. Men in broken shoes sauntering by, faces shining with sweat. Cyclists on creaky bicycles, one holding a transistor radio to his ear as he peddles away. An old man in a patched jacket wearing a conical lampshade as a hat. The din of shouted conversations. A phalanx of policemen in combat fatigues striding towards the station, swinging long batons. The crowds part, like dense shoals of fish making way for a shark. Two female constables bring up the rear, also swinging batons. They chat and laugh, like any women out on a stroll.

No shark-like menace in me, apparently. At a bus depot my car is suddenly enveloped; nervously I inch forward through a sea of bodies. I jump when someone slaps the car's roof. Playfully, one hopes. Forty years now seems an eternity. I surreptitiously push down the door lock with my elbow, at the same time feeling a growing irritation at my paranoia. I chide myself: this is Africa. Crowded, noisy. Chaotic.

IV

Hazel and my mother go back a long way. They were the same age and close friends from childhood. I remember a lively woman, always bright and cheerful. Naturally beautiful; auburn-haired and fair-skinned with violet eyes. The only white person I knew who proclaimed herself to be African. She had a little curio shop-cum-tearoom on the main road in Que Que that never did very well because the tourist trade at that time was too small. Her parents farmed in the upper Insiza River Valley, not far from Whitestone. They were among those few farmers Errol and Lydia knew personally who were killed in the war. Ambushed at the gate to their farm one night after attending a function at the Fort Rixon Club.

She was a regular presence at Sunnyside. As far as white women went in Rhodesia, Hazel cut an eccentric figure; she wore brightly coloured kaftans, fezzes and other exotic attire; she didn't shave her armpits and occasionally braided her hair like an Ndebele maiden. I remember once she painted her hands with henna. A weirdo before weirdos. Like Lydia, she smoked liked a chimney. I was besotted with her. If ever there was a damsel of my boyhood dreams it was chain-smoking, hairy-armpitted Hazel.

Childless, unmarried, I suppose she lavished her maternal affections on Max and me. She was fascinated by what made boys tick and amused by our idiotic rivalry. To my chagrin, she seemed to like Max more. She loved his relentless determination, the way he fanatically

42

honed his skills, spending mindless hours dribbling a soccer ball between chairs out on the front lawn or bowling at the stumps my father painted on the garage wall. She would pitch up at Que Que Junior School to watch him play soccer. He always scored goals and Hazel's cheers could be heard above those of the parents on the sidelines. She would come to my games too, more, I think, for a chuckle than the promise of any Peléan spectacles on my part. As a player I tended to direct operations from a largely stationary position on the field. And when a rare opportunity came for me to deliver, I'd cock up. A cross kick would find me unmarked in front of the goal. I'd let fly with an almighty kick, miss the ball completely, and land on my backside. Howls of dismay from my teammates. Groans from the parents. And out of the corner of my eye, Hazel almost collapsing with mirth on the sideline.

In dress and manner, Hazel was a Rhodesian anomaly. She was also that most suspect of creatures – a *liberal*. She harboured crackpot notions of racial equality and freedom for all. People shook their heads behind her back. But she was bright and articulate, hard to beat or belittle in an argument. She and my father used to argue a lot, playfully. You might have thought they'd have little to argue about, given Errol's own liberal leanings. I think both of them just enjoyed the intellectual stimulation, though I remember her exclaiming once: 'Oh, Errol! You're *so* exasperating! What *do* you really believe in?' My father seemed perplexed by the question.

Since theirs was a friendship that had carried through from childhood, Lydia and Hazel knew each other intimately and never felt any need for pretences. I remember how they always chaffed each other, giggling like adolescents, each giving as good as they got. Close, like sisters. She almost seemed part of the family; she accompanied us to functions at the sports club or on picnics at Sebakwe Poort or Dutchman's Pool. Although I have no recollection of any antagonism between her and my parents, there must have been a falling out during this time at Que Que. When we moved to Salisbury and Bulawayo we saw Hazel only occasionally, once or twice a year. And after we moved down to South Africa we saw no more of her. For a while she used to send us a card every Christmas. Then she stopped. The memories of her began to fade and, like Lettah, there came a time when she belonged to another life.

If Hazel graces my memory as a sweet damsel, Vic Baldwin lurks as a brute. He had a big cattle ranch called Thorn Drift south of a range of hills called the Great Dyke, a fifty-kilometre drive over rough dirt roads from Que Que. My father had become acquainted with Vic through his work as a Connex extension officer. Once in a while we would spend a weekend on the ranch. As we pitched up in front of the Baldwin's crude rambling homestead, out would come burly, bristle-haired Vic with his booming voice, followed by his timid wife, Iris, and four rough, bristle-haired sons. Lots of loud laughter and hearty banter. Vic always pulled the same stupid trick when he shook hands with Max and me. He'd crush our hands in his big paw and keep on pumping away. 'Ow! Let go,' he'd cry in a high-pitched girly voice. His house was full of dead animals, large and small, decrepit souvenirs from old hunting safaris. The profusion of horns, skins and tusks littering every room gave the place the slight whiff of carrion. The side tables in the lounge were made from chopped-off elephant feet. Especially grotesque was the dining room with its array of kudu and sable heads staring glassily from the walls. A mangy lion's head was mounted above Vic's place at the head of the table. Its jaws were parted in what was meant to be a snarl, but it looked more like it was about to eject a fur ball. But the worst for me was the miserable vervet monkey he kept chained to a pole in the dusty backyard next to the kitchen. At the top of the pole was a little box with a hole in it, the monkey's only shelter from the elements and the stones Vic's boys threw at it.

The boys' names were Hugo, Todd, Martin and Cecil – Thpethal Thethil, as his brothers called him because of his lisp. They were tough, barefoot, bush-wise – typical farm boys. While Vic and Iris entertained my parents, this coarse foursome would whisk Max and me, the townies, off into the bush. It usually ended in me copping some good old bullying. Hugo, the oldest, was the worst. While the others held me down, he'd pee all over me and then roll me around in the dirt. He rubbed my face in wet cowpats. I had a wild temper and would scream and struggle in helpless fury. Great entertainment value. They went easy on Max because he had the nasty habit of fighting back. And Max never did anything to stop them picking on me because it was normal to bully younger boys, and he had always been partial to doing a bit of it himself.

Bullying came easy to the Baldwin boys. After all, they were taught by an expert. They lived in fear of Vic. Prone to frightening rages, Vic flogged them unmercifully for the smallest things. Our visits to the ranch always ended up with at least one of them getting a serious hiding. Once our two families travelled in tandem up to Kariba for a holiday. All I remember of that trip is Vic's frequent stops to cut a stick to hit his sons with.

The beatings were not confined to his sons. I discovered this during a weekend visit to Thorn Drift. On our arrival there was the customary loud merriment from Vic; the usual bone-crushing handshakes and girly voice begging Max and me to let go. Vic had bought a new rifle and was keen to break it in. So us men and boys spent the afternoon blasting away at empty paraffin cans perched on a fence near to where the monkey was chained. The poor creature sat shivering in its little box on top of the pole, nattering away to itself in terror. Naturally, when it came to marksmanship, Vic and his boys put the Coles to shame. Vic guffawed at our abysmal efforts. The rifle was so heavy I had to rest it on a tree stump; the kick left a bruise on my shoulder that lasted weeks.

After the shooting practice, we gathered under a marula tree at the front of the house for a braai. Servants started the fire; they brought drinks for the grown-ups. The boys ran around playing games in the gathering darkness. Then Vic's headman approached through the gloom, hat in hand. He said something to Vic in Shona. Vic got up from his chair, excused himself and went off with the headman. Vic's sons told Max and me to shut up and follow them. We snuck around through some bush and came up behind the tractor shed. There, hidden by some trees, we could see all the farm workers and their families gathered in front of the shed. A hurricane lamp glowed on the ground, lighting everyone's faces from below.

Vic was standing to one side with the headman. He had a long quirt called a sjambok in his hand. He was talking in Shona. The assembled people listened quietly, their eyes downcast. Then Vic barked an order and the headman called out some names. Five boys, none older than twelve, stepped forward fearfully. Hugo whispered to Max and me that they had been caught stealing fruit. One by one they were made to bend over while Vic thrashed them, four to six strokes each according to age. He took huge swipes, pausing between each stroke. The smaller boys had to be held still by the headman. The air rang with their cries and the moans of anguish from the families forced to watch. It seemed to go on forever. Vic's sons' eyes gleamed as they watched. While the last boy, the smallest of the group, was being flogged, a woman, presumably his mother, ran forward and stood between him and Vic, begging him to stop. Vic bellowed at her to move. She refused, so he laid into her, lashing her across the legs and shoulders in a wild fury. The way she hopped around shrieking made Vic's sons giggle. Then a man leapt forward and grabbed Vic's arm. There was a tussle. I could hear Vic panting and swearing loudly. Bloody black bastard this and Kaffir that. The man just held Vic's forearms and glared into his eyes. Vic roared with fury. Then the man let go and just stood there, resigned to what was coming. Vic dropped the sjambok and went berserk. He punched and kicked the man and the man just took it until he fell to the ground, groaning. Vic went on kicking him until he was exhausted. Hunched over with his hands on his knees, he ranted at the assembled people. Then he picked the man up by the scruff of the neck and shoved him in the direction of the road. He kicked the woman's backside and gestured for her to follow the man. The woman and the boy, and two other children, joined the man and they made off into the darkness, the children crying.

When Vic rejoined my parents at the braai he behaved as though nothing out of the ordinary had happened. If anything, he appeared more jovial than usual. I wondered what my father thought of his skinned knuckles.

We had many other farmer friends, none of whom were brutes. But I couldn't rid myself of the sight of Vic kicking that man on the ground. Or of the way he took his time flogging the boys, or of that woman hopping around, shrieking. My eyes had been opened for the first time to another side of the world I lived in.

It's a mystery that Hazel and Vic live under the same roof. I can only imagine that it comes down to expedience; elderly whites in Zimbabwe, whose income has been reduced to nothing by inflation, taking practical measures to survive.

Hazel's house in Sable Avenue is set among granite kopjes luxuriant with wild fig trees in a typically large garden. I arrive around noon and park in the shade of a spreading flamboyant tree flanking the driveway, climb the stone steps to the front door and knock. The shrill whine of insects and chirruping of birds seems deafening as I wait. The heat is oppressive, heavy; my shirt is damp with sweat. I notice a gardener nearby scrubbing the walls of the swimming pool with a long-handled brush. He calls across that I should knock again. He taps his ear. 'No good,' he says.

I knock again, louder this time. The door opens. Momentarily, I experience the weird feeling that I'm dreaming. Before me stands Hazel – not the aged Hazel I was expecting to see, but the young Hazel of Que Que, so long ago. The same auburn hair and quizzical violet eyes, the haughty aquiline nose, the clean strong line of her jaw. Alluring in a floral bikini top with a pale blue sarong around her waist. African bangles on her arms, fair skin peeling on the shoulders – Hazel was always reckless with the sun. I stand there speechless.

'You must be Frank. My mother's just been telling me about you. I'm Clara – Hazel's daughter.'

A Scots accent. A few tiny wrinkles at the corners of her eyes suggest she is older than she looks. Mid-thirties perhaps.

'Clara? My God, I thought I was in a time warp. You look just —'

'Like my dear old mother?' An exasperated smile.

We shake hands. Clara looks past me at the gardener cleaning the pool.

'Jeremiah! Are you nearly finished?'

'Nearly finished, missus,' the gardener calls back.

Clara turns back to me. 'This bloody heat's killing me. Come in. The old fogies are in the lounge.'

She leads me inside to a lounge adorned with African craft — masks and shields, drums, straw mats and batik wall-hangings. A huge granite boulder spotted with white and orange lichen, part of one of the kopjes outside, protrudes through one wall. A fan on the ceiling blows a blue fog of cigarette smoke towards me.

I recognise Hazel immediately. Despite her grey hair, now cropped short, and her stooped, thinner frame, her face has retained its somewhat haughty character. The lines and wrinkles around her eyes and mouth lend her a serene, composed air. She laughs. 'Well I never! Frank Cole. You're the spitting image of your father!'

'Oh, great. Another look-alike,' Clara remarks.

'Hello Hazel,' I say.

Hazel comes forward and kisses me on the cheek and hugs me. Her body feels like a bony old bird.

'Look who's here, Vic!' she says.

A frail old man is seated in a chair next to a screen door that leads onto a patio. I barely recognise him. Once a hefty bloke with a big gut, Vic Baldwin now looks almost emaciated. His still thick, spiky hair is cotton white; just the cowlick at the front has a yellow tinge — presumably from tobacco smoke, if the piled ashtray on the table next to him is anything to go by. With the help of a walking stick he leans forward to get up.

'Please don't get up,' I say. 'How are you, Vic?'

It took an absurd act of will not to call him Uncle Vic, in the obsequious manner of my youth. Vic sinks back in his chair. He shakes hands tiredly.

'Old and buggered,' he says. He eyes me closely. 'Hell, isn't he a chip off the old block, Hazel?'

Hazel pats a chair next to her. 'Sit down, Frank. Isn't this heat revolting! If the boy wasn't cleaning the pool, I'd invite you for a swim. Clara, why don't you put on some clothes and join us?'

Clara shakes her head. 'I'll join you in a moment, Mom. Right now I'm going for a swim, Jeremiah or no Jeremiah.'

She pulls open the screen door next to Vic and goes outside onto the patio. She removes her sarong and then skips down to the pool and dives in. A refreshing spectacle, I have to say. The gardener continues to brush the walls as she swims.

'I wish she wouldn't display herself like that in front of Jeremiah,' Vic grumbles.

'Oh, leave her be, Vic.' Hazel sighs and turns to me. 'You wouldn't have met Clara before, would you? Of course not. She was born after you left Rhodesia. How time flies!' She claps her hands. 'Well, isn't this a surprise? So you Coles are all Aussies, hey? To what do we owe the honour of your presence, dear boy?'

'Pure coincidence, actually. I had no idea either of you were in Bulawayo.'

'I suppose the last you remember of us is from the Que Que days. Dear me, a lot of water has passed under the bridge since then, hasn't it, Vic? I bought this place back in the seventies, when I moved from Que Que. I was lucky. In those days people were leaving in droves. I got this house for a song. Didn't I, Vic?'

Vic cups his ear.

Hazel almost shouts: 'I said, I got this house for a song!'

Vic grunts. 'Fifteen thousand dollars. You know what you can buy for $15,000 now? Bugger all. Not even a used toilet roll.'

'Dear me, Vic, the comparisons you make!' Hazel gestures at the big boulder protruding into the room. 'Isn't it clever the way they designed this house, Frank?'

'It's lovely.'

Vic snorts. 'Lovely? *Lovely?* A stupid bloody rock sticking into your house? Ridiculous, if you ask me.' Hazel frowns at him. He sighs. 'But I suppose everyone to their own taste. So, tell me, Frank, what are you doing with yourself these days?'

Vic's eyes acquire a hint of incredulity as I summarise the ins and outs of life as a Rottnest Island bus driver.

'To each his own,' he says. ' How're your folks? Haven't heard from them in ages. When last did you hear from them, Hazel?'

'Oh, I don't know . . . we lost touch during the war years, I think. That's right, shortly after I moved to Bulawayo. Before Clara was born. God, was it that long ago?'

I fill in the spaces of the blank years. When I talk about my mother's death, Hazel's eyes cloud.

'It's been tough on Dad,' I say. 'He took a big knock. We all did.'

Hazel buries her face in her hands. 'I'm so sorry to hear about your mother. I had no idea.'

Vic nods. 'Ja, man. Just shows you, people should keep in touch.'

Hazel gets up and leaves the room.

'Shame,' Vic says. 'Hazel and your mom used to be close.'

Hazel returns, blowing her nose in a handkerchief. 'I'm sorry,' she says, clearing her throat. 'I wasn't expecting such bad news. Would you like a drink? Vic likes a beer at midday.'

'A beer would be nice.'

She turns to go but Vic stops her. 'Sit, woman, for God's sake! What do you employ bloody servants for?' He turns to the kitchen and yells, 'Daphne!'

A distant voice answers, 'Nkosi.'

'Bring two beers. Tshetsha!'

'Yebo, nkosi.'

Vic points to a drinks cabinet against the wall. 'Do me a favour, Frank. Could you pour Hazel a half glass of sherry? It's my job usually but my old legs are giving me hell today.'

'It's gout giving you hell,' Hazel says, sitting down. 'If you drank less beer you'd be out running marathons.'

'Life's one big marathon, woman. And I've finished my race.'

Hazel laughs. 'That's what I love about you, Vic. Your eternal optimism.'

I get up and fix Hazel's drink. The maid, Daphne, enters with a tray carrying two cold quarts of beer and two glasses. She places the beers on the side tables next to Vic and me and goes back to the kitchen. Hazel lights two cigarettes and hands one to Vic. 'You don't smoke, do you, Frank?' she asks.

I shake my head. 'Gave it up.'

'Good boy,' she says. 'Filthy habit.'

Vic raises his glass. 'Well, here's to your mother, God bless her. Cheers.'

We drink and reminisce about the old days in Que Que, before, as Vic puts it, the kaffirs came along and ballsed everything up. Since both Hazel and Vic are hard of hearing, it is a loud conversation, with many repeated questions, at times escalating almost to shouting. In her matter-of-fact way, Hazel explains that she sold her parents' farm in the Insiza Valley after they were killed during the war. With the proceeds she established a new craft centre opposite Central Park in Bulawayo, and when the tourist market picked up in the early eighties it became very successful – she had more demand than she could cope with. With Zimbabwe's recent troubles, though, she's been battling to make ends meet. I ask about Vic's family. His wife, Iris, died of cancer years ago. The sons have all moved overseas. Hugo and Cecil are doing very well as businessmen, apparently; Todd and Martin are doing less well, though neither are bus drivers. The conversation is interrupted momentarily when Clara comes back inside through the screen door, still dripping. I catch the smell of chlorine as she moves past.

Hazel rolls her eyes. 'Clara! Why don't you dry yourself off before coming inside?'

'Sorry, Mom. I forgot my towel,' Clara replies, disappearing down a passage.

I tell them of my visit to Kwekwe. When I describe the state of our old house, Vic laughs. 'What did you expect? That, my Aussie friend, is what kaffirs do. Bugger things up. We make, they break.'

Vic's body may have diminished but not his big booming mouth. A frown of irritation forms on Hazel's forehead. She puts a finger to her lips and shushes him.

Vic looks at me, eyes wide with mock fear. 'Hazel's worried about the servants reporting me to the police. You're not allowed to call a kaffir a kaffir these days.'

'One day they'll drag you off and give you a good flogging,' Hazel says. 'It's probably what you deserve.'

Vic guffaws. 'I'd like to see them try! I'll call a kaffir anything I damn well like!' From the kitchen comes the sound of an oven door opening. The smell of roast beef comes wafting through. Vic sniffs loudly, catarrhine nostrils flaring. 'Sweet Jesus, that smells good!'

Hazel turns to me. 'So what brings you back, Frank?'

I explain the reasons for my journey. When I get to the subject of Lydia's will, Vic acquires that incredulous look in his eye again. He slaps his hands on his thighs. 'Jesus H bloody Christ! Now I've heard everything! Fifty thousand Aussie dollars! God knows what that is in Zim currency. What on earth got into your dear mother's head, man? Who ever thought of giving a kaffir that sort of money?'

The consternation on his face makes Hazel laugh. 'Oh, stop being such a miserable old so and so. I say, well done, Lydia. What a nice thing to have done.'

'Wake up to yourself, woman! You might as well take that money and flush it down the toilet. And for what? A bloody nanny she had God knows how long ago!' He shakes his head. 'No, sorry, I've never heard of anything so damn ridiculous!'

Daphne comes through to tell us lunch is ready. Hazel helps Vic to his feet and we carry our drinks through to the dining room. We sit at an oak table, with Vic at the head. On the wall around us are pictures of Hazel's family and friends, including one of Errol and Lydia at their wedding, where Hazel was maid of honour. Just one photograph of

Vic, Iris and their four boys taken next to the marula tree in front of their house at Thorn Drift. Clara comes in, wearing a short skirt and t-shirt, her wet hair brushed back. Vic puts his glasses on and begins to carve a small side of beef, while Hazel dishes out the potatoes and vegetables – homegrown, she explains. It seems Zimbabwe's suburban backyards have become small subsistence farms. Vic lifts a few slices of meat between the carving knife and fork onto each plate. We pass the gravy around and eat.

For the sake of conversation, I tell them about my drive around the city. 'Quite amazing. Nothing seems to have changed all that much. No development – Bulawayo's still her old self.'

Hazel swallows a mouthful behind her hand. 'Yes . . . and yet everything has changed. I wish you'd seen Bulawayo during Operation Murambatsvina. Parts of the city looked like a tornado went through it. The market stalls in 5th Avenue and near the City Hall – complete devastation. The shantytowns – gone, bulldozed into the ground. Mugabe's grand plan to clean up the cities. I don't suppose you people in Australia even heard of Murambatsvina.'

I nod. 'We saw a fair bit on TV.'

'It means *clean up filth*,' Clara says. 'Just an excuse for Mugabe to persecute his political opposition. He knows the urban poor are against him.'

Hazel nods. 'Those poor people . . . it's hard enough trying to make a living in this country. Fifth Avenue used to be a thriving market place –'

'Ag, what are you complaining about?' Vic interjects. 'Those bloody market stalls were just clogging up the streets with their junk. Never paid taxes. It's about time someone cleared them out. We never allowed it in the old days, did we?'

Clara bursts out laughing. 'Now I've heard everything! Vic seeing eye to eye with Mugabe!'

Hazel lets out a slow breath. 'Vic . . . Vic. No wonder this place is such a mess. First, the people had to deal with the likes of you – then Mugabe.'

'Christ, they were happy when they had to deal with the likes of me. They had jobs. Money. Food in their stomachs.'

'Well, you know how I feel about it. You just say things to annoy me.' Hazel returns her attention to her food. 'At least we've got the elections coming up.'

Vic thumps his fists down on either side of his plate, knife and fork clasped upwards. 'What is it with you and elections? You see that bastard rig every single one. Terrorise the opposition. And still you think: Ooh, the *people* are going to vote him out. Christ almighty. We should've hung him when we had him in jail.'

'I'm not going to argue with you. Frank's here. Let's talk about something nice. Where are you staying, Frank?'

'Milton Ogilvy. An old university friend.'

Vic laughs with his mouth full. 'Ogilvy? That shyster! His firm handled my case. Useless bastards. Bloody lost everything —'

'No, they didn't,' Hazel cuts in. 'They won your case. Legally, your ranch still belongs to you. It's not the lawyers' fault the veterans thumb their noses at the law.'

Vic grunts. 'How're you surviving there at Milton's? I hear he doesn't drink. Never trust a man who doesn't drink, I say.'

Clara rolls her eyes. 'Another original pearl of Baldwin wisdom.'

'I'm sure Frank's getting along just fine,' Hazel says. 'An alcohol-free stint would do you a world of good, Vic.'

'What's that?'

'I said an alcohol-free stint would do you a world of good!'

Vic points a fork at Hazel. 'Do me a favour, woman. If I ever have to give up the grog, just put a bullet through my head, okay?'

Hazel laughs. 'The last of the old Rhodesians. You're a dinosaur, Vic. When you die they'll stuff you and stick you in a museum!'

Vic smiles as though pleased with that prospect. 'So, Frank, what's your next move, boy? For all you know, this munt you're looking for is dead and buried.'

'Have I missed something?' Clara says.

'Frank has come all this way to give some old nanny 50,000 Aussie dollars.' Vic laughs incredulously. 'Can you bloody believe it?' He stares upward, as if for divine help.

Hazel waves a hand at him dismissively. 'What Vic's saying is that Frank's here to deliver a generous gift of money his dear mother left in her will to a maid, Lettah, who was once part of their family.'

Clara gives me a quizzical look.

'Part of their family!' Vic scoffs.

I continue: 'The last we heard of Lettah was that she'd gone back to my grandparents' farm. I hope she's still there. If she isn't, maybe someone knows what happened to her.'

'I still think it's a ridiculous idea,' Vic grumbles.

'I just want to lay the matter to rest, whatever the outcome.'

For a while we eat without speaking. Just the scrape of knives and forks and Vic's chomping. We finish our beers. Vic rings a bell. Daphne appears and Vic asks for more beer and a glass for Clara. The beer comes and we fill our glasses. Clara takes a long swig and stifles a belch. 'That's the one positive thing I'll say about Zimbabwe,' she says. 'The beer's good, even if the choice is limited.'

Vic smiles at her affectionately. 'Now there's something we can agree on.'

'There's something I wanted to ask you, Vic,' I say. 'Remember Brak Malan from Que Que? I heard he worked for you for a while. Any idea where he might be?'

Vic puts his knife and fork down. He raises his hands in the air and begins to clap. For an uncomfortable moment I think he is mocking me. Then he laughs. 'Brak Malan? Old Brak's a happy clappy. Born-again. Last I heard he was up at Kariba running a camp for God-botherers.'

'Brak went religious?'

He cups an ear. 'What's that?'

'You're saying Brak went religious?'

'Ja, man. I don't know what it is with those army blokes. Like a damn disease. I told him it was a crock when he worked for me. We had a few arguments. He buggered off eventually to preach the word.

55

Haven't heard from him since. Bloody waste. The bloke was a good mechanic when he stayed off the grog.'

Hazel says: 'Have a heart, Vic. Some of those army boys had a hard time.'

Vic waves his hand in disgust. 'Ag, what! Killing a few munts?'

Clara stops eating and stares at Vic. She seems about to say something but doesn't.

'Pity Brak wasn't a big tough guy like you!' Hazel says.

Vic grunts, waves his hand again and resumes eating.

'When are you going to Whitestone?' Hazel asks me.

'Hopefully tomorrow, first thing.'

'Would you mind terribly if I tagged along? It's been a while since I've been that way. You might find me useful. I know the area and speak the lingo.'

I shrug. 'Fine by me.'

Vic puts down his cutlery again. He slaps his forehead with a big sun-spotted hand. 'Have you completely taken leave of your senses, woman? What do you want to go gallivanting around the countryside for? Haven't you got a business to run here in Bulawayo?'

'Clara's perfectly capable of running the shop, Vic. She's been doing it for the past year. God knows, there's not that much to do these days anyway. It's not as though we're overrun by tourists.'

'Clara doesn't know her arse from her elbow! And those kaffirs who work for you are stealing you blind!'

Clara rises abruptly from the table and leaves the room without a word. We hear a door slam down the passage.

Hazel gives Vic a hard stare. 'You're being offensive now. I want you to apologise to her —'

Vic begins to object.

'No, Vic. I want you to apologise. And if I want to go to Fort Rixon with Frank, I'll go. I don't have to ask your permission.'

Vic holds out his hands in a helpless gesture. 'I'm just trying to look after you, girl. What happens if you run into a bunch of war vets, hey?'

56

'I'll be giving war veterans a wide birth, Vic, if that's any consolation,' I say.

After lunch we move back to the lounge. We chat about mundane everyday matters: the food and petrol shortages, inflation, the flood of people leaving the country. Vic's eyes begin to droop; soon he is snoring in his chair. I take this as a cue to leave.

Hazel accompanies me outside. 'Don't mind Vic,' she says.

'I wasn't expecting him to be any different.'

She smiles. 'My God, you look just like your father. What time are you leaving tomorrow?'

'About seven-thirty. Are you serious about coming?'

'I'll be waiting.'

She waves as I drive off.

In the four years that my family lived in Bulawayo, we rented a double-storey Mexican-style hacienda in Hillside, along Percy Avenue, not far from where Hazel now resides. Driving past, the old place looks much as I remember it: terracotta-tiled roof, white stucco walls, palm trees out in front. A curious oddity, even among the eclectic array of Bulawayo's suburban dwellings.

Further down Percy Avenue, another strange apparition appears: a medieval castle, stone turrets and all, nestling in a big wooded estate. An utterly bizarre English fantasy plonked on African soil long ago when the outposts of the British Empire seemed safe and secure. When we lived in Hillside the castle was empty and served as a fabulous battleground for the neighbourhood boys, our imaginations inflamed by the *Ivanhoe* series on TV, with Roger Moore in the lead role. Here, pint-sized Crusaders in cardboard armour, brandishing wooden swords and shields, fought and died, shrill of voice, and lived again to fight another day.

The castle has since been transformed into an up-market hotel. Zimbabwe seems a place of startling contradictions. Rare sprouts of improbable wealth in a vast morass of poverty. Not much in between.

I'm dogged by a lingering anger, ignited when Vic raised his hands mockingly above his head and clapped at the mention of Brak Malan. That is the thanks Brak receives from the old Rhodesian he fought to protect and preserve. Brak and his wild comrades with the corpse in the background ... when it comes to what soldiers must do in war – to killing – a curtain descends in me, behind which I have no desire to look. I have no idea of even how to think. All I can do is surmise that everyone is different. To some, perhaps, it's as easy as stamping on a cockroach. To others, a weight they must bear all their lives.

I drive up into the terraced parklands that surround the Hillside Dams, another boyhood haunt. I park under a tree and sit there with the car doors open, letting through a faint breeze. The main dam is dry; it looks to have been empty for some time; reeds and yellow grass sprout from the cracked-mud basin. Across the dams some kopjes emerge from a carpet of bush and trees. I used to explore these kopjes and once came across a beautiful frieze of San paintings – Bushman paintings, as we called them then. Kudu, eland, sable. Running hunters with bows and arrows. At the time, I had no idea how ancient the paintings were.

The beer I consumed at lunch has made me drowsy. I close my eyes and a fitful sleep returns me momentarily to Australia. Back on my bus route around Rottnest Island, I announce drop-off points on the intercom with smart-arse aplomb. 'Next stop, ladies and gentlemen: Nancy Cove – for you heaven-seekers. Stark Bay, for the wild ravers. Catherine Bay, for the genuine Rottnest connoisseur.' My tourist passengers stare blankly back at me through the rear-view mirror.

When I wake the afternoon shadows are long; the last of the sun catches the tops of the kopjes across the dams. Drowsy, lethargic, I get out of the car and walk across the causeway to the other side of the dam. I wander up through the kopjes, trying to find the rock face with the San paintings, but I can't. I pause on a rock ledge and look out towards the city. Bulawayo's tallest buildings glint. A distant growl of traffic. I breathe in the scent of the surrounding bush, strangely similar to human sweat. A faint whiff of smoke. I listen to the chatter of some weaver birds in the trees around the dam and the long, peaceful mantras of doves.

I feel I've only just arrived.

On my way back to Milton's I contemplate buying some beer at the Hillside shops. A quiet sundowner is something I've grown to relish back home in Perth and see no reason why this little ritual should be abandoned. After all, isn't the cottage in which I've been installed neutral territory? Surely Milton won't be offended if I stock the small bar fridge with a few beers and consume them privately, away from Ruby. There must be room in Milton's new world for compromise. But I picture the rigmarole of sneaking into the cottage with my illicit contraband and consuming it in surreptitious gulps, one guilty ear primed to the sound of approaching footsteps, and decide against it. Better to clear it with Milton first.

The two service stations en route are closed. I glance at the petrol gauge; the tank is just under three-quarters full. Enough, surely, to get to Fort Rixon and back tomorrow. Not more than 250 kilometres, I would guess. I continue on to Kumalo. The maid, Precious, unlocks the gate for me; I drive in and park under the carport next to Milton's car.

Milton and Ruby are in the lounge watching the news on satellite TV. Vernon is in his room, doing homework. Milton equips me with a sturdy glass of Coke and we sit and watch TV. Blood and mayhem in Baghdad. An escalation of fighting in Afghanistan. Lots of leftie tut-tutting by Milton and Ruby.

'If it's all about fighting terror and getting rid of horrible dictators,' Ruby asks, 'why haven't they put the boot to Mugabe's rear?'

The bulletin concludes with the story of a Frenchman who has taught a parrot to sing the *Marseillaise*. 'How symbolic,' Milton mutters, switching off the TV. 'So, Franco, how was your day? Did you get hold of Vic Baldwin?'

I nod. 'I had lunch with him and Hazel Kent, in fact.'

'How's the old warthog?'

'Age has not wearied the tyrant's tongue, sad to say. Though he does seem a bit perplexed by what's going on in this country.'

Milton laughs. 'Perplexed? Vindicated, you mean. When he sees what Mugabe's done to this place it must convince him that everything he ever stood for is right. Bloody ironic, hey! Mugabe's defining legacy: vindicating the likes of Vic! Was he able to help with your friend?'

'Apparently Brak went up to Kariba to join some Christian sect. No big deal. I've got someone else to find first.'

'How did you go with Geoffrey this morning?' Ruby asks.

'No records. He reckons the farm is my best bet. Talking of which, did you manage to get hold of that cop?'

'Chombo? Yes, I did. He'll be at the police station in the morning. I've told him you're coming.'

'Hazel Kent's decided to come with me tomorrow. She knows the place like the back of her hand.'

'Just don't go nosing around places without checking with Chombo first.'

'Ja, better to err on the side of caution, Franco,' Milton says. 'If something looks dicey, give it a miss. Especially with an old lady in tow. I take it you've got a bit of forex on you.'

I nod. 'US dollars, mostly.'

'Take some with you. It's amazing how cooperative people get in this country when you flash a greenback in front of their eyes. But for God's sake don't overdo it. You don't want to get yourself mugged.'

I blow out my cheeks. 'Sometimes I wonder what I've got myself into.'

Ruby laughs. 'You'll be all right. Just do what Chombo says.'

After dinner Milton walks outside with me to the cottage. The night sky is ablaze with stars. Milton stops at the pool and lifts the cover off the filter. He fiddles around with the engine. The engine starts, humming somewhat erratically.

60

'Bloody thing keeps packing in,' Milton says. 'I've been thinking of turning the pool into a fishpond. Breed some trout or bream.'

I gesture at the tennis court with its flourishing vegetables. 'Why not? Seems like you're on a self-sufficiency roll. I never figured you for a gardener.'

'More a necessity than a passion, I assure you.'

'Your passion, as I recall, was propping up the bar and talking literature.'

'Ja, in another life.'

'That reminds me: there's something I wanted to ask you, Milton. Would you mind if I kept some grog in the cottage? I don't want to rock the boat if it's a problem.'

Milton puts the filter cover back on and stands up. His face is in darkness.

'Ruby won't have any drinking in the house. I doubt if she'd like it in the cottage, either. I'd prefer you not to but feel free, if you must.'

I'd prefer? If you must?

'Surely you're not totally against drinking? I mean, I can understand Ruby's position —'

'Ruby's position is my position, Frank.'

The small thought that Milton is a teetotaller for convenience fades from my mind. I make light of it. 'It's just weird, seeing you after all this time. A pillar of sobriety!'

'We can't go on being students forever, Franco. Sad as that may be.'

What is this — a reproach? In the darkness I can't tell.

There is a long silence. Then Milton laughs softly and puts his hand on my shoulder. 'Drink, if you must, boyo. All I ask is that you respect Ruby's feelings. It's a big deal for her. Just the smell of the stuff freaks her out.'

I lie in the darkness, unable to sleep. My head swarms with the terrible images of Zimbabwe's farm invasions that for a while made the world recoil. Crops on fire. Homesteads besieged. A fox terrier keeping vigil next to the bullet-riddled body of a farmer. Workers chased down, hacked and clubbed to death. Petrified children cowering beside raped and beaten mothers. A cow flailing about on the floor of a burnt-out dairy, hock tendons slashed. The war veterans: gloating thugs, brandishing axes, pangas – veterans only of a war against their helpless own. I fret. What will tomorrow hold?

My thoughts turn to my father. A real veteran. Who fought in the Second World War battles that raged in North Africa, including the one that claimed Lydia's brother. Always my measure of men. What would he make of this? What would he do in my shoes? In my mind's eye, he looks at me with his unflinching gaze. Now Lydia moves into vision beside him. Opposites, yet inseparable. Errol tall, lean. Eyes a clear sky blue. His gaze outward, beyond himself. Steady, fearless, honest. Impatient with foolishness. Lydia short, burgeoning at the hips. Eyes like bottomless green wells, teeming with anxious thoughts.

V

I'm running an hour late, after a protracted but fruitless search around Bulawayo for petrol. Milton came to the rescue by siphoning some from his car, insisting it was of no great inconvenience, since his firm had taken to purchasing its own fuel via blackmarket sources — a measure adopted by many companies, apparently.

The sun has just broken clear of a rosy bank of clouds on the horizon when I arrive at Hazel's house. Hazel and Vic are waiting outside. Vic clad in slippers and a frayed green dressing-gown, a thick fur of white chest hair protruding. He is brandishing his walking stick and issuing instructions to the gardener who listens patiently beside a wheelbarrow. For a moment I imagine him naked beneath the gown, not an easy thought so early in the morning. Hazel looks quite Blixenesque in safari-style khaki shorts and shirt, straw hat and stout walking shoes. A leather bag hangs from a strap around her neck. I decline her offer of a quick cup of coffee and apologise for being late. Vic raises his stick in farewell as we depart.

Hazel lights a cigarette and chats away as we exit Bulawayo along an avenue lined with bedraggled palm trees and bougainvilleas, past the old drive-in, now overrun with acacia bush, past dusty smallholdings, brickworks and cement silos. In the distance a row of electricity pylons marches towards Harare; scraggly gum trees mark the position of railway sidings. There is little traffic on the road.

The car soon fills with a fog of cigarette smoke. I open my window.

Hazel coughs. 'If you don't want me to smoke, just say so.'

'I don't mind,' I lie.

Hazel asks more about my family; I talk about the Pietermaritzburg days, before our move to Australia. She is amused by my touchy sarcasm when it comes to Max's achievements and Errol's baleful opinion of my school career. She becomes wistful when I talk about my mother. When I finish she is pensive, then she shakes her head as if dispelling a bad thought.

We drive on in silence for a while. Hazel finishes her cigarette and stubs it out in the car's ashtray. She gestures at the passing countryside. 'It's amazing to think of what was going on here barely a century ago. The Matabele Wars. Rebellions . . . God, this soil is drenched in blood.'

I nod. 'Not much has changed, apparently.'

Hazel lights another cigarette and takes a long drag. 'What a struggle it must've been for those settler families . . . Amazing! This nondescript bush. That people have fought so violently for it.'

The turn-off to an army barracks flashes by. We pass a police car with a large dent in the right front fender parked under a tree. Behind the wheel, a policeman sits fast asleep, his mouth agape.

Hazel heaves a weary sigh. 'I suppose he is more effective that way.'

I laugh. 'I bet the cops are never short of petrol.'

'Depends on what you need them for. God help you if you need them for law and order. Nine times out of ten their vehicles are empty or broken down. Lots of petrol, though, when it comes to breaking up opposition rallies. Or for presidential motorcades.' Hazel snorts with disgust. 'What a circus this place must seem to you. And the worse it gets, the harder it'll be to turn it all around.'

'I thought you were pinning your hopes on the elections.'

'I only say things like that in front of Vic to keep a semblance of optimism alive. Make no mistake, the elections will be a farce. Mugabe's already terrorising the opposition. I hear his militia have started setting up torture camps. The opposition leader's hiding in

South Africa, scared he'll get assassinated if he returns. Vic's right. Mugabe will never relinquish power. He'll only go by force.'

'I don't get the impression revolution's in the air.'

'No, you're right. I thought Murambatsvina would've been the last straw, but it wasn't. People just meekly succumbed. Everyone's too broken, too defeated. And there's no one to turn to. The whole of Africa aids and abets Mugabe, despicable tyrant though he is. That, to me, has been the most disappointing thing. That so few Africans speak against him.'

'I don't know how you stick it out here, Hazel.'

Hazel takes a last drag on her cigarette and stubs it out. 'It's not all gloom and doom. Mugabe's old. If a bullet doesn't get him, old age will.'

We turn off at Whites Run Road and drive south-east along a rutted dirt road that makes the car's suspension gibber. Just a few crumbling stretches of tar across concrete culverts over dry streams. At a road-side store we branch off along a road heading due east, taking a longer route along the Amanzamnyama River past Hazel's old family farm. A group of men lounging on the store's veranda watches as we drive past. 'Nothing better to do than sit around drinking beer,' Hazel huffs. 'Where they find the money, I don't know. Slow down, Frank. These roads have seen better days.'

No exaggeration. The road has not been graded in years. At times I must slow to a crawl to negotiate holes and eroded dongas. The fences alongside are broken or have been pilfered, allowing the bush to encroach. We encounter no other vehicles. The surrounding lands are parched, desolate. The only signs of life, some women on the roadside walking along in single file with cans of water on their heads and a lone, tick-covered cow foraging among small plots of withered maize stalks beside a dry stream.

'Vic would cry to see this,' Hazel says.

'I must say, Hazel, it came as a surprise to see you two together.'

Hazel chuckles. 'I suppose it would. If someone told me fifty years ago that I'd be living under the same roof as Vic Baldwin, I would've laughed out loud. He's mellowed a bit since you last saw him, don't you think?'

'Not really.'

Hazel laughs. 'Believe me, his bark is bigger than his bite.'

'I think you've been very kind, taking him in.'

'Kind? Good Lord, he's not a charity case. His boys, Hugo and Cecil, send him a monthly stipend that more than covers his needs. In fact, lately I've had to rely on him to keep the wolf from the door. No, Frank, Vic doesn't need me to look after him. I asked him to move in. When you get to my age, it's nice to have company.'

'And Clara? Where does she fit into the picture?'

Hazel sighs. 'Clara . . . Clara. My troubled child. I was married to a lovely Scotsman for almost nine years. A lovely but extremely *trying* Scotsman. A gallery owner, based in Edinburgh. We met during a trip he made here in eighty-one – just after Mugabe took over. He was here collecting Shona carvings. We fell madly in love and got married. Along came Clara. Then we started to realise why we shouldn't have married. I wouldn't live in Britain permanently. I tried but couldn't stand it. My God, that *weather*! So we found ourselves conducting a hopeless relationship on opposite sides of the globe. He was also a drinker – a gentle drinker, mind you, but when he drank he liked the odd roll in the hay with other women. So we divorced – amicably. He died two years ago of a heart attack.'

'Sounds like Clara had a complicated upbringing.'

'I suppose it was. When she was a child I thought she'd be better off doing her schooling in Edinburgh and spending her long holidays here. So I wasn't the most attentive mother, and I think it shows in her sometimes. A bit of a restless spirit, I'm afraid. Can't seem to settle down.'

'What are her plans? I mean, will she take over your business?'

'It's not a business worth taking over. The idea was that she'd take over her father's business. Unfortunately for her, when he died all the women in his life started squabbling over his will. He left a lot of debts too. Once everything was divvied up, she got very little.'

'How long is she planning to stay here?'

'I don't know. As long as it takes to get bored, I suppose.'

We arrive at the boundary of the old Kent farm, marked by the corner post of a nonexistent fence. When the homestead comes into view, I pull over and wait as Hazel gets out and crosses the road to the farm's entrance. She leans against a gatepost and gazes at what remains of the house, two hundred metres away. Just crumbling walls sticking out above the long grass and thorn trees. A ruptured rain tank nearby enveloped by bougainvillea creepers with magenta flowers, lending the shimmering brown landscape a splash of colour. There is a powerful stillness, now that the rattle of the car has ceased. Hazel stares at the ruins of her old home for a long while. Then she glances down at the broken gate lying in the grass beside the entrance, and bows her head. It occurs to me that this is where her parents died. One dark night, shot to ribbons as they stopped here to open the gate. It was never established if they were still alive when the killers torched their car. Found the next day by a neighbour passing by.

Hazel comes back to the car, dabbing her eyes with the back of her hand.

'Are you okay?' I ask.

She nods. 'It's always a bit sad coming here. You wouldn't remember my parents, would you?'

'I remember what happened.'

'I can understand people wanting their land back. But it hurts to see the way the old place has gone to ruin. It makes their deaths even more senseless.' She gives a dismissive wave of her hand. 'Anyway, you can't cry over spilt milk. Let's go.'

We link up with the Nsiza road and continue south. Finally the small settlement of Fort Rixon appears against a range of low, thickly wooded hills. We reach an intersection marked by a sign listing the farmers' names from the district – obsolete, as Hazel points out – and cross a cattle grid into the settlement. Just a few dusty buildings straddling the road: a store, a small school, the police station and a handful of near-derelict houses, hidden behind acacia scrub. It's almost ten o'clock; already Fort Rixon's inhabitants have succumbed to ennui, taking refuge in the shade of verandas and trees, resigned to another day of sweltering heat. The only establishment in apparent good nick is the police station, easily located because of its radio mast and four-metre-high security fence – indeed, the only place that has undergone something of an upgrade since I last passed through here as a boy. Shaded by big jacaranda trees, the red-brick buildings and grounds are immaculate, gardens and parking areas demarcated with whitewashed stones. Outside the charge office a Zimbabwean flag hangs limply at its mast.

We are stopped at the gate; I explain the purpose of our visit to the policeman on duty and ask the whereabouts of Inspector Chombo. The constable points towards the jail where an officer is talking to a group of convicts, each equipped with a gardening implement. We park in front of the charge office and walk around to the jail.

Inspector Julius Chombo is an imposing man of middle age. Khaki peaked cap perched well forward on his forehead. Neatly pressed khaki trousers, a grey short-sleeved shirt with a blue lanyard around his left shoulder. Shining insignia on the epaulettes, shoes boned like mirrors. An old jagged scar across one cheek. Not a man who favours exercise, judging by his bulging midriff. Ruby has informed me that Chombo is a Shona, yet he speaks IsiNdebele fluently if his rapid orders to the assembled convicts are anything to go by. He finishes and dismisses them. The convicts saunter off in their thick, faded brown prison garb, presumably to begin another day of raking and weeding around the police station precincts.

I introduce myself and Hazel; we shake hands. Chombo's gleaming jowls bunch around a jovial smile. 'Ah! Ah! Magistrate Ruby's Australian friend – g'day, mate! How'ya goin', mate?'

Nonplussed by this jolly welcome, I grin stupidly in response.

Chombo laughs. 'You must tell Ruby that I miss her chocolate cake.' His eyes gleam wistfully at the thought. 'Tell her she must come and have a picnic with me at the dam. The dam is empty, but no matter.'

We follow him back to the charge office. He instructs a young female constable behind the counter (whose moniker, I gather, is 'Fashion') to make tea. He ushers us along a corridor to his office. We sit facing each other across a desk strewn with folders, the working parts of a rifle laid out on an oily newspaper, and a silent computer. On the walls there are maps and aerial pictures of the region along with the obligatory presidential portrait. One of the maps still has the Rhodesian names of towns. A few framed photographs of Chombo among colleagues and one of him saluting the Police Commissioner, Augustine Chihuri, at a passing-out parade.

As we wait for the tea, I explain my mission. I place the old photograph of Lettah on the desk. Chombo listens without interrupting. He writes a few notes on a pad. Constable Fashion enters and places a tea tray on Chombo's desk and departs. With a curious dainty efficiency, Chombo pours the tea. We drink.

Chombo gets down to business. He screws up one side of his mouth and taps the photograph with a stubby finger. 'When was this taken? Thirty? Forty years ago?'

'It's the only picture I have. Maybe someone from that time will recognise her.'

Chombo blows his cheeks out and shakes his head slowly. 'If she is alive then she would be, what? Seventy? Eighty?'

I nod. 'In that vicinity.'

He asks more questions: How long did she work for my family? Where did we live during her employment? What year did she return to the farm? Small details. I answer as best I can. As Chombo notes down my answers, I begin to suspect he is merely going through the motions. His questions seem perfunctory, sceptical. If it were not for his past association with Ruby would he even bother with this?

The questions cease. Chombo stares at the photograph on the desk, then at me. 'Who knows? You may be lucky, Mr Cole. This Lettah Ndlovu might still be alive. She might still live in this area. But

I don't think so. I've worked in this district for sixteen years and I've never heard of this woman. I know this district. It's my job to know everyone here. I'm sorry to say this, but I think you are wasting your time. She has probably died or moved away.' He holds up his hands in a helpless gesture. 'You mustn't hope too much. The world has changed since this photograph was taken. It's anyone's guess what has happened to her.'

'Indeed,' Hazel says. 'She might well have moved away. Or fallen ill and died. And there's always the possibility that she was a victim of the army. It's common knowledge that the 5th Brigade cut a swathe through this area back in the eighties during Gukurahundi. The police would surely have knowledge of what farms were affected by that campaign.'

Her blunt comments bring a blunt expression to Chombo's face. He stares at her, then smiles. 'I wasn't in command here in the eighties, madam. But as far as I understand, the soldiers only came to Matabeleland to restore order. Their job was to find the bandits who were killing people. Killing white farmers, too, as you may recall. They were not here to harm innocent people, especially women. If any innocents died it was at the hands of the dissidents.'

Hazel laughs dryly. 'Inspector Chombo, forgive me, but we all know what went on when Gukurahundi came to Matabeleland. Atrocities were committed. Thousands were slaughtered. You can't deny this.'

An amused, half-plaintive expression appears on Chombo's face. 'That is only your opinion, madam. If you check the facts I know you will change your mind.'

I hold up my hand. 'Look, I'm not interested in what went on in this country twenty years ago. I just want to find Lettah. Or find out what happened to her, so I can resolve the matter of the will.'

Chombo leans forward on his elbows, his fingers interlocked. 'Will? You mean this woman has received an inheritance?'

I nod.

'This inheritance — what figure are we talking about?'

70

I hesitate. 'Fifty thousand dollars. Australian.'

Chombo's eyes assume the glazed expression common to Zimbabweans engaged in mammoth tasks of currency conversion. A figure is computed: Chombo raises his eyebrows and blinks. I can almost hear the ring of a cash register. 'Hmm . . . a lot of money for one poor old woman.'

Hazel and I look at each other. Hazel smiles.

With a look of firm resolution, Chombo slaps his hands on his desk. 'Well, then, we must do our utmost to find this woman. Perhaps I can receive a commission for my efforts, if we do find her?'

I don't answer.

Chombo laughs. 'Only joking, my friend. You Australians! What's happened to your sense of humour, hey?'

'Who knows?' Hazel says, winking at me. 'If all goes well perhaps there will be a little bonsella.'

Chombo gives her a warm smile. 'Rest assured, I will leave no stone unturned. I'd start right now this minute, if I could. However, I'm very busy today. I must attend the magistrate's court this afternoon. But you can still visit the farm where this woman was last seen.'

'Is it safe for us to visit?' I ask.

'Don't worry, you will be safe. I know the farm. Whitestone. I know all the farms in this area. You can go with my constable. I know the man who is in charge at Whitestone. Dlomo – a good man, committed to the objectives of the government. If he sees the constable he won't make trouble for you.'

'Yes, but will he mind us asking questions?'

'People respect the law in Zimbabwe, Mr Cole. I'm the law in this district. If I send my constable with you there will be no trouble.'

Chombo is in a generous mood. He offers the use of a police van. We go outside, collecting Constable Fashion along the way (I had in mind a slightly more robust-looking police escort, but there you go). The monotonous *tink-tink* calls of barbets are loud in the trees. The convicts are down on their haunches in the gardens. Constable Fashion minces along in a tight-fitting regulation green skirt and new pair of shoes. Chombo discovers the van has no petrol. Apologetically, he rescinds his offer of transport.

We climb into my car. Constable Fashion up front next to me, Hazel in the back. Before leaving, I say to Hazel: 'Are you sure you want to come along? I told Vic I was going to give the war vets a wide birth. I don't know what to expect at Whitestone.'

Hazel dismisses my concern with a wave of her hand. 'What? And leave me here to be entertained by the good folk of Fort Rixon? Oh, come, come, Frank! You're as bad as your mother. You worry too much.'

We drive east along the Shangani road. Hazel puffs away in the back, IsiNdebele spouting from her mouth like smoke signals as she tries to engage Constable Fashion in conversation. From my rudimentary grasp of the language I deduce that Hazel's questions are mostly related to the occupants of Whitestone. But Constable Fashion is a woman of few words. She sits stiffly in her seat, staring sullenly ahead, her monosyllabic replies terse and evasive – it's clear that this jaunt is not her preferred option. Eventually Hazel desists, concentrating instead on a running commentary of the scenery around us.

We enter the hilly country of the eastern Insiza River Valley; a profusion of exfoliating granite kopjes bursting from dense msasa-gondi woodlands and open grass plains. Hazel likens the kopjes to the tops of bald heads rising from a tawny sea. Constable Fashion's attention is aroused at last. She turns to Hazel. 'It's interesting that you make this observation,' she says in English. 'The old Ndebeles used to call this land Amakhandeni.'

Hazel laughs. 'Well I never! The Place of Heads. Isn't that poetic!'

This seems to break the ice between them. It appears at least some of Constable Fashion's earlier hostility stemmed from an aversion to being spoken to in IsiNdebele by a white person, as though it marked her as an uneducated country bumpkin. She explains how many of the settlements in the area originated from Matabele garrisons set up by the old chief Mzilikazi way back in the nineteenth century. I suspect Hazel is au fait with this history; the way she murmurs in wonder is, in my book, mildly patronising. Not that Constable Fashion seems to notice. The conversation moves to more mundane things. On the subject of women's fashion, the constable proves aptly named. We listen to a passionate denunciation of skinny models like Kate Moss and Posh Beckham. 'Girls like boys,' she concludes succinctly.

Pale brown dust billows out behind the car as we head towards a distant rampart of hills. The encroaching bush has reduced the road to a single-vehicle track. The land is tinder dry; parts are blackened by recent fires. The last time I traversed these roads was with my parents almost forty years ago. The sour-dry smell of elephant grass wafts in through my open window, evoking memories of the thatched home of my grandparents. Of holidays spent on Whitestone. Cyril and Betty sitting together in the evenings playing Solitaire with worn-out cards, slowly sipping their brandy, chirping away like old roosting birds. The hiss of hurricane lamps and the distant thump of drums from the headman's kraal, a mile away. Cyril used to say that if you couldn't hear the drums, there was trouble afoot.

Cyril was a fine storyteller. He had lived what Betty called 'a colourful life' before settling down with her to eke a difficult living from the unforgiving Insiza Valley soil. After a few brandies, Cyril used to tell Max and me stories about the early days in Rhodesia. Amusing stories, often repeated with slurred embellishments that contradicted earlier versions, but no less entertaining. And after a bit more brandy, he acquired a gleam in his eye and referred to Betty as his little 'dumpling'. Betty would get coy and pat his hand. A scamp, old Cyril. Happy with his lot in life.

Betty also had her ways. Once Max and I were left alone with her while Cyril was away at a cattle sale in Gwelo. Some workers spotted a mamba in the tractor shed and ran to the house to call the nkosi. Finding only Betty, their expressions grew sceptical – they knew Cyril was handy with his shotgun, but Betty? Standing imperiously on the veranda, arms akimbo, Betty listened to them calmly. Then she went inside and a few minutes later, to everyone's astonishment, emerged clad head to toe in her husband's attire — khaki shirt and long trousers with braces, his big boots and worn-out hat with the stained zebra skin band. Shotgun at port, she descended the veranda steps and marched grimly towards the shed. Sighting the snake coiled around a rafter, she blasted away at it, succeeding only in perforating the corrugated iron roof and destroying a paraffin lamp hanging from a beam. The snake slithered down and made a leisurely escape into the nearby bush. Betty returned to the house, ignoring the laughter of the workers, her job as Nkosi done.

Small, lost histories . . .

The road skirting the Dhlo Dhlo Ruins is in such poor condition we are at times forced to inch across rock-strewn patches and dongas. We cross the range of hills that separates the Insiza River Valley from the Shangani River catchment and head south. The track is now strewn with sandy patches; I worry that we may get stuck but Constable Fashion assures me she has traversed these roads in police vehicles with no problem.

We pass forgotten landmarks of countless childhood visits to Whitestone. Farms of my grandparents' neighbours. The hulk of an old Ford truck abandoned in a field. The small dams, now dry, built to catch the run-off from the hills. Roadside ramps where cattle and sheep were loaded onto trucks that took them to the abattoir in Gwelo. Familiar, yet changed. Ominous. The lands are haunted by absence, by emptiness. Devoid of livestock or crops. Devoid of old trees — the avenues of eucalypts that graced farm entrances, gone. Abandoned buildings, derelict shells. The squatter camps themselves are empty, but for a few women listlessly carrying out chores with babies on their backs or with toddlers in tow.

'Constable, where are the people?' I ask. 'Where are the men? I see just a few women and children.'

'The men are looking for work.'

'In Gweru? Bulawayo?'

Constable Fashion nods.

'Why are they not working on the farms?'

'There is no rain.'

'In our time,' Hazel says, 'you put a little aside to see you through.'

Constable Fashion stares ahead, sullen again.

Reaching the Whitestone turn-off, we enter over a cattle grid and drive across a flat stretch of woodlands, the grass between the wheel tracks scraping underneath the car. As we round the kopje my grandfather called Betty's Bluff, the farmhouse and outbuildings come into view. Just as they used to be, almost: the crude, simple house built of stone and cement blocks, the grey thatched roof; smoke wafting from a makeshift boiler adjacent to the kitchen – a forty-four gallon drum perched above an open fire. The place seems bare, strangely naked, and I remember it used to be surrounded by trees. My grandparents had a particular fondness for flamboyant trees. There were at least a dozen of them around the house, along with cypresses and fruit trees, native msasas and the beautiful mountain acacia. All gone. Cyril and Betty were fastidious about keeping the house and gardens spick and span. They employed gardeners to tend the orchards and the flower and vegetable beds; every leap year the house and sheds were whitewashed. Back then, the homestead was an oasis of green amid the vast brown swathes of bush. Now it's a barren sore on the land, the gardens bare and dusty – all that grows is a dense stand of cactus trees behind the house. Just the poles and rusted gates remain of the security fence that was built in the war years. There are a number of square mud adobes next to the sheds; the only new buildings visible. A rusted Datsun van with one wheel missing stands up on a jack in front of the house. A Zanu-PF flag hangs like a rag from a pole in the centre of the bare ground that was once the front lawn.

I stop the car. Constable Fashion sighs impatiently as I reach into the glove box for my camera and take a couple of shots of the old place through the window. We drive on. As we approach the house, a pack of starving dogs scrambles towards the car, barking incessantly.

People emerge from the buildings. Compared to the other farms we have passed, Whitestone appears to accommodate a fair-sized community. Constable Fashion informs us that it had been the 'centre of operations' for the local war vets, and is now a 're-education centre'.

About twenty people, most of them men, gather as I stop in front of the house. A man in tattered blue overalls carrying an axe hurls a stone at the milling dogs, hitting one which starts yelping; the rest quieten and slink off. The other men make threatening gestures at the yelping dog; it cowers and limps off. The man with the axe circles the vehicle, peering at Hazel and me with a perplexed look. When he sees Constable Fashion he straightens up and shouts something to a young woman on the veranda who calls inside. After a while, a tall man wearing baggy cargo shorts and a soiled AC/DC t-shirt emerges. Gingerly, he limps down the stairs, yawning and indignant, muttering to himself. He has the irritable morning-after expression of a binge drinker, something I've occasionally seen gazing back at me in the mirror. But the man's face softens when he spies Constable Fashion climbing out. He smiles slyly while they exchange pleasantries in IsiNdebele, mostly, I gather, of a lurid sort.

'Fashion, my darling!' he calls in a heavy rasping voice. 'Your bottom grows in size and beauty.'

'Aibo, Dlomo — wena!' Constable Fashion giggles coyly.

'Who have you brought here to visit us, sweetie pie?'

Hazel and I are introduced. Constable Fashion explains my intentions, mentioning Chombo's name.

The sly smile is still there. Speaking in English, he asks: 'Your family owned this farm?'

I nod. 'My grandparents owned it long ago.'

'Oh, so it must be like coming home, not so?'

I'm uncomfortable beneath Dlomo's red-eyed stare. I notice his legs are covered with white scars. 'My home is in Australia, not here. I'm just interested in finding a woman who once lived here. Lettah Ndlovu — she would be an old woman now.'

The smile fades. 'There are no Ndlovus here.'

76

'Yes, but perhaps someone knows where she is. If she is still alive.'

'There's no one left on this farm from that time.'

'I'd still like to ask some questions.'

'What is your business with this Ndlovu?'

'She once worked for my family.'

Without turning Dlomo reaches out and clicks his fingers. He barks an instruction. The young woman on the veranda runs down the steps and, almost grovelling, hands him a pack of cigarettes.

'Why are you looking for this woman, after all this time?'

'It's a family matter.'

'That does not answer my question, Mr Cole.'

'So I can give her an inheritance.'

'Not that it's any of your business,' Hazel mutters.

Dlomo looks askance at her, then returns his gaze to me. He lights a cigarette, takes a drag and coughs. 'Inheritance? You mean money? How much?'

'A sizeable sum.'

'Don't waste my time, Mr Cole. I must know what we are talking about here if I'm going to help you.'

'Fifty thousand Australian dollars.'

That blank look. The cash register blink. 'Mayibabo! That's a lot of money for one old Rhodesian slave. Where is this money?'

'The money is in Australia. In the bank. It can be released to this woman only if we find her.'

'And how much will you pay to ask questions?'

I sigh. A game must be played. 'Inspector Chombo said nothing about paying to ask questions.'

'You cannot expect a free ride, Mr Cole.'

'Fifty US dollars. That's all I can afford.'

Hazel gives a scornful laugh. 'And what makes you think you deserve anything at all? Only criminals would seek to benefit from what doesn't belong to them.'

I glance at Hazel, concerned that the heat might have robbed her of her senses. Dlomo also looks at her, the sly smile on his face exfoliating into a sneer. He mutters in IsiNdebele, 'Perhaps the reason for this Ndlovu's disappearance is that she possessed an impertinent tongue.'

'Quite possibly,' Hazel replies in kind. 'Those who tell the truth are never welcome among crooks.'

Am I missing some subtle diplomacy here? Do African thugs welcome being publicly rebuked by old white ladies? Not according to Dlomo's irate body language. Constable Fashion intervenes impatiently. 'The umlungu, Mr Cole, is happy to pay to ask questions. But we must get on with it. I don't have time to waste. Chombo expects me back at the station by noon.'

Dlomo's smile returns. 'No need to hurry, plump dove. Perhaps I can entertain you while the umlungu conducts his investigations?'

Constable Fashion laughs. 'Aibo! With your entertainment a girl can get the Sickness.'

Dlomo protests: 'AIDS? No! No! I make love only with virgins.'

'Are we free to ask questions?' I ask.

Dlomo holds his hands out magnanimously. 'Zimbabwe is a free country, Mr Cole. Once I've received my fee you can ask the people on this farm anything you want. One of my men will accompany you so the questions can be answered fully.'

I reach into my back pocket and take out a small wad of notes. I count off fifty dollars and hand it to Dlomo. 'I'm sure we don't need any help,' I say.

'You have paid me to ask questions. It's my duty to see that you get answers.' Dlomo turns to the man with the axe. 'Zuma, go with the umlungu. Make sure his questions are answered.'

The man, Zuma, raises his axe in salute.

Dlomo turns to Hazel. 'You see, old lady, I am a man of honour. There are no criminals here.'

'Yes, I can see,' Hazel says, smiling. 'I can see that honour wears a short skirt in your world.'

Dlomo stares at her. 'Be careful how you tread today. Old people are prone to accidents.' He turns and limps back into the house.

Exasperated, I glare at Hazel. She gives me an innocent look.

'My, my!' she says. 'More your mother by the minute.'

We follow Zuma along a path through the stands of cactus trees to the rear of the house. I'm peeved that we appear under the direction of Zuma but there's no choice in the matter. Already he has given instructions that no photographs are to be taken, insisting that Hazel and I leave our cameras in the car. I wonder if they will still be there when we get back.

'What are those scars on Dlomo's legs?' I ask Constable Fashion.

'He was wounded in the war,' she pants. 'Phosphorous bomb.'

'An actual war veteran,' Hazel says. 'How extraordinary.'

After a few hundred metres it becomes apparent that Constable Fashion's tight skirt and stout new shoes are causing extreme discomfort. Faced with the bleak alternative of returning to the house and the attentions of Dlomo, she soldiers on, wincing with every step. But soon her chafed thighs and feet are too sore to continue; she retires from the expedition and hobbles off, wide-legged, skirt hiked up over her thighs, back towards the house. We continue in single file: Zuma up front, Hazel, then me. Every so often Zuma is halted by a coughing fit. He bends over double as he coughs, spitting dark gobs into the grass. Hazel, puffing away on a cigarette, shakes her head as though bemused at how people abuse their bodies. The bush screams with insects. Sweat trickles down my face; I pant. My physical condition galls me, particularly as Hazel strides along effortlessly ahead of me. The deft gait of her thin white legs reminds me that she was an avid bushwalker back in the Que Que days.

The path winds through some dense bush between two kopjes, emerging onto a ridge above a wide shallow valley. We follow the ridge and come to the workers' compound, nestled among some msasa trees. Built by my grandfather for his unmarried workers, the compound consists of a long block of rooms with a corrugated iron roof flanked by two smaller buildings – a kitchen and an ablution block. Never an aesthetic wonder, it was nonetheless whitewashed regularly, like the other buildings on the farm, and my grandparents set aside land nearby for the workers to grow plots of mielies and vegetables. Betty, with customary eccentricity, even gave them seedlings to grow flowers around the buildings and offered prizes for those who kept the best gardens – a challenge the men, strange to say, responded to with competitive fervour.

Now, with depressing inevitability, we are confronted by squalor and neglect. The buildings have become hovels, blackened by smoke and grime. The corrugated iron roofing of the kitchen and latrines is gone. Doors and windows are missing. In the past chickens, pigs or goats might have scampered away at our approach; now there are just two starving dogs that gaze listlessly at us from where they lie in the shade next to the kitchen building. Faces appear at the doorways of the rooms.

Zuma comes to a halt in front of the building. He whistles loudly. The people emerge. About twenty ragged, emaciated souls, the children hiding behind the adults. A baby suckles at a withered breast. Some of them appear to have a skin disease; their arms and legs are covered in white flakes.

'Heavens above, isn't this pathetic,' Hazel whispers.

The people gather before Zuma, eyes downcast. There are three men; the rest are women, teenage girls and infants. Most look sick and frail. Zuma speaks too quickly for me to follow. The people nod.

Hazel takes over. 'Thank you, Zuma,' she says, stepping forward in front of him. 'We can manage from now on.'

Zuma glares at her. He starts to say something but Hazel waves him aside and turns to the people. She indicates for them to sit. She beckons me forward and we sit facing the group. Zuma stands to one side, glowering.

'I better do the talking,' Hazel says under her breath. 'These people won't understand your Fanagalo.'

I nod.

Speaking IsiNdebele, Hazel asks who can remember the old days on the farm. The people stare at her in nervous silence. Even the young ones appear old.

She asks again: 'Can anyone remember the old people who owned this farm – the Metcalfs?' She points to me. 'This man is Frank Cole. His grandfather, Nkosi Cyril Metcalf, owned this farm.'

Silent stares. Zuma crouches on his haunches, drumming his fingers on the axe between his legs. He spits.

'Mr Cole is looking for a woman who lived here,' Hazel says.

I take the photograph of Lettah from my shirt pocket and hold it up for the people to see. I give it to one of the men who looks at it, then passes it to the man sitting next to him.

'This photograph is from long ago,' Hazel goes on. 'Please look at it, all of you older ones. The woman's name is Lettah Ndlovu. Her father was headman here. Solomon. Does anyone remember the Ndlovus? Please do not be afraid to speak. Mr Cole has a gift for this woman, that is all. That is Mr Cole's purpose here. To give this woman a gift.'

Hazel singles out the oldest man, a sallow individual with a sunken chest. 'Indhoda, will you speak with us? You look old enough to remember that time.'

The man looks at her, then returns his gaze to the ground.

'Do you remember Lettah Ndlovu?' I ask. 'Do you remember her father, Solomon Ndlovu, the headman?'

The man looks at me. There is a brief intensity in his gaze; for a moment I think he is about to say something. Then he looks down again and shakes his head.

'Umgazi,' he says.

'Umgazi,' the people around him echo. 'We do not know this woman.'

Hazel glances at Zuma, then turns to me. 'We're not going to get anything out of them with that idiot hanging around. They're terrified of him.'

'Shall I tell him to push off?' I say.

81

Hazel shakes her head. 'I doubt he'd listen. He's Dlomo's eyes and ears. They've got wind of a bit of money and want to be in on the action. Anything these people know, they want to know. We're in a bit of a predicament, Frank. I've no idea if they have anything helpful to tell us. But I don't want to push the issue if they're afraid to talk. God, these poor souls! Look at them. What they must have endured at the hands of this scum.'

I glance at Zuma. He gazes back blankly.

'Okay,' I say. 'Offer them a reward, then we'll go.'

Hazel turns to the people. 'Perhaps you have forgotten about this woman, Lettah Ndlovu. I know there have been other owners of this farm since the Metcalfs, but Mr Cole is offering a reward – a handsome reward – if someone comes forward with information that enables us to find Ndlovu. US dollars. If your memory returns you can tell Inspector Chombo at the police station in Fort Rixon. He will contact us and we will give you the reward.'

I get to my feet. 'Thank you for your attention. I hope you can still help me.'

Zuma approaches. 'Are you finished with these people?'

'We're finished,' Hazel replies.

Zuma dismisses the people with a wave of his hand. They stand up and shuffle back into their hovels.

'I want to talk to the other workers on this farm,' I say.

'There are no other workers,' Zuma says.

'What? In the old days there were at least twenty men and their families here.'

Zuma shrugs. 'They have gone.'

'Gone? Gone where?'

'You are not my interrogator. They have gone – that's all you need to know.'

'I want to see Ndlovu's kraal.'

'There is nothing to see. There is no kraal.'

Hazel takes me by the elbow. 'Come on, there's no point in talking to him. If you remember where the kraal was let's just go.'

There used to be a path from the compound to the headman's kraal, but it has long since vanished beneath bush and grass. Once again, I follow my instincts. I vaguely remember the location of the kraal – down near a bend in the river, in a north-facing lea of Betty's Bluff. Ignoring Zuma, we walk in the direction of Betty's Bluff. The noon sun burns down, hot and heavy. Sweating profusely, I swat irritably at flies, cursing them. Hazel chuckles behind me. 'Shame on you, Frank! Mistreating Africa's precious wildlife like that!'

Zuma follows fifty metres behind. We listen to his coughing and hawking. Angered by this unexpected deviation, he cleaves off the top of an ant heap with his axe as he wades through the long grass. I think of the people we have just encountered and imagine the sort of pedagogy they experienced in Dlomo's re-education centre. I've read horror stories about such places, better described as torture and rape camps. The abject resignation on their faces suggests they have suffered a frightful atonement. Atonement for what? For working for white farmers? As we approach the dry river course, I notice many of the smaller trees alongside have been pushed over. I point them out to Hazel.

'Elephants,' she says.

'You're joking,' I say.

'No, I'm serious. Escapees from the game reserves. Apparently, there're hundreds of them following these old water courses.'

'That's incredible.'

Hazel laughs. 'Isn't it wonderful? Roaming free.' She glances back at Zuma. 'Until these goons get in on the ivory trade.'

We follow the river course through a forest of msasa trees, our feet crunching on their spiral pods strewn on the ground. We emerge onto an open plain and wade through chest-high grass until we come to the place where I remember the Ndlovu kraal to have been. I recognise the grey granite rampart of the bluff and the wild fig and mountain acacia trees that formed a backdrop to the kraal, and the steep-banked river nearby, now just a winding snake of white sand and rocks. As I recall, there were seven huts belonging to Solomon

Ndlovu and his family, set out in a wide semi-circle with Solomon's at the apex. The huts were thatched with circular ridges and the exterior walls were painted in traditional blue and white zigzag designs. There was also a storage hut nearby built on stilts to keep their grain clear of damp and bugs. A few maize and vegetable plots straddled the river, surrounded by sapling fences to keep the cattle and goats out. Solomon Ndlovu had chosen the site for his kraal well. The towering bluff shielded it from the afternoon sun in summer; in winter it basked in late sunshine.

The hot, ripe smell of the bush tugs me into the past. Whenever we visited Whitestone during holidays, Lettah used to take Max and me to the kraal to meet her family. We'd pay our respects first to Solomon who taught us to shake hands the African way, gripping thumbs. Solomon had two wives and five children – three sons and two daughters – of whom Lettah was the oldest. The sons all worked on the farm; the other daughter was a late arrival and wasn't much older than Max and me. Lettah said there had been three others – twin boys who died in childbirth, and another sister who was bitten by a snake. She explained the hierarchical layout of the huts, how seniority determined who lived closest to Solomon. The interior of the huts smelled of smoky thatch and dry dung floors. We'd sit around the fire while Solomon told us stories and his wives cooked up a feast of sadza, the maize meal porridge that is Africa's staple meal, and goat stew, or a chicken, feet and all in the pot. His calloused hand scooping out some sadza from the three-legged pot over the coals, squashing it into a ball and dipping it into the stew. Taking a bite and sighing with delight. Handing the rest to me, saying, 'Eat this, Nkosana, and tell me what better pleasures exist in this world.'

Now, from where we approach through the long grass, it appears that nothing of the kraal remains. Just the bluff, the bush and the eternal whine of insects.

'Are you sure this is the spot?' Hazel asks.

I nod. 'This is the place. Everything's gone.'

Not quite everything. I almost stumble over the barely discernible rings of earth denoting where the huts had been, now overgrown with grass and sickle bush.

We stop and stare in silence at the remains. Hazel lights a cigarette and takes a deep drag. Zuma watches nervously; he keeps his distance, waist deep in the yellow grass. I wonder if his nervousness is prompted by a fear of the spirits that haunt this space. I crouch down and poke through one of the mounds with a stick, unearthing a rusted spoon and a melted transistor radio. Hazel crouches down next to me. She picks up the spoon and rubs it between her fingers. I prize the melted radio out of the mound and turn it over fearfully, as though it might suddenly come to life.

Hazel stands up. She looks around and shrugs. 'We can only speculate, Frank. There could be half a dozen explanations for this. These remains are old. This bush would've taken years to grow over like this. It's certainly possible that this is the 5th Brigade's handiwork. They liked to make examples of those in positions of authority. Unfortunately Lettah's father, being a headman, would have fitted the bill.' She raises her hands and drops them. 'We can't say for certain that Lettah was even on the farm at the time of Gukurahundi.'

I go over to the remains of Solomon's hut, now hidden under an impenetrable thicket of sickle bush. I scuff at the mounds of dirt beneath the bush, then desist, suddenly fearful of what lurks beneath. Fearful that I'm desecrating something. Staring up at the sheer-sided bluff, I'm overwhelmed by a sense of dread and defeat; the task of finding Lettah in this God-forsaken country seems fraught with menace. I turn and walk over to Zuma who now sits in the grass, invisible save for a glimpse of his blue overalls. Hazel follows behind.

I pretend to be affable. 'Zuma, is there anything you can tell me about what happened to these people?'

Zuma groans as he slowly gets to his feet. 'I'm not from these parts.'

'Yes, but perhaps you heard what happened here. Surely you would have heard something from the people who worked on this farm.'

'The people who worked here when this happened have all gone.'

'But surely you've heard something? You said *when this happened*. When what happened?'

Zuma just stares at me blankly.

I sigh, exasperated. 'For God's sake, man! People can't simply disappear! Someone must know!'

Zuma continues to stare back. Hazel whispers in my ear. 'Perhaps an incentive is called for.'

I take a twenty-dollar note from my pocket. 'I will pay for information. Any information.'

Zuma looks at the money. He blinks. Rubs a thumb along the blade of his axe. Our helplessness dawns on me fully; fear surges through me.

Hazel, too, senses danger. 'We're wasting our time, Frank,' she says, her voice quavering slightly. 'Come on, let's go. *Inspector Chombo* is waiting for us.'

The heavy emphasis on Chombo's name appears to have an immediate effect. The malevolent gleam in Zuma's eye disappears. He stretches and yawns elaborately. Smiles, brown-toothed. 'The people here were killed for supporting the dissidents. That's what I heard. That is all I know.'

'All the Ndlovus?' I ask. 'The whole family?'

'That's what I heard.'

'What happened? How were they killed?'

'I don't know. They were killed. Punishment for traitors.'

'No one from the family survived?'

'That's what I heard.'

'No witnesses?'

Zuma shakes his head.

I look at Hazel. She shrugs.

'Okay,' I say. 'Let's go.'

Zuma does not move. A staring match ensues. I hand him the twenty-dollar note, muttering, 'Fucking thieves, the lot of you.'

*

Constable Fashion has been whiling away the time in Dlomo's thrall, gingerly sipping from a bottle of beer, her big bottom draped over the veranda wall. Dlomo reclines, legs splayed, on a ruptured sofa a few feet away from her, a row of bottles on the floor next to him. One hand gesticulates grandly; the other strokes the thigh of a frozen-looking girl sitting on the armrest. Two other women watch from the doorway.

The thin dogs bark at our approach and the same throng of people that greeted our arrival earlier emerges from the adobes near the house. Constable Fashion leaps to her feet when she sees us. 'You are back!' she cries with relief. She waddles to the stairs, looking at her watch. 'Why are you late?'

'Thula!' Dlomo yells at the dogs. They cower and slink off around the house. He gets to his feet, scratches his crotch and limps over to the stairs. Wrapping an arm around Constable Fashion, he chaffs her: 'Where are you going, my darling? We are making such beautiful conversation, you and me.'

'Ai! Suka wena!' She laughs nervously, slipping from his grasp. She descends the stairs and makes smartly for the car. Dlomo watches with a drunken leer. 'What I'd give to unbutton that pretty uniform, sweetie pie.'

'Hayi, uSathane!' she hisses.

Dlomo shouts from the stairs, 'What can you report, Zuma? Did our guests find what they are looking for?'

Zuma stands beneath the stairs, staring at the ground. 'No one can remember the Ndlovu woman,' he replies.

'Just as I expected,' Dlomo says. 'You have your answer, Mr Cole.'

'It's more a case of no one wants to remember,' I say. 'Lettah Ndlovu and her family once lived on this farm. No one can deny this. All I want is to know what happened to her.'

I look at Zuma. He continues to stare fixedly at the ground.

Dlomo waves his hand impatiently. 'If the Ndlovus lived here, as you say, then they are old history. Rhodesian history. Of no importance.'

'Of no importance only to those with no regard for innocent life,' Hazel says.

Dlomo's face grows weary. 'It seems exercise has not curbed your tongue.'

'People here know what happened but are too terrified to speak.'

'Terrified to speak? How can that be, old lady?' Dlomo taps his head. 'Perhaps your faculties are not in proper working order. People are free to speak here.' He turns to the gathered throng. 'Hey, wena! This old Rhodesian says no one is free to speak. Is this so? Are you deprived of freedom?'

The people jeer. 'Aikona! No!'

Dlomo turns back to us. He holds the palms of his hands out. 'You see? Everyone is free to speak in Zimbabwe.'

I sigh. 'My offer is there. If anyone can help us find Lettah Ndlovu there will be a reward. That's all. We're finished here now.'

Constable Fashion opens the car door. She taps her watch. 'We are late!'

The sly smile creeps back onto Dlomo's face. 'You are breaking my heart, my darling. My true love, don't leave me!'

We climb into the car. Happily my camera is where I left it. Dlomo limps around to Fashion's side and peers in the window. 'Come again soon, sweetie pie. I will wait for you.'

He blows a kiss. The people laugh.

Fashion stares straight ahead. 'Hurry up! Drive!' she snaps.

As we drive past the throng of people, Zuma raises his axe and with mincing steps dances around in a circle.

'Fuckwit,' I mutter.

Not far from the farm's entrance a man waves us down. I immediately recognise him as the sallow older man from the compound. I pull over and he comes around to my window. His shirt is drenched in sweat, he is breathing heavily. I imagine he has run some distance through the bush to intercept the car.

But as I wind down my window, he sees Constable Fashion. He takes a step back, his face assuming a stony blankness.

'Sakubona, Indoda,' I greet. 'Can I help you?'

The man nods but says nothing.

Constable Fashion blurts out impatiently. 'Hey, wena! Ufunani? What do you want?'

The man just stares at the ground.

'What's the matter with you, man?' Constable Fashion demands. 'He's drunk. Let's go. I can't waste my time.'

'Perhaps the poor fellow wants a lift,' Hazel says.

Constable Fashion shakes her head vigorously. 'No! No! This man is drunk. We must go!'

'We are on our way to Fort Rixon,' I say. 'Would you like a lift?'

'Yes, sir,' the man replies.

'What do you want in Fort Rixon?' Constable Fashion asks impatiently. 'You are going there to steal, not so? What's your name?'

'I don't steal, sister.'

'What's your name?'

'Ntombela.'

'Don't be so suspicious, dear girl,' Hazel says. 'He looks a perfectly decent fellow to me and this is our car, after all.' She leans over and opens the back passenger door. 'Ngena, indoda.'

Ntombela climbs in. His sweat smells like cut sisal. Constable Fashion winds down her window and gazes morosely out at the countryside as we drive on. Hazel chats away with Ntombela, as though he were a complete stranger. She asks about his family. How many children. How old. Ntombela plays the game, answering politely, succinctly. Constable Fashion sighs, shifting uncomfortably in her seat.

The real reason for her short temper soon becomes clear. The beer she consumed with Dlomo has prompted an urgent call of nature. She orders me to stop. As we come to a halt, she bolts, buttocks heaving, across the road and disappears behind some trees. Dust envelops the car. We hear the slither of elastic against skin. A hissing torrent.

89

Seizing the opportunity, I turn to Ntombela. My voice lowered, I say, 'If you have something to tell me, you must tell me now.'

'For this information you promised money.'

I nod. 'Yes, I will give you money.'

'I recognise the woman you are looking for. It was a long time ago, but I recognise her. I was present when they killed her family. I am the only one left on this farm who was present.'

'Dlomo and Zuma both said there was no one on the farm from that time.'

'That's what they believe. But I was there when the soldiers came.'

'5th Brigade?' Hazel asks.

Ntombela nods.

'Quickly, tell me what happened,' I say.

'The soldiers burned the whole family. The headman, Solomon, his wives and their children and their grandchildren. Eh-ja, even the little ones, the abantwana. Twenty-two people. All put into one hut that was set alight.' The man closes his eyes. 'I will never forget the scream-ing. Until I die, I will never forget. That's what the soldiers promised the ones who watched: that we will never forget until we die.'

I feel a sudden vertigo. 'You're telling me Lettah Ndlovu was among those who died?'

Ntombela shakes his head. 'No, sir. This is what I've come to tell you. A more terrible thing befell her. First the soldiers made her light the fire that burned her family. Then they raped her and then they cut her to make her laugh. Her name became uMahleka.'

I look at Hazel. Hazel shrugs and shakes her head.

Ntombela does something dreadful. With his fingers he pushes the corners of his mouth into a grotesque smile.

'uMahleka. It means a woman who always laughs.'

'I don't understand,' I say.

'Lettah Ndlovu was not burnt with her family,' Ntombela repeats quickly. 'The soldiers allowed her to live because living was worse than death. She left the farm. She went away.'

'Where did she go?' I ask.

Ntombela glances across the road. He shrugs.

'Where did she go? Surely someone knows!'

'I don't know. That's all I can tell you, sir. Please, you must not come again to ask questions. If you come again it will be very bad for us. They hurt us for any reason. We live in fear all the time.'

'But if I come with the police —'

Ntombela laughs bitterly. 'The police are dogs, like Dlomo. I have no more information.'

A rustle of bushes. Constable Fashion emerges from the trees.

'Quick. Give him some money,' Hazel says.

I fish in my wallet and hand Ntombela a bundle of banknotes. Feverishly, he thrusts the money into his pocket.

'Are you sure you can't tell me anything more? Please, I must find this woman,' I say, turning away from Ntombela and gazing casually ahead as Constable Fashion waddles across the road.

'That is all I can tell you, sir,' Ntombela replies. He opens the door and climbs out. 'My father worked for your grandfather, Mr Cole. Long ago. He said Nkosi Metcalf was a good man.'

Constable Fashion comes around to her door. She eyes Ntombela. 'Where are you going now?' she snaps.

'Oh, sister, I'm feeling very sick.'

'Aibo! Wena! Why do you waste my time?'

'I'm very sick, sister.'

No longer niggled by a bursting bladder, Constable Fashion ekes a drop of compassion. 'Sick? You look sick, indoda. You are sweating too much. Maybe you have the Sickness. You must go home and rest.'

Ntombela nods and begins to shuffle off down the road.

Constable Fashion climbs in the car and slams the door. She laughs. 'It is just as well. Hayi! That man smells too much!'

It's three o'clock when we arrive back at the police station. Inspector Chombo's busy day appears to have ended early; the convicts are back in their cells, the gate and charge office are unmanned. We find Chombo and two other policemen in his office, dutifully imbibing the contents of a bottle of brandy. The office reeks of booze and cigarette smoke. We are welcomed back with bleary-eyed conviviality. Chombo's two companions immediately direct a barrage of ribald banter towards Constable Fashion as she collapses, exhausted, into a chair in the corner. She heaves a morose sigh at the prospect of more drunken crap from men.

Chombo lifts the quarter-full bottle of brandy and offers us a drink. Hazel and Constable Fashion decline; Hazel frowns when I accept — tired and frazzled after a long day, I'm not about to close the door when opportunity comes knocking. Chombo pours me a stiff tot. 'Plenty more where that came from,' he says, handing me the glass. He gestures at two empty seats. 'Please sit.'

Hazel and I sit.

'So, did you detectives have any success?' Chombo asks.

I sip the neat brandy, uncertain of whether to engage in any serious discussion, since Chombo seems about to confirm at least one of Newton's Laws, the way he teeters on his chair.

Hazel beats me to it. 'No luck, I'm afraid,' she says.

'Well then,' Chombo says. 'We will have to double our efforts, won't we!' He raises his glass. 'Here's to finding the lost Lettah! If I find her where shall I post her?'

He cackles wildly. I shiver with pleasure as the brandy blazes a trail into my gut.

Hazel asks: 'May I use your toilet, Inspector?'

'Of course, my dear old Rhodesian lady. Fashionista! Show our madam the toilet.'

Constable Fashion wearily extricates herself from the attentions of the other policemen. Hazel follows her out the office. We drink. A short while later Constable Fashion returns and resumes her seat in the corner.

'Oh yes!' Chombo exclaims. 'I forgot. I have found some petrol for you.'

'There's no need,' I say. 'I have enough.'

Chombo guffaws. He turns to the other cops, hands outstretched helplessly. 'You can see our friend from Australia has no experience in Zimbabwe!' The other cops laugh. He turns back to me. 'When someone offers you petrol in Zimbabwe, my friend, it is a gift from God Almighty.'

I bow my head. 'It's very kind of you. Thank you.'

Chombo gets ponderously to his feet and, whistling away, lumbers out the office. He comes back with a greasy jerry can which he hoists triumphantly aloft. 'You are in luck, my friend!'

Hazel returns. She scolds Chombo: 'That toilet is absolutely disgusting! Has no one ever heard of soap and a scrubbing brush here?'

Chombo assumes a look of contrition. 'There is always room for improvement in this world, madam. Fashion, you heard what the lady said. Tomorrow you must find some soap and scrub the toilet, you hear me?'

The other cops laugh. Constable Fashion gives Hazel a deadly scowl.

Hazel gives me a nudge. 'Come on, finish your drink.'

I knock the last of my brandy back — a bold act which brings tears to my eyes. We wait outside as Chombo fumbles around with a funnel and decants the petrol into my car.

I ask: 'If someone wished to seek sanctuary around these parts, where would they go?'

Chombo laughs. 'You think your lost Lettah was looking for sanctuary, Mr Cole?'

'I must explore every possibility.'

'If people are looking for sanctuary, they come to the police. That is what the police are here for. We are guardians of the people.'

He says this without any trace of irony. He shakes the last drops into the funnel. I thank him and shake his hand. Hazel and I climb in the car. Before we leave, Chombo peers into my window. His breath reeking of brandy, he says, 'Keep me informed about your progress,

Mr Cole. Remember, I'm in charge of what happens in this area, okay?'

I nod and we depart.

We take the Insiza road back towards Bulawayo. Twenty kilometres from Fort Rixon the car suddenly loses power. It splutters and backfires, recovers briefly, then gives up the ghost. We shudder to a standstill beside a row of gum trees across a culvert over the Insiza River. I sit dumbstruck as the stark reality of our predicament begins to register. Again and again, I turn the ignition, to no avail.

I slam the steering wheel with my hands. 'Fuck! Fuck it!'

I get out, open the bonnet and stare blankly at the engine, fuming, clueless. The silence around us is broken by the ticking of the engine as it cools and the infuriating call of a cuckoo in a nearby msasa tree — *I'm so saaad!*

Hazel comes around to the engine. She leans in and fiddles around with the battery leads. Opens the distributor cap. Peers close. Then she straightens up and shakes her head. 'Dirty petrol — that's my guess. Carburettor's probably clogged. Chombo's parting gift, no doubt.'

I curse again. Hazel opens the boot and rummages around. 'No tools of any kind here, not even a wheel spanner,' she calls.

She comes around again to the front. 'And by the way your spare wheel's flat.'

I slap my hands on my thighs. 'Fuck!'

Hazel thrusts her hands in her pockets. There is a look in her violet eyes that bores straight through me. 'This swearing of yours. Fuck this. Fuck that. It's quite a habit among your generation, isn't it?'

'Be fair, Hazel. My generation didn't exactly invent the word.'

'No, you didn't. You just made it common-speak. Decent men of my generation would never talk like that in front of a lady. Did you ever hear your father swear in front of your mother? I don't like it, Frank. It's disrespectful.'

I laugh plaintively. 'Oh come on, Hazel! It's not meant —'

'No, Frank. I don't like it and there's no excuse for it.'

I stand there, embarrassed. 'Okay, Hazel, I'm sorry if I offended you.'

She reaches out and pats me gently on the shoulder. 'Apology accepted. Now, let's see what we can do about our predicament.'

It's late afternoon and shadows from the gum trees stretch into the bush across the road. I feel lethargic, thirsty. The after-effects of my tipple with Chombo. The Insiza River, I note, is dry. Not even stagnant pools mark its course. Not that I'd chance drinking water from these bilharzia-infested rivers.

Hazel scrutinises her phone. 'No signal,' she says.

'Someone will come along, sooner or later,' I say. 'They could tow us back to Fort Rixon.'

'Seen any cars on these roads today? Besides, what's the point of getting towed back to Fort Rixon? Who can help us there? Chombo?' She points at a nearby kopje. 'Let's see if we can get a signal up there.'

We climb over the single strand of barbed wire that is left of the roadside fence and trudge through the bush towards the kopje, a kilometre away. We haven't eaten all day; my stomach rumbles noisily. Hazel smokes as she walks. I marvel at her sprightliness; she seems indefatigable – if she were a car she would run on the smell of an oily rag. She gestures out at the surrounding lands. 'This all used to be prime cattle country. Now look at it. Nothing! Aside from the few tick-infested beasts we saw this morning, have you seen any cattle? The fraud of these land invasions is just so tragic. That imbeciles like Dlomo inherit these beautiful farms.'

I pant. 'Wasn't it always inevitable, Hazel? Do you really believe the idyll could've gone on forever? A tiny minority of whites owning Zimbabwe's best farmland? Wasn't that what the war was all about? Returning the land to its rightful owners?'

'Rightful owners? Dlomo?'

'Well, who then? People like Vic? Or perhaps you've forgotten how Vic used to treat his workers.'

Hazel gives me a sharp look. 'My, but you're in a self-righteous mood, aren't you? Not every farmer was like Vic, you know. Your grandfather – did he ever abuse his workers? My parents certainly didn't. Don't tar everyone with the same brush, Frank. Besides, are the workers any better off now under the likes of Dlomo?'

I sigh, exasperated. 'Hazel, you can repeat the sad old story of whites losing their land until you're blue in the face. No one's interested. To outsiders, the story is simple. British invaders stole the land; oppressed Africans rose up and took it back. End of story.'

'Yes, and that's the problem with you outsiders. The story's not so simple. You forget that whites in this country are no longer British colonials. They're African, born and bred. They have a right to be here. You forget that white farmers paid for their land legitimately. They or their forebears spent a lifetime paying off loans. You forget that white farmers once fed the nation and half of Africa. They provided stable employment to hundreds of thousands of people. But you outsiders only want the simple story, hey? Evil whites oppressing poor dispossessed blacks. That's all you want to hear, isn't it?'

'Hazel, if you want to defend Europe's colonial land-grab in Africa, that's your business. I'm just saying that Zimbabwe is small fry in the big scheme of things. Outsiders don't spend their lives pondering the complexities of life here. Mugabe gets away with all his shenanigans because no one gives a damn —'

Hazel silences me with a wave of her arm. 'I don't want to hear any more, Frank. I'm too old to stomach smart-alec outsiders talking about things that are so tragically important to people here. There are *real* people suffering here. Not just statistics. Do you realise that you are, in effect, defending Mugabe?'

'I'm not defending him —'

'You are, Frank! You *contaminate* the air by defending that bloody barbarian!'

'I don't agree —'

'No more, Frank! Change the subject, please!'

We climb the kopje in silence. I seethe with frustration. I don't believe that I do subscribe to a simplistic view of Zimbabwean politics. At the same time I'm mortified that Hazel is offended. Why should her opinion of me matter so much?

It's a fairly easy climb up the kopje. Hazel reaches out a hand for assistance only when we scale the last rock dome to the top. We stand there for a while looking down on the land. The sun is low on the horizon; the Insiza Valley winding south in the distance is in deep shadow, a violet anguine smudge. We can see the car on the road near the culvert with its bonnet up and, further afield, almost submerged beneath a carpet of gold-grey bush, the ruins of yet another farmstead. The long, faint sigh of a plane passes overhead heading north.

Hazel puts her glasses on and checks her phone. A weak signal, thank God. She hands it to me. 'Here, try your friend, Milton. I don't want to phone Vic. He'll just get into a panic. He's not supposed to drive with his bad heart.'

Still smarting from her rebuke, I retrieve the slip of paper with Milton's number on it from my wallet. It rings for a while before Ruby answers and tells me Milton is caught up at work.

'When he gets back tell him we're on the Insiza road, about twenty kilometres from Fort Rixon.'

'Okay,' Ruby says. 'Just sit tight.'

I hand the phone back to Hazel. 'Might as well go back to the car.'

'On second thoughts, I'd better give Vic a ring,' she says. 'He'll go just as bonkers worrying if I'm not back by dark.'

She calls Vic. The expected tirade follows. 'No, Vic, we're fine,' she replies. 'I've got big, brave Frank here to look after me. Milton Ogilvy will come and get us as soon as he gets off work. No need to worry. Oh, for heaven's sake!' Hazel holds the phone at arm's length while another rant ensues. 'No, Vic,' she says firmly. 'You will not come and fetch us. I won't speak to you if you put one foot in that car — it's *my* car, remember?'

The conversation ends abruptly and we start back to the car. By the time we reach the road the sun has gone down. We sit in the car listening to the bleating of guinea fowl and the noisy roosting of weaverbirds fussing around their round grass nests in some thorn trees along the river. Hazel pushes her door out wide and lights a cigarette. I'm embarrassed by my stomach's garrulousness.

Hazel pats me on the leg. 'We should've packed a picnic, hey?'

'I'm dying of thirst more than anything,' I say.

We wait as the darkness encroaches. No other vehicles come by. The only sign of human life comes in the form of two girls driving a decrepit donkey laden with firewood in the direction of Fort Rixon. I wave and greet them through the window as they approach; the girls nervously return my greeting and quickly continue on their way. The air is cool outside, a relief from the afternoon's heat. Up ahead, where the road rises to meet the low horizon, the white thorn of a crescent moon pokes through the membrane of night. Dwindling birdcalls.

Hazel appears to be enjoying herself. 'This is such a treat,' she says, cupping her ear at the far-off yapping of a jackal. 'I grew up with these sounds.'

'Must be bittersweet,' I say.

'I've never been one to dwell on negatives.'

'My mother also grew up with these same sounds.'

Hazel nods. 'When I was a girl I used to believe that people are united by birdsong. Our souls are forever connected to those who grew up hearing the same birds. I believed that's why your mother was like a sister to me.' She laughs. 'I used to believe in lots of things when I was girl.'

'Would that have made Lettah a sister, too?'

'In hindsight, yes.'

'Hindsight?'

Hazel chuckles. 'Your mother and I were *Rhodesian* girls, for heaven's sake! Our sisterhood was exclusively white, dear boy. I'm honest enough now to admit that black people were never included – never even considered! – in my childhood notions of soul-connectedness. Besides, I was never close to Lettah like your mother was.'

'What happened between them, Hazel? My mother and Lettah. I

just remember Lettah was like one of the family. Next thing she was gone.'

'Could've been anything. Your mother had a stubborn streak, you know. She'd never turn back on a decision. I wouldn't make too much of it.'

'It's just strange. She didn't even confide in my father.'

'Typical Lydia, I'm afraid. I'm sure you probably know that your mother kept matters of the heart – the deep, serious stuff – to herself. I knew her almost as well as I knew myself. We grew up together, connected by birdsong.' Hazel giggles and elbows me. 'You probably think I'm rather odd! One of those . . . what do you call them? New Age types. But it's true. We went to school together, we shared boarding school dormitories. I knew what made your mother tick. Lydia had the biggest, kindest heart I've seen in anyone, but she was also a brooder with the memory of an elephant. If someone upset her she found it hard to forgive and forget.' Hazel pauses, taking a drag on her cigarette. 'Lydia . . . your mother was quite a complex bundle.'

I smile and shake my head. 'My mother's moods . . . the whole thing's so bizarre. How Lettah – someone so close – could be summarily dismissed from our lives. Never a word of explanation in forty years. And now for me to be sent on this mission of atonement. All those years, carrying that silent guilt.'

'That's Lydia. What's important, though, is that she's tried to put things right. It may be a lifetime too late, but at least she came around to it. There's redemption in that, I think.'

'Complex beasts, you females.'

Hazel laughs. 'My dear boy, you have no idea!'

We are silent. I must confess, Hazel's cigarette smoke is troublesome for all the wrong reasons. Right now, I can think of nothing more desirable than a nicotine hit. Make that a cold beer too. Hazel puffs away, musing.

'The one thing you should know about your mother is that she was extremely insecure. *Painfully* so. If she felt her position was being threatened or undermined in any way . . . heaven help whoever was in the firing line. Which is where I happened to find myself, unexpectedly. I was also summarily dismissed.'

'When? In the Que Que days?'

Hazel nods. 'Again, it came from nothing much. Lydia was insanely jealous of your father. If any woman so much as looked at him, she'd have a fit. I thought I was exempt from suspicion. But I wasn't. I adored your father. Don't get me wrong — I adored your father as a friend. He was a breath of fresh air in crude colonial Rhodesia. It was always intellectually stimulating to be in his company. And, believe me, Frank, that's all it was — intellectually stimulating. Unfortunately, that wasn't how Lydia saw it. She thought I was beginning to occupy a special place in your father's life. I became a threat. Another single female out to steal her man. So I was banished. That's why I lost contact with you.'

I feel a slow, gentle sadness — knowing what Hazel says is true, but loving my mother even more for her faults. I turn and gaze out at the dark bush.

Hazel puts her hand on my arm. 'I'm not saying this to get back at Lydia, Frank. I loved her dearly, and still do. It was pure animal instinct — Lydia wouldn't allow anything to come between her and Errol. I understand that. I'm just sorry she wasn't able to see that no other woman was ever a threat. I don't think she knew how deeply your father loved her.'

We lapse into silence once more, the sadness welling up again in me. I think of how fiercely protective Lydia was of her family. Her family was her life, pure and simple. If there was fault in that, it was divine fault.

'It must be strange for you,' Hazel says. 'Here, searching for Lettah. I mean, what do you feel for her? Is she solid enough in your memory to feel anything?'

I shake my head. 'It was awful to hear what happened to her today. But to be honest, I still couldn't fully connect with her. The distance between us is too great to make it personal. I don't know if I'm making sense.'

'It was all so long ago.'

'It's the same as how I feel about this country. I recognise it but don't feel part of it.'

Hazel takes my hand and squeezes it. 'Hopefully that will change.'

We wait, silent with our thoughts, until headlights appear beneath the crescent moon ahead. As the vehicle, a Volkswagen Beetle, nears and catches my car in its beam, it slows almost to a stop, then does a crazy wheelspin and roars towards us, skidding to a halt in a cloud of dust on the opposite side of the road. Vic's grinning head pokes out the driver's window, already revelling in Hazel's inevitable reprimand, for which he is not kept waiting.

'When are you going to grow up?' Hazel yells past me. 'Mr Superman, hey? You bloody men! Little boys, the lot of you! And what about poor Milton Ogilvy, hey? He's probably on his way right this minute.'

Vic laughs. 'Ag, don't get your knickers in a knot, woman! You would've sat out here all night waiting for that shyster to arrive. I rang him and told him not to worry. What's the problem?'

'Your heart, you big baboon! What happens if you have a heart attack, hey?'

Vic looks at me helplessly. 'Christ Almighty. That's the thanks I get. Can't win with women, hey?'

He does a U-turn and reverses back in front of my car. Hazel and I get out. Vic emerges with a rope. Leaning on his walking stick, he instructs me where to tie the rope to both vehicles. When I'm finished he inspects my handiwork. Much wheezing and grunting as he tugs each end of the rope, muttering, 'Where did you learn to tie a rope? Girl Guides?' Then he straightens up and dusts his hand off on his trousers. 'By the way, your happy clappy friend phoned.'

'Brak Malan? Really?'

'Ja, quite a coincidence, hey? Haven't heard from the ungrateful bastard for two years and now he just phones out of the blue, looking for work. I told him even if I did have work I wouldn't give him any.'

'Did you tell him I'm looking for him?'

Vic nods. 'Ja, I told him. He got all excited. Keen to see you. He's on some smallholding out near the Matopos. Only been there a short while apparently. Gave me a phone number.'

We prepare to depart. There is some argument about who is to drive Hazel's car. Vic wins because according to him he's the only one in the vicinity who 'knows his arse from his elbow'. He and Hazel climb into the VW, I get into the Nissan behind. Vic starts up the VW. As we ease into motion, I see Hazel lean across and give him a long kiss on the cheek.

The mysteries of this world . . .

VI

My hippy girlfriends in Perth that my mother disdained were, without exception, devotees of mysticism of one sort or another. Palmistry was top of the list. The simian line on my right palm elicited much morbid interest; at least a few of them expressed surprise that I was alive, not to mention arguably sane and out of jail. Coincidence was another big ticket item. They believed that coincidences were signs that a big hand was out there guiding all things. I was deluged with useless information. Fluke associations between the King James Bible and Shakespeare, for instance, or Mark Twain and Halley's Comet. On a personal note, it was observed that I have the same birthday as Vincent Van Gogh – March 30th – who was born on the same day as his brother, also called Vincent, who died at childbirth exactly a year before.

All this mumbo-jumbo left me wondering: why do I attract these spaced-out souls? Do I, despite my obvious scepticism, project a spiritual thirst? The fact is, I don't waste much time with intangibles, though I can see how, for some, it might provide a warm fantasy of existential purpose, something to stave away the terrors of nothingness.

Still, the way my meandering path has led to chance encounters – Hazel, Vic, and now Brak – leaves me wondering if coincidence is indeed the way of the world. No divine hand. Just chance.

*

I wake at first light from a dead sleep and lie comatose amid the early-morning sounds, my thoughts slowly gathering. Thank God the ordeal of being towed back to Bulawayo is behind me. The stretch from where we broke down to the main road seemed endless. The atrocious condition of the Insiza road made it impossible for Vic to maintain a consistent speed; he braked and accelerated incessantly, the tow rope slackening then jerking tight. After a while I got a bit cranky, thinking Vic might be doing it on purpose. I could picture him laughing up front there with Hazel. Giving the townie a hard time, as his sons used to do long ago. But once we made it to the tar road it was a relatively comfortable run into Bulawayo. I gave a silent cheer as we passed beneath the broken sign that welcomes travellers to the city, its sputtering coloured lights festooned with birds' nests: *Zim..bwe In..pe.dence 1980.*

The sun rises; another hot day in the offing. Donning my swimmers I go outside to the pool and swim a couple of lengths. I'm showered and dressed when Precious brings my morning tea. She greets me with her toothy smile; I thank her and sit at the table making notes in my diary, summarising the events of yesterday. Never by nature a methodical person, I can only guess that such a tidy approach to my mission here is motivated by the uncomfortable feeling that Lydia is watching me like a hawk from the heavens.

Precious calls from the house to let me know breakfast is ready. I find Milton at the table, reading a newspaper. Ruby and Vernon are seated at the end of the table; Ruby is helping Vernon with some last-minute homework. A bustle of activity and the sound of Precious singing from the kitchen.

Ruby looks up and smiles. 'Morning, Frank. How are you after yesterday's dramas?'

'Can't complain. Warm this morning, isn't it?'

Milton puts the newspaper down. 'Ja, these summers seem to get hotter every year. Must be something in all this global warming stuff. Since when did you turn into a fitness freak, hey? Swimming at six in the bloody morning! I'm impressed, boyo. Damn near got out of bed to watch.'

'It obviously doesn't take much to qualify as a fitness freak in your book.'

Vernon looks up from his homework, grinning. 'I'd like to see you up swimming at six in the morning, Dad. I'd have to video you for anyone to believe it.'

He and Ruby laugh.

Milton wags a finger at him. 'You just get on with your homework and don't interrupt your elders, okay?'

'Yes, O physically uncoordinated one.'

Milton smiles and turns to me. 'Sorry it was left to Vic to help you out last night.'

'I'm glad you didn't have to go to the trouble.'

'I phoned the bloke who services my car. Jervis. He reckons it'll be dirty fuel, for sure. Common problem these days. Says it'll probably be quicker to just get it fixed than wrangle with the hire company – but check with them first.' Milton reaches for a piece of paper in his shirt pocket and hands it to me. 'That's Jervis's number if you want to give him a ring. The other one is your friend, Malan. Vic phoned this morning with it.' He pauses. 'None of my business, Frank, but be careful of these old war relics. Some of them can be bad news.'

Precious serves breakfast, porridge followed by omelettes on toast. Milton chomps away with his customary relish. I'm only halfway through when he finishes. Scraping up the last morsels on his plate, he laments, 'Always sad to see the end of a good meal, don't you think? So what's on your itinerary, Franco?'

'God, the old brain's in a bit of a whirl after yesterday. I guess putting a missing person's notice in the newspapers is top of the list.' I look at Ruby. 'Your colleague – whatshisname? Geoffrey – also suggested I stick up some posters around the townships. All depends on how soon I can get my car fixed.'

'Don't bank on that being today,' Milton says. 'When it comes to fixing stuff things are a bit on the slow side here in Zim. Why don't you drop us off in town and use our car. Save a lot of hassle. My secretary could give you a hand with that newspaper notice.'

'I'd hate to impose on you, Milton.'

'It's not imposing. The car just sits idle at the office all day.'

Ruby gives a wave of her hand. 'Oh, don't even think about it. Milton's just buttering you up in case we pitch up on your doorstep in Australia one day.'

Precious waves goodbye from the gate as we drive off. I'm crammed in the back with Vernon, Rosie and Geldof, all very proper in their school uniforms. Rosie gives me a big smile, as radiant as her mother's. A solemn hello from Geldof before he returns his attention to Vernon beside him. It's soon clear that they worship Vernon and compete for his favour. In no time he exhorts them to a round of songs including, for my benefit, the first verse and chorus of 'Waltzing Matilda'. Geldof demonstrates a fine, sweet voice, quite unlike that of his famous namesake.

We bounce and rattle along. The Cortina has obviously seen better days. A virulent eczema of rust covers the roof and bonnet; an old pair of roof racks seems permanently corroded into place. Wonky suspension. Not that I'm fussy about cars; I'm just intrigued that Milton still spurns the trappings of wealth. For amid the shabby mass of exhaust-belching rattletraps that constitutes the bulk of Bulawayo's traffic, there are a surprising number of brand-new luxury cars. Mercedes Benzes, BMWs, top-of-the-range four-wheel-drives. When I point them out, Milton just shrugs and says, 'There're always those who make fortunes out of chaos.'

We drop the kids off at their school in Burnside and proceed into the city. Ruby gets out at Tredgold House; Milton and I drive on to his office in Jason Moyo Street. We climb the stairs to the fifth floor of an eight-storey block. Milton tells me, panting heavily, that after being stuck twice during power failures he never uses the lifts. We enter the office suite of *Braithwaite, Ogilvy & Hall*. I'm introduced to Milton's remaining partner, Barry Braithwaite, a short, jovial man with a white moustache, a dead ringer for Alf Garnett. The other partner,

Hall, has recently migrated to New Zealand. The walls of the suite are covered with large abstract expressionist paintings which Milton explains were done by Barry's brother who lived in New York in the fifties. The less-than-swanky suite also seems from that decade. When Barry hears I'm from Australia he jibes, 'Not another Afro-Australian! They should change Perth's name to Zimbabwe-by-the-Sea. Half the bloody country lives there these days. I'll probably wind up there too, the way things are going.'

'Come, come, Barry,' Milton says. 'How could you leave *all of this*?' He waves an arm around the suite.

Milton introduces me to his secretary, Mrs Mkize, who occupies a small reception area next to his office. He shows me into his office, a neat, sparsely furnished space with photographs of tourist spots on the walls – a vast Matobo vista, the Victoria Falls in full flow, a sunset over Kariba. Smaller photographs of Ruby and Vernon stand on his desk next to a computer. He rummages in a cabinet and extracts some files. 'I've got a meeting in five minutes. Make yourself at home. Ask Mrs Mkize to do the newspaper ad. She knows the ropes – just give her the details.' He opens one of the desk drawers and takes out a roll of masking tape and puts it on the desk. 'You'll need this to stick your posters up. What else? Oh, feel free to use the phone. Just dial zero for an outside line.' He hands me the car keys. 'Remember to pick up Rosie and Geldof from school. Don't worry about Vernon – he's got a lift with friends. Ruby and I'll cadge a lift home with Barry.'

'Thanks, Milton.'

Milton pats me on the shoulder and says in a stilted Australian accent, 'No worries, mate.'

I phone the car hire company and speak to a woman whose voice becomes wearily philosophical – no doubt, my little problem is a familiar one. She is abrupt and pragmatic: *officially* the company would need to collect the car, assess the problem and determine responsibility, which could take a while – and there are no spare vehicles available for at least a week; *unofficially* I could get it fixed myself – if it's dirty petrol it wouldn't be too expensive – and it would be as though this telephone conversation never took place.

I try the mechanic Jervis's number. It rings and rings; I'm about to hang up when Jervis answers. In a long, expletive-ridden diatribe, Jervis promises to fetch the car from Milton's address but says it will probably take a few days to fix – he has quite a backlog since the last 'dipshit' mechanic who worked for him quit and 'gapped it' to South Africa. He now has only a couple of 'munt appies' there to assist him to whom 'pulling cars apart is as fucking natural as nature itself, but when it comes to putting them back together again – non fucking comprendo!' According to Jervis, anyone with any skill and half a brain has already left the country – an astute, though personally unflattering observation. I tell him the keys to my car have been left with Precious.

Not feeling especially confident of the Nissan's speedy restoration after Jervis's tirade, but resigned to circumstance, I set about designing a poster on Milton's computer. I scan a close-up of Lettah's face and set out the necessary information underneath: her name, the offer of a reward for reliable information and Milton's home phone number. I print off a copy and take it through to Mrs Mkize. I ask her to run off thirty copies on the photocopier and arrange the newspaper notices. Mrs Mkize eyes the poster critically. 'Leave it with me,' she says.

I return to Milton's office and with sudden trepidation dial Brak's number. Would I even recognise him after all this time? No reply. On impulse, I try my father's number, not expecting to get through. I'm startled when he answers almost immediately: 'Hello, Errol Cole.'

'Hello, Dad. It's Frank.'

'Good Lord! I was just wondering how you were getting on.'

I provide a summary of events so far. He gives his customary 'mmph' as he digests each fact. He agrees that the prospects of finding Lettah don't appear good. His voice becomes animated when I tell him about Hazel and Vic. He asks for their phone number and promises to give them a call.

'Look after yourself, son.'

'Don't worry,' I say.

I leave some money for the overseas call in an envelope on Milton's desk, collect the posters from the secretary and go downstairs, the reassuring timbre of my father's voice still ringing in my ears.

There was never much cause for us to venture into Bulawayo's townships in the time of Rhodesia. Lettah was a live-in maid, as were the others that appeared after she had gone. My parents would sometimes drop Lettah off at her friends' places in the old townships of Makokoba or Thorngrove on the weekends; my mother also liked to occasionally browse through the textiles and pottery at the Mzilikazi Craft Centre. These visits had the nature of air strikes – in and out, no hanging about. The townships were another world; my parents imagined dangers lurking there for unsuspecting whites. As Rhodesia's political situation deteriorated those dangers became increasingly real, ultimately making the townships a no-go zone. In this, my parents were no different from other white Rhodesians: hiding a subliminal fear of the real face of Africa by averting their eyes from it, by living separate to it.

From the few occasions that I accompanied them I vaguely remember endless rows of small box-like dwellings, identified by numbers stencilled on the façades. Crammed together along narrow streets; all the same, poor and shabby. Scraggly hedges or low fences sectioned off tiny front yards, no more than a few metres deep. A few trees provided meagre screening and shade, little gardens offered splashes of green. Always chock-a-block with people. Endless processions of pedestrians and cyclists. Barefoot children in ragged clothes running along next to the car, laughing and waving. Thin dogs barking. Carts harnessed to donkeys dozing in the sun.

Poverty was never a stranger to Bulawayo's townships back then, but now it is a virulent fungus, clinging to everything. People stare as I drive slowly along the crumbling streets. Abject, empty stares. I pass the same shabby brick boxes with their stencilled numbers. The brave little gardens. Thin dogs bark and ragged children play in the streets. The same streets, the same dwellings. Just poorer . . . much poorer.

Mrs Mkize has applied her deft hand to the layout of my poster. Among other embellishments, she has added an ornate border around Lettah's photograph, giving it a bizarre Baroque touch. I stick posters up near taxi ranks and bus terminals, outside community halls. I tape them to trees and telephone poles in the residential areas. I do so perfunctorily, working on the vague assumption that Lettah or someone who knew her may have ended up here. Wherever I go, people gather around, watching me, talking among themselves. Pointing at the photograph of Lettah, they ask: who is this person? Why are you looking for her? And then, always, the other questions: have you got work for me? Please, Sir, I am strong — I can work hard. Can you give me money, Sir? Please, I am hungry, my children are sick . . .

I feel my foreignness. I've no idea of what lurks beneath the surface of things here. Like a wretched miser I ignore the pleas.

Outside the old Stanley Hall, where Joshua Nkomo and his followers once gathered to plot revolution, I'm approached by a policeman. He takes a poster from me, saying nothing. He scrutinises it. I explain my purpose with a forced air of breezy good cheer. He just looks at me, hands the poster back and walks off.

On an outer fringe of the townships, I drive along a road that I think will take me back into the city; instead, it leads in the opposite direction, around some small granite outcrops and over a stony ridge. A wasteland suddenly opens up before me. I stop the car and stare out at the desolate scene, acre upon acre of what must have been a shantytown. A ghost place. The homes of an entire community razed, reduced to rubble and charred debris, disappearing into the ground beneath encroaching bush and grass. I walk down into this wasteland, following the still-visible tracks of bulldozers until I stand amid the wreckage. Twisted sheets of corrugated iron, collapsed mud walls, smashed bits of furniture. Everywhere the glint of broken glass. A crushed felt hat with weeds growing through the crown. A piece of a woman's shoe with a plastic flower buckle. A flattened wire cage full of chicken skeletons. The faint stench of rot. A thin dog noses around a short distance away. The only sounds are of distant traffic and the eerie squawking of scavenging ibises that I don't remember seeing around Bulawayo in the old days.

A packet of stale salt and vinegar chips and a bottle of too-sweet orange juice suffice for lunch. Then on with the job: a brief and fruitless chat with an official from the Department of Social Welfare before pinning posters to church noticeboards around the city. At a Catholic church I obtain a list of missions in Matabeleland.

As I head towards the school in Burnside to pick up Rosie and Geldof, I'm buoyed by a sense of progress. That my elation may stem from simply going through the motions and not from any tangible outcomes, does not concern me unduly. Adverts, notices . . . I have my doubts if any of it will bear fruit.

I arrive at the school five minutes late. Rosie is waiting at the gate. When she sees the car she turns and calls Geldof, who is playing soccer with friends on the nearby playground. He comes galloping across to the car, horse and rider both, one hand gripping imaginary reins, the other whacking his rump. His mates laugh and yell after him. Rosie prattles on all the way to Kumalo about the animals the school accommodates — rabbits, guinea pigs, three sheep. A concerned soul, she launches into a small tirade against whale hunting. Geldof, now less nervous in my presence, listens with a puzzled frown.

'Do you have cane toads in your house, Mr Cole?' Rosie asks. 'My teacher says Australia has lots of cane toads.'

'Your teacher is right. But I don't have any in my house.'

'*My* teacher,' Geldof interjects, 'has no toenail.'

'No toenail?' I say.

'Yes, it was cut off by the doctor. It was ingrowed.'

Rosie gives an exasperated sigh and stares out the window.

Back at the house, I see the Nissan has been taken away. Precious tells me that Jervis had problems getting the winch of his tow truck to work. She laughs and whistles. 'That man, Mr Jervis – aibo! God will not allow him to talk like that in heaven!' She hands me a telephone number on a piece of scrap paper.

'It is urgent,' she says. 'A policeman – Chombo.'

I try the number three times before getting through. Chombo greets me with a barrage of droll Australianisms. He tells me he has people right around the country searching for 'the Ndlovu woman'; he himself has made extensive enquiries around the district, as far afield as Gweru. There are a few leads he wishes to follow up on. He needs more detail about Lettah's background. For half an hour I tell him what I know of Lettah's origins, her family, and the period of her life that she spent with my family – much of it a repeat of yesterday's discussion. I provide more detail about my family, the names of my parents, my father's occupation, even the vehicles we owned. The more information, the better, Chombo says – that way we will know for sure if we find this woman.

'These leads,' I say. 'Do you have anything solid?'

'I can't say, Mr Cole. I don't wish to give you false hope. I've spoken to people from the district. I've been to Whitestone myself. There's nothing definite. Just a few possibilities.'

'You went to the farm? Who did you talk to?'

Chombo laughs. 'Please, Mr Cole, don't get excited. You must be patient. Let me do my job.'

'Let me know immediately if there are any developments, Inspector.'

'Of course, Mr Cole. I'll leave no stone unturned. But please remember one thing: this is my case. My case alone. You are lucky that I'm willing to help you. I can assure you no other policeman will waste his time looking for one lost old woman from the bush. If this woman is to be found, I will find her. So you must keep me informed about everything you know. Any small detail may help.'

'Thank you, Inspector. I appreciate your efforts.'

Encouraged by this exchange, I spend an hour or so phoning the missions on the list I got from the Catholic church. None has any record of Lettah.

I try Brak's number again. A woman answers and I ask for Brak.

'Is that Frank?' the woman asks.

'Yes, a blast from Brak's very distant past.'

'I know. I've heard nothing else from Brak since Vic told him you were here. I'm Regina, by the way – Reggie. Brak's wife. He's not in right now.'

'When's the best time to reach him?'

'Evenings, mostly. But, look, why don't you drop by this evening? Give him a surprise. We live out on the Matopos road. Not far. He's dying to see you. I won't tell him you called.'

'My car's getting fixed, but give me the directions. I'll see what I can do.'

I write the directions down in my diary.

'Your car's getting fixed?' Reggie says. 'Ag, Frank, man! Brak would've done it for nothing. That's what he mostly does these days – fixes cars for nothing.'

She giggles wearily.

'Wish I'd known, Reggie.'

'See if you can make it this evening. We can do a braai.'

Brak was an only child. Despite this, his parents were never over-protective; in fact, his father, Piet Malan, a coarse but kindly Afrikaner, liked to stoke the fire of adventure in his son's heart, equipping him with air rifles, crossbows and hunting knives, among many other indulgences my parents disapproved of. Brak loved hunting and boasted a huge collection of bird wings pinned to a board in his bedroom, all carefully labelled, the trophies of his exceptional marksmanship. A skill not shared by me. My reputation for marksmanship was set in stone the day I shot him in the ankle when he foolishly straddled a tin can we were using for target practice. The pellet had to be surgically removed. The doctor and Brak's parents were not amused; Brak was more contemptuous than angry.

Brak's other great boyhood love was cars. If you went over to the Malans' place in Que Que the chances were you would find him lying underneath some jalopy alongside his father. I'd crawl underneath and watch the two of them fiddling around, not that anything other than grease ever rubbed off on me. Brak's father did a lot of grunting and cursing in Afrikaans and seemed amused when Brak grunted and cursed too. Jou moer! Jou lelike fokken moer!

Piet would do just about anything to see a smile on Brak's face. He even built him a little racing car, modelled on the kind that Stirling Moss used to drive. They called it the *Silver Bullet*. Piet graded a racetrack in the bush behind their house, a bumpy circuit about a kilometre in length. He yelled encouragement as Brak sped around the track, the *Silver Bullet*'s engine belching clouds of exhaust smoke. Piet used to time him with a stopwatch and noted down the times in a little black book. They let me drive too, but I was never brave enough to hit the speeds Brak reached. I was just honoured to be part of the team.

Brak seemed to have everything a boy could dream of – guns, knives, even a proper racing car. I was exasperated by my own parents who frowned on such largesse. My father thought Brak's racing car was a dangerous and unprincipled extravagance. When he heard that I'd been driving it, he fretted that I would come to grief. But he never forbade it, derring-do being the often hazardous prerequisite of a Rhodesian boyhood. Lydia also disapproved, though her disapproval was mostly based on a snobbish (and, as it turned out, unfounded) fear that I might develop a love for engines and turn into a *mechanic*. Her boys would earn a living with their heads, not their hands.

She and Errol need not have feared. My brief affair with engines and speed was cut short one day when Brak lost control of the *Silver Bullet* and ploughed through a row of sisal plants into a cactus tree, which spurted a sticky white sap all over him. Everyone was amazed that a cactus tree could do so much damage. The *Silver Bullet* was mangled beyond repair. As for Brak, there was a brief panic about the cactus tree sap that had gummed up one eye – rumour abounded that it caused blindness – but he suffered no ill effects after he was hosed down with water. He also had to get the sharp black points of the sisal plants dug out of his back and shoulder by the same doctor who'd removed the pellet from his ankle when I shot him; the doctor by this stage had come to accept that Brak Malan led a harebrained and perilous existence.

We kept in touch when my family moved away to Salisbury and Bulawayo. We spent a few school holidays together; when we met up it was always like old times. But when my family moved down to South Africa contact was limited to occasional letters. We took separate paths, meeting again just once when the Malans went down to Durban for a holiday. We were in high school; Brak had grown tall and rangy, towering above me. He sported a long fringe that hung above his eyes, as was fashionable in Rhodesia. Compared to my negligible athletic pursuits, he'd become a champion long-distance runner and played fullback for the Rhodesian Schools rugby team. He showed me some photographs of a big buffalo cull he and Piet had taken part in at Wankie Game Reserve. Gory images of blokes holding rifles and bottles of beer next to slain beasts. One of Brak and his father skinning a carcass, shirtless, their arms covered in blood.

I tend to remember Brak for these things. Guns and engines. Things that led to skinned animals, to the legs of a corpse. For some reason it's been easy to ignore his other side. Beneath the hard shell lurked another Brak, beguilingly complex and sensitive. His mother, Muriel, was a red-haired Englishwoman from Suffolk who made it a condition of her marriage to her rough Afrikaner husband that English would be the language spoken in their home. She had refined tastes. She loved classical music and from an early age cajoled Brak into taking piano lessons. A prodigious natural talent was unearthed. He could play Chopin before his feet could touch the pedals. His parents bought him a piano and a guitar. He mastered the guitar without taking lessons. You could ask him to play anything and he would bash it out. Elvis, Cliff Richard, the Beatles. I remember him doing a beaut version of 'Ferry Cross the Mersey' by Gerry and the Pacemakers, my favourite song of that time. I'd listen to him, mesmerised, envious.

Brak's real name was Dwight — that was the name Muriel gave him, after her father. That was the name he blushed bright red to at school rollcalls, and which only the girls teased him for, knowing they wouldn't get clobbered. Brak was a nickname given to him by his father. In Afrikaans it means mongrel. His father meant it as a dig at Muriel's English airs and graces, but it stuck.

I didn't anticipate becoming an encumbrance to Milton. The incidentals — the telephone calls, the use of his car, meals — are mounting up. When Milton and Ruby return from work I offer to reimburse them, but this is refused. Pushing the envelope of money I left on his desk into my shirt pocket, Milton retorts: 'Hang on to your money, boyo — maybe we'll come knocking on your door in Australia one day.' Moreover, he is adamant it's no inconvenience for me to use the car this evening. He draws a detailed map of the Matobo Road, showing how to reach Brak's place.

I set off at dusk, stopping at the Hillside shops to buy some beer. Beyond the outer suburb of Burnside I encounter few other vehicles. A bus grinding along at snail's pace. Another one broken-down on the side of the road, its passengers waiting next to it. Expressions of resigned forbearance. A few people on bicycles or on foot heading away from the city. A woman sits on a blanket next to a small pile of tomatoes and carrots at a deserted bus stop, hoping for a late customer.

The land around is flat and densely strewn with acacia bush, some areas burned black from recent fires. I pass the landmarks Milton noted on his map: the Umganin and Khami river crossings, the defunct Matopo Rock Motel and the agricultural research station. Piles of rubbish have been dumped on the roadside, no doubt by Bulawayo residents frustrated at the city's sporadic garbage collection.

My headlights illuminate the eyes of goats and donkeys nibbling at the bushes alongside the road. In the far distance, I can just make out the blue outcrops of the Matobo Hills, hazy in the last light. I muse over the confusion of names for this rocky wilderness — Matobo, Matopo, the Matopos. A small reminder that Zimbabwe is a chameleon still changing colour.

About thirty kilometres from Bulawayo, I pass a superette and bottle store and turn right onto a dirt road. I travel another three kilometres before turning left across a cattle grid onto a property called Pilgrim's Rest. A few hundred metres further on I come to a house surrounded by a security fence. I stop to open the gate. Out of the gloom a huge dog comes bounding towards me, barking ferociously. I go back to the car and hoot a few times. A man appears against the lighted doorway of the house. He calls gruffly, 'Shuddup, Cracker!'

The dog, a Rhodesian ridgeback, stops barking but remains at the gate, snarling. The man approaches, illuminated by the car's headlights. A bearded giant with a balding pate. The face of a street fighter; a broken nose and a deep crescent scar around his right eye. He wears tattered khaki shorts and a stained t-shirt with *Bulawayo Bottlers* emblazoned across the chest. Barefoot.

'Can I help you?' he calls.

'Brak?' I call back.

He stops in his tracks, a look of surprise on his face. Then he yanks open the gate. 'Frank? Shit a brick! Howzit you bloody old mangy mongrel!' He lumbers over to where I'm standing next to the car, pumps my outstretched hand and slaps my back. A heavy stench of sweat.

Brak stands back. 'I've been trying to figure out the last time I saw you. Must've been at least thirty years ago, hey? Long time between drinks, man! Hell, I wouldn't have recognised you — age has not treated you kindly, my friend.'

I laugh. 'I was wondering how to say the same thing tactfully.'

Indeed, he is not remotely the person I remember. That tall, rangy, red-haired kid, body whittled down to sinew and bone by sheer boundless energy, is now an unkempt behemoth, the bulk around his neck and shoulders, along with that unruly salt and pepper beard, giving him the look of a bloated wildebeest.

'We've got some major catching up to do, china. But first things first. Come inside and meet Reggie. My ball and chain.'

I follow him through the gate. The dog lopes along with us, growling sideways at me. 'Oh, for Chrissake, Cracker,' Brak mutters. In the fading light I can see no garden to speak of, no lawn, just some rockeries with a few struggling plants along the perimeter of the security fence. The house is plain, basic. Unplastered cement block walls in a simple rectangular plan, a wide veranda at the front. Corrugated iron roof. A water tank to one side, enswathed by a trumpet creeper. A windmill behind a garage with two carports, separate to the house. In one of the carports the hulk of a minibus stands up on blocks. In the other an old Datsun sedan.

We skirt an ancient Land Cruiser parked in the drive and climb the front steps to the house. We enter a lounge furnished with a few worn chairs and a couch grouped around a TV set. Bare cement floor covered by a couple of frayed straw mats. A few photos on the walls, one of which I recognise to be of Brak's parents, Piet and Muriel. An oil painting of African huts and baobabs silhouetted against an orange sky. Above the fireplace, a small framed print of Jesus standing on the waters of Galilee, gazing heavenward.

'Hey, Reggie!' Brak calls. 'Look what the cat dragged in!'

A dark-haired woman in her early forties appears at the kitchen door, cigarette in hand. She reminds me vaguely of Joan Baez – attractive dark eyes, a wide mouth, irregular teeth. Denim dress and yellow sweater. A few extra pounds around the hips. She smiles and affects surprise. 'So, you must be the famous Frank.'

We shake hands.

Brak plonks a dirty paw on her shoulder. 'Eat your heart out, china. I bet you never imagined Brak Malan would score a sexy goddess like this, hey?'

Reggie laughs coyly. 'Jeez, but you can talk rubbish, hey.' She removes his hand from her shoulder. 'Ag, Brak, look at your hands, man!'

'Roll out the barrel, doll. Me and Frank have got some catching up to do.'

'Barrel? In your dreams. Wine or sherry is about all we can offer.'

'Is that all we've got? No beer?'

'You know there's no beer. You also know who finished it all.'

'Oh, Jesus, Reggie. Had I known Frank was coming tonight . . .'

Reggie winks at me. 'Just as well you didn't know, babe.'

I come to the rescue. 'I've got a few quarts in the car.'

Brak's eyes light up. 'China, you're a bloody star. It'd be a mission to get any hooch at this time of night.'

Reggie gives Brak a knowing look. 'As long as we don't overdo it. Hey, my sweetness?'

Brak pecks her on the cheek. 'That's right, doll. As long as we don't overdo it. How 'bout a braai? Have we got any meat, sugar cube?'

'Just as well I defrosted some earlier.'

Brak transfers his hand to my shoulder. 'I tell you, this chick's psychic. Always one step ahead of me. Come on, let's get a fire going. Where'd you say those beers were?'

I follow Brak outside. While he goes off to the garage to fetch the braai I get the beers — half a dozen quarts — from Milton's car and take them through to the kitchen. Reggie is cutting up some salads; I offer her a beer but she has already poured herself a glass of wine. She finds me an opener and puts the rest of the beer in the fridge.

'You may be wondering why I didn't get some booze, knowing you were coming,' she says. 'It's not a bad thing to limit Brak's intake, believe me.' She pats my arm. 'He's been carrying on like a big kid since he heard you were here. It's not like I want to spoil his fun. But I have to watch him.'

Back outside, I put the bottles down on the stairs and take in the fine spray of evening stars. Brak returns from the garage dragging a forty-four gallon drum cut in half and mounted on wheels, which he positions in front of the veranda steps. We each fetch an armful of logs and kindling from a woodpile around the back of the house. There he points out a thriving vegetable garden running off water from the windmill, established by the owner who, Brak says, has gapped it overseas. It strikes me that Zimbabweans show off their vegetable patches like others might show off a new car or patio.

We dump the wood next to the drum. Brak rummages around in the old Land Cruiser and retrieves a newspaper. The front page is emblazoned with a large photograph of Mugabe's face behind a pontificating finger. With a look of grim satisfaction, Brak scrunches the page into a ball, puts it into the drum and piles kindling and wood on top of it. He takes some matches from his pocket and lights the paper. Flames crackle up, sparks popping, through the kindling. Once the wood has caught properly, Brak piles some bigger logs on top, dusts his hands off and sits down next to me on the veranda steps.

I hand him a beer. We clink bottles.

'Cheers, china. Good to see you, man.'

I nod. 'Who'd have thought, hey?'

Brak laughs wryly. He takes a deep swig, stares up at the stars and sighs. He reaches into his pocket and pulls out a pack of cigarettes. Flicks the bottom of the pack, making a couple of cigarettes pop out, and holds it out to me. 'Smoke?'

'No, thanks. I quit a while ago.'

Brak lights a cigarette, one eye squinting at the smoke. 'Filthy bloody habit. So what brings you to our happy country?'

Once more, I explain my mission. The whole story, from my mother's will to yesterday's visit to Whitestone. Brak listens in silence, smoking and swigging his beer. When I finish he just sits there looking up at the stars. For a moment, I wonder if he has been listening at all. Then he says: 'Sorry to hear about your mom. She was a good old bird.' He taps the end of his cigarette. 'I remember that nanny of yours, Lettah ... shit, what is it about this country? Everybody's story's the same. Nothing but bloody pain and sorrow. I feel sorry for the munts. For ordinary munts like Lettah. Never get a break. For them things just get worse, never better.'

He takes another deep swig. Belches. 'Ah! That hit the spot. God bless alcohol. Ja, I dunno, Frank. I dunno what to suggest. Half the bloody country's gone missing. Your nanny's a drop in the ocean.'

'I'm not expecting miracles. I stopped by at our old neighbourhood in Kwekwe.'

'Hillendale? I used to go back there now and again, just for old time's sake. I suppose your place is in ruins too.'

I shrug.

Brak smiles. 'Ja, what can you do? Those were good times, hey, my china? I remember that nanny – Lettah. Nice munt. Always laughing.'

Always laughing. uMahleka. Thoughts of what might have happened to Lettah at the hands of the soldiers leap suddenly to mind. Lighting the fire that incinerated her family. Listening to their screams. I quickly shove these thoughts away and listen instead to Brak as he reminisces about the old days. Reggie comes out with a tray of meat and salads which she places on a table nearby. She goes back inside and returns with a half-empty demijohn of red wine and sits on the step next to Brak, tucking her dress up between her legs.

'Uh-oh, the party animal's here!' Brak says.

Reggie gives a sarcastic snort and lights a cigarette. She slaps at a mosquito on her arm. 'Bloody mozzies. Where's that insect muti? Don't you boys get bitten?'

'Stand next to the fire,' Brak says. 'The smoke will chase them away.'

Reggie smooches him on the cheek. 'Why stand next to the fire when I've got you to keep me warm, my darling. My big cosy teddy bear.'

Brak grins, embarrassed. 'Get bitten then.'

'How're your folks, Brak?' I ask.

'Both passed away. They moved down to South Africa when Mugabe took over. My old man died of a heart attack about fifteen years ago. Mom came up and lived with us for a while, but then went back because the health system here was so bad. She had emphysema – too much bloody smoking. Reggie's a nurse. She went down and cared for her until she died. Eight years ago, I think.'

Reggie puts a hand on Brak's knee and blows a plume of smoke out into the night. 'Your mom was a real lady.'

'And you, Brak? What've you been up to all these years?'

Brak gets up and throws a couple of logs on the fire. He puts the grid over the flames to burn clean. His eyes gleam in the firelight.

'Ja, it's a long story, china. A long story of cock-ups.'

'Come on, babe!' Reggie says. 'It's not all gloom and doom.'

Brak taps the grid with a fire fork to make the dried grease fall off. He sticks the prongs of the fork into the grid and comes back to the stairs next to Reggie. Lights another cigarette. He laughs. 'Actually, there's a short story too. Once upon a time, after the war in Rhodesia, an unqualified mechanic called Brak Malan went from job to job trying to make a buck in beautiful Zimbabwe. Things didn't work out. The end.'

Reggie sighs. 'Don't be so negative, man.'

Brak looks at me. 'I wrote to you a couple of times when I was in the army, didn't I?'

I nod. 'It was the last contact we had.'

'After we lost the war I went off the rails. I don't know ... just couldn't adjust. In the war our dads fought they came back home heroes. The shit stuff they did was exorcised through parades and commemoration services. We didn't have that privilege. We just had to get on with living with the enemy. The people we used to call terrorists were now rubbing our noses in *their* parades and commemoration services.'

Brak drains the last of his beer and belches again. 'Anyway, I went a bit wild. Drank too much and caused a lot of strife. Got my face rearranged one night in a bar in Harare and ended up in hospital. That's where I met Reggie.'

Reggie shakes her head. 'You should have seen him, Frank. Half dead. Cracked skull – just about every bone in his body broken. Blood everywhere. But the drunken idiot was still singing Rhodesian army songs at the top of his voice. I had to sedate him to shut him up!'

Brak laughs.

'It was no bloody joke at the time!'

'You're right, doll. I was a mess. Not the nicest bloke to be around in those days. The long and short of it was while I was in hospital some priest came by and talked to me. I found Jesus.' Brak clicks his fingers. 'Just like that. Born again. Seemed the only way I could get rid of my demons. After a stint working for Vic Baldwin, Reggie and I ended up in a little mission up at Kariba called Gospel Path.'

'Vic said something about you preaching.'

'Preaching? I couldn't preach to save my life. No, I just tried to help the munts. Taught them how to fix cars. A bit of woodwork. Reggie helped out in the mission's clinic.'

Reggie jabs him in the ribs. 'Ag, man. You missed out the romantic part. How you fell in love with me and begged me to marry you.'

'Ja, Frank, you have to understand I was a bit brain damaged at the time. I wasn't in a fit state to make rational decisions.'

Reggie gives a high-pitched giggle and slaps him on the shoulder. 'Jeez, you lie! I tell you, Frank, he was down on his knees begging me.'

Brak escapes from any further sentimental reminiscences by getting up and going over to the fire. He rustles the coals around with the fork. 'I reckon we can chuck the meat on now.'

'Still looks too hot to me, babe,' Reggie says.

'Ag, what do you know about braais, hey? Let an expert get on with his job.'

'Expert on what? Charred meat?'

Brak dismisses her criticism with a wave of his hand. He gets the plate of meat and returns to the fire. Slaps the steaks and boerewors on the grid. They begin sizzling immediately. I have to agree with Reggie: it seems a huge fire for the amount of meat he is cooking.

I fetch more beer from inside. I hand a bottle to Brak and sit back on the stairs with Reggie. Brak gulps the beer, gazing intently up at the stars, as though searching for one that might provide guidance. Attracted by the smell of meat, the dog, Cracker, appears out of the darkness and sidles up with a big tongue-lolling smile behind Brak. He spies me on the stairs and emits one huge, brainless bark. Brak, unaware of the dog's presence behind him until that moment, jumps a foot in the air. 'Jesus Christ Almighty!' he bellows.

Reggie and I clutch our stomachs, laughing. Using the Lord's name in vain does not appear to be verboten for Brak, the Christian.

Brak brandishes the fork at Cracker who backs away, crestfallen. Relenting, Brak crouches on his heels and beckons the dog. 'Come here, big boy. It's all right, old fella. I'm sorry. I know you're just doing your job.'

Cracker comes over and rubs jowls with Brak.

'I tell you, that dog gets more attention than me,' Reggie says. 'Watch that meat, Brak. We can't afford to waste it, man!'

Brak straightens up, knees clicking. He starts turning the meat over. 'Ja, as I was saying, before I was so *rudely interrupted* . . .' He gives Cracker a glare. Cracker wags his tail. 'Reggie and I ended up at the mission up at Kariba. Things went well for quite a while, hey Reggie? It was good up there, hey?'

Reggie nods. 'Ja, it was a good time. Calm, tranquil. Like being in the eye of a storm, I suppose. How long were we off the grog, Brak?'

'The whole time we were up there. Five years, I think.'

'Jeez, didn't seem that long! Maybe I just liked you sober.'

'Ja, it was a circuit-breaker, I suppose. I'll be frank with you, Frank . . .' Brak pauses to allow his trite pun to sink in. 'My drinking got pretty bad at one stage. Scared myself shitless sometimes with the things I got up to. Brawling, losing jobs, traffic offences. The grog earned me a decent-sized rap sheet.'

'So what happened?' I ask. 'How come you didn't stay up at Kariba?'

'What happened? Murambatsvina, that's what. There we are trying to get ourselves sorted out, trying to help the poor munts get a start in life, and one day Mugabe's heroes of the revolution come along and bulldoze it all down. The whole mission – flattened. Burned to nothing. All our work up in smoke. So I threw in the towel. Had to get away before I did something stupid. I'm not one of those Christians who can turn the other cheek.'

'What possible purpose could be served by destroying your mission?'

'It's the way Mugabe's always operated, china. Terror and intimidation. He sees the missions as agents of subversion. Stoking the fires of revolution.'

'I just don't get it. Wasn't he educated in a mission?'

Brak grunts with disgust. 'Look, Frank, the one thing about Mugabe nobody seems to recognise is that he's just a miserable bloody coward. All this violence has only one purpose and that's to save his own skin. He'd rather destroy the whole nation than relinquish power and face the consequences.'

'Ag, man, watch the meat, Brak!' Reggie calls.

The boerewors has ruptured, the spurting fat causing a sudden conflagration. Reggie runs inside and comes back with a jug of water and Brak douses the flames. Reggie rolls her eyes at me as she sits down again. 'I tell you, Frank, if I left it to him we'd be eating charcoal tonight.'

Unperturbed, Brak continues his train of thought. 'Any Rhodesian back in the seventies could've told you what a dirty little terrorist Mugabe is. We told the world what he'd do once he got into power. The world wouldn't listen and what you see in Zimbabwe today is the result.'

I'm about to respond by saying that despots are what you get when you deny people their political voice, but find the sense to refrain. Instead, I nod and say, 'Yes, it's a sad state of affairs.'

'Let's not talk politics,' Reggie says.

'You're right, Reginald,' Brak agrees. 'Bugger politics.'

He whistles a merry tune as he turns the meat.

'Do you still play the piano?' I ask.

He frowns. 'Piano? Jesus. Haven't touched a bloody piano since I left school.'

'I remember you used to play all that classical stuff. Chopin, Beethoven . . . do you still play the guitar?'

'He used to, when we first started going out,' Reggie says. 'In our wild days. You used to serenade me with beautiful love songs, hey, babe? After a few snorts. Now your old guitar just sits in the cupboard gathering dust.'

'Ja, playing guitar always seemed tied to getting drunk. I told you to sell the damn thing, Reggie.'

'He used to compose such nice songs, I swear. I'm sure you could be famous if you wanted to, babe.'

Brak laughs. 'Christ, the one thing I do know in this world is my own limitations.'

'Ja, but you could serenade me, at least. Be nice to hear you play again.'

'Forget it, sugar pie. If you want vibes why don't you get that ghetto blaster I bought you.'

Reggie goes inside and comes back with a CD player and a stack of CDs. She rummages through and selects Joni Mitchell's *Blue*. Joni's sweet, lilting voice sings out into the darkness. Reggie closes her eyes and sways her head. She sings to some of the verses, adding a sweet melisma to Joni's pure notes.

Brak finishes cooking the meat. We eat on our laps on the steps. Along with the meat there is sadza, lettuce, green beans and tomatoes. Reggie apologises for the limp lettuce, saying their vegetable garden around the back nearly 'vrekked' during a recent heatwave. I'm too busy savouring the rough, bland taste of sadza to notice anything amiss, surprising as I never had any particular fondness for it in the past.

Cracker lies salivating at Brak's feet, waiting impatiently for the titbit of boerewors Brak has done for him. When it has cooled down enough Brak throws it off into the dirt. 'Bugger off now, you bloody freeloader,' he mutters. Cracker dives after it and devours it in a second with snapping chops.

'As if we can afford to feed that dog good meat,' Reggie says.

'Ag, he does a good job, looking after us, Reg. Don't you, Cracker, my big brave boy.'

Reggie scoffs. 'That big baby wouldn't hurt a mouse.'

After eating, I get the last two beers from the fridge and we sit looking out at the black bush, drinking. Reggie has been going slow on the wine. When Brak and Reggie light up cigarettes, I find the craving too much. Shamefaced, I ask for one.

'Just don't blame me for getting you started again,' Brak says.

'Tell us about yourself, Frank,' Reggie says. 'What do you do for a crust there in Australia?'

I tell them about my teaching career and offer an abridged version of my failure as a writer. My attempts to joke about my job as a bus driver fall on deaf ears. The more I talk, the more disgusted I feel with myself. Fifty years old and still putting on fronts. Brak and Reggie just listen, saying nothing. I suddenly feel quite inebriated; my voice begins to slur. I light another cigarette when it is offered.

When my soliloquy tails off, Brak says, 'You should stick with the writing, china. Don't give up.'

'If anyone should be writing, it's you. At least you've got something to say.'

Brak shakes his head. 'No way.'

The beer is finished. Reggie affects a yawn and suggests some coffee.

'Told you she's wild,' Brak says. 'Won't you get Frank and me a couple of glasses, my sweetness? I'm sure Frank is dying to sample that expensive wine there.'

Reggie gives Brak a serious look. Brak laughs plaintively. 'Come on, Reginald! It's not everyday ol' Blue Eyes drops by. The night's still a puppy, man!'

'Okay, but I'm watching you.'

Reggie goes inside to fetch the glasses.

Brak laughs. 'Christ, she watches me like a bloody hawk.' He leans over and puts his hand on my shoulder. 'Good to see you again, china.'

'Likewise,' I say.

'Those Que Que days were good, hey?'

'The best.'

'Why don't you sleep over tonight? Spend a few days.'

'Can't. I've got to get Milton's car back to him. Maybe when my car's fixed.'

'What's wrong with your car?'

I explain. Reggie comes back with two glasses. Brak fills them to the brim with wine and hands one to me. He moves to top Reggie's glass up; she shakes her head and puts her hand over her glass.

'Pity you didn't get hold of me earlier,' Brak says. 'I would've done it for nothing. Who's fixing it?'

'Some joint called Prospect Autos. Thanks, anyway.'

'Why don't you come out Friday evening?' Reggie says. 'Stay the night.'

'I'd love to,' I say.

We drink and talk. After a while, Reggie finishes her wine. She yawns and gets up. 'Good night, Frank,' she says. 'I'll leave you two to reminisce. Don't make it too late, Brak.' She goes inside. Brak and I continue talking. The level of the demijohn drops. Now that Reggie's gone I notice the level of our language drops too. We just stand and piss on the ground in front of the house, causing me to reflect fuzzily on the undervalued contribution of women to civilised behaviour.

We finish the wine. Brak goes inside and comes back with a bottle of sherry, about three-quarters full. He swigs the sherry straight from the bottle and passes it to me. We are both more than a little drunk. As we gradually flatten the sherry, Brak's conversation dwindles into a morose silence. His eyes grow troubled; he seems to be making a physical effort to prevent dark secrets from bursting from his mouth. I make small talk, trying to steer the mood towards lighter things. When we finish the sherry Brak just sits there, grinding his teeth.

He goes inside and practically turns the house upside down looking for more booze. There is none. He comes outside again. 'Fuck-all grog left in this joint,' he says. 'Next time you come, my china, we'll do a proper job.'

I get up to leave. Brak spits out at the darkness. Then he clasps me to his chest. I'm startled to see tears streaming down his face.

We walk to the gate. Another bear hug before I get in the car. In my haste to go, I reverse into a fence post. Brak guffaws and slaps his thigh. Nothing like a little mishap to lift one's spirits. He goes round to the back of the car and inspects the damage. He yells: 'Just a little scratch, man! Milton won't even notice!'

I drive off, cocooned by drunkenness.

VII

My drunken slumber unlocks a subconscious bedlam. One unruly dream, among the deluge, commits to memory: I have a wife and a frightening brood of children – a dozen at least. I am a hairy brute, Neanderthal, with nothing to do but eat and fuck. My faceless wife cringes at the sight of me, yet is compelled to procreate. Children are the wall around her soul. On and on we go, the stained mattress squeaking. Beside the bed, a half-eaten roast boar with a shrivelled apple in its mouth. Through the window I can see our kids squabbling in a dreary suburban backyard. A weird bird sits on the windowsill watching us. At first I think it's a kookaburra, then I see it has a face like a lynx.

On and on. My faceless wife beneath me. The clamour of kids outside. The bird on the windowsill . . .

I wake to a commotion. Precious is shouting: 'Hayi! Hayi! Wena! Aibo!' Dogs in the neighbouring properties begin a riot of barking. A flurry of footsteps. I wrench open the bedroom curtains. The rising sun blinds me momentarily, then I find myself staring into the face of a stranger running past the cottage with a pumpkin under one arm – stolen, I assume, from Milton's vegetable patch. The man is in rags, barefoot. For an instant, our eyes meet. There is a frightening expression in his eyes, a wild desperation brimming with violence.

I stare back stupidly, aware that the cottage door is unlocked; I feel my body go limp — am I one of those animals that feigns death when threatened? But the man sprints away with an ungainly limp to the concrete wall at the end of the garden. He jumps up and looks over, reaping a roar of canine invective from next door. He runs to the side wall; that has broken glass cemented into the top. He is cornered. He turns back towards the house. Precious is standing outside the kitchen brandishing a frying pan. The intruder draws a knife from his pocket and advances on her. High-pitched wails from Rosie and Geldof who watch the scene, wide-eyed, through the servants' quarters' window.

I stumble to the door and wrench it open. The man slows and almost saunters past the cottage, still gripping the pumpkin under one arm. He wags the knife at me like a finger. Smiles malevolently, shakes his head. Don't even think of trying anything with me, his eyes say. Yes, I will stick this knife in you just for the sake of a pumpkin. Milton emerges from the kitchen in his pyjamas and yanks Precious inside by the arm. 'Let him go!' he shouts at me.

The man heads around the main house. He vaults over the front gate, and is gone, the air still aloud with dogs barking.

Only now do I realise that I'm still dressed in yesterday's clothes and am packing a rather nasty hangover. I close the door and lie down again, my head throbbing. Last night seems a blur. I do a quick damage assessment; an inveterate denialist, I conclude that not enough alcohol was consumed to feel quite so wretched. No, my hangover must be due primarily to smoking. My system was unprepared for a deluge of nicotine. I groan with despair at having given in to temptation. Four years abstinence up in smoke, literally.

There is a knock. Precious with my tea. I greet her and take the tray. 'It'll be nice to see your frying pan put back to proper use,' I say.

Precious laughs, her teeth white as maize pips. 'Hayi, nkosi! I am making breakfast now.'

'You shouldn't take such risks with thieves. They're desperate.'

'Yebo, nkosi. But still they should not steal. It is against God.'

'Please call me Frank, Precious. None of this nkosi business.'

'Okay, baas.'

I close the door, aware that I've made no progress in liberating Precious from the linguistic yoke of the past. The title *baas* is worse than *nkosi*, in my book. I won't rock the boat in future. I drink the tea while writing in my diary. Summarising what I can recall of last night, I'm assailed by the sudden memory of Brak guffawing after I had reversed into the fence post. I freeze with dismay. God, how could I be so irresponsible? I can barely remember driving home. Seeking an excuse for my folly, I blame the mishap on my queasy distaste for male intimacy. Brak's bear hug caused my careless haste in driving away. I loathe what used to be the distinctly un-Anglo practice of men hugging and petting each other. Tired of me harping on the subject, one of my hippy girlfriends once called me 'anal retentive' – how do people come up with such revolting terms?

I gulp back my tea. A work siren goes off in the distance. I shower quickly and dress in clean clothes, then hurry outside. The car is parked where it should be, only slightly askew. Milton is loading a cardboard box of files into the boot. He sees me approaching.

'Howzit, Franco. Hope you enjoyed the entertainment this morning. Nothing like a little pumpkin stealing to spice up one's day.'

'I'm beginning to give up on the idea of a leisurely lie-in here in Bulawayo.'

A dimpled grin. 'It's not the first time my vegie patch has been raided. I suppose it's because we don't have a dog. I feel sorry for the poor bastards. I'd do the same if I was in their shoes.'

'I suppose so.'

'So, how was the grand reunion, boyo?'

'Pretty good. Brak's certainly a different kettle of fish to what I expected.'

I cast a glance at the back bumper. The damage is negligible – just a tiny kink. Still, I come clean. 'Look, Milton, I'm terribly sorry, man. I bloody well reversed into a pole last night.' I lean down and rub the kink with my finger. 'Here – this little ding. I swear it was so dark –'

'Ja, I noticed. Don't worry. It's just a nick.'

'I feel terrible, Milton. Let me get it fixed. It's the least I can do.'

'Franco, forget it. It's no big deal. I'm not about to deliver a sermon on the evils of alcohol, if that's what you're worried about.'

Embarrassed, I don't reply.

Milton laughs. 'I told you to watch out for these ex-army types. What's the story with your car? When will Jervis have it fixed?'

'I'm not sure. He seems to have a bit of a backlog.'

Milton kicks one of the tyres. 'Well, the old girl's still at your disposal in the meantime. By the way, your new cop friend, Chombo, phoned last night. Wants you to give him a call. Wouldn't say what about.' He looks at his watch. 'Might be a bit early to catch him, but give it a try.'

I go inside and phone Fort Rixon police station. The line is engaged. After several attempts a terse voice recognisable as Constable Fashion's answers. Chombo isn't in yet, she says. Try later.

During breakfast the phone rings. Ruby answers. She engages in some light-hearted banter before she calls me, rolling her eyes as she hands me the receiver. 'Chombo,' she whispers.

Chombo sounds very distant.

'Phew!' he exclaims. 'You have no idea how hard I have been working on your case. I've been through all the records here. All the files. What a job!'

'I appreciate your efforts, Inspector.'

'Ja, but I need your full cooperation, Mr Cole.'

'You have my full cooperation, Inspector.'

'I don't think so, Mr Cole. It's very disappointing. You see, I've been to Whitestone again to interview the workers. It seems that one of the workers has been withholding information from me.'

'Withholding information?'

'Ntombela — do you remember him?'

I pause. My head throbs. 'What man is this?'

'Come, come, Mr Cole. Of course you remember him. You paid him for information, not so?'

I heave a sigh. 'Look, Inspector, I'm not going to beat about the bush. Yes, I paid Ntombela for some information. But it was dated information – it tells me nothing of where Lettah Ndlovu might be today. I thought it was irrelevant.'

'I agree and disagree with you. Ntombela's information is dated and irrelevant. But it is also incorrect. You must realise the man has AIDS, Mr Cole. His brain is not functioning right. Therefore we can take his information with a pinch of salt, not so?'

I try to remain civil. 'I don't follow your point, Inspector.'

'The point, Mr Cole, is that if you want me to help you find this Ndlovu woman, then you must be honest with me. You must tell me everything you know. You must withhold nothing. I haven't got time to waste with people who are not being straight with me, do you understand?'

'I'm sorry. I didn't think I was being devious in any way. I appreciate your efforts in helping me.'

Chombo seems satisfied with my apology. 'That's all right, Mr Cole. I just want you to know the way I work. Everyone must be open and honest, okay? However, I didn't contact you just to complain. As I said in our last conversation, I've had some promising outcomes to my other investigations around the district. It's too early to provide details, but I thought I would just let you know that I'm making good progress – just so you don't give up hope. What I need is a few more small details about your family . . .'

'Progress? What progress? Please tell me.'

'Be patient, Mr Cole, it's too early to say. Who knows? I might be on a wild goose chase. I need to make sure about my investigations before I can tell you anything. I have a few more questions about the movements of your family while you were with this woman . . .'

'Fire away.'

I go through another round of questions about my family. He asks me if I can remember any mannerisms that Lettah had. Anything at all. He assures me this is for the purposes of identification. All I can tell him is that she was always laughing. I find myself apologising for knowing so little.

When he finishes, I say: 'Inspector, this man Ntombela. I hope he's not in any trouble. It's my fault for not informing you of what he told me. He's not at fault.'

Chombo laughs. 'Trouble? Why would I persecute this sick man? What good would that do? He has AIDS. No, it would be inhumane for me to punish him more. Ntombela is of no consequence to me, Mr Cole.'

'I don't want him to suffer because of me.'

'He will not suffer because of you. Of course, I have confiscated the money you gave him. His ill-gotten gains.'

'Why? Surely —'

'He obtained this money by deception. Fraud. I cannot allow this. He's lucky I have not charged him for this crime.'

'And this money — will I be reimbursed?'

'Of course. We can sort that out at the end. I'm sure you under-stand, Mr Cole, my investigations have not been without cost.'

'Is there anything that can be done for Ntombela, to help ease his sickness?'

'Forgive me for saying it, Mr Cole, but what you ask for is naive. If you want to help Ntombela then you must also help all the other people on the farm who have AIDS. And while you're about it, you can help everyone else in Zimbabwe. The millions like Ntombela. No, Mr Cole, Zimbabwe does not need foreigners coming here like knights in shining armour to help us poor Africans. We can help ourselves. You must concentrate on finding your old servant. That is your responsibility.'

After dropping Milton and Ruby off at their offices, I proceed along Fort Street to Prospect Autos near the railway station. Along the way I buy *The Chronicle* from a street-corner vendor and scan the advertise-ment pages. My notice is there; the tiny image of Lettah's smiling face among several other missing persons. It will run for two weeks.

Jervis's business premises are typical of Bulawayo's semi-industrial fringe: a long bare cement block workshop and poky adjoining office. A concrete perimeter wall with razor wire along the top. A scruffy guard dog chained to a pole. Staffordshire terrier cross, by the look of it. My Nissan is standing with four other vehicles in the yard outside the workshop. The yard is a quagmire of grease and old engine parts. A young man in blue overalls – one of the apprentices, I imagine – is levering the tyre off a wheel with a badly damaged rim next to a drum of water. I park in the street and cross the yard to the office. Even at this time of the morning it's unbearably hot. I sniff the air; for someone so divorced from the mechanical world, it intrigues me that I've always liked the smell of disembowelled engines. The result, perhaps, of those hours I spent lying under greasy hulks with Brak and his father, listening to them grunting and cursing. My hangover lingers.

The office is empty. An old computer hums at the end of a grubby counter strewn with invoices and some welding rods. A once-white enamel bar fridge jiggles in the corner. For a minute I'm transfixed by the office wall behind the counter boasting a bizarre frieze of old *Scope* centrespreads pinned around the obligatory presidential portrait. Boobs, bums and Mugabe. I could never have imagined Mugabe as *Hefner-esque*.

I exit the office. The apprentice working with the wheel sees me and points with the lever at the workshop. There I find Jervis and another apprentice beneath a Toyota up on a hoist. They have their backs to me. Jervis is short and stocky, middle-aged. He grunts loudly as he wrestles with a spanner. Curses and blasphemes with immaculate diction: 'Bloody hell! Jesus Chrrrist! Who on God's bloody earth tightened this fucking bearing? Some bloody Jap sumo wrestler, I bet!' He strains again at the spanner, the veins in his neck bulging, his close-cropped grey hair glistening with sweat. 'Jesus Chrrrist have mercy! Mary! Mother of God!'

The apprentice bursts into laughter, his hand cupped to his mouth. Jervis pauses, then brandishes the spanner at him. Mud brown eyes magnified by thick black-rimmed glasses. 'What are you laughing at, hey? You think I pay you to laugh?'

'No, sir!' the apprentice replies with a valiant attempt at a contrite expression.

Jervis nods his head knowingly. 'Ja, that's right. Just stand there and laugh while I do all the bloody work, hey?'

'No, sir!'

Jervis notices me standing there. He hands the spanner to the apprentice. 'Okay, Benjamin – Mr Fucking Know-it-All – when I come back I want that thing loose. Loose – not stripped, okay? Uzwile na?'

'Yebo, nkosi.'

Jervis approaches me. 'Lemme guess: Milton's friend? Frank, is it?'

I nod. 'Thought I'd just drop in and see what the score is with my car.'

Jervis's magnified eyes are bloodshot and bleary beneath a saturnine brow. He points at the other vehicles outside in the yard. 'I got those to do first. Got their owners breathing down my neck as well.'

'Thought I'd just check.'

'Ja, I'm sorry. Things are bloody slow, man. You can't get parts. You can't get fuck-all. As for labour!' He waves an arm to indicate the apprentice pounding on the tyre rim outside. He sighs wearily. 'Oh, for fuck's sake, Morris!' he bellows. 'I want that wheel in one piece, man!'

Morris nods and laughs. Clearly, Jervis is a benevolent tyrant.

Jervis slaps his thighs wearily. 'Why I bother. Sometimes I feel like a one-legged man in an arse-kicking competition. So, where're you from, Frank?'

'Australia.'

'Australia, hey?' He proceeds to walk laboriously in a circle, as though dragging something heavy with one leg. 'Where's your bloody ball and chain, man?'

His shabby pantomime is so ridiculous I have to laugh.

He taps his temple with a stubby finger. 'Just visiting, hey? What sort of bloody pervert would want to visit Zim, for Chrissake? What's your next stop? Iraq? Afghanistan? You don't sound like an Aussie. What happened to the g'day, mate, and all that?'

'I'm from here originally.'

'Ah, the plot thickens. Ja, you bastards who buggered off and left us to kaffirdom. To tell the truth, I wish I'd gapped it long ago. Now I'm too fucking old.'

I follow Jervis over to my car. He pops the bonnet and leans over the engine. 'Haven't had a chance to look at it yet, but if it's dirty fuel we'll have to clean the whole system out. Petrol tank, carburettor, fuel pump, jets, filters — the works. Not a difficult job, just time-consuming.'

He closes the bonnet. 'Sorry for the delay. I don't like to stuff people around.'

'I can wait. But if you're looking for a mechanic, I happen to know one who's at a loose end.'

Jervis looks at me sceptically. 'You're bullshitting me! A mechanic? Here in Bulawayo? I've already turned this fucking town upside-down looking for a decent grease-monkey.'

I nod. 'Old mate of mine. Just moved here from Kariba.'

Jervis shakes his head and laughs. 'You got a phone number?'

Hazel's shop, Zambezi Pride, is on the corner of Park Street and Leopold Takawira Avenue. It occupies a long thatched building set among some jacaranda and syringa trees abutting Bulawayo's Central Park. People lie like dropped fruit under the trees, staring languidly at passers-by. Some garrulous women sit weaving straw mats on a wide brick courtyard outside the shop's entrance. They greet me with smiles and continue their banter.

The shop smells of smoke and straw. A wild profusion of craft merchandise greets the eye. Fans suspended from the rafters above whirr loudly. Mugabe's portrait is positioned between two tie-dyed sarongs, like a hippy icon. Hazel and Clara are seated at a counter in the centre of the shop, busy sorting through some silk-screened t-shirts with a young Ndebele woman with intricately braided hair falling to her shoulders in clusters of beads. Clara sees me and waves. 'Hi Frank.'

I wave back. 'Hope I'm not intruding.'

Hazel stares pointedly around at the shop, empty of customers, and says, 'Intruding? We could do with a few intruders.'

She introduces the young woman as her assistant, Vera Ndube. Vera gives me a smile, eyes bright and mischievous. 'So this is Frank. Hazel has been telling me *all* about you.'

'You're no doubt aware that my mother is the town gossip,' Clara says.

'Oh yes,' Vera says. 'When it comes to eligible bachelors, Hazel is Bulawayo's social encyclopaedia!'

Hazel peers at Vera over her glasses and smiles. 'Girls, girls, just where do you think I get all my gossip from? Would you like a cup of tea, Frank?'

I nod. 'Tea would be nice.'

Hazel turns back to Vera. 'Won't you make us some tea, deary? Make a pot for the ladies outside too. Milk and sugar, Frank?'

'Just a drop of milk, please.'

'Angifuna itiye eletshukela,' Hazel says.

Vera winks at me. 'Yes, madam. He no want sugar.' She goes through to an adjoining kitchen where she begins a hearty rendition of Madonna's 'Like a Virgin'.

Clara giggles. 'We can always rely on Vera to provide the authentic sound of Africa, can't we, Mom?'

Hazel pushes one pile of t-shirts aside and starts going through another. 'She's a bright girl. In any normal country she'd have the world at her feet. I'm surprised she's still here.'

'Don't tempt fate, Mom. If you keep treating her like a maid she will push off somewhere else.'

Hazel glances at Clara, vexed.

'Don't look at me like that, Mom. It's true.'

'Perhaps I should've asked you to make the tea.'

'Mom . . .'

Mother and daughter stare at each other.

I gesture at the shop's cluttered merchandise. 'I was expecting your shelves to be empty, like every other shop.'

Hazel lets go of her daughter's eyes. 'It's mostly old stock. With the tourist market gone, it just keeps piling up. If it wasn't for the little money I've got invested overseas I'd have closed the doors long ago. Zambezi Pride is practically a charity these days.'

'Hazel!' Vera calls from the kitchen. 'The milk's sour!'

Hazel sighs. 'Oh God.'

'Black tea's fine,' I say.

'Make black tea, then!' Hazel calls back. She turns to Clara. 'Why don't you show Frank around while I finish sorting this stuff. Oh, Frank, your father phoned me last night. It was lovely to hear him again. His voice hasn't changed a bit.'

Clara and I browse through the shop's fabulous plethora: straw mats and baskets, batiks, dyed and crocheted garments and bags, beadwork, masks, stools and drums, calabash cups and rattles, armies of soapstone carvings. Clara demonstrates (to my layman's ears) an impressive knowledge of just about everything on display, from technical process to tribal or functional significance. She is wearing a loose white cotton dress, unbuttoned at the top, revealing a sweaty cleavage. Close up, her musky perfume is oddly familiar, though I can't think why. She shows me some shirts with garishly printed African motifs, which I pretend to like. She selects one emblazoned with a roaring lion with a great shaggy mane and holds it up against me. She nods. 'Aye, it's you, Frank. Definitely you.' I don't know how to respond to her teasing. Another whiff of her perfume and it comes to me: it's the same kind that Hazel used long ago. Weird.

I pick up a small soapstone elephant and rub my thumb over its surface, textured to resemble hide. 'I love these carvings. Such an eye for detail.'

'Bashed out by the dozen, as you can see.'

'Still, I think they're great.'

'Then you would've wept to see what happened during Murambatsvina. All the township workshops . . .' She gives a sweep of her hand. 'Wiped out. Thousands of carvings, just like these, smashed to pieces. Destroyed. So bloody vindictive. Those people outside – those weavers and the others hanging around – they were once self-supporting vendors. My mother tries to keep them going with little commissions she knows will never sell.'

Vera comes through with four mugs and a large billycan on a tray. She sets the mugs down on the counter and goes outside with the billycan. We hear her call: 'Omama, itiye!'

Clara and I sit on stools at the counter. Hazel hands me a mug of tea. 'Any progress with Lettah?' she asks.

'Nothing yet. I've had a couple of conversations with Chombo. He says he's following up on some leads, but won't elaborate. Just a matter of waiting, I guess.'

Hazel blows on her tea and sips it gently. 'Let things take their course. Don't waste your time fretting. If finding Lettah is meant to be, it's meant to be.'

Vera returns and sits next to Clara. She smiles at me and raises her mug of tea. 'Here's to you, Frank. Zimbabwe's rarest species – a visitor! Who knows? If you stay long enough we might even make you an honorary Zimbabwean.'

Clara laughs. 'I'm sure that's high on Frank's wish list.'

Hazel fans herself with her hand. 'God, it's hot! I'm not sure that tea's the best thing right now.' She gazes up at the spinning fans suspended from the rafters. 'Sometimes I wonder if those have any effect at all.'

'That's what I've been trying to tell you, Mom,' Clara says, exasperated. 'They just blow the hot air back at us.'

'Yes, well, there's no money for air conditioning.' Hazel turns to me. 'Did you get hold of your friend?'

'Brak? I caught up with him last night.'

'I remember him from the Que Que days. Tell him I haven't forgiven him for murdering half of Rhodesia's bird population with that damn pellet gun of his. Naughty little blighter! He probably doesn't remember me.'

'I'll tell him.'

She gives my arm a squeeze. 'You'll let me know if you do get word about Lettah, won't you?'

'Of course I will.'

'I've been thinking a lot about your mother. She had the kindest heart. It'll be a shame if your search comes to nothing.'

We drink our tea. The last remnant of my hangover, a stubborn lump of pain at the back of my head, throbs briefly, then implodes to nothing. The only physical symptom I have left to remind me of last night is a slight queasiness in my stomach. Outside we can hear the women cackling with laughter.

Vera raises a finger. 'That, good citizens, is the sound of hope.'

Back at the cottage, I offload the soapstone elephant and some other bits and pieces I ended up buying at Zambezi Pride (including the shirt with the roaring lion's head). Precious brings me some tea and tells me Jervis phoned. I drink the tea, then go across to the house to return his call. It takes Jervis a while to answer; as I wait, the dapper image of Mugabe among the *Scope* pin-ups springs to mind, only to be rudely supplanted by Jervis's myopic, saturnine visage as he bawls into the phone, 'Ja! Prospect Autos!'

It turns out that Brak came into town immediately after Jervis rang him. Jervis was duly impressed when, by way of a test, he asked Brak to have a look at my Nissan. When Brak expertly assessed the problem and checked the cylinder heads for cracks (thankfully, ruling out a worst-case scenario), Jervis offered him a job on the spot. Brak agreed to start once he'd finished a freelance job he was doing.

'So I phoned just to tell you we'll probably get your car on the road sooner than I thought,' Jervis says. 'The way I see it, we kill two birds with one stone. Your car gets fixed sooner and your china Malan gets a job. Cheeky bastard, though. Started muttering about my bloody dog. Telling me dogs should never be chained up. I said, right, Mr Fucking Dog-Expert-Hero – *you* unchain that mongrel. Which your bloody idiot friend proceeds to do. Or tries to do. Got a nice little bite on the hand. A good nip.'

I spend the rest of the morning lying on the bed in the cottage, reading some old newspapers I found in one of the cupboards. My stomach churns noisily. I find the political babble of these state-controlled papers strangely entertaining. We are presented with Mugabe as International Statesman, forging links with such venerable nations as Iran and North Korea. He is frequently quoted. In defining friend or foe, he makes persistent reference to identity. When it comes to the question of whites claiming their right to Africa, his racist essentialism is blunt: whites are not indigenous to Africa, therefore can never be African. Africa is for Africans. Zimbabwe for Zimbabweans. Except that it's not just whites who are excluded from belonging. In his rants there are the millions of black Zimbabweans, referred to as 'excess people' or the 'nation's trash', that also bear his wrath. The cruel irony of it is oddly captivating. Propaganda's horrible burlesque.

Navel-gazing about identity has always seemed an exercise in futility to me. Yet reading these awful diatribes, the question of belonging starts to scratch at my conscience. What am I? Born in a country that no longer exists. Born in Africa, nonetheless.

I feel suddenly lethargic, drained of energy, as though in the throes of a second bout of jet lag. I lie on the bed, looking up at the ceiling, thinking of Lydia, of her stubborn faith in me.

At noon Precious brings a steaming plate of sadza and gravy. The last thing I feel like in this stifling heat, but I sweat through it, thinking of how Lydia used to chide Max and me when we wouldn't eat our food. Think of all the starving people in the world, she would say. And I would wonder how my eating would alleviate their suffering.

Yet afterwards I feel decidedly better; my stomach has at least stopped churning. I change into my swimmers and apply some sunscreen to my face and shoulders. A knock on the door. I open the door, expecting it to be Precious to collect the lunch things. It's Clara.

143

'Have I come at a bad time?' she says.

'No, no,' I stammer.

Her eyes quickly scan the interior of the cottage. 'Mmm, so this is your wee den, hey? Thought you might like to join me for a swim. I do a few laps at the municipal pool every day at lunch time.'

'You must've read my mind. I was about to have a dip here.'

She glances at the algal waters of Milton's pool, the flutter of a smile on her mouth. 'Your choice: me or the frogs.'

'Hang on, let me grab a towel.'

The only thing that has changed at Bulawayo's old municipal swimming pool is its address, Samuel Parirenyatwa Street having replaced Borrow Street. Everything else is the same: the white-gabled entrance, with its arches and columns and green corrugated iron roof; the jacarandas outside; inside, the pool surrounded by lawns and huge, shady trees; the sharp smell of chlorine, the shrill racket of birds in the trees. Another Rhodesian oasis.

The pool is quiet; just a few other swimmers doing laps. Clara tells me that the lunch period is the best because you miss the kids that come in school groups in the mornings and chaotic mobs in the afternoons. She disappears into the change rooms and returns wearing a snug-fitting black Speedo. She reaches into the sports bag over her shoulder and hands me a pair of goggles. 'You better use these. The chlorine's a bit strong sometimes.'

'You should realise I'm past my physical peak,' I say.

She gives my thickening midriff an amused glance and puts her bag down on a bench next to the pool. 'It's never too late to turn back the ravages of time. See that fellow over there?' She points at one of the swimmers, a muscular specimen, churning tirelessly through the water. 'That's Allan. One of Bulawayo's dying breed of white businessmen. How old do you reckon he is?'

'Haven't a clue.'

'Fifty-five.'

Clara arches an eyebrow. Enough said.

We take two empty lanes. Clara dives in and starts swimming: a slow, mincing freestyle, as though hating getting her face wet. This ungainly display fires up my confidence. A chance to impress lies begging, swimming being the sole small feather in my sporting cap. I dive in and begin the butterfly leg of an intended medley. Halfway across the pool I power Spitz-like past Clara. Even Allan, two lanes down, might have been impressed, were he not engaged in adjusting his goggles strap in the shallow end. Sad to say, this heroic burst fizzles out like a damp squib; by the end of that first length I can barely clear the water with my arms. Clara minces past me. A prissy little tumble turn and she swims back, pausing just once between strokes to grin at me. I change to freestyle and manage only eight lengths in total. My persistence in achieving even that, I confess, was due mainly to catching the occasional glimpse of Clara's bottom as she cruised past, kicking those long legs. Twice, I took a breather to demist my goggles.

Shaking from exertion, I climb out of the pool and lie baking in the sun on the side while Clara finishes her quota of lengths – thirty, I believe. The effort has left me feeling faint; I lie on my back, eyes closed, acutely aware of my mortal limitations, at the same time unable to rid myself of the memory of those long legs and wobbling bum. Lust . . . the tawdry old devil stirs. I should take care not to make a spectacle of myself.

I open my eyes at the thud of footsteps next to me. Allan, fifty-five and rippling with muscles, strides past. 'Enjoy your paddle?' he asks.

Paddle? Is Adonis having a dig?

'Can't say that I did.'

'Ja, well, no pain no gain,' he says sagely and heads off to the change rooms.

Clara finishes her swim with a sprint. In one movement she pulls herself up and out of the pool, her bum landing with a wet plop on the cement next to me. 'Youch! That's hot!' she exclaims, squirming. 'Phew! How're you feeling, old man?'

I groan.

She laughs. 'Don't worry. It's amazing how quickly you can get into shape if you just keep at it.'

Such kind encouragement.

'So, Clara. How do you cope with life in this weird town?'

'What do you mean cope?'

'What's there to do in Bulawayo? Do you have a social life?'

'I suppose if you compare it to the social life I had overseas, you'd have to say Bulawayo is, well, *different*. People tend to congregate at each other's houses. Braais, braais, and more braais. But, believe me, people know how to party here. Desperate times make for desperate partying! I go out occasionally with Vera – you know, Vera from the shop?'

I nod.

'She's introduced me to Bulawayo's wee artistic community. Trouble is, I love art but I'm all thumbs when it comes to doing it. I don't really fit anywhere. So to answer your question: no, I don't have much of a social life. It does get boring, but it's no big deal. I didn't come here for a *social life*.'

'Why did you come here?'

Clara gazes up at the cloudless sky. 'Oh, God . . . why did I come? Have you got all afternoon, Frank?'

'If needs be.'

She laughs. 'Okay, I'll try to summarise it for you. When my father died I was given a comfortable inheritance. Comfortable enough not to have to work for the rest of my life. He left me his gallery and two expensive properties. But he, silly man that he was, had married two other women after my mother. They successfully contested his will and I ended up with a tiny fraction of my original inheritance. I was faced with two options: stay in the UK and try to forge a new life for myself – I was over thirty and not really qualified to do anything, so that was the hard option. Or I could go somewhere else, somewhere cheaper, where I could survive off what was left of my inheritance.'

'So you chose Zimbabwe, of all places.'

'Mom was here, so it was a straightforward choice. Zim's always been a sort of second home. But there were other reasons why I left. Personal reasons. A few failed relationships. So, Frank, I'm an *escapee*!

Footloose and fancy free.' She laughs emptily and drums her fingers on the cement. 'I really was rather spoilt by my father. He let me do as I pleased. And when he was gone the rug was pulled out from under me.'

'And Zambezi Pride? You seem to like working there.'

'Aye, I do. I can see why African craft has always been a passion for my mother. But she's not making any money and so many people have come to depend on her. You heard her going on about the shop being a charity. She's not exaggerating.' Clara slaps her thighs. 'That's it in a nutshell. Clara's silly little life. What about you, Frank? Have you a silly little life you can tell me about?'

'Sillier and littler.'

'Oh, come on! I've told you mine!'

I deliver an abridged version of my life. To the point, verging on colourless. Clara listens, pursing her lips sceptically. She shakes her head, gives that flutter of a smile. Then she starts to prod and probe; soon she wheedles things out of me that are usually kept under strict lock and key. My failed relationships. My aspirations to be a writer.

'Nobody told me you're a writer,' she says.

'I *was* a writer. Or, rather, an aspiring writer.'

'At least you tried to be something. More than I can say for myself.'

'Don't be so hard on yourself.'

'I'm just being honest. Being straight with yourself makes life easier sometimes.' Her eyes rest on my outstretched hand. She leans forward and scrutinises the lines on my palm. She nods slowly. 'Hmm . . . interesting.'

'Don't start.'

She laughs and slaps her thighs again. 'I suppose I better get back to the shop. Can't leave Mom and Vera to handle *all* those customers on their own.'

She goes over to her bag on the bench nearby. On impulse, I say: 'I'm going to a braai at my friend Brak's place tomorrow evening. Out near Matobo. Staying over and coming back the next day. Would you like to come?'

Clara thinks for a while. 'Wow, a braai. Will he mind me coming?'

'I'm sure he won't. I'll let him know.'

'Okay, that would be nice.'

Can life be so simple?

For the rest of the afternoon I feel like I'm standing under a rainbow. I fetch the kids from school with a happy heart. Rosie and Geldof natter away animatedly in the back, more comfortable in my presence now. I watch them through the rear-view mirror, amused as Geldof acts the clown, sucking in his cheeks and squinting. As we pass a tearoom I decide to treat them to an ice-cream. I park the car and give them some money. They run into the shop but return empty-handed. No ice-creams. No soft drinks either. I send them back inside to get something else – sweets, anything, I say. They come back each with a fistful of bubblegum.

We return to Kumalo, big pink lungs billowing from their mouths.

The evening is close, sultry. The city secretes a dirty sweat. Possible thunderstorms have been forecast for the weekend, but tonight, like every night so far, there is not a cloud in the sky. I yearn for rain. Even the smell of rain – anything to freshen this dead air.

After a potato souffle supper, Milton, Vernon and I go for a dip in the pool; Ruby stays inside watching *Judge Judy* on satellite TV. Milton floats about on his back, belly glistening, like a hairy dugong. The water is tepid. We are joined by Rosie and Geldof who paddle around on the steps at the shallow end. Rosie is wearing the sort of bloomer-like costume girls wore in the fifties.

After our swim, Milton and I sit in plastic chairs next to the pool. The evening rings with Rosie's and Geldof's shrill voices. Their eyes and teeth glint in the gloom. Vernon is trying to teach them how to swim. Their ungainly efforts, punctuated by much spluttering, send him into fits of laughter.

Milton smiles as he watches. 'Vernon would make a good sports coach. Plenty of patience and good humour.'

'What would you know about sports coaches?' I say.

He laughs, dismissing my jibe with a wave of his hand. I bring up my plans for the weekend. No problem with the car, Milton says. Ruby has half a dozen friends and relatives who can lend them a vehicle if needs be.

'I hope you don't think I'm taking liberties, Milton. I'm sure Brak won't mind picking me up if it's inconvenient.'

'Liberties? For Chrissake, Frank, if you say that again I'll bloody kick you. I wouldn't say the car's available if it wasn't.'

Rosie and Geldof scream with delight as they take turns riding across the pool on Vernon's back. Milton calls: 'Hey! You lot! Keep it down, okay!' They quieten for a few seconds before the decibels rise again.

Milton shakes his head. 'Should've known I was wasting my breath.'

'Vernon's a great kid,' I say.

'He's a blessing.'

'Must've been a big thing adopting him. A big decision.'

Milton doesn't reply. His expression becomes sombre, reflective.

'I don't mean to be intrusive.'

'I know. But you can never imagine what it took. What we went through makes him more than flesh and blood in my eyes. I don't even think of him as adopted. It still makes me bitter to think of it. There he was, almost dead when they found him, skin and bone, an orphan, desperately needing medical attention, and we had to fight pig-headed bureaucrats tooth and nail to give him a loving home. To save his life — to *give* him a life. The crap Ruby and I had to put up with from Social Welfare. Stonewalling. Reverse racism. They just couldn't accept seeing a black kid with white parents. That's all it came down to. They'd rather have seen him dead. If we weren't in the legal game he wouldn't be here today.'

'He's lucky you hung in.'

'He's lucky. We're lucky. He's the reason I stay in this country. If he can survive, Zimbabwe can.'

'Wouldn't you all be better off leaving?'

'And go where? Australia? Forget it. Vernon and Ruby were born here. Why the hell should we leave?'

'I would've thought simple self-preservation might be reason enough. Sorry, Milton, I don't see how anyone would *choose* to live here when there are other options.'

'Who knows, Franco? Maybe we're all a bit crazy.'

Milton stretches his arms and looks up at the stars. We are silent for a while. Then he turns to me, the shining circles of his glasses giving him the look of a night beast. 'I've thought about leaving. Often. Finding a nice little democracy somewhere in the world to settle down and live happily ever after. The trouble is I really don't think the so-called Free World out there is quite what it's cracked up to be. Nothing solid about it. Too full of fuck-all.'

'Well, you've chosen a pretty diabolical alternative. I'll stick with the Free World, thank you.'

Milton laughs dryly. 'Don't you ever get sick of all that nothingness? All that moral relativism? No more right or wrong. Everyone just floating around. No more truth, just deconstructions of truth. No limits to self-indulgence. Everyone just following the path of least resistance. Slaves to self-interest, to excess. Always the coward's choice when it comes to hard decisions. Where even the church vacillates and compromises so the flock can do as it pleases.'

'My God, Milton, there's a place for you among the Quakers, I'm sure.'

'Ha, ha. The point I'm making is that the Free World is doomed to extinction in a quagmire of excess.'

'Surely it all depends on how you define excess —'

Milton laughs. '*Define excess* . . . shit! There you go, proving my point! No truth, just endless deconstructions.'

'If you'll let me finish. The West doesn't have a mortgage on excess. I could name quite a few non-Western countries that I would consider excessive, especially here in Africa. Zimbabwe is bloody well awash with excess. Excess power. Excess corruption and cruelty. Excess poverty and death. Despots like Mugabe are just gluttons for excess.'

Milton cocks his head in assent. 'But you're missing my point. I'm not extolling the virtues of tyrannies. What I am saying is that I prefer to live where things like right and wrong are clear. Where good and bad are straightforward, simple.'

I can't help the terseness in my voice. 'So you'd rather live under the thumb of Africa's Hitler just because it's easier to recognise right and wrong? That's just plain bloody idiotic. I can't believe that a lawyer can even argue such nonsense. What happened to all that stuff we used to talk about as students? Democracy, freedom of speech?'

A note of irritation enters Milton's voice too. 'Ja, ja. Democracy. Freedom of speech. All very nice. The problem, boyo, is that democracies have just ended up in a chaotic free-for-all in which only the rich and the intolerant thrive. A nebulous mess. For all Zimbabwe's terrible faults, for all its terrible cruelties, at least truth is clear here. Here we witness the best and worst of human behaviour. Right and wrong are unequivocal.'

'You're being absurd, Milton. Give me the nebulous mess of Australia any day. What you're saying is perverse!'

'Simmer down, Franco. Don't judge me for the choices I make.'

'I'm not judging you. I'm appealing to your sanity.'

'Ja, well, you live your life, I'll live mine.'

Milton turns to the kids in the pool and claps his hands. 'Come on, that's enough! Out you get. School tomorrow.'

Rosie and Geldof groan and slowly clamber out of the pool. Vernon does a slow length under water and climbs out at the deep end. They dry themselves off and walk off towards the house.

Milton slaps at a mosquito. 'We all follow our instincts, Franco. Or we should, anyway. For better or for worse. But let's change the subject. Tell me about your writing.'

I sigh. 'There is no writing. I gave it up years ago. I'm sorry I lied to you. It was just too much of a humiliation to admit failure. I guess I made the coward's choice.'

Milton puts a hand on my shoulder. 'I know, Franco. A blind man could've seen you'd packed it in. If you'd been writing there would've been *something* to show me after all this time, hey? Why did you give it up?'

'I could ask you the same question. We both used to write, remember?'

'That's true. Reprimand acknowledged. I just lost it – lost the passion. I don't know why. Maybe this place just eclipses writing. Why did you stop?'

'Simple. Writing is storytelling. Writers have to have someone to tell their stories to. I couldn't find any listeners. End of story.'

'Writing's your hard choice, Frank. I hope you change your mind.'

'I hope you do too.'

He smiles. 'The world lost nothing in me not becoming a writer.'

'You know that's crap.'

Another silence.

Ruby calls from the house. 'Anyone for coffee?'

We get up and go inside.

VIII

On Friday I receive a call from Geoffrey Dlamini, the man from the Births and Deaths Registry. He tells me he has made enquiries about Lettah around the country. He lists a string of government departments and agencies he has consulted. No luck. The little flame of hope that flickered on hearing his voice sputters and dies. He asks about my visit to Whitestone; I reply with a brief summary. I thank him for his trouble and ask how much I can pay him. 'There's no obligation,' he says simply.

Before fetching the kids from school I stop off at Tredgold House. I find Dlamini in the same office, tapping away at his computer. Behind him, Mugabe stares down from his portrait on the wall, the reflected ceiling fan making his eyes flicker. The thump of stamps as the two officials at the counter process another endless queue.

I hand him an envelope. 'A token of my appreciation.'

He stands up and takes the money with both hands, puts it in his inside jacket pocket. A wry smile. 'Thank you, Mr Cole. However, I feel guilty taking money for my fruitless efforts.'

'I'm sure you did your best.'

Dlamini pauses. 'There was no response to the newspaper advertisement?'

I shake my head.

'Nothing?'

'Nothing from the notices I put up in the township either.'

He nods thoughtfully. 'Mmm . . . but you say the policeman in Fort Rixon is making progress. Chombo.'

'That's what he says. Nothing solid yet, though.'

'Perhaps he will have better luck than me. I hope so. In the meantime I will keep looking. There may be something I've missed. You never know.'

I thank him again and leave.

I set off for Brak's in the early evening, looking game in the shirt with the roaring lion's head. I stop at the Hillside shops for a crate of bombs (Bulawayo vernacular for quarts of beer) and some wine before dropping in at Hazel's house, just on six o'clock. Clara is still getting ready. I have a sundowner, a couple actually, with Hazel and Vic in the lounge while I wait.

Hazel is pleased with tonight's arrangement. 'It'll do Clara a world of good to get out and about,' she says. 'She's become a bit of a social recluse.'

Vic slurps his beer and snorts. 'Social recluse? Don't exaggerate, woman! What about all those parties she goes to with her homo friends?'

Hazel heaves a weary sigh. 'Just once, Vic, it would be nice to hear you say something positive. Just once. I know Clara's lifestyle irritates you – you should be glad Frank's taking her out. At least she'll be out of your hair for a while.'

'I am glad. Christ, I'm ecstatic. The only thing that worries me is the choice of venue.' He gives me a bleary stare. 'Ja, you be careful of that Brak. Rough as a dog's knee. I'd never allow my daughter anywhere near that bastard.'

'Good gracious me!' Hazel laughs. 'Isn't this a case of the pot calling the kettle black!'

Foolishly, I enter the fray. 'I don't think he's as rough as you make out, Vic. Did you know Brak could play Chopin on the piano when he was six years old?'

Vic's expression tells me two things: not only hasn't he a clue who Chopin is but in his book males and music make for a dodgy mix. 'Chopin? I don't care if he can play bloody Chopsticks! Doesn't change the fact he's rough as guts. I should know – he worked for me for three years.' He squints at me through a minute aperture between thumb and forefinger. 'That close to a kaffir, I tell you.'

'Now you're being offensive, Vic,' Hazel says.

Clara appears in jeans and a floral blouse, her hair loose on her shoulders. A small overnight case in one hand and a bottle of wine in the other. She stares at my shirt. 'I didn't think you'd actually *wear* that!'

'Oh, I think that shirt looks lovely,' Hazel says. 'Hey, Vic? Don't you think it makes Frank look strong and manly?'

Vic cups his ear. 'What's that?'

'I said, don't you think Frank's shirt makes him look strong and manly?'

'Hmmph! A strong and manly fairy, maybe.'

'I've got plenty of beer and wine in the car, Clara,' I say.

'Better safe than sorry,' she replies.

It's almost dark when we depart. I accelerate as we leave the city precincts. We're running late; Brak had said to come before sunset. An image of Brak flits into my head, huge, feral – how astonished my father and Max will be to see how he has turned out after all these years!

'Damn!' I exclaim, thumping the steering wheel.

'What's the matter?'

'I forgot my camera. My mind's like a sieve.'

'Don't worry, I've got mine.'

The lights of Bulawayo recede behind us. Clara relaxes back in her seat. She chats away and I relax too, glad to be in her company, thinking how much I like her Scots twang. We cross the Khami River and wind up through some low hills. Darkness has set in; there is no traffic on the road. The headlights barrel through the blackness, picking up small swarms of insects. A sign of rain? A few kilometres before Brak's turn-off, I accelerate up a rise, listening to Clara describe how she once broke her leg in two places skiing in Switzerland when she slammed into a Japanese tourist who had stopped mid-slope to photograph the view. She lifts her hands, mystified. 'Just bloody well stood there, *docilely*, as I ploughed straight into him!'

I imagine the poor Japanese tourist on that snowy slope. Slowly lowering his camera, eyes blinking in astonishment at the yodelling Scotswoman bearing down on him. Why was the onus on him to get out of the way?

The donkey appears so suddenly over the rise, I have no time to brake or swerve. A momentary vision of it standing, *docilely*, in the headlights before we collect it head-on. Clara yelps and grips my arm. I duck instinctively as the animal is catapulted into the air. A loud crack against the windscreen. Violent tumbling above as we skid to a bumpy standstill at the side of the road. The engine shudders and stalls. A long, seething silence. Just one headlight shines off into the long grass in front of the car, dust swirling in its beam. The windscreen on the passenger's side is crazed around a hole the size of a cricket ball.

Clara just sits there, eyebrows raised, open-mouthed. Glass fragments on her lap. I ask: 'Are you okay?' She nods dumbly. I look back through the rear window. Nothing but blackness. I get out. Aside from the beam of the single headlight, it's pitch dark. I search around the car on rubbery legs. The donkey – if it *was* a donkey – has vanished, inexplicably. Did it somehow survive the collision unscathed? Has it taken off intact into the bush? The force of the impact would seem to negate any such possibility. I stand in the darkness, stupidly trying to piece things together, wondering if I've gone mad. How could a donkey, not the tiniest of beasts, simply disappear?

Something is trickling down the rear window, giving off a pungent scent of . . . urine? I lean closer – it *is* urine. Glancing upwards, I'm confronted by a sight that makes my jaw drop. There on the roof, silhouetted against the headlight's glare, is the mystery donkey.

Bizarrely, it has landed upright on its belly, facing forward like some goofy figurehead. Stone dead.

Clara gets out and stands next to me. She follows my transfixed stare.

'Oh, my God,' she says.

I attempt to free the animal, but its hind legs are jammed fast, splayed under the roof racks. The bolts fastening the racks to the roof are rusted tight, impossible to loosen with my fingers. I open the boot to look for a spanner. The raw stench of beer assails me. I groan. The boot is awash with beer foam and broken glass.

'Oh shit,' Clara says. 'This is not getting any better, is it?'

Indeed not. Rummaging around for a spanner, I cut my finger on some broken glass. There are no spanners. With a growing sense of desperation I climb up onto the roof and try again to wrench the donkey's legs out of the racks. I wrestle and heave, grunting with strain, to no avail.

Clara watches me, her hand over her mouth.

'Is there anything I can do?' she asks.

I shake my head. 'Just as well it's dead.'

Clara shudders. 'Poor wee thing . . . you shouldn't drive so fast on these roads.'

'Oh Christ. Now I stand accused of donkey murder.'

I climb down and inspect the front of the vehicle. Aside from the broken headlight, the bumper and front grill are slightly buckled. I stand there looking at the beast atop Milton's car, with its gentle head lolling between its front legs, as though snoozing, wondering if a bigger fuck-up was humanly possible.

Clara finds a tissue in her bag for my cut finger. We get back in the car. I start the engine. Thank God, at least *that* is in one piece. Bearing our beast of burden, we drive on slowly. Clara begins to laugh. Soon she is in hysterics. I glance at her, thinking it may be delayed shock.

'I'm sorry,' she gasps, holding her stomach. 'It's just I can't get that expression of yours out of my head. When you first saw it up on the roof. I thought your eyes were going to pop out!'

Another bout of hysterics.

'Hilarious,' I mutter.

By the time the whole grotesque ensemble arrives at Brak's place the car smells like a brewery sidelining as a knacker's yard. I stop to open the gate. The dog, Cracker, comes bounding up through the darkness barking like a buffoon; he quietens when I call his name. I drive slowly up to the house. The veranda lights are burning and music is coming from inside. A fire flickers in the half-drum braai near the veranda steps. Brak and Reggie appear at the front door. They stand there, open-mouthed, as I pull up. Brak whistles in wonder and lumbers down the stairs, a smile spreading across his hairy dial. His right hand is bandaged; his left clasps a beer bottle.

'Holy snapping arseholes!' he says, shaking his head. He turns to Reggie, still in the doorway. 'Hey, Reginald! Frank's brought his own meat, doll.'

Reggie has her hand in front of her mouth. 'Ag no, man, Frank!'

Feeling a prize idiot, I climb out. Brak opens Clara's door. 'These Aussies, hey!' he goes on. 'No class. The least he could've done was skin the damn thing.'

Clara laughs and gets out. I can see this is not something I will live down any time soon. I'm about to introduce her when Cracker spies the donkey for the first time. Lit up by the veranda lights, it must make a pretty impressive sight to canine eyes, perched up there, legs splayed, head leering down, a row of teeth bared on one side like a bashful grin. After a shameful backward leap, Cracker glances uncertainly at Brak, gathers himself, and proceeds to circle the car, barking oafishly. Brak guffaws. 'Cracker, you bloody hopeless mutt!' He reaches up and runs a hand over the side of the donkey. 'Shame. Still warm, poor little bugger. Probably just standing there minding his own business and along comes ol' Blue Eyes.'

Finally, I introduce Clara.

Brak shakes her hand gently with his bandaged paw. 'Howzit, Clara.'

'Nice to meet you, Brak.'

'Och aye! A lassie straight from the Glens, hey?'

Reggie comes down the stairs. She gives Clara a peck on the cheek. 'Hi, I'm Reggie. I'm so glad you came. Now I won't feel outnumbered. Are you okay?'

'I'm fine,' Clara says.

Brak goes around to the front of the car. 'Christ, what happened, china?'

I explain the mishap as Brak inspects the damage. He nudges the bumper with a bare foot. Takes a swig of beer and belches. 'Ag, it's bugger-all, man. Couple of scratches. Leave it with me. I'll fix it in no time. But we can talk about that tomorrow. Let's get your gear out. By the way, lekker shirt, china.'

Clara and Reggie giggle.

'I'm serious,' Brak says. 'Just my style.'

I open the boot. A great breath of warm beer wafts out. Brak snorts. 'Phew! Bloody hell! What's going on in there – Oktoberfest?'

'I'm afraid there was some collateral damage,' I say.

'What is it with you and cars, man? You got some personal vendetta or what?'

Reggie peers in the boot. 'No big deal. A bit of spilt beer.'

I shake my head. 'A bit of beer? You forget my friends are rabid teetotallers.'

Brak kicks the back tyre with his bare foot. 'Ja, we better clean up this jalopy or you'll be in Shit Street, my friend. We'll need some soap and rags, Reginald.'

'Bring your stuff inside,' Reggie says.

Clara and I grab our bags and follow Reggie inside. She shows us to separate rooms along a passage. Taking me aside, she whispers: 'I just assumed you wanted your own rooms.'

'You assumed correctly.'

'These days you never know,' she says.

Reggie notices my cut finger and, once a nurse always a nurse, washes it in Dettol and sticks a plaster around it. Clara stays with

Reggie in the house; I return to the car. Brak lifts the crate of beers from the boot. He carries it over to the fire and puts it on the ground. It turns out only two bottles have been broken. A matter of some joy to us both. He opens a quart with his teeth and hands it to me. 'There, might as well put that to good use.'

'Haven't they heard of twist tops in this God-forsaken place?'

'China, the only thing with a twist to its top here is our president.' We stand there staring at the flames in the braai. Brak hawks and spits. 'Tell me something, Frank, as one old man to another. How the bloody hell did you score a chick like Clara? You've only been in this country two minutes.'

'For crying out loud. No one's *scored* anything. She's Hazel Kent's daughter. Remember Hazel from Que Que?'

'You know, I thought her face was familiar. That friend of your Mom's. Always at Sunnyside. Hazel, hey? Shit, now there's some ancient history.'

'Hazel lives with Vic Baldwin.'

'True's God? I always thought she was a bit weird.'

A waxing moon is just beginning to rise over the eastern horizon and the sky above is silver with stars.

I gesture at Brak's hand. 'Jervis tells me you and his dog got acquainted.'

Brak grunts. 'That poor bloody thing. Can you imagine the life it leads? Chained to that pole, day in, day out.'

'Looks like the dog appreciated your sympathy. When do you start work?'

'Monday. I've managed to get the other jobs I was busy with out of the way. I appreciate it, buddy. I owe you.'

'Owe me for what?'

''Cause of you I got that job.'

'Bullshit. You don't owe me anything.'

Reggie and Clara come back with a bucket of hot water foaming with soap and some old towels. Insisting that the 'boys' stand aside, Reggie sweeps up the broken glass in the boot with a brush and dustpan and begins mopping up the beer. Brak manfully opens a beer for Clara with his teeth. We watch Reggie, sipping our beers. When she finishes, she says: 'That's the worst of it. We can give it another sponge tomorrow. Brak, do something about that bloody donkey, man. It's giving me the creeps. You'd better hurry. That fire's nearly ready.'

She squashes the towels into the bucket and goes back inside the house. Brak drains his beer and puts the bottle next to the crate on the ground. Then he walks off to the sheds and returns with a torch, some tools and a thick plastic bag.

'Gimme the keys,' he says. 'I know where we can ditch the critter.'

I hand Brak the car keys.

He turns to Clara. 'You look just like your mother. Serious.'

'Mmm, so I'm told,' Clara says.

'Just relax here with Reggie. We won't be long.'

Clara digs an elbow in my ribs. 'Oh, aye, men's business, hey?'

Brak smiles. 'Put it this way: it won't exactly whet your appetite.'

'Let me take a quick photo before you boys go. Come on, I insist.'

Ignoring my protestations, she runs inside and returns with her camera. She positions Brak and me in front of the car. Brak puts his arm around my shoulder and brandishes a beer bottle. I muster a half-hearted smile. Brak and me in front of my handiwork: a dead donkey and a pranged car – one for the album. As the flash goes off I pray fervently that this picture will never find its way into Milton's hands.

Brak and I climb in the car and take off into the darkness. He drums his fingers on the steering wheel and whistles as he drives, warbling the notes. A few hundred metres down the road he turns off onto a rutted dirt track that soon peters out into nothing but bush. The one headlight pierces the darkness, lighting up the sparse scrub. The flat ground is bare and sandy in patches. The prospect of getting stuck – yet another stupid calamity to explain to Milton – is a grow-ing worry; I can only hope Brak knows what he is doing. Brak takes out a pack of cigarettes and offers me one. 'What the hell,' I say. We light up. Brak jabbers away nonstop, slurring the odd word. He reckons whistling is an underrated musical form and cites John Lennon's 'Jealous Guy' as evidence. He commences a chirpy rendition.

The headlight picks up a cluster of thorn trees ahead. Brak swings the car around in a wide circle and reverses back towards the trees. 'This'll do,' he says. 'I saw a jackal and her pups around here a few days ago. Might as well give them a good nibble. Between them and the vultures, there'll just be bones in a week.'

I shine the torch while Brak loosens the roof racks with a shifting spanner. We free the donkey's legs and let it slide off the side of the car. The donkey emits a long bubbling wheeze as it flops heavily onto the ground. Brak fastens the racks back on the car. Then he fishes around in his tool box and extracts a long knife. He slices the skin down the hind legs. It takes some sawing before he is able to tear the hide free. He asks me to hold the leg still. With bloody hands, he starts butchering the rump and haunches. 'Cracker'll eat anything,' he says, by way of explanation. I'm reminded of that photograph of him and his father skinning buffalo. Brak grunts and pants as he saws away. 'Man, this is thirsty work! At least old Cracker will be all smiles.'

Feeling slightly nauseous, I watch as Brak cuts the meat away to the bone and drops it into the plastic bag and loads it in the boot. He wipes his bloodied hands on his t-shirt and shorts. We drive back to the house.

The girls are sitting on the steps next to the fire.

'Ag, no man, Brak! Look at your shirt!' Reggie complains as Brak dumps the bag of meat next to the braai. 'I'll never get that blood out!'

'It's just an old t-shirt, doll. How about a beer, Frank?'

'Would you mind if I gave Milton a ring first?' I ask.

'Help yourself. Phone's in the lounge. I'll get the meat on so long.'

The phone is on a sideboard in the corner of the lounge. I dial Milton's number and stare at some photographs of Brak and Reggie on their wedding day on the wall above the sideboard. Reggie is slimmer; a looker with her party girl smile and highlighted hair. Brak stares casually at the camera. Mullet hairstyle and cocky demeanour. The wildness in his eyes makes me wonder what Reggie's parents thought of the union. As I wait, Brak comes through to the kitchen carrying the bag of donkey meat. I hear the freezer chest open and close. He walks past again, swigging a beer.

Milton answers. After I explain the accident, he heaves a long sigh and says, 'These things happen, I suppose.'

'I don't know what to say, Milton. It really was unavoidable.'

'Ja, I know. Livestock on the roads is a big problem. Don't worry, the car's insured.'

'Brak says he can fix it.'

'Whatever.'

I don't tell him about the beer. The slightly terse tone to Milton's voice implies that bad news should best come in instalments.

I join the others outside next to the fire. The air is cool and Reggie has snuggled up under Brak's arm. Clara hands me the half-full quart of beer Brak opened for her earlier. 'Finish this,' she says. 'I've switched to wine.' Brak turns the meat – steaks, chops and boere-wors – in a folding grid. A hefty slab of donkey meat sizzles on one side of the braai. Cracker sits patiently at Brak's feet, watching every move.

'It's lovely and peaceful out here,' Clara says. 'You must be close to Matobo.'

'The property backs right onto Matobo,' Reggie says. 'We were lucky, hey Brak? The owner went overseas in a hurry and needed someone to look after the place. We just happened to be around at the right time, hey, honey bunch?'

Brak nods. 'Ja, it's magic. You'll get the grand tour tomorrow.'

'No war vets or other creepy-crawlies?' Clara asks.

Reggie taps her head. 'Touch wood, no. The big guy upstairs has been looking after us. I suppose there's not much in it for the vets. Only a few acres. Too small and infertile to be worth stealing. The only thing of interest would be the house. So far they've left us alone.'

Brak scoffs. 'War vets. Bloody thieving scum, that's all they are. Better not start their shit here.'

'Nothing you can do about it if they do,' Reggie says.

'Everyone just lets those bastards run riot. Time someone put a bullet up their backsides. They could all do with an extra arsehole.'

'As if this country needs any extra arseholes,' Reggie says. 'Let's change the subject, babe. Politics just gets everyone angry. Come on, watch that meat, man.'

'Everything's under control, doll.'

Far off, a donkey hee-haws in the darkness.

Brak cups his ear. 'Listen . . . maybe that's some kind of donkey resurrection. You never know.'

Reggie shakes her head. 'Poor little thing. Maybe it's his mate calling out.'

'Don't donkeys mate for life?' Clara asks.

I hold my hands up. 'Okay, okay! Enough!'

Brak laughs and turns the meat once more. 'We're just about ready to rock and roll, Reginald.'

Reggie goes inside and returns with a large steel tray. Brak takes the slab of donkey meat in his fingers, holds it briefly above Cracker's nose and hurls it off into the dirt. 'There you go, my puppy,' he says. Cracker charges after it. He takes the other meat off the fire and tips it onto the tray Reggie is holding. We help ourselves to meat and salads up on the veranda then we sit on the stairs and eat. Brak flattens the last of his beer. He goes inside and fetches two cold quarts from the fridge. He opens them with his teeth and sets one down on the steps next to me.

'Take it easy, babe,' Reggie says. 'You don't want to finish all your grog in one night, do you?'

'Ag, don't nag, man,' Brak says, flicking the beer caps off into the darkness.

'Ja, and what have I told you about opening beers with your teeth? Don't complain to me that they're giving you hell! You bloody men! Where were you when God dished out brains, hey?'

Brak grins, serrated teeth glinting in the firelight. 'Reggie, gimme a break, doll. It's not every day that a bloke's long-lost friend drops in for a visit.'

'You know where it ends if you go too far. That's all I'm going to say.'

Having bolted down the donkey meat, Cracker reappears and hovers around next to Brak, doe-eyed. 'Christ, you're a guts,' Brak mutters. He finishes a chop and tosses the bone out across the driveway. Cracker bounds off; soon we hear the popping sound of bone breaking. Brak stretches his leg out and points to a tiny blue scar next to his ankle. 'Remember that?'

I smile. 'Who could forget such an historic feat of marksmanship?'

Brak swivels his leg towards Reggie and Clara. 'Hey ladies, check out where my *best friend* shot me. Serious. One day when we were kids ol' Blue Eyes here just decided to pump me full of lead!'

'One pellet, to be exact,' I say.

Reggie kisses the tips of her fingers and touches the tiny scar. 'Poor little Brak. I'm sure you weren't doing anything stupid, hey.'

Brak turns to me. 'You see the sort of sympathy I get? Nurses! Bloody callous, I tell you.'

Reggie laughs. 'Don't worry, Frank, there's many a time that I've felt like pumping him full of lead too! Like when he drinks too much.'

'Ja, okay. I get the message, doll. I wasn't planning on a major piss-up tonight. We've got a big hike tomorrow and I don't want to be babelaas.'

'Yes, but you know you've got no control once you get going.'

'Okay. Okay. Okay! Frank and I'll have a couple more, then we'll call it a night. I told you, I don't wanna be hungover tomorrow.'

The word *hike* is still flashing red and luminous in my brain. 'No one said anything about a hike.'

Brak plonks his bandaged hand on my shoulder. 'Don't worry, china. I meant a drive. A little tour of our backyard. I wanna show you a really lekker place. Special. You'll enjoy it. Both of you.' He looks at Reggie. 'You see Miss Matabeleland here? It's where I proposed to her — hell, Reginald, when was that now? Twenty years ago, at least!'

Reggie reaches over and kisses Brak on his bearded jowl. He blushes. They light up cigarettes and reminisce about their early years when life was full of hope and promise. The distant flashing lights of a plane pass by overhead, its sound following behind. Cracker comes and lies on the step next to Brak. Then Reggie begins clearing up the plates and bottles. Clara and I move to help her. She waves me away. 'You sit and talk to Brak,' she says.

Brak watches Reggie and Clara go inside. 'Best thing that ever happened to me, that girl. An angel from heaven, I swear . . .'

'So what about kids? I'd have thought there'd be a whole tribe by now.'

The look of pain on Brak's face takes me completely by surprise. His voice is barely a whisper: 'Ja, that was the plan. But Reggie miscarried her first one. A boy. After that she couldn't have kids. We thought of adopting, but I was so fucked-up it just wasn't a proposition.'

'Sorry to hear that. I had no idea.'

Brak tilts his bottle and half empties it in one gulp. 'Shit happens. Life dishes out the good and the bad. All so bloody arbitrary. I can't accept that God plans these things. He's there only for us to deal with it all.'

He finishes his beer in another gulp. He goes inside and returns with two more. We drink in silence, the ghost of the lost boy on Brak's shoulders. Reggie and Clara come back outside. Reggie has a dusty guitar under her arm.

Brak groans. 'Oh, for Chrissake.'

The girls sit down next to us. Reggie leans the guitar against Brak's arm.

'Put that thing away, doll. Let's not embarrass our guests.'

'Come on, Brak!' Clara pleads. 'Reggie's been boasting about you.'

'Ag, man. Reginald . . .'

'Better than talking politics,' Reggie says. 'That's what we always end up doing, don't we?'

'Let me finish my beer first. Christ, Reggie . . .'

We talk and drink. The moon slowly crosses the starry sky. Clara is surprised when Brak offers me a smoke and I take one.

'Brak's a bad influence,' I say.

Brak laughs. 'Hey! I said don't blame me!'

'No wonder you were so pathetic at the pool yesterday,' Clara says.

'Pathetic? I didn't think I fared too badly, considering.'

She gives me a wry smile.

Then Brak takes the guitar and tunes it. He plays a few chords and fancy riffs. His bandaged right hand, doing the strumming and picking, appears to cause no impediment. Ordinarily, fireside sing-alongs are not my thing. But tonight is different. Maybe it's the beer, maybe it's the fact that Clara has shifted closer, but the sounds coming from Brak's guitar are nothing short of enchanting. He begins a set of chords with intricate picking that I recognise as the preamble to the Beatles's 'Blackbird'. Then he sings the words in a strong, clear tenor. Reggie sits next to him, eyes closed. Clara smiles and slips her hand under my arm. We listen, spellbound. I'm astounded, not just by his virtuoso guitar skills, but that a voice so sweet and pure could emanate from someone seemingly so rough and uncouth. Brak finishes the Beatles song and immediately launches into Stephen Stills's acoustic masterpiece, 'Black Queen'. The nimbleness of his fingers across the frets is incredible. Marvellous. Then he just stops. Abruptly, in mid-song. He lays the guitar down on the steps between his feet, his face masked by a strange blankness. His mouth opens; his lips shine with spit.

'Are you okay, babe?' Reggie asks. 'Don't stop now.'

'That was so beautiful,' Clara says.

Brak just stares blankly at the flames. Then, as though a wider malevolence is at work, the house lights go out. Just the firelight and the stars give form to our faces.

'What's the matter, babe?' Reggie asks.

Brak shakes his head, as though waking from a dream, and gets to his feet. 'Sorry folks, my fingers are killing me.' He gingerly prods the fingertips of his left hand. Laughs gruffly. 'Shows how long ago I picked up a guitar. Better start up the generator, otherwise everything in the fridge will go off.'

He disappears around the side of the house. We wait in silence and a short while later we hear the generator start. The lights return, getting brighter as the generator revs up.

Brak reappears, apparently composed. 'Who's for a grog, hey?'

I raise my hand. Clara nods.

'Not for me, babe,' Reggie says. 'I'm hitting the sack. We've got a big day tomorrow, remember.'

Brak takes Clara's glass inside.

Reggie stands up. 'Help yourself to coffee or tea, if you want.' She wags a finger at me. 'You make sure that big baboon gets to bed soon, okay?'

She goes inside. Clara shuffles closer.

'Brak was amazing, wasn't he?' she says.

'While it lasted.'

'Aye, pity he just stopped like that. It's been quite a night.'

'It sure has. Sorry about the donkey drama.'

Clara shrugs. 'Donkeys, drama . . . c'est la vie.'

Brak returns with Clara's wine and two quarts. With the generator drumming in the background, we drink and talk. Brak's festive spirit has waned; he seems tired, drained. He asks Clara a few questions about Vic and Hazel and sits quietly listening to her replies, nodding his head. Cracker sidles up to him and lies with his big slobbering muzzle on his leg. Brak scratches his ears. 'Shame, puppy,' he says. 'Just a big puppy, hey?' Cracker's tail thumps against the step.

Clara finishes her wine and gets up. 'I'll leave you boys to it.' She motions me back when I start to get up. 'See you in the morning. Thanks for a nice evening, Brak.'

'No trouble,' Brak says.

She goes inside.

Brak shakes his head. 'What's it with women, hey? How come they know exactly when to pull the ripcord. Built-in intuition, I swear.'

I yawn and stretch my arms. 'Well, I'm about to follow suit. Been a long day.'

Brak smiles. 'Come on, Frankie boy, don't leave me in the lurch now. We'll have one more after this and call it quits. Talk to me, china. Tell me about Australia. Tell me about anything. Just talk, man.'

I talk while Brak grinds his teeth. I tell him about Australia, about the sense of freedom I felt when I first arrived in Perth. About not having to live with the burden of perpetually defending my right to exist, like people in Africa seem to do. The flames in the braai die down.

Brak just grinds his teeth and swigs his beer.

Then he says: 'Tell me, Frank. What are you, hey?'

'What do you mean?'

'I mean, *what are you*? What nationality? Where do you belong? What place?'

'Oh Christ, I don't know. I'm a mongrel, I suppose.'

'Have you ever felt that you belong? That you're part of some place?'

'Maybe as a kid. I don't know. I really don't think about it all that much.'

Brak shakes his head. 'You see, that's something I can't understand.' He lights a cigarette and leans forward, resting his elbows on his thighs. He takes a deep drag and blows an angry jet of smoke between his knees. 'You talk about a right to exist. I know Zimbabwe's a fuck-up. Common sense says pack up and bugger off. Forget about this damn place. Greener pastures and all that shit. But then I start to think: why the hell should I leave? I was born here – I have a right to be here. I'm African. This is my place.'

Why the hell should I leave? I'm reminded of Milton. Brak's opposite. United in their claim to Africanness.

'I'm sorry, Brak. I can't get all pumped up about place and belonging. It's beyond me.'

'Just as well you gapped it then, Frank. Australia sounds just right for blokes like you. Me? I'm African. I belong here. I have just as much right to be here as anybody. As much right as fucking Mugabe himself!'

I shrug. 'Everyone's entitled to their opinion. Personally, I don't see how we can truly belong anywhere outside of Europe. We don't have a claim to any place outside of Europe that goes beyond a few centuries of colonial rule. That's nothing compared to the cultures that have existed here for thousands of years. It may seem perfectly logical to you to claim Africanness, but to blacks we will always be interlopers. When whites were in charge, did we ever call ourselves Africans? No, we called ourselves Europeans, British, whatever – never Africans. Sounds a little contrived to start now, don't you think?'

Brak stares at me. Another person. I burn under his stare.

'*It may seem perfectly logical* . . . don't give me that shit, Frank! I don't wanna hear that gutless crap. Some of us learned our Africanness the hard way. We fought a fucking war and lost everything. Everything! But we stayed. We didn't run – we stayed! That's how some of us learned our Africanness. How we *earned* our Africanness. Others fucked off. Ran away to Britain and Australia like bloody rabbits when the going got tough. The people who deserve to be here stayed. So don't talk to me about what is or isn't African, okay?'

'Jesus, Brak. Take it easy, man. I'm only making a point.'

'I hate it when people like you start lecturing me.'

People like you? Unnerved by his anger, my mind flounders. Yet I can't restrain my tongue: 'I'm not lecturing you, Brak. Call yourself whatever you bloody well like. Who gives a shit? I'm not going to sit here arguing with you.'

Brak swigs his beer, nodding, as though my words have confirmed certain suspicions. 'That's your solution to everything: when it gets too hard – just give up and run away. Never stand for anything, hey? Where were you in the war? When Rhodesia needed people to stand up and be counted. Hiding away in South Africa while others did the dirty work. Know what I think of that, Frank?' He hawks and spits on the stairs. 'That's what I think.'

I react with anger: 'Listen to you! Christ, it's been *thirty years* since that stupid fucking war! Wake up to yourself, man!'

Brak leans forward; for an instant, I think he's about to **throw** himself at me. The same vacant look that stared at me from that photograph with the corpse. But he settles back. His voice is cold, quiet: 'Fuck you, Frank!'

'For Chrissake, Brak! What's got into you?'

He starts to say something, then clamps his mouth shut and gets up. He picks up the guitar and walks off into the darkness, Cracker following discreetly. I'm about to go inside when I hear him smashing the guitar. Savage, splintering, resonant blows. Cracker comes running back into the firelight and looks back at the darkness, whining softly. Then Brak reappears, carrying remnants of the guitar in the crook of his arm. He lifts the grid off the braai and heaves the remnants onto the coals. The steel strings squawk and twang in the heat. Then he turns and climbs the steps past me and goes inside.

I sit watching the guitar burn, dumbstruck.

I dream again of the wife I never had. She is standing in a forest of oaks and spruce, wearing a floral cotton summer dress that bells out to the ground. In the background, illuminated by a splash of sunlight is a house with little Russian domes; ice stalactites drip from the eaves. She waves at me and says goodbye, her voice resonating in the trees. Her face hidden in shadow. She turns and walks towards the house. Nothing tells me that she is my wife. Yet I know that she is, and that we are parting forever. Parting forever from the wife I never had. The sense of loss is unbearable.

I wake, breathless. Outside, I can hear the crickets sing and the faint drumming of the generator. The stars pour a meagre light through a crack in the curtains. There is a brown water stain on the ceiling that resembles a flaccid flower. I cannot dispel the image of the woman, my wife, in that long dress. I cannot dispel the sence of loss.

I wake to the sound of voices outside. I lie for a few minutes in a state of groggy paralysis, my throat raw, my stomach queasy.

A rooster crows amid the busy clucking of chickens. I get up and pull the curtains aside, shielding my eyes from the sudden white blast of sunlight. The room commands a sweeping view of Matobo's turbulent mass of hills, some miles distant. The vista flickers behind heat waves. In the driveway, Brak, Reggie and Clara are busy tending to Milton's car. A few hens fossick around. A small square of black plastic has been duct-taped over the hole in the windscreen. Brak is attempting to lever the bumper straight with a pole. Reggie, looking sporty in a bright red tracksuit, stands on a chair, washing the blood and urine from the roof. Clara is bent over in the boot, scrubbing away, a singularly attractive sight to seedy eyes in her petite jogging shorts. A blurred memory of Brak's odd belligerence breaks through. For a second I wonder if it was a dream.

I have a quick cold shower and dress in jeans and a t-shirt. I join the others outside, shamefaced at being the slacker. Reggie and Clara have done a commendable job of cleaning out the boot. They have unclipped and removed the carpet, taken out the spare wheel and tools and scrubbed the lot. The carpet is hanging over the veranda wall in the sun. Reggie has sprayed a disinfectant in the car to get rid of the smell of beer and urine. 'All your friend will notice is his car's cleaner than it used to be,' she says.

In the clear light of day, Brak is less optimistic about the damage than he was last night. 'Ja, china, I dunno,' he says, wiping his hands on his shorts. 'The dents on the bonnet and roof are nothing. The radiator and bumper can be straightened out. But you'll definitely need a new front fender and headlight. And a windscreen.'

'Milton said it was insured.'

'Even if it's insured you can still sit around forever waiting for parts. But let's not jump to conclusions. We'll see what Jervis says on Monday.'

'Thanks, Brak. I feel like a malingerer. You should've woken me up.'

Brak slaps a hand on my shoulder. 'Let sleeping malingerers lie — that's my policy. Come on, Reggie, let's get some breakfast into this boy.'

No hint of last night's anger. It's as though nothing happened.

We enjoy a hearty breakfast of fried eggs on toast and some of last night's leftover boerewors – a near cure for hangovers, I can vouch. Then we climb into Brak's Land Cruiser and head off along a bumpy track towards Matobo. It's a squash up front: Clara and Reggie sit crammed between Brak and me, Clara half on my lap, an unexpected pleasure. I did offer to ride on the back but Brak said it would be too rough and dusty for elderly city slickers like me. Just a short jaunt anyway, he assured us. He rummages around in the glove box for some tapes, selects Bob Dylan's *Blood on the Tracks* and sticks it in the cassette player. As soon as the music starts, he begins humming along, tapping his fingers on the steering wheel.

Brak's idea of a short jaunt is eccentric, to say the least. On and on we drive, following an endless maze of dirt tracks that disappear into the western Matobo range. At one point Brak swerves to avoid a mongoose crossing the road. Instinctively I reach out to steady Clara on my lap, grabbing a chunk of her rear in the process. Clara looks at me with feigned outrage and laughs at my mortified expression.

Soon we are enveloped by the unruly wilderness of colossal granite kopjes. Dylan's nasal American whine seems an incongruous accompaniment as the Cruiser winds its way through thickly bushed ravines, dust billowing behind. I peer up at the rock faces, stained orange and green by lichens, wondering if Dylan ever stops to think that somewhere in Africa his reedy voice echoes among lonely canyons. The air through the open window is warm, filled with pungent fragrances. The dormant smell of parched foliage, like the breath of an old man. The acrid reek of fire-blackened vleis.

Reggie surprisingly rattles off names like a tour guide: mukwa, munondo and gondi trees. Dassies and klipspringers. Hartebeest, impala, tsessebe . . . names rich in origin, amalgams of Africa and Europe. I remember the many excursions I made as a boy into this sublime wilderness. Family picnics at World's View, Rhodes's gravesite. The boy scout jamborees – all those little white boys, bedecked in scarves and badges, assembled beneath the old pale blue Rhodesian flag with the Union Jack in the corner, singing 'God save the Queen'. How, as little Rhodesians, we roamed these hills free inside our colonial cage. Innocent in the withered hand of Empire . . .

Brak points at a giant kopje looming in front of us. At its summit stands a cross. 'That's Nungu,' he says. 'IsiNdebele for porcupine.' He explains that the cross was erected by an intrepid bunch of Christians years ago. We climb a steep, winding track around a kopje adjacent to Nungu, emerging on a high ridge. Brak parks the Cruiser in the shade of a wild fig tree. The drive has taken well over an hour.

The sun beats down; the air is hot and still, loud with insects. My right leg, having borne the happy burden of Clara's bottom, has gone numb. Clara slings her camera around her neck and ties her hair back with an elastic band. She is wearing a black gym top, her midriff bare. Brak grabs a knapsack from the back of the Cruiser. We follow him a short way along a path up through some dense bush to a ledge shaded by a sharp overhang. The ledge commands a breathtaking view of Nungu's great dome, immense and serene, across a deep ravine before us. The overhang is covered in San friezes — pale eland and kudu; a rhinoceros; groups of running hunters. Brak reaches in his knapsack and removes a thermos flask and some plastic mugs. He pours some coffee and hands the mugs to us. We sit there, taking in the San paintings and the endless undulating wilderness below. Brak gestures out at the vista. 'Nice, hey? Our secret spot, hey, doll?' He raises his mug. 'Cheers, dears.'

We raise our mugs and sip the hot coffee.

Reggie smiles wryly. 'So, Frank, now you know where this galoot pledged his undying love for me. Down on his knees. Right here.' She jabs the rock with her finger. 'This is where my whole life came undone.'

'Thanks, Reginald.'

She punches his shoulder with a tiny fist.

'Hey! Don't make me spill, man!'

'Such a big baby, aren't you, my cherub.'

She pinches his hairy jowl. He gazes at an eagle circling in the distance. 'Look at him, just floating up there. I'd like to give hang-gliding a go sometime. Just take off and soar like that eagle.'

'With that stomach you'd probably soar like a stone,' Reggie says.

Brak smiles and swigs his coffee, his eye still on the eagle. Reggie leans against him, resting her head on his shoulder. Watching them, I feel a pang of envy.

We are silent for a while. Birdsong carries up from the bush far below. Then Clara gets up and closely inspects the San paintings. She takes some photos. 'My mother would love to see these,' she says. She stands at the edge of the ledge, her trim form stark against the sky. She takes a few more shots then sits with her back to us, her legs dangling over the ledge, gazing out into space.

I go across to her. Clara sneaks a photo of me as I sit down with an old man's groan. 'You and that damn camera,' I grumble. 'Come on, let me take one of you.'

'I'm hardly as photogenic as you.'

'Ha. Ha. Come on. Your turn.'

She hands me the camera. I take a shot of her on the ledge, looking like she's been ringbarked in that gym top.

Clara smiles and takes my hand. 'Isn't this place beautiful?'

Far off, on the western horizon, some thunderheads are building. A cool breeze caresses my face. Brak's eagle soars past, hanging effortlessly on an updraught. My spirits seem to lift with it. If I had the eyes of an eagle I might see all the way to Europe or Australia. Is this how Rhodes felt a century ago when he decided to make Matobo his grave? He, who could see from Cape to Cairo. Next to Clara, I close my eyes and for a small moment let go of the world . . .

My reverie is broken by Reggie's giggling. Like trickling water. I turn to see Brak's wildebeest head nuzzling the crook of her neck. She shivers and squeals, gives his beard a tug. I look up, watching the vapour trail of a plane disappear behind the looming storm clouds. The wind in my face carries the faint smell of rain.

*

On the way back to the house the first big drops start splattering against the windscreen. Soon there is a solid downpour; the Cruiser's wipers barely cope. The blue-black sky is split by jagged flashes of lightning; thunder cracks and rumbles. Rain drums down on the roof, drowning out any conversation. The windows quickly fog up with the four of us crammed in the front. Reggie wipes the windscreen down with an old rag she found under the seat.

Brak has his window half open to help demist the windscreen. He sniffs in the dank smell of wet earth. 'They should bottle that scent!' he yells, his beard glistening from the spray coming through the window.

There is something miraculous, cleansing, about it. The smell of expectation, newness. Of hope. But then I'm reminded that the word *cleansing* can be anyone's metaphor. Murambatsvina. Gukurahundi. The removal of people, a different cleansing. Final solutions lurk in purity.

We arrive back at the house late in the afternoon. Brak splashes through puddles in the driveway and parks in front of the house next to Milton's battered Cortina. I groan at the sight of it. Brak says: 'Don't beat yourself up, man. It's not the first time a car's hit an animal in this country.'

We find Cracker cowering under a table on the veranda, petrified by the lightning. Inside, we discover there has been another power cut. With the air of someone going about a routine chore, Brak ambles off to start the generator. Clara is keen to get going but Reggie insists on a cup of coffee before we leave, so we sit around the kitchen table, killing a bit more time.

'When does your plane leave?' Brak asks.

'In a couple of weeks.'

'Why don't you come and stay with us until you go?'

'I'd like to. It's just convenient being at Milton's. Maybe later.'

'The offer's there, china.' Brak yawns and stretches. 'Jesus, I'm buggered. What's for supper, doll? Roast donkey?'

Reggie gives a muffled shriek. 'Oh, man! Don't remind me! Frank, you have no idea what a fright you gave me driving in here with that poor thing on your roof! True's God, I nearly died!'

Brak grins. 'Ja, china, you sure like to do things in style, hey.'

The phone rings. Reggie gets up and goes through to the lounge to answer it. She calls: 'Frank, it's Milton!'

Brak flicks his fingers. 'Oh-oh. Now you're in for it.'

I take the phone from Reggie.

Milton sounds excited. 'Where've you been, Franco? I've been trying to get hold of you all day.'

'What's up, Milton?'

'Chombo called. He's found Lettah.'

As we drive away, I glance back and catch a quick glimpse of Brak and Reggie standing on the veranda, watching us depart in the rain. Brak has his arm around Reggie's shoulders; Cracker sits at his feet. I beep the horn a couple of times; Brak raises his bandaged hand and waves. I drive slowly along the muddy road. Just the driver's side windscreen wiper is working; Brak removed the other one so it wouldn't scrape off the plastic duct-taped over the hole.

By the time we reach the tar road the rain has stopped and shafts of sunlight are breaking through the clouds. The countryside sparkles. The grass seems incandescent as it waves beneath sudden gusts of wind.

Clara opens her window and takes a deep breath. 'Well, that was an interesting wee sojourn!' She laughs. 'Oh, man! One thing's for sure – it wasn't dull!'

'I can see you have a perverse taste in adventure.'

'Brak's a bit crazy, but Reggie's nice.'

I almost tell her about Brak's strange behaviour last night, but think better of it. After such a pleasant day it seems an aberration best forgotten.

Clara pats my leg. 'Seriously, I had a great time.'

'Donkey and all?'

She laughs and kisses my unshaven cheek. 'Aye, donkey and all. Got any more wild excursions lined up? When are you going to Fort Rixon?'

'Soon as I can organise another car.'

'I'm sure my mom won't mind you taking hers. She'll be wanting to go too, I'll bet. Mind if I tag along? I'm dying to meet this famous Lettah of yours.'

Back in Hillside, I suffer the humiliation of explaining the state of the car to Hazel and Vic. As I talk, Vic shuffles around the car, leaning on his walking stick, harrumphing and shaking his head, his worst suspicions about me apparently confirmed. When I tell them the good news about Lettah, he is positively outraged when Hazel and Clara announce their intentions to accompany me to Fort Rixon. Not only that: before I even get the chance to ask, Hazel volunteers the use of her car.

Vic rolls his eyes heavenwards. 'Sweet merciful bloody Jesus! Are you certifiably insane, woman! Has this bloke's record with motor-cars made no impression on you yet? No, I won't allow it. You're not going, either of you!'

'Oh yes, we are,' Hazel replies calmly. 'There's absolutely no need for you to work yourself into a state about this, Vic.'

'That's two cars he's buggered up in the space of a week! I've got every good reason to work myself into a state!'

'No, you haven't. Because I'll be driving.'

And that was that. I climb back in the car. 'Thanks again,' Clara says. She leans through the window and gives me a long kiss on the mouth, an event not missed by Hazel or Vic. Both have pert smiles of amusement as they wave goodbye.

It's dark when I pull into Milton's. The outside light comes on and Milton emerges from the house. His bespectacled eyes scan the car, lingering on the patched-up windscreen. Before I can explain anything, he says: 'How was the weekend, otherwise? How did Clara bear up to your special brand of entertainment?'

'I think she's a bit of an adrenalin junkie.'

'Would have to be, hey?'

I just sigh and hand him the car keys.

'So, what have you done to my old girl?'

We walk around the car; I point out the damage, describing the accident in detail. Milton laughs dryly. 'You should put *that* in a book,' he says.

I wonder what it would take to make him spitting mad. Even when I open the boot and explain the mishap with the beer, only a slight frown appears on his forehead.

'Tell me, have you got a thing with cars, boyo? Some kind of auto-phobia, maybe?'

'Sorry about this, Milton . . . I think I'm bloody jinxed.'

Milton shakes his head. 'Ag, forget it, man. Except for a poor inno-cent burro, no one got hurt. That's the main thing. My insurance will fix it up. Life in Zim is one continual accident. We'll get Jervis to have a look at it on Monday. I reckon you've become his number one client.'

IX

We have been waiting outside the police station in Fort Rixon since 8 a.m., the time Chombo suggested we meet when I phoned him last night. He made a big deal about giving up his Sunday to accommodate my private business. But, he finally said, what is one Sunday in his life when it comes to solving the 'bountiful riddles of the past'. His flamboyant choice of words reminds me of his president's dreadfully erudite proclamations. Learned English mocking English.

Given the paranoia that infects Zimbabwe's security forces, it surprises me that no one is on duty at the police station. No sentries, no jailers. Intriguing, too, that none of us – not even myself, the newcomer – complains about Chombo's tardiness; we've automatically resigned ourselves to that ubiquitous constant of African life: waiting. At least this time we've come prepared with a thermos of tea. Sipping the tea from plastic mugs, we pass the time in pleasant conversation. I sit up front in the VW with Hazel; Clara lounges on the back seat. The doors are open wide. Chain-smoking, Hazel has been lamenting the relentless drought – none of yesterday's rain made it as far east as the Insiza Valley. She can't remember it ever being so hot and dry. Already, the morning air is stifling. Fort Rixon's dusty scattering of buildings lies comatose. Roosters crow feebly, a dog barks. An endless torpid whine of insects. A muffled chatter of voices from the jail, the only sound of human life. Behind a distant hill a pillar of smoke rises into the still air. Another veld fire burning unchecked.

I reflect on my quaint predicament, sandwiched, as it were, between Hazel and Clara as their feisty chitchat flies back and forth. More like sisters than mother and daughter, the way they tease each other. I also dwell on the momentous occasion that awaits. Soon I will be face to face with Lettah. All going well, I, Frank, will fix what was broken between her and my mother. I will restore what was lost and Lydia will rest in peace. And I will return to Australia, to bask in my father's and brother's approval. Mission accomplished.

Around nine o'clock, two constables saunter up the road. One unlocks the security gate to the police station, the other approaches the car. We greet him and ask after Chombo. 'You arranged a time to meet the inspector?' he asks.

'Yes,' I reply. 'Eight o'clock.'

The constable looks at his watch. 'Maybe he will come soon,' he says. He laughs and enters the police station. We overhear him informing his colleague that the umLungu outside has arranged a *time* to meet Chombo. A burst of laughter.

Constable Fashion arrives, attired in blue combat fatigues, the trousers so tight her gait is restricted to small, dainty steps. She eyes us warily beneath her cap as she passes the car. Without returning Hazel's wave, she clambers up the front stairs into the charge office. Ribald banter and laughter ensue. There is a commotion in the jail: a banging of pots and the convict's cheers at the arrival of their jailers — presumably breakfast is in the offing. After a while one of the constables emerges from the charge office, yawning lustily. He exits the security gate and walks off back down the road. Hazel's cell phone rings. 'No, you big oaf,' Hazel sighs. 'We're perfectly capable of managing without you, Vic . . . Frank is quite capable, thank you. I'll have none of your facetious comments . . .'

The bickering continues for a minute before Hazel hangs up. I realise, finally, that the thing she loves most about Vic is being exasperated by him.

'I don't know what you see in that man,' Clara says.

'You should exercise just a teeny bit of tolerance, my dear.'

'*I* should exercise tolerance? What about *him*?'

Hazel lights another cigarette.

'You should stop smoking, Mom. Imagine your lungs.'

Hazel blows a plume of smoke out the window. 'Anything else?'

I ask: 'Hazel, do you think we'll recognise her? After all this time.'

'Lettah? I don't know.'

'The more I try to picture her face, the more elusive it becomes. I hope your memory's clearer.'

Hazel shrugs. 'It may be up to her to recognise us.'

At last, two hours late, Chombo pitches up, a passenger in an old Dodge truck that comes rattling down the road, apparently stuck in low gear. He slaps the door a couple of times and waves the driver on. The truck whines on past us, spewing exhaust smoke. Chombo lumbers up the road, his ponderous step appearing to lag slightly behind the forward tilt of his big belly. A hot air balloon dragging its basket along the ground. We climb out and exchange greetings. Sweating profusely, he rubs the dust off his boned shoes on the back of his trousers.

'Hayi! This sun is too much!' he complains.

There is a flicker of disappointment in his eyes when he sees Hazel but he quickly musters a smile. 'Ah, we meet again, madam. To what do I owe the honour of a second visit?'

'Only your limitless charm, Inspector. Allow me to introduce my daughter, Clara.'

Chombo shakes hands with Clara. 'Oh, yes, I can see the resemblance. Is this world brave enough to cope with both of you?'

Clara regards him uncertainly. He cackles loudly and ushers us into the police station. Constable Fashion glowers at us from behind the counter as we follow Chombo to his office. Her worse than usual bad temper, Chombo explains as he pulls up chairs around his desk, is due to being on the Sunday roster. We sit. He wipes the sweat from his face with a grubby handkerchief and sits behind his desk. 'Fashionista!' he bellows. 'Make some tea for our important guests!'

'No milk!' comes the terse reply.

Chombo holds his palms out helplessly. 'What's wrong with the farmers in this country that they cannot even produce milk for our tea?'

'Perhaps they don't have farms and cows,' Hazel says.

Chombo laughs 'Ah, what would life be without old Rhodesian ladies with sharp tongues? Reminding us Africans of our place in the world. Would you like black tea, perhaps?'

'I'm sure Mr Cole would like to get down to business,' Hazel says.

I nod. 'Yes, I would, if we may. You say you've found Lettah Ndlovu?'

As though scarcely able to believe it himself, Chombo shakes his head. 'Hayi! My friend, you have no idea how much trouble I've been to finding this woman. I have been to every farm, every village, every kraal in the district. Shangani . . . even Gweru. Searching, searching for this Lettah Ndlovu. And all the time she is right here under my nose!'

'Here?'

'Here! Ten minutes from Fort Rixon!'

'Well I never!' Hazel says. 'That's wonderful news. And there I thought Zimbabwe's police were next to useless!'

'Mom . . .' Clara says.

Chombo lowers his eyes; he strokes his chin, abashed.

'How did you manage to track her down?' Hazel asks. 'Were there records? Was it word of mouth?'

'Work, madam. Lots of very hard work.'

'Are you sure it's her?'

'Dear lady, do I look incompetent?'

Fearing a reply, I quickly ask: 'Can we see her now?'

Chombo nods. 'Of course. But first I must caution you. Ndlovu is not the woman you remember. She's not the woman in the photograph from the old days. She's very old.'

'I'm expecting her to be old,' I say.

'Old? She'd be about the same age as me,' Hazel says. 'It's not as though we're Egyptian mummies!'

'Some bear the ravages of time better than others,' Chombo replies sagely. 'Her memory is not a hundred percent. It took me a long time to confirm that she is indeed the Lettah Ndlovu you are looking for. Only she would know certain things from the past.' He stands up. 'No point sitting here wasting time. Just one problem. There are no police vehicles for our use. All are broken.'

'Must be something in the fuel,' Hazel muses innocently.

Chombo sighs wearily. 'Eh-ja . . . what can I do? I must ask you a favour —'

'Not to worry,' Hazel says. 'We can use my car.'

Chombo plonks his cap back on his head and we walk out into the hot glare of the morning. Three convicts are sitting in the shade of a jacaranda tree outside the jail, scooping sadza out of a black pot. I note how thin these men are and wonder how often the luxury of a proper meal comes their way. 'Don't think I can't see you lazy bastards doing nothing,' Chombo growls as we pass by. The men laugh nervously. One of them pipes up: 'Hau, Inspector, it is Sunday. The day of rest.'

'Look at me,' Chombo says. 'Do you think I rest on Sundays? Always on the job. Always!'

Hazel hands over the role of driver to me and gets into the back with Clara. With Chombo issuing directions from the passenger seat next to me, we drive off back in the direction we had come, turning left after the store onto the Insiza road. Hazel points out the landmarks of her youth to Clara: the Jeannette Schur School, the old Dhlo Dhlo farmstead, the roadside graves of a pioneering family now overgrown with long grass. So sad, she says, that all this history is simply vanishing. I catch Clara's eyes in the rear-view mirror; she winks and smiles. Chombo lounges back in his seat. He laces his fingers behind his neck and stretches, yawning cavernously, his joints cracking. Pointing at the column of smoke in the distance, he tells us of two children who perished in a veld fire just three weeks ago. He chats about the mundane problems of police work. The thing that drives him mad is stock theft. The cases are endless, the paperwork too much. Ruefully, he shrugs and shakes his head. In the end you just give up, he says. I fully expect a barbed remark from Hazel, but she just listens quietly in the back, one eyebrow raised.

I pay scant attention to Chombo's waffle. I'm thrilled at the prospect of reporting back to Errol that the job is done, that my mother's faith in me was well placed. At the same time, I'm apprehensive. What will meeting Lettah again evoke? After all she has been through, will she bear any resemblance to the person I knew? How will I appear to her? How will I be received?

Something else niggles me too.

I ask: 'Inspector, that man from the farm – Ntombela – how is he? When we last spoke, you said he was sick.'

'Ntombela? Oh, yes. Henry the Fourth.'

'Henry the what?'

'Henry the Fourth,' Clara says. 'HIV. Geddit?'

Chombo guffaws. 'Hayi! These Australians are too slow, man! What's required in this country is a sense of humour, Mr Cole.'

'I apologise for my deficiencies, Inspector. But Ntombela – how is he?'

'He is six feet under the ground.'

For a few seconds there is just the sound of the tyres rumbling over the corrugations in the road.

'What? He's dead?'

Chombo nods. 'Eh-ja.'

The tone of good cheer has not left his voice.

'But I spoke to you only –'

'Mr Cole, you must not worry yourself about things that are beyond your control.' He gestures out at the passing countryside. 'Four out of ten people here have the Sickness. AIDS is everywhere. Your Ntombela is a drop in the ocean.'

'Where did he die, Inspector?' Hazel asks. 'Was he given treatment?'

Chombo sighs impatiently. 'From what I hear, he died in the night. On the farm. His family woke up and he was dead. That's all. Finished. Now let's not be distracted from the happy event that lies ahead. We must be positive in life.'

In the mirror I see Hazel make a face at the back of Chombo's shaved head, her childish impudence a curious measure of our place in the scheme of things here.

Chombo directs me off the Insiza road onto a narrow track that winds up through some forested hills. We pass through tinder dry glades that smell like old tea leaves, the scream of insects growing louder as we slow down over rough sections of the track. The bush thins as we descend into a small, arid valley. We pass empty, shimmering pastures and deserted kraals, coming at last to a T-junction, next to which stands a long ramshackle building. Chombo tells me to pull over in front of the building. Hazel recognises the place as Harrie's General Store from the old days – Bob and Mavis Harrie, she says, used to run a thriving business selling anything and everything from blankets and horse bridles to beer. The tired ghost of this business can still be discerned in the remnants of red lettering on the building's flaking façade. Only the façade appears intact. The veranda to one side of the entrance has collapsed; the corrugated roof, too, seems in imminent danger of caving in; the exterior walls are cracked and peeling. A group of people – a man, three women, and some children – peers through the doorway as we arrive. There are no other signs of life: no dogs or fowls, no livestock in the pastures behind the old store.

We climb out into the hot glare. The people emerge from the store. All look half-starved; they appear to be expecting Chombo. They greet him nervously and the women and children promptly disappear around the back of the building. Chombo introduces the man to us as Gumede; he is Lettah's distant relative – a cousin of a cousin, Chombo explains. Gumede shakes my hand, African style. With Ndebeles it's a sign of respect to look down when greeting someone; Gumede's downcast eyes, however, seem more the product of defeat than custom. He is an emaciated wreck; prematurely aged, wizened, yet probably no older than forty. He breaks into a terrible coughing fit. When he finishes, I half expect bits of lung to be hanging out his mouth. He commences to roll a cigarette in newspaper, nonetheless.

'Aibo, Gumede!' Chombo chides him. 'You have one foot in the grave, my friend. Where is MaNdlovu?'

'Phakathi — inside,' Gumede rasps, gesturing at the dark interior. 'She is waiting.'

We follow him inside. Our steps echo in the huge, empty room that was once the shop. A strong smell of wood smoke. A couple of ruptured mattresses on the cement floor at one end and some blankets strewn over flattened cardboard boxes at the other. A few pots surrounding the embers of a fire on the floor near the open window. Some bare shelves along one wall. 'I always had the impression Harrie's shop was tiny,' Hazel reflects, her voice echoing.

Gumede leads the way down a passage. A gaping hole in the roof above provides a splash of hot light on the passage floor. A bicycle minus one wheel leans against the wall. The doors to the rooms on either side have been removed from their hinges. Glimpses of more beds on floors, small belongings. A foul-smelling toilet, loud with buzzing flies. At the end of the passage Gumede halts and gestures to a room on his right. 'She is here,' he rasps before breaking into another coughing fit.

We follow Chombo inside. The room is small, lit by a single window with broken panes. An iron bed and a rickety table and chair are the only items of furniture. A battered leather suitcase and some cardboard boxes are stacked against the wall. An old woman sits on the bed, her eyes fixed on her clasped hands resting on her lap. She is barefoot and wears a dark blue headscarf, a threadbare orange dress and a grey shawl fastened around her shoulders with a safety pin. A surge of expectant joy rises in me.

'Sa'bona, MaNdlovu,' Chombo greets her, placing emphasis on her name. 'Kunjani — how are you, MaNdlovu?'

She looks up at him and nods. She glances quickly at Hazel, Clara and me before staring down at her calloused hands again. A square of light on the bare cement floor at her feet illuminates her face from underneath. She is ancient; her sunken eyes surrounded by a maze of deep lines, none of which appear the product of laughter. Her face is like the desolate terrain outside, eroded by neglect. There is nothing about her that I recognise.

Chombo stands over her. 'MaNdlovu, are you not happy to see the nkosana from long ago? Come, greet Mr Cole. This is Frank. He is the same boy that you knew long ago. This is a time to celebrate, MaNdlovu!'

The woman looks up again. She gives me a trembling smile. 'Sa'bona, nkosana Frank,' she whispers.

Standing in the doorway, Gumede breaks into another coughing fit. He disappears. We hear him stumbling outside, coughing and spitting.

'Lettah?' I say, my voice choked. 'Is it you, Lettah?'

She looks at me and back at her hands.

'Aibo, MaNdlovu!' Chombo exclaims impatiently. 'Mr Cole has come a long way to find you. He asked you a question. You are the person he seeks. You are Lettah Ndlovu, are you not?'

Hazel interrupts: 'Oh, don't badger her like that, Inspector!'

Chombo gives Hazel a frustrated glare. 'I'm just asking MaNdlovu to identify herself. She is old and senile. Her memory needs encouragement.' He turns back to the woman. 'Tell them. You are Lettah Ndlovu.'

She nods. 'I am Lettah Ndlovu.'

I go down on one knee. I put my hand on hers. She flinches. 'Do you recognise me, Lettah?'

She continues to stare downward. 'You are nkosana Frank.'

'I've wondered what became of you, Lettah. Do you remember the time when we lived in Que Que? Do you remember the house we lived in? Do you remember my parents?'

'I remember.'

'Can you tell me anything about that time?'

'You are the son of Mr and Mrs Cole. Errol and Lydia.'

She labours over the pronunciation of the names. My heart begins to wilt.

'Do you remember my brother?'

188

She nods.

'Maxwell? You remember Max?'

'A-heh. I remember Maxwell.'

Chombo beams. 'That's right, MaNdlovu. You remember Mr Cole's family. Four altogether, is that correct?'

She nods. 'Errol, Lydia, Maxwell, Frank.'

I stand up. A long silence ensues.

'Is there anything you want to tell me?' I say. 'Do you wish to ask me any questions?'

She shakes her head.

'Do you remember me?' Hazel asks.

The woman looks up at Hazel, the lines on her face contorting with confusion. She glances helplessly at Chombo.

Chombo's voice has a flustered, frantic ring. 'What are you talking about? What have you got to do with this?'

'I asked her a simple question, Inspector.' Hazel replies. She turns again to the woman. 'Do you remember me?'

'She is senile!' Chombo yells. He taps his head with a finger. 'Her memory is full of holes! She can only remember the big things!'

Hazel ignores him. 'Do you remember my name? I was a friend of Frank's mother, Lydia – her best friend. If you are Lettah then you would remember me.'

The woman's eyes are fixed on her hands again. She doesn't answer. I feel both pity and anger.

Hazel persists. She moves closer to the woman. 'Hazel Kent – that's my name. Look at me. Do you remember me? I was Lydia Cole's friend. I went to school with her. I visited the farm, Whitestone, often. Surely you would remember me?'

The woman doesn't look up.

Clara takes her mother's arm. 'Mom, don't . . .'

Hazel pulls her arm free. 'No, Clara. There's something wrong here. You are not Lettah Ndlovu, are you?'

Chombo slaps his thighs in exasperation. The woman jumps at the sound. 'Damn it!' he yells. 'This woman is senile! It's not her fault she can't remember everything! She remembers what is important, doesn't she? She remembers Mr Cole here. She remembers his parents, his brother. She remembers where the Coles lived — she even remembers the car they drove. Tell them, MaNdlovu! Tell them what car the Coles owned.'

The woman looks frozen.

'Tell them, MaNdlovu! The Coles owned an Opel car, not so?'

The woman nods. 'A-heh. Opel.'

'What colour?'

'Green.'

Chombo gestures at her like a barrister resting his case. 'You see? She *is* Lettah Ndlovu!'

'If she can remember the colour of a car then she can remember me,' Hazel says.

'She is Lettah Ndlovu!'

'Does she have papers to this effect, Inspector?' Hazel asks calmly.

'Papers? What are papers? We can find papers! Look, old Rhodesian, you have no idea how hard I have worked to find this woman. I have put everything aside to find her!'

Hazel meets Chombo's wrath unflinchingly. 'I'm sure you worked very hard to find this woman. I'm sure that a reward for your efforts never entered your head. I'm sure that a cut of the inheritance was the furthest thing from your mind. But, unfortunately, this woman is not Lettah Ndlovu. Contrary to your belief, not all old people are senile. I'm blessed with an excellent memory.' She gestures at the woman. 'This is not Lettah. I remember her face. She had broad features. Her eyes were wide apart, not close together like this woman's. She had beautiful straight teeth, not crooked with big gaps like hers. One of her front teeth — this one,' she bares her own teeth and taps an incisor, 'was chipped when a donkey kicked her as a girl. There was also a small scar on her top lip caused by that kick. I know people change with age. But there's nothing of Lettah in this woman. Nothing!'

Chombo explodes. 'Fuck off, you old troublemaker! What do you know? It's for Cole here to decide who is who. He is the one who is important here, not you. Fuck off! Get away from here! You are mad!'

Hazel gives Chombo a withering stare. Then she turns to me. 'Don't waste your time with this, Frank. Come, Clara, let's wait in the car.'

Clara hesitates.

'Go with your mother!' Chombo barks. 'Mr Cole and I have business to finish here.'

Hazel and Clara leave. There is a terrible silence in the room, broken only by the sound of Gumede hawking and spitting outside. The old woman is trembling. I want to reach out and comfort her. But I just stand there.

Chombo slaps his thighs again. He jabs a finger at me. 'MaNdlovu, who is this man? What is his name? What is his father's name? What was the address you worked at in Que Que? And Salisbury? And Bulawayo, before they went to South Africa?'

I hold up my hand. 'Please, Inspector. Please, let's not persist with this. Clearly, this is not the woman I'm looking for.'

Chombo thunders: 'MaNdlovu! Tell Mr Cole who you are! Where you come from!'

'This woman is terrified, Inspector. Please leave her alone now. I've heard enough.'

Chombo's shoulders slump; he becomes conciliatory. 'Let's not jump to conclusions, Mr Cole. Your friend is old and too full of opinions. Old people forget. They confuse some with others —'

I shake my head. 'Please, Inspector. No more. My instincts told me this is not Lettah when I first saw her. But my heart wanted to believe, so I allowed this pretence to continue.'

'Pretence? What is this pretence you speak of? Are you accusing me of something, Mr Cole?'

I'm unnerved by the lurking menace in Chombo's voice and curse my tactlessness. His eyes burn into me; I struggle to meet his stare. My eyes drop to the holstered pistol at his belt. Terrible possibilities race through my head. I see our shallow graves dug up by wild animals, our bones scattered in the veld, never to be found. I must play this carefully. I look at the woman. She stares at her trembling hands. I can hear Gumede outside succumb to another coughing fit.

I turn back to Chombo, fighting to meet his livid glare. 'I'm only saying this woman is not Lettah Ndlovu.'

'I hope that is all you are saying, Mr Cole. It would be very dangerous for you to accuse me of anything improper. Let me be clear on that matter. I won't stand for it.'

'I'm not accusing you of anything. This business is finished as far as I am concerned.'

'Finished? And what about all my hard work finding this woman? All the extra hours I spent on your case. You have no idea how much work I have done for you. And this is the reward I receive. Accusations that I'm dishonest.'

'I'm not accusing you of anything, Inspector. I've no doubt you worked hard finding this woman.'

Chombo moves across to block the doorway. 'And who will pay for my hard work?'

'I'm expected to pay for police work?'

'This is not only police work, Mr Cole. This is a private investigation. I have worked for you in my spare time.'

'What of the money you confiscated from Ntombela? You have been paid for this already.'

His eyes narrow. 'What are you saying now? That I have stolen money from you? I'm warning you, this is very dangerous.'

'I'm not saying you have stolen anything –'

'You better be careful, Mr Cole.'

'All right,' I sigh. I take a wad of hundred-dollar bills from my pocket. 'This is all I have on me, so please don't ask for more. I think you'll agree that what I give you more than adequately compensates you for your investigation.' I peel off all but one of the bills and hand the money to Chombo. Chombo looks at the notes disdainfully, then thrusts them in his shirt pocket. I stoop next to the woman and place the other bill on her lap beside her hands. 'I'm sorry,' I whisper.

She makes no move to take it. Chombo lurches across and snatches it off her lap. 'Useless fool!' he snaps at her. 'You've done nothing for this.'

He turns to me and gestures at the door. 'I've had enough of your shit. You and your fucking Lettah Ndlovu. Take me back to the police station.'

We drive back to the police station in a seething silence. Chombo sits next to me glaring out the window, an expression of angry indignation on his face. Every so often, he glances at his watch — clearly, time waits for no policeman in Zimbabwe. Clara's face in the rearview mirror is strained, frightened. Beside her, Hazel gazes calmly ahead. She hums a few strains of Acker Bilk's 'Stranger on the Shore'.

At the police station, we are mercifully spared a prolonged parting of ways. Chombo gets out and stomps around to my window. 'I don't want to see you or that old bitch here again. Believe me, if you come here I'll make life very difficult for you. Do yourself a favour, Cole. Go back to Australia.'

Her broken tooth. And the scar on her lip. Hidden in the photograph by the way she turned her head. It was not shyness that caused Lettah to present a three-quarter profile to the camera when that one clear photograph was taken all those years ago – no, she wished only to hide these small disfigurements. Hazel's memory has opened my own. It's as though a fogged-up window to the past has been wiped clean. I can see her face, clear and precise. Laughing, always laughing, her straight front teeth white and square, except for the one with the diagonal break. The small scar slanting across her top lip, where the tooth broke through, stretched smooth like shiny plastic.

Lettah — always laughing.

uMahleka.

*

193

Hardly a word has been spoken since we left Fort Rixon. Turning onto the tar road to Bulawayo, Hazel rolls down her window, allowing a blast of air to enter the car. Steering with one hand, she lights a cigarette and takes a couple of deep drags. Then she reaches across and pats my arm. 'You must be disappointed.'

I look away. 'Disappointed? That bastard . . . I'm sick of this place. Everywhere you look there's some bloody crook on the take. How can this country ever come right when everyone's corrupt? It's hopeless. Maybe people are getting what they deserve.'

Hazel gives me an amused stare, then turns her eyes back to the road.

'You're mad to stay here, Hazel!'

'Oh, now I'm mad too. On top of being corrupt and getting what I deserve.'

Clara interjects: 'He's just letting off steam, Mom.'

'Is he? Sounds pretty high and mighty to me.'

A long silence before I recant: 'Sorry, Hazel. I had no right to go off like that.'

'Don't apologise,' Clara says. 'I'd be pissed off too.'

Hazel nods graciously. 'Your anger is understandable – appropriate – I suppose, given the circumstances. And you're probably right. We *are* mad, staying here. Poor old Chombo – my God, what a fool! How did he ever imagine he could pull off something like that?'

'Poor old Chombo?' Clara says 'He's a crook, Mom!'

'Yes, I know. The trouble is, my dear, there're Chombos everywhere. Frank's got a point. Everywhere you look it's the same story. Remember when they devalued the currency? Mugabe's way of fighting inflation – no problem, just print new money with a few zeros chopped off and make the old currency illegal. And what did the Chombos do? They went and bought herds of cattle from unsuspecting poor rural folk with the old illegal cash, leaving them destitute. I'll give you that, Frank: Zimbabwe is a classic case of power corrupting, absolutely.'

I rub my brow. 'I wanted so much to believe that poor woman was Lettah. If it wasn't for you I might well have fallen for it.'

'You'll just have to keep on looking,' Clara says.

I sigh. 'No, that's it, I'm afraid. I'm not pinning my hopes on anything any more. I'm finished with this bloody business. Chombo was my last hope.'

'Maybe tomorrow you'll feel differently,' Hazel says.

There is a police roadblock outside Bulawayo. The usual show of blank-faced authority. An officer carrying a rifle approaches the car and asks for identification. My Australian passport appears to arouse suspicion; the officer asks me my business in Zimbabwe. I go through the rigmarole: I'm on holiday, visiting friends. Hazel verifies this. Not a journalist? I shake my head. You were born here? I nod. The officer purses his lips thoughtfully; he gives my passport a sharp flick with his finger and hands it back. He walks slowly around the car, peering through the windows. We wait, staring ahead. He comes around to my window and asks: are you enjoying your stay in Zimbabwe? Wonderful, I reply. We are waved on.

Hazel lights another cigarette.

'What were they looking for?' I ask.

'Who knows? With the elections around the corner, it's probably just to remind us who's in charge. But you never know from one day to the next. You get used to it.'

We arrive at the house in Hillside. I'm in no mood for a dose of Vic, but Hazel insists that I stay for lunch. We find Vic lounging on a deckchair on the veranda, watching the gardener brush the sides of the pool. He is dripping wet, the white hair on his head and chest plastered flat. He looks almost emaciated in a baggy pair of blue swimmers, wrinkled folds of skin hang from his bones like furled sails. We pull up chairs and sit. Hazel lights two cigarettes and gives one to Vic. The maid, Daphne, brings a tray of drinks. Sherry for Hazel. Beer for Clara, Vic and me. The gardener continues with his brushing. Some weaverbirds are noisily building nests in a tree next to the pool.

'Bloody pests,' Vic grumbles. 'Wish we could fumigate the little bastards.'

Hazel sighs. 'Oh, Vic. Why can't you just appreciate nature's wonders?'

'Nature's wonders, hey? All that crap they leave on the slasto? Jesus!'

Hazel rolls her eyes. 'Tell Jeremiah to go and have lunch now.'

'That lazy munt hasn't finished yet.'

'I don't care. I don't want him hovering around while we have lunch.'

'Oh well, if you want your pool full of algae . . .' He barks at the gardener: 'Jeremiah! Lunchtime. Go on, hamba!'

The gardener lays the brush on the slasto next to the pool and walks off towards the house. Vic takes a deep drag on his cigarette and blows the smoke slowly out his nostrils. He turns to me. 'How about a swim? I can lend you a costume.'

'Thanks, maybe some other time,' I reply.

'I'm dying for a dip,' Clara says. 'Come on, Frank.'

I hesitate, then shrug. 'Okay, if you insist.'

'My old costume's in the laundry,' Vic says.

Clara finds me Vic's faded maroon swimmers; I change in the bathroom. On my way outside I bump into her emerging from her room in her bikini and sarong. Our eyes meet, we pause, standing close in the passageway. She takes my hand.

'I'm really sorry about the way things turned out.'

Her voice is husky, pent-up. She is so close I can smell her sweat-damp hair. A vein in her neck pulsing. My skin tingles. We can hear Daphne singing in the kitchen as she prepares lunch.

I shrug. 'That's life, I guess.'

We go outside and dive into the pool. I blow the air from my lungs and lie on the bottom, eyes closed, for a few seconds. It feels good to wash the sweat of a lousy day from my skin. Then I feel the weight of Clara standing on my back, her feet making wiping motions; I've become a submarine mat. I heave her off and rise to the surface. Some infantile splashing and giggling before we emerge from the pool. Hazel watches us with a smile as we resume our seats on the veranda. Vic says: 'Come on, drink up. Your beer's getting flat.'

We drink. A big yellow smile is smeared across Vic's face. 'Hazel's been telling me the sad tale of the corrupt cop and the impostor nanny. I was wondering why no one seemed keen to talk about your little jaunt.'

'Yes,' I reply. 'I received a sobering lesson in moral bankruptcy today. Enough to lose the last vestige of faith I had in humanity.'

Vic erupts with laughter. Great mulish hee-haws. 'Oh, Jesus Christ, what did you expect? When are you going to wake up, man? This is Zimbabwe! These cops are all crooks. Give them a whiff of money and I swear they'll murder their own bloody mothers!'

'We live and learn, don't we?' I say.

Vic guffaws, slapping his leg. 'You know, sometimes you have to hand it to these munts. When it comes to thieving they're in a class of their own. World champions. And they've got a never-ending supply of suckers willing to be conned. When that Chombo goon saw you coming along he must've rubbed his hands in glee.'

'Don't tease him, Vic,' Hazel says. 'It's not a joke.'

'Jesus, woman! Of course it's a joke. Even funnier than Lydia handing out all that loot to a bloody nanny no one remembers.'

'Gee, aren't you a sensitive fellow,' Clara says.

'Just stating the obvious, girl. The one thing I've learned in my time is how a munt's brain ticks. These bloody crooks only survive because people like Frank are born every second.'

I'm suddenly sick of it all. Sick of my fruitless mission. Sick of this damn country. Sick of toeing the line with Vic. I put my glass down and get up. 'I'm not going to listen to your bullshit, Vic. Sorry, Hazel, but I've had enough crap for one day. I better push off before I get into an argument.'

'Oh, Frank . . .' Hazel says.

'Sit down, man,' Vic says. 'Jeez, you're a touchy bugger, hey?'

'Vic, I'm not a bloody kid anymore. I'm not going to sit here and listen to you carry on. All these stupid jibes about my mother, about me —'

'What are you getting uptight for? I'm only joking, man!'

'You always go too far, Vic,' Clara says. 'Enough's enough, man!'

Vic dismisses it all with a wave of his hand. 'Ag, sit down, Frank. I'm only joking, for God's sake. I can't help it if I've always been a straight shooter.'

I remain standing. 'Straight shooter? I wonder how long your sense of humour would last if I did a bit of straight shooting.'

Vic just looks at me, that big yellowy smirk across his dial. Hazel tugs at my elbow. 'Come on, Frank. Vic meant no harm. It's just the way he talks. Sit down. Relax. Let's change the subject, okay.'

Vic raises the bottle of beer. 'Ja, relax, man. Have another beer. Don't get all worked up over nothing. At least that bastard didn't fleece you of all your money. Look on the positive side.'

I sit down again, feeling foolish at my outburst. Vic reaches over and tops up my glass. He chuckles and shakes his head. 'Man! This bloody country has a way of getting under anybody's skin – even liberals.' His eyes widen in mock horror. 'Sorry, no offence!'

I take a deep, comforting swig of beer. When Hazel lights another cigarette I cadge one off her. She raises her eyebrows with surprise, but says nothing.

'So where to now, Frank?' Vic asks.

I shrug. 'Home, I guess.'

'When does your flight leave?'

'In a couple of weeks. I'll see if I can bring it forward.'

Hazel says: 'Why? You might as well just relax and enjoy yourself. Catch up with your friend, Brak. Do a bit of sightseeing.'

'I'm not sure if I deserve a holiday after this fiasco.'

Hazel laughs. 'You *are* just like your father! That Calvinistic streak! So what are you going to do? Sit around at Milton's and mope until it's time to go?'

'I don't know.'

Daphne appears with a tray of cold chicken and sweetcorn. Hazel dishes out the food; soon the air is loud with the clacking of Vic's dentures as he chomps away. After lunch we have another beer. Clara and I swim. When we emerge Hazel and Vic are snoozing in their chairs. We dry ourselves off.

'I'd better get going,' I say, wrapping the towel around my waist.

Clara nods. I get changed in the bathroom. When I emerge she is waiting in the passageway. We stand there. Me uncertain, Clara decided. Without a word she moves up close. Slipping her hands under my arms, she pulls me to her. I can feel her breath on my neck. I try to think of something to say but words elude me. The sound of Daphne and Jeremiah talking in the kitchen seems a thousand miles away.

It happens. She leans forward and kisses me. Our mouths open, she presses hard against me. We totter back into her room; she kicks the door shut. I push my hands down under her wet bikini, the feel of her gooseflesh skin arousing me. She undoes my trousers; they fall to my ankles. She grabs my shirt and pulls me back towards her bed. Hobbled by my trousers, I stumble; we sprawl onto the parquet floor. A self-conscious moment in which I imagine my ludicrousness, floundering around upon her, backside thrusting. She wraps her legs around my waist; we heave and pant away, her flesh squeaking on the parquet, moans rising.

The tide recedes. We lie there, shuddering in the last throes. I wonder if Daphne and Jeremiah heard anything.

'Jesus Christ,' I wheeze. 'Where in hell did that come from?'

'No idea,' Clara replies.

We laugh. After the events of this morning I don't care where it takes me.

Despite having lent an unwitting hand to Chombo's preposterous ploy (after all, who put me in touch with him?) Milton and Ruby reveal that they are amply endowed with that strangely perverse sense of humour common among Zimbabweans. The blatant shenanigans of the powerful elite seem to provide a perpetual font of dark amusement to ordinary folk, long starved of conventional farce. As I relate the morning's fiasco, seated in Milton's lounge with portable fans blowing a gale, their response is, first, incredulity, then laughter. Milton feigns outrage: 'No! Chombo – corrupt? A crooked cop in Zimbabwe? My God!'

As they chortle away, I glumly lament my haplessness. In the space of a few days, I have gone from responsible citizen to clown. Ruby, gathering herself, shakes her head. 'I'm sorry, Frank. We shouldn't laugh. It's just the audacity of it! Just shows you, hey? Even the ones you think are okay. Poor Frank. I'm sorry we got you into this mess.'

'That bastard should be in jail,' I grumble.

'No chance of that,' Milton says. 'One thing I'll guarantee you, if you so much as open your mouth the only bastards who'll end up in jail will be you and that poor old girl he conned into playing Lettah.'

I sigh. 'It's just a pity it had to end on this note. Chombo was my last hope.'

'You did your best, Franco.'

'It's not your fault he's a crook,' Ruby says.

'Ja, just another thief in Mugabe's grand kleptocracy,' Milton agrees. 'Be nice to see them all in jail. Wipe the slate clean and start again. Can't wait for the elections.'

Ruby laughs. 'When were you born, Ogilvy? Yesterday? You don't honestly believe the elections will change anything, do you?'

I get up. 'Mind if I call my father? He'll want to know where things stand.'

'You know where the phone is,' Milton says.

The phone in Perth rings and rings. I'm about to hang up when Max answers, breathing hard – no doubt, he has sprinted from the house to my father's cottage in the back garden. He tells me Errol is out having drinks with some friends at the bowling club. I explain the day's events and ask him to pass on the bad news to Errol. 'Tell him I'm finished here. I've done what I can.'

'That's too bad,' Max says. 'Though I'm sure you're not completely unhappy with the price of failure.'

'What do you mean?'

'Well, with failure comes a nice little windfall, hey?'

'Get your arse over here if you think you can do any better.'

Max laughs. 'Only kidding, man! It was a crazy idea in the first place. So when are you coming back?'

'I don't know.'

'Might as well make it an official holiday.'

'Piss off, Max. Just tell Dad, okay?'

I go to the cottage and shower. Then I lie on the bed, my head teeming with thoughts. Chombo's chicanery. Ntombela. The ramshackle store. Gumede rolling a cigarette with newspaper, coughing. The old woman, so pathetic in her guise as Lettah. Chombo's anger, his threats. Vic's bullshit. And Clara . . . the smell of her, her intense look, the irresistible tide . . .

She eclipses everything. It's light outside, but I doze off, exhausted.

X

'Fucking hell!' Jervis blurts out, staring at the Cortina. He pushes his thick glasses up along his nose, his bloodshot eyes baleful. 'What is it about you bloody Aussies, hey? Nothing's safe with you okes around, man!'

We – Jervis, Milton, Brak and I – are standing around the Cortina in front of the workshop. Brak is kitted out in a new pair of navy blue overalls with *Prospect Autos* across the back. First day on the job.

'Frank's a walking goldmine, Jervis,' Milton says. 'You should be down on your knees kissing his feet, my friend, not insulting him.'

Jervis scrapes at some peeling paint around the broken headlight with a filthy fingernail. 'Reminds me of a munt who worked for me years ago. Broke a brand new bloody anvil . . .'

Ah, the dreaded broken anvil. I'd forgotten the countless times I'd heard this same solemn myth when I lived in Africa. In my reckoning, if you melted down all the broken anvils that must litter the African veld you would have enough raw iron to build another Sydney Harbour Bridge. I should have known it would appear somewhere in Jervis's repertoire.

We hear out his version of the grim fable that has survived unscathed into the postcolonial era. In the background, his appies, Benjamin and Morris, are buffing up a sky blue station wagon, well clear of any anvils.

'. . . and I swear to God, that fucking anvil was in two pieces, man. *Two pieces!*' He holds up two stubby fingers, black with grease. 'I wouldn't've believed it if I didn't see it with my own two eyes!'

He stares at us with touching incredulity. Dutifully, Brak shakes his head.

'Jervis, you're a walking time warp,' Milton says. 'Just give me a damn quote, man. And don't try to crook the insurers either!'

A look of outrage. 'Crook the insurers! Listen, my friend, I don't crook anybody. As much as I'd like to.'

He slips a sheet of carbon paper under the first page of a grease-stained pad and proceeds to inspect the car.

Brak goes over to the chained dog. He squats down, just out of reach. 'Howzit, big fella. How's my big puppy?' he says gently. The dog watches him uncertainly at the end of its chain, growling.

Jervis gives him an exasperated glance. 'For Chrissake, Brak. You got your Aussie mate's *other* car to get back on the road. Make sharp!'

Brak straightens up slowly and ambles over to the Nissan in the workshop. He beckons Benjamin and they begin to fiddle around under the bonnet. I watch them for a while.

'Ja, it's nothing,' Brak says. 'Jets are all gummed up. We'll drain the tank and clean out the carbs. A day's work. She'll be ready to roll this afternoon.'

I find Milton and Jervis in the office. Jervis is busy adding up some figures on a calculator. Milton is gazing up at Mugabe's portrait among the bevy of *Scope* centrefolds. He smiles wryly, dimples showing. 'I wish my old philosophy lecturer could see this. All that syntactic crap about context and meaning suddenly makes sense.'

Jervis points at the fridge rattling away in the corner. 'You okes wanna beer?'

Milton shakes his head. 'It's ten in the morning, Jervis. What do you think we are? Alcoholics or something?'

'Fucking girly boys,' Jervis growls.

With a final blunt jab of his finger, he finishes his calculations and writes down the total on his pad. He pushes the pad across the counter in front of Milton. Milton scrutinises the figures.

'Jesus! Daylight bloody robbery!'

Jervis looks hurt. 'You know what parts cost in this country! And that's just an approximate figure. With inflation like it is, it could be twice that tomorrow.'

Milton laughs. 'Only kidding, Jervis. I'll check if it's okay with the insurers. When can you have it fixed by?'

Jervis's brow contorts in deliberation. 'Two weeks. What's today? Monday . . . I can probably start on Wednesday.'

'Two weeks? Christ.'

Jervis smiles. 'That's if I can get another headlight here in Zim. If I have to order one from South Africa it could take even longer.'

I drive Milton to his office in a 'courtesy vehicle' Jervis provided for half the going hire rate — since I was paying, he reluctantly dropped the proviso that I was not to get behind the wheel. We travel a mere fifty metres down the road before the reasons for the cut-rate fee become apparent. Without exaggeration, the vintage two-cylinder DKW, algae green in colour, is a death trap: the steering pulls hard to the right; the second gear doesn't work; the brakes require pumping. The bodywork is rotten with rust and flaunts the telltale signs of a number of collisions. The interior reeks of lavender toilet freshener.

By chance, Milton's partner, Barry Braithwaite, is standing on the kerb outside the office block as we arrive, scanning the front page of a newspaper. Milton chuckles indulgently. 'Watch his face when he claps eyes on this heap,' he says. With that distinctive *ring-ting-ting* of a DKW engine, I pull up sedately at the kerb. Barry lowers his newspaper and stares at us, eyebrows raised.

Milton gets out casually. 'Greetings, Braithwaite.'

Barry nods. 'Greetings, Ogilvy. Nice to see one's business partner arrive in a style commensurate with the status of his profession.'

'Yes, you can never overestimate the confidence it bestows on our clients.'

Barry smiles and taps the newspaper. 'Have you heard the news? Tsvangirai is coming back to contest the elections. Arrives tomorrow.'

'Brave man. Looks like an interesting time ahead.'

'Succinctly put, Ogilvy. Zanu-PF has already started its campaign. The usual story. Opposition rounded up and tortured. Militia thugs running riot. I don't know why Mugabe persists with the farce of holding elections. He'd save everyone a lot of pain and misery if he just declared himself president for life.'

'Maybe there's a limit to just how far he can rig this one,' Milton says. 'We shall see.'

The same group of weavers are sitting in the courtyard outside Zambezi Pride when I arrive. The same welcoming smiles. Nice mats, one of them says, patting a pile next to her. The shop is quiet. I find Hazel and Vera among the wood and soapstone carvings, re-pricing the stock. Vera's chirpy demeanour seems to have evaporated; she gives me a brave smile and resumes her work.

Hazel takes me aside. 'I think she's figured out these new prices amount to a fire sale. She knows I can't afford to keep going.'

'You're closing down?'

Hazel nods. 'I'll go broke if I don't. Vic and I talked it over last night.' A tired smile. 'Or rather, Vic held my head under the cold tap of reality. For years now I've topped up the business with my dwindling overseas savings. You simply can't run a business based on the tourist trade if there are no tourists. Even at these giveaway prices we won't sell anything.' A burst of laughter from the women outside. Hazel glances towards the door. 'I don't know how I'm going to break the news to those old girls. I was up all night agonising over this.'

'I had no idea it'd come to this.'

She raises her hands and drops them. 'You can't stand against the tide forever. African craft has been my whole life. It breaks my heart.'

I find Clara sorting through piles of mats.

'Aha, a tourist!' she says, smiling. 'This is your lucky day, sir. Mats, mats and more mats, going cheap. My dear mother could never refuse a good mat.'

'Looks like she's going to have to.'

Clara's smile fades. 'Did she tell you?'

I nod.

Clara shrugs and sighs. 'Aye. Zambezi Pride means so much to her. And to a whole bunch of other people too. But what can one old lady in a craft shop do?'

'I know. It's crazy.'

She laughs sadly. 'My dear mother . . . such guts and optimism. The way she just hung in, hoping things would change . . .'

The garrulous chatter of the women outside stops abruptly. We glance across at the shop's entrance. Two policemen have entered. Pistols and batons strapped to their belts. One slaps his hand down on the counter twice. Hazel stops what she's doing and speaks with them; a mumble of IsiNdebele I can't follow. She takes out a black book from under the counter and flips through pages, pointing at rows of figures. Three youths, one sporting a green beret and a t-shirt with a crowing rooster on the chest, now also enter the shop. They wander around, picking up objects, laughing. Doped-up or drunk, it appears. They greet Vera in a mockingly polite manner. Sakubona, nkosikazi. Hallo, kunjani, missus? They chaff her, pointing at prices. Hai, kuyadula lapha! Much too expensive, missus. Vera returns their greeting; she pretends to be amused by their banter as she continues with her work, eyes averted, her fear palpable.

'Green Bombers,' Clara whispers. 'Youth militia.'

I follow her over to the counter. The policemen stare at us from beneath their low cap visors as we approach.

'What's going on, Mom?' Clara asks.

Hazel turns, smiling, and says, 'These two gentlemen of the law are just checking to see if my books are in order and that I'm not exploiting anyone. And I've given an iron-clad assurance to the contrary.' She turns back to the cops. 'In fact, you'll be happy to know that we're more than halving our prices. No use doing things in half-measures, I always say.'

One of the cops mutters something to his colleague. They laugh, then turn away and wander briefly about the shop. Disinterested glances at the array of wares. One carelessly spins a postcard rack around.

'Nothing worth looting,' Hazel says under her breath. 'Looks like our custodians of law and order are on another spree. They go around from business to business, helping themselves to whatever they want. Happens a lot these days, I'm afraid.'

The policemen make for the door, beckoning the youths. The one with the beret dallies next to a display of soapstone carvings. Knowing our eyes are on him, he picks up a small warthog and inspects it closely. Then looking straight at us, he curls his hand around the carving and slips it in his pocket. The same spaced-out, defiant look as he follows his friends towards the door.

'One day you'll pay for that,' Hazel says nonchalantly. 'Full price.'

He gives her a hard stare and leaves.

'One day you'll pay full price for opening your mouth, Mom,' Clara says.

By the time Clara arrives, I've already completed fifteen laps, almost double my last sorry effort, and have been sunbaking on the poolside, chatting to Allan, the fifty-five year old Adonis. Allan tells me he is leaving for Canada next month. The rest of his family are there already, he says; he stuck it out all these years, for what?

Clara emerges from the change rooms. She greets Allan and puts her towel and bag down next to me, adjusts her goggles, and dives in. I watch her swim, noticing that her mincing style seems lethargic, lacking purpose. I turn over and lie on my back. The sun seems to burn with a special intensity today. I imagine it to be Lydia's glare. Her anger at my capitulation. That I have given up my mission at the first real obstacle.

Clara has stopped swimming and is climbing out of the pool.

'Hey, what's up?' I say. 'Don't be a slacker now.'

She smiles and removes her goggles. 'Not in the mood,' she says, flopping down on her stomach next to me.

We are alone. Allan and the other swimmers have gone. The trees around the pool are loud with birds. I look at her wet skin, the way her black Speedo clings to her. As a younger man I might have been anxious to know what is going on in her head; now I'm curiously acceptant, fatalistic, expecting the dream to dissipate.

After a long silence, she says: 'Sorry, I'm just a bit upset. Vera, all those women my mother supports . . . the looks on their faces when she explained the situation to them.'

'How long before she closes the door?'

'A month. Maybe two.'

'Vera will find her feet somewhere else.'

'Vera maybe. But the others haven't a hope. What do they do? And here I am in the wake of it all, the white lady, lying next to a bloody swimming pool!'

'Lady? Don't give yourself airs.'

She laughs and looks away. 'Be serious.'

'It's not your fault. Or your mother's.'

'That doesn't make it easier, Frank.'

Another uncomfortable silence. Clara presses her eyes closed with her fingers.

'Vera said a group of opposition supporters – people she knows from the township – were rounded up yesterday by the cops and taken to the police station. They were made to lie on the floor and were beaten for five hours. Five hours! Most of them women. Some with children. The kids were just shoved in a corner while their mothers were beaten. Can you imagine it? Watching their mothers scream for mercy. I'm sick of this fucking place!'

'Maybe you should get away for a while. Why don't we go someplace together? Victoria Falls? Kariba? My car will be fixed today. Come on.'

Clara looks at me hesitantly. 'My mother will probably need some support while she winds up the shop. I don't particularly want to go sightseeing right now.'

'Just a suggestion.'

'I appreciate it, Frank. Not now though.'

She lays her head on her arm and closes her eyes. The backs of her legs are turning mottled red under the sun. She breathes deeply. I'm wondering if she has fallen asleep when she speaks: 'Will you write about me one day?'

I laugh. 'Why? Does it worry you?'

'You'll probably cast me as a fickle temptress.'

'I'd never make you fickle, Clara.'

'I *am* fickle. I have a bad track record.'

'Why don't we just play it by ear?'

Clara smiles and, eyes still closed, reaches out. I take her hand and kiss it.

'You're so gallant,' she says.

Gallant? Now there's one for the books. Lydia would have been proud.

Just after five Milton drops me off at Prospect Autos and *ring-ting-tings* his way towards home in the DKW. My Nissan stands ready in front of the workshop, next to Brak's Cruiser; it's been washed and the tyres blackened. The appies, Benjamin and Morris, emerge from the workshop and saunter past me towards the gate. Approaching the office I hear loud voices and laughter.

I enter a blue fog of cigarette smoke and beer fumes. Jervis and Brak are seated on opposite sides of the counter, a vanquished army of quart bottles at their elbows. Jervis, looking every bit the squalid bartender, is first to see me enter.

'Hey, Matilda!' he yells. 'How about a little waltz, hey?'

Brak turns on his seat. 'Howzit, china! Pull up a stool, man.'

Both stare at me with glazed eyes.

'Nice to see the sober work ethic is alive and well in Zimbabwe,' I say.

'Bugger the work ethic,' Jervis says. 'Our work ethic is . . . sympathetic. Sympathetic to the pathetic. Sympathetic to the pathetic melancholic alcoholic who likes to frolic.'

Brak laughs. 'You're a fucking poet, Jervis.'

'How much do I owe you?' I ask.

Jervis pushes his thick glasses up the bridge of his nose. 'Fuck, I'm too pissed to worry about that now. Pay me tomorrow. As a valued customer do us the honour of sharing a beer with us, man.'

'Might be better if I just picked up my car and left you boys to it.'

'Come on!' Brak insists.

'Ja, come on, Matilda!' Jervis says. 'What's the hurry, man?' He cups a hand to his mouth and whispers to Brak. 'Bloody Aussie. Can't wait to get back to the Gay Mardi Gras, hey?'

He erupts into laughter.

Brak smiles wryly. 'You're a man of great wit and tact, Jervis.' He turns to me. 'Come on, Frank. Don't leave me in the lurch here.'

'Okay, just one.'

'Not hard to twist his arm, hey?' Jervis says. He takes out a quart of Zambezi Lager from the fridge, opens it and shoves it across the counter. He does a little dance in front of Mugabe's portrait and the frieze of pin-ups. Wagging his grease-stained backside, arms jerking like pistons.

Brak looks at me. 'See what you got me into, hey? More than one wire loose in this oke's head. Seriously.'

'Just remember who's boss around here, my friend,' Jervis growls, settling back into his chair.

I pull up a stool. The three of us clink bottles and swig our beers. Jervis gives a hefty belch, simultaneously mouthing 'Bulawayo'. Brak shakes his head, laughing. One day on the job, and he and Jervis are just about joined at the hip.

'Good to see Zimbabwe's woes aren't causing undue concern here at Prospect Autos,' I say.

Jervis waves his hand. 'Ag, what can you do but go with the flow? I believe in providence, my friend. I have great faith in our government. There will always be pissed Zanu-PF stooges with pranged government cars for me to fix. Never-ending supply. Politicians plus alcohol plus motor vehicles equals paydirt. Not to mention the odd Aussie who comes along. My business is safe.'

'Is everything okay with my car?' I ask.

'Going like a Boeing. So when can we expect it back again? What new auto atrocity will you commit?'

'Who knows? Maybe I'll have a go at that mobile brothel you conned me into renting.'

A nicotine-stained grin. 'Mobile brothel, hey? My friend, many a true word is said in jest. You got no idea how much, shall we say, rec-reation of a sexual nature that baby's seen. Man! I used to naai myself silly in that car —'

'How? On the gearstick?' Brak asks innocently.

'Fuck off, Malan. Bloody wiseguy. Many a sweet damsel lost her virginity in that little jalopy. Those springs got a good work-out —'

Brak scoffs: 'Ag, don't talk shit, man! What self-respecting woman would ever get in a car with you?'

Jervis waves a stubby finger. 'No lies, my friend!' He leans close, his voice conspiratorial. 'I'll tell you blokes a story. I made a complete bloody arse of myself on one such occasion, man. Literally. There I am at the drive-in, parked on that hump, you know, with the speaker in the window, making love not war on the back seat with a nice fat matron from one of the boarding schools. Naked as the day we were born, car springs going berserk. Everything going lekker like a cracker, when all of a sudden the fucking car starts rolling forward . . .'

He pauses for dramatic effect, bleary eyes magnified.

'Coitus interruptus big time, I tell you. Ja, there we go, hey, straight down the dip towards the car in front. Matron still has me in a scissors grip. Bloody speaker gets ripped off the pole. I untangle myself from the matron who starts to screech like a banshee and I dive over the front seat, trying to grab the handbrake under the dash. Picture the scene, boys. A wild matron screeching, me with my arse hanging over the seat trying to grab the handbrake. Too fucking late. Bam!' Jervis whacks his fist into his palm. 'We pound straight into the car in front. Big commotion. And what does the oke behind us do? Switches on his bloody lights, illuminating my arse over the seat! Nice big shiny ring for all to see. Anus horribilus. And, of course, the joker starts hooting, and soon the whole bloody drive-in is hooting and laughing. Christ, I never lived that one down, hey. The whole of Bulawayo was talking. I was a fucking laughing stock, man!'

Brak guffaws. 'Oh, Jeez! Have you no shame, man? No wonder they shut the place down.'

Jervis grins. If little horns sprouted from his dirty crew-cut hair, I wouldn't have been surprised. He gets up and does his little jig over to the fridge. 'Come on, girls. Who's for another grog? Drink up, Matilda!'

And so the deluge. How easily my flimsy defences are breached; how feebly I surrender. Soon I'm as drunk as my pie-eyed companions – not surprising since I haven't eaten since breakfast. A cosy buzz spreads through me; I seem to float in a piss-warm pond, not a care in the world. After all, wasn't I entitled to unwind now that my search for Lettah is over? Did I not give it my best shot? Things distort. Brak and Jervis's huge, strangely endearing, faces bulge and contract like anemones. Every so often, Mugabe's dour visage, magnified among tits and bums, peers over Jervis's shoulder. A fellow devil. I know that soon this warm pond will spill over and the plunge will commence. Down, always down. Still I drink.

It's dark when we go outside to relieve ourselves. We stand together in front of the office, slaking down the still-hot concrete surface of the work yard, watching the urine funnel off to a drain. The grubby rituals of men.

Brak spies the chained dog. 'Only a bloody savage leaves his dog chained up like that, Jervis. You should be ashamed of yourself, man.'

Jervis looks exasperatedly up at the stars as he does up his fly. 'Ag, for crying in a fucking bucket, I'm sick and tired of you carrying on about that bloody dog. If you want him, take him. My gift to you, okay? Happy Christmas.'

Aside from the dog, whose name is Gator, Jervis supplies us each with a pack of Marlboro cigarettes from a stash he keeps under the counter and four cold bombs for the road. The 'plan' is to leave my car at Prospect Autos, sleep the night at Brak's and pick it up tomorrow morning when he goes in to work. I phone Milton from the office – he doesn't sound too impressed, probably because he can hear the inebriated laughter of my companions in the background.

With Gator tethered in the back of the Cruiser, wearing a make-shift rope muzzle, we hit the road. I'm just about to open one of the beers when Brak decides to stop off at what he says is one of Bulawayo's few remaining up-market waterholes where you can drink among civilised folk – such as himself, he adds with a laugh. Even to an ine-briate, *up-market* is not a term that readily springs to mind as we enter the bar, empty but for three young white men playing darts. Floor littered with cigarette butts. Walls festooned with smutty cartoons, ancient rugby memorabilia and some mounted animal heads – kudu, zebra, a moth-eaten lion. Brak orders drinks. He eyes the young blokes playing darts. 'Any chance of a game, boys?' They size us up; what they see amuses them, apparently. They beckon us over. Two are tough-looking fellows with pumped physiques in tight t-shirts. Military-style trousers. Sideburns shaved into thin angular strips. One sports a silver nostril ring. I prove a woeful partner to Brak; on one occasion I miss the board completely, causing much hilarity. My brain now seems to operate in short, sporadic bursts, as though wired to a defective battery. Still I drink. The beers keep coming courtesy of my US dollars which the bartender, a tired-looking geriatric in a rumpled safari suit, accepts with alacrity.

Everyone is getting on just fine when I stagger off to the toilet. Down a passage, through a noisy swing-door, into the foul ambience of excreta. The urinal is overflowing with yellow piss and cigarette butts. I lurch into a cubicle. As I pee, the toilet bowl seems to grin up at me demonically.

Back in the bar, things are no longer hunky-dory. Loud bicker-ing has commenced between Brak and the guy with the silver nostril ring. Something about earning the right to wear army apparel. 'What is it,' Brak asks, a malevolent glint in his eye, 'about you bum bandits and uniforms?' This does not go down well with the boys in camouflage. The one with the nostril ring, looking more like a bull by the second, ups the ante.

'Bum bandit? Say it again, you old prick, and I'll boot your balls so hard you'll ring like a fucking pinball machine.'

Brak just lounges smiling against the bar, lapping it up. I lurk on the periphery. After having my nose broken by that yobbo in Australia, I know that I have no fighter's instinct whatsoever. The stupidity of our situation begins to register. What am I doing here, carrying on like some low-life? And yet, inexplicably, I begin to mouth off like a stroppy barfly. 'Grow up, you idiots! Pick on someone your own age!' – even as I say it, I wonder what possesses the drunken mind.

They eye me, the puny geezer with a broken nose, with amused contempt. 'Stay out of it, fuck face,' one of them warns. Enough said. They turn back to Brak who still leans casually against the bar, grinning like a fat old mongoose in a chook pen. Some ritual posturing. Snarling, snorting, pawing the ground. Yet none of them appears game enough to initiate hostilities. It's not just that Brak is still the biggest guy in the room. There's something in his stare that stops them. A look in which there is no fear.

Engrossed by this unfolding stupidity, I forget that I'm holding a glass of beer; it slips suddenly from my grasp, exploding into fragments on the floor. Brak jerks into a crouch, back to the bar, fists up and ready. I almost laugh at the theatrical absurdity of it – him poised there, head weaving from side to side behind clenched fists, like some mothballed prize-fighter. The three amigos, though, now look decidedly unenthusiastic; none seems keen to take on this big smiling lunatic, yet none wishes to lose face either. The old bartender yells at us to take it outside.

Out we go to the car park. I hear myself chirping again, berating the young men for their lack of respect for their elders – ironic, considering deference to seniors has never been a notable feature of my own behaviour. A heavy blow to my back sends me sprawling to the ground. I look up to see Brak backing up against the Cruiser, that scary smile still on his face. Behind him, Gator roars with muffled rage, straining at his tether. He has managed to partially remove the muzzle, enough to allow his jaws a decent purchase on any stray human body part.

Brak cracks his knuckles and beckons the men forward. 'Come on, you gutless wonders. If I don't tear you apart, my little pooch will. Come on, you big heroes!'

He reaches into the pocket of his overalls and takes out a clasp knife. Without taking his eyes off the men, he lobs it to me.

'Get on the back, Frank. Cut the dog loose if you have to, okay?'

I pick up the knife and stagger to my feet, the palms of my hands skinned; I clamber aboard the Cruiser and crouch well out of Gator's reach. It occurs to me that cutting Gator's tether might expose me to a serious mauling, but I take comfort in the fact that Gator's eyes are fixed on the men standing nervously around Brak. With one hand Brak reaches behind and rustles under a tarpaulin on the back of the Cruiser. He pulls out a short wooden pole and brandishes it at the men. 'Okay, boys! Time to back up the big talk. Come on, who's first to be a tent peg?'

The amigos start muttering among themselves, wanting no part of this madman or his dog.

Brak taunts them: 'What's the matter, boys? Big fucking talk, hey? Come on, just me against you.'

'Fuck this for a joke,' says one.

'Ja, let's piss off,' says another. 'This old prick's seriously insane.'

I almost cheer with relief. A sensible outcome that leaves our honour and hides intact.

But Brak has other ideas. He suddenly lunges forward and clouts the one with the nostril ring square on his crew-cut pate. A ringing *toonk*. The man staggers back clasping his head, groaning. Brak takes a wild swing at the other two, misses and nearly falls. Before he can recover, they pile into him. Kicks and punches. Wild curses.

The pole clatters across the ground under the Cruiser. He with the nostril ring recovers sufficiently to join the fray. Gator tugs wildly at his tether as Brak disappears beneath a scrum of bodies. I crouch helplessly in the back of the Cruiser, fearful of where this might end, picturing Brak and me laid out on a morgue slab, covered in cuts and bruises, the tags around our toes reading: *Cause of Death – Seriously Insane Old Prick*. A loud yelp; one of them leaps back, examining his arm. 'Jesus, the old fucker bit me!' The others take no notice; one has Brak pinned down on the ground with a forearm across his neck, the other starts punching him in the face. Brak twists his head, trying to avoid the blows. Panic-stricken, I decide to cut Gator loose. I move closer and grab the tether. Gator turns, his throat rattling. He scrambles towards me; I retreat beyond his reach, wondering what the hell to do next. Brak is taking a pounding. Am I expected to leap into the fray?

Then from within the melee comes a terrible breaking roar. Brak bellows like a wounded beast, as though all the pain and hatred in his life were given voice at once. It seems to paralyse the men – even Gator stops his tirade. Eyes darting with fear, the amigos fall on Brak as if their lives depend on holding him down. But nothing can contain the beast. Brak erupts from the tangle of bodies, eyes wide, insane, bloodied mouth roaring. In a flurry of blows he fells two, the meaty crack of fist against face resonating around the car park. They lie bleeding on the ground, staring groggily after their friend who has taken off down the road in a limping run.

Brak shouts after him: 'Hey! Where're you off to, chicken shit?'

He looks at me, breathing heavily. Laughs. 'Fuck, is that it? After all that hunna-hunna!'

He retrieves the pole from under the Cruiser. The two on the ground cower as he brandishes it at them. 'Go on, fuck off before I get serious,' he pants.

They get slowly to their feet. One holds his jaw as they retreat down the road.

Brak turns to me, laughing like a madman. I'm still crouched in the back of the Cruiser, unable to fully believe how this has turned out. Not that Brak has emerged unscathed. A trickle of blood from a cut on his eyebrow runs down his cheek into his beard; blood oozes from his mouth. He inspects his right hand; his knuckles are bleeding and the gash where Gator bit him days ago has opened up. The dog strains at his tether, his paws scrambling on the Cruiser's rusted tray. Brak looks at him affectionately. He wipes his bloody hand off on his overalls and reaches out slowly towards the dog. Gator's ferocious growling subsides, then stops. Brak gently strokes the dog's muscular neck. He removes the makeshift muzzle. Then he leans forward and rubs his head against Gator's — an act of profound stupidity, in my estimation. For a moment the two just stand there, heads together. Gator's crinkled tail starts to wag. He licks the blood from Brak's face.

'Thanks, big fella,' Brak croons. 'Good boy. You wouldn't let me down, would you, big boy?'

Then he straightens up. 'Come on, china. Let's get the fuck out of here.'

My drunkenness has started to lift. 'Maybe you should drop me off at Milton's.'

'Bullshit. Night's still a puppy. Don't fade on me now!'

We stop at another hotel. It's after midnight when we emerge, completely blotto, laden with a crate of beer Brak wangled on tick. With Brak whooping, we roar off into the night.

No surprises that Reggie is less than impressed by the feral company that skids to a halt in front of the house, especially after Brak rammed down the security gate rather than open it. Funny at the time, I have to say. Cracker is also unimpressed; he circles the Cruiser, outraged at Brak's treachery in bringing such a disreputable cur home with him — I refer to Gator, of course. The dogs glower and snarl at each other. A small blessing that Gator is restrained; it's my guess he'd make short work of Cracker, given half a chance. Reggie stands at the top of the veranda steps, arms folded, as we disgorge from the Cruiser, bottles clinking. She is furious.

'Where the hell have you been, Brak? I've been worried sick about you, man!'

'What's that, honeybunch?' Brak says, swaying on his feet.

'I said where the hell have you been?'

Cracker starts barking at Gator. Brak yells: 'Cracker! Shuddup!' The dog cowers. Brak stumbles and nearly falls as he leans over to pat him. 'I'm sorry, my big puppy. I brought you a friend. You and Gator can be chinas, like Frank and me, hey?'

'Where've you been, Brak? Answer me.'

Brak straightens up. 'Ag, don't nag, doll. Frank and me were just celebrating. A couple of beers, that's all.'

Reggie glares at me. I stand beside Brak, smiling like a halfwit, holding the crate of beer as though it were an offering. I imagine we make a comical, endearing sight, and that shortly Reggie will drop her feigned outrage and be her normal good-humoured self. Instead, she bursts into tears and runs back into the house.

Brak looks at me, flummoxed. 'Now what?'

He follows her inside and a short while later a shouting match ensues.

'You're out of control, Brak! I can't live with it again!'

Brak laughs plaintively. 'One night! You won't even allow me one little night on the town! For Chrissake, Reggie!'

'You know what it leads to. Look at the time! One o'clock in the morning! You've just started a new job and you're already asking to get fired!'

'I can't help it if my boss asked me to have a couple of beers with him after work. It's no big deal, doll!'

'No big deal, hey? Look at your hands! Look at your face! You and your bloody fighting. Don't tell me everything's okay. You know the score with your drinking. I can't go through this again!' She starts sobbing. 'It's too much! I knew it wouldn't last. Fuck you, Brak!'

I put the crate down on the veranda and walk away, not wanting to listen, wishing I hadn't come. I stagger over to the gate and try to fix it back on its hinges but it seems buckled beyond repair. I sit in the dirt next to the fence, looking at the house. They are still yelling. The stars above start to whirl; soon the whole damn universe is whirling and wobbling out of kilter. I keel over and retch into the sand.

Then the yelling spills out of the house. Reggie charges outside, suitcase in hand. She flies down the stairs, stops and screams, 'Bastard! You promised!' at Brak standing in the lighted doorway and runs off to her Datsun. She flings the suitcase into the back, reverses out of the carport and tears off down the driveway, gears grating. What she might have thought when the headlights caught me lying in my vomit next to the gate, I shudder to think.

Brak watches her car disappear into the darkness, then turns and goes inside. After a few minutes he comes stumbling out again with a plastic bowl and a pot that he puts on the back of the Cruiser next to Gator. Gator drinks thirstily from the bowl, then starts to wolf down some food in the pot. Brak watches him as he eats. Cracker creeps out from the shadows and starts growling again. 'Cut it out, boy,' Brak says. 'That's enough now.'

As though suddenly remembering me, he yells: 'Hey, Frank! Where're you, china?'

I get unsteadily to my feet and stagger back down the drive to the house. As I appear in the pool of light below the veranda, Brak says: 'Where you been, china?'

'Evacuating most of my internal organs against your fence.'

His bleary eyes rest on the vomit stains on my shirt. He laughs. 'Shit, I thought you Aussies could drink.'

'Not this Aussie. What's up with Reggie?'

Brak waves his hand dismissively. 'Ag, you know women. Fly off the handle about nothing . . . Where're those beers, man?'

'Christ, Brak. Shouldn't we be calling it a night?'

'Don't you start now. Come on, china.'

He spies the crate I left on the veranda and opens two bottles

219

with his teeth. We drink on the stairs, looking out at the stars. Brak belches after each long swig. My stomach heaves at the taste. Gator has been noisily licking the bottom of the pot, banging it around on the back of the Cruiser. Now he peers over the side and sees Cracker lying on the step next to Brak. The growling and snarling recommences.

Brak yells: 'Hey! That's enough! Shuddup!'

'What are you going to do about them?' I ask.

'Ag, they'll get used to each other. I'll keep Gator tied up for a while.' He jabs Cracker with his boot. 'I'm scared he'll make mincemeat of this poor idiot. Hey, Crackerjack? Won't that be sad?'

Cracker looks up at him with doe eyes, his tail thumping against the step. Brak scratches his ears. 'Don't worry, boy, you're still my number one.'

We drink and smoke, flicking our cigarette butts out into the yard. I seem to have reached an odd point where I'm drinking myself sober, whereas Brak's voice has become increasingly slurred and incoherent. He gazes out at the dark bush. Dark swellings on his face, dried blood in his beard. Skinned knuckles. He starts that awful teeth-grinding. 'Ja, bloody women,' he mutters, shaking his head. 'Can never figure them out. Different fucking species.'

'Where did Reggie go?'

'Dunno. She's got some friends in town. I couldn't give a shit.'

'Maybe we should call it a night —'

'For Chrissake, Frank! I said don't start. How's your beer?'

'I'm okay.'

Brak opens another beer for himself. He laughs. 'Shit, that Jervis is a bloody reprobate, hey? Wonder how his head's gonna feel tomorrow.'

'A question we might well ask ourselves.'

'Too late, cat's out the bag and the horse has bolted.' He laughs and slaps me on the back. 'Amazing, hey? How we've just slotted together again. Like those Que Que days were yesterday.'

I nod, though it hasn't been quite so seamless for me.

'You're my best china, Frank. I mean it. I reckon your first friends are always the best friends.'

The prospect of a drunken sentimental journey down memory lane at this time of the morning fills me with dread. I wonder about his other friends. Why do he and Reggie seem so alone in the world? I think of my own tiny social circle back in Australia – my family, a few acquaintances from my teaching days, those footloose hippy lovers – and realise Brak is not alone among the friendless. Not that it's bothered me before.

Exhausted from a long, tumultuous day, Gator has fallen asleep on the back of the Cruiser. His snores are interrupted by occasional little yelps.

Brak laughs. 'Probably dreaming he's still chained to that pole at the workshop. What do you dream about, Frank?'

'Dream about?'

'Ja, other than big-breasted women.'

'I wish. Lately, I seem to have this recurring dream that I have a wife. A wife with no face. Always leaves me feeling like I've lost everything.'

Brak takes a deep drag on his cigarette. 'How're things with whatshername – Clara?'

'I'm too old for her.'

'Bullshit. Either you click or you don't. Fuck-all to do with age.'

'Ja, well, what will be will be.'

I realise I have unconsciously readopted the word *ja* into my vocabulary. How much else of this place have I reclaimed? We sit there listening to a jackal yapping in the darkness. Brak grinds his teeth. He pulls the case of beers closer and, before I can decline, opens a bottle and hands it to me. 'What a pleasure, hey? Drinking with your oldest china.'

'What do you dream about?'

Brak takes a deep swig and sighs. 'Oh fuck, I dunno. Big-breasted women mostly. Nah . . . sometimes I dream about my folks. Me and my old man buggering around with cars. Remember that racing car we built? The *Silver Bullet* — fucking unreal, hey?' He laughs wistfully. 'Best old man any kid could want. My mom too. Dreamt once I was sitting next to her, playing this massive fucking piano. Size of a damn house. Playing some complicated tune together. She'd lean over and kiss me on the cheek when I got it right . . .'

His voice falters. He closes his eyes and pinches the bridge of his nose between thumb and forefinger. He is quiet for a while, then continues in a choked voice: 'And I always wake up feeling shit because it's all gone. Nothing left. No family, no kids, nothing. Alone in the fucking universe.'

'You've got Reggie.'

'She's gone too, china.'

'Come on, Brak. She'll be back. She worships you, man!'

'Fuck her. I don't wanna talk about her.'

'That's the grog talking. She's the best thing that ever happened to you. That's what you said the other night.'

'Fuck her!'

Brak slips into a reverie, grinding his teeth and nodding his head. Over in the Cruiser, Gator snores away. Brak's eyes close; he breathes deeply, noisily, through his boxer's nose. For a moment, I think he has nodded off but then he starts talking in a low mumble, as though to himself.

'I also have a recurring dream. I wish it would go away, but it doesn't. Always the same shit dream.' A long, tremulous sigh. 'It's a helluva thing, you know. A helluva thing to have blood on your hands. To have taken life. You can never know till you've done it yourself. I killed a lot of people, Frank. A *lot* of people, and I feel fuck-all about most of them. Most of them were terrorists, Mugabe's boys. I feel fuck-all about them. It was war. Us against them. I hated those bastards then and I hate them now. Can't help it. Especially now, when I look at the fuck-up they've made of this place. But some of the people were innocent. Ordinary munts. Sometimes women and children. Usually they got caught in the crossfire, it wasn't deliberate. I never deliberately aimed a weapon at any civilian — I can swear

222

to that. I accept that I killed innocent people. I feel shit about it but I don't blame myself. My army unit was just a killing machine. Towards the end of the war we were thrown into battle every fucking day, sometimes three times a day. Kill, kill, kill. Stonking gooks. That's all we were wired to do. I believed in what I was doing and I was always with other guys when we killed. And the war machine condoned it. Awarded me a fucking Bronze Cross. We were all cogs in the machine. We did what we had to do.'

Brak takes a drag on his cigarette and flicks the butt out across the driveway. 'Reggie hates it when I flick stompies into the garden. Reckons it's *uncouth* . . .' He laughs. 'Ja, where was I?'

'You were talking about killing . . . about blame.'

He lights another cigarette. 'Blame . . . the point I was making is that in war responsibility for killing rests with the machine, not the men. In every situation I was in the decision whether to kill or not to kill was made for me by the machine. Every situation except one. There was one time where I was on my own and the choice was mine. No one else. We hit this terrorist camp in the mountains along the Mozambique border. Big bunch of gooks, about sixty of them. This was towards the end of the war when the bastards were pouring in from Mozambique. I was part of a stopper group. Our job was to nail the ones who escaped the main assault. All goes well. Camp gets hit. Gooks get stonked. We lie in wait across a small valley, their only escape route. All of a sudden, this pathetic bunch of terrified terrorists comes balekering out of the killing ground towards us. They were desperate. Heavy firefight. Bullets fucking everywhere. One of them manages to break through our line and I chase after him down this valley. Thick bush. The fucker's wounded and I'm following his blood spoor.'

He drinks and sighs. 'Ja, this is the shit part. Hunting is intuition. Instinct. I find the fucker hiding in some bushes next to a stream. I almost walk right past him, but then I sense him watching me; I turn and lock eyes with him, and he knows he's fucked. He's lost his rifle, unarmed. If he had a gun I probably wouldn't be here telling you this story. He's been shot through the leg, his pants are drenched in blood. Barefoot, his clothes are rags. A pathetic sight, man. I've got my gun on him and he starts cowering, absolutely terrified. Starts begging. Please, baas. Please, sir. Please, master. Please don't kill me. He crawls to me on his hands and knees, begging, begging. Please, master, don't kill me. He says some weird shit. I am my father's son. I am my mother's son. Please don't kill them. And I had the choice. The power over life and death. I was no longer protected by the machine – the decision was mine. I could've walked away. Could've taken him prisoner. But I didn't. I shot him. Shot him between the eyes, so close it burned his skin. Blew the back of his head off. That was my choice. That was the power I exercised. When he hit the ground like a sack of meat, I knew it would haunt me. And it does. I hate closing my eyes at night because I know he's waiting for me. Waiting for me to follow him down that valley of death. Waiting for me to find him there under that fucking bush. I see him there begging on his knees. I am my father's son. I am my mother's son. Please don't kill them. Fuck . . .'

Brak scuffs at some dried mud on the step with the heel of his boot. He wipes his eyes with his sleeve. 'I must seem like a bloody freak to you, hey? You were lucky, Frank. It could've been you sitting here telling me the same fucking story. You could've been one of us. You never had to carry the weight of this stuff, china.'

'I've no illusions about that, Brak. Believe me.'

He takes a huge swig of beer, almost draining the bottle. 'I don't blame Reggie for fucking off. It's like I fell off a cliff a long time ago and never stopped falling. I'm falling inside. Can't stop falling.'

I shake my head. 'I don't know what to say. This is out of my league.'

'Nothing to say. Reggie reckons I should go to a shrink.'

'Maybe you should.'

'Nothing anybody can say can bring me back to that moment when the choice was mine.'

A wave of tiredness overwhelms me. I put my bottle down on the step, unable to drink any more, unable to respond intelligently. Like everything else in this place, Brak's story is beyond me. I'm moved by the dreadful pathos of it, by the excruciating angst in his voice – yet it's also the oldest story in existence: young men marching off to war, sacrificing their bodies and souls for noble and ignoble causes, learning the value of life by destroying it, finding wisdom always in hindsight, in the terrible aftermath. Brak's story is not the first of its kind, nor will it be the last. Still, I feel deeply unworthy of making such judgements. There is a fatalistic conviction that, as a man, I have no right to talk of such matters because I have not learned life by destroying it. Men only acquire substance and wisdom through rites of destruction. We build by tearing down.

'You once sent me a photo of you and some army mates. There was a corpse in the background – just the legs showing. Barefoot, bloody trousers. Was that the same incident? Was that the man you shot?'

Brak shrugs and shakes his head. 'There were a lot of photos and a lot of corpses. Might've been. I don't remember sending you any photo.'

'Reggie's right, you need to talk to somebody about this.'

'I'm talking to you.'

'A professional. Someone who can stop you falling.'

'No one can stop me falling.'

Brak takes another two beers from the crate.

'Not for me, Brak. Please, I really can't manage any more.'

He opens one bottle with his teeth and spits the cap down the stairs. 'Suit yourself. All the more for me.'

I look at my watch. 'Come on, let's crash. It'll be daylight soon.'

'You're like an old woman!'

'You've got work tomorrow, Brak. Don't you think –'

Brak waves me away. 'Jesus Christ! Quit nagging. Fuck off and crash if you want to!'

I glance at him, sitting there grinding his teeth. I get up and pat him on the shoulder. He grunts but doesn't look up. I go inside to the spare room. I manage to pull off my trousers and shoes before collapsing on the bed. The room begins to whirl. I pass out, gripping the spinning mattress.

The wife I never had lies unconscious on a hospital bed. I sit beside her, caressing her forehead. Huge red rubber tubes protrude from her abdomen. They pulse and bubble through a colossal machine next to the bed. Through an open window, I can see, far below, a great ploughed field. A winter sky swarming with crows. Our tribe of kids charges about the field on horses, wild savages attacking each other, their war whoops barely audible above the noise of the machine. My wife is naked. She smells like fresh flowers as I lean over her. At last I can see her face. She is beautiful, yet she seems ancient; her skin has the craquelured texture of an old painting. She babbles away in her sleep, her words lost amid the clanking and hissing of the machine.

Sirens. Down below, police cars and an ambulance converge on the field. One of the kids lies on his back. The top half. The lower half is still seated astride his horse, which canters around in circles. The other kids watch from a distance as the cops and the ambulancemen stand there, perplexed.

Brak's shouting wrenches me from sleep. It takes me a while to register where I am. In the darkness I can just make out the water stain on the ceiling resembling a flaccid flower. The curtains are open; outside there is a pale strip of dawn light along the horizon. Brak is lurching around the house calling for Reggie. Heavy stumbling. Loud thumps against the walls. The crash of furniture. His voice an anguished bray.

'Reggie! Reggie, where're you, doll?'

I lie in the darkness, listening, half-awake. I feel wretched: my mouth tastes foul; my head throbs. Outside, the generator drums; dogs are whining. Dogs? A sudden memory of Gator unleashes a confused flood of images: Jervis's demonic face. The brawl at the hotel. Reggie's angry departure. The spinning universe. More stumbling and crashing. More anguished braying.

'Reggie! Where're you, doll?'

Brak's shadow briefly eclipses part of the thin rectangle of yellow light around the closed door. The slap of a hand against the wall outside in the passage. Heavy footsteps breaking into a faltering run. A crash of breaking glass. A tormented wail. I'm about to get up when the shadow returns. I lie there watching as the shadow pauses, swaying across the strip of light. I can hear Brak's laboured breathing.

The door bursts open. Brak stands there, silhouetted against the light, swaying on his feet. He teeters up against the door jamb and almost falls over. Though his face is in shadow I feel his eyes fix on me.

'Who the fuck are you?'

I stare back. 'Hey, Brak. What's going on, man?'

'Where's Reggie? Who the fuck are you?'

'What —?'

'You heard me. Who the *fuck* are you?'

'Come on, Brak! What's your case, man?'

Brak fumbles around on the wall and switches on the light. I sit up, momentarily blinded.

'For Chrissake, Brak!'

He is grotesquely drunk, nearly toppling over as he leans forward, peering at me stupidly, mouth agape. Still in his work overalls and boots. Eyes glazed, angry. I don't know what he is seeing. Certainly not me.

He staggers forward. 'Who the fuck are you? Where's Reggie?'

I get to my feet. 'What the hell's the matter with you, man? I'm Frank! Remember? Frank — your friend? Your china? Reggie went into town, remember?'

He sways at arm's length from me, teeth grinding. I hold up my hand. 'Whoa! Come on, Brak! Back off, man! It's me — Frank!'

Brak stares at my bare legs protruding beneath my vomit-stained shirt. He thrusts a wavering finger in my face. 'Where's she? Where's Reggie? You've been screwing her, hey?'

'What?'

He bends over and looks under the bed. Then he straightens up unsteadily and faces me again. He nods, certain of something.

'Oh, for God's sake, Brak! What's your bloody problem, man? Reggie's not here! Back off!'

'You've been fucking her, hey? My wife.'

'What are you talking about? Back off, man!'

A long, wild stare. He thrusts out his jaw. Taps it. 'Big man, hey? Just walk into my house. Come on, big man. Hit me. Gimme your best shot.'

'Fuck off, Brak! Get away from me!'

'Just walk into my house and fuck my wife, hey? Come on.' Taps his jaw. 'Now's your chance. Come on, big man. Hit me. Better do it now 'cause you're not gonna get another chance.'

'Brak, this is Frank! Frank – from Que Que!'

As I speak, his eyes follow my lips, his mouth opening and closing as though repeating my words. He looks down, nodding, contemplating something. And I don't even see it. An explosion of white light in my skull. I reel back against the wall, stunned. My left ear big and burning. A caged roar behind clenched teeth. He hurls himself at me, hands grasping for my throat. Berserk. We grapple. He swings a punch and misses, grabbing my neck instead in a head-lock. That insane braying. I feel the power in his arm closing like a vice, crunching the vertebrae in my neck. I struggle wildly, yelling at him to stop.

'Cut it out, Brak! Fuck off, man!'

His face presses against mine, his eyes bore into me. Reeking terribly, he grunts and pants as he wrestles with me, heedless of my cries. We stumble and crash around the room. A table breaks under our weight. He grabs my head and butts me hard between the eyes. I feel the skin split, my nose crack. I gasp for breath, tasting blood, warm, metallic. He flings me to the cement floor. I roll as he kicks at my head; he misses and falls on top of me. The stench of his sweat and panting breath. A sharp stabbing pain in my chest. Growling like a beast, he bites my shoulder. I scream in agony. He pounds my head against the floor. Tries to gouge my eyes. Terror surges through me. Brak is possessed by a fury so immense, so unstoppable, I cannot see how I'll emerge from this alive. He straddles my chest; punches me again and again in the face, but is too close to land a solid blow. He straightens up and swings at me with all his might. I jerk my head to the side; his fist cracks against the floor, the momentum of the blow tips him over. Frantically I wrestle out from under him and get to my feet. Grabbing a broken table leg I smash it down on him, again and again. No effect, except to enrage him more.

It's only Brak's drunkenness that saves me. He labours to his feet, slips and falls, whacking his head against the floor. A resonant *whump*. He lies there, dazed. I hit him as hard as I can across the head with the table leg and run for my life. I flee through the house, barely registering the carnage of broken and overturned furniture. Out on the veranda, the first thing I notice is that Gator is loose. He and Cracker are milling around on the veranda, old enmity apparently forgotten. Just my fucking luck to have this bloody brute of a dog loose and me, covered in blood, fleeing his master, his saviour. I picture myself being chased down and savaged, torn to pieces. But the dogs just bark and yelp in confusion as I sprint barelegged, barefoot down the drive. Cracker construes it as some sort of game and frolics along with me until we reach the broken gate where I stop and yell at him: 'Go home! Go on, *voetsak!*' Another bygone bit of vernacular that leaps to my tongue. He stops and looks at me with a hurt expression. I pick up a stone and make as though to throw it. 'Go on, *voetsak!*' Go home!' Crestfallen, Cracker turns and slinks off back to the house.

I keep running down the road, turning every so often to glance back. After a hundred metres or so the adrenalin that has sustained me thus far drains suddenly from my body, as though from a rupture.

My legs buckle; exhausted, I collapse on the side of the road and crawl under some bushes, gasping for breath.

I wipe the blood from my eyes with my shirt. My tongue flops around my parched mouth. Only now do I realise the soles of my feet are bristling with thorns. One by one I pull them out. I lie there, struggling to catch my breath. In the growing light I watch the house. The dogs mill around the front door, whining in the still morning air. A pair of doves starts calling from some thorn trees close by.

I wait. The sand in which I lie is cool and soft. Relief at having escaped the house floods through me.

Then Brak lurches from the house, a rifle in his hand. He staggers up and down the veranda, pointing the gun wildly. Incoherent raving. The doves cease their morning song. Brak stumbles down the veranda stairs, sprawling headlong onto the driveway. The gun goes off; a sharp whine as the bullet ricochets off into the bush. The doves burst from the thorn trees with a clatter of wings. Cracker scoots around the house, yelping, tail between his legs. Gator approaches Brak warily and gently licks his face. Brak clambers slowly to his feet, cursing loudly, and staggers over to the garage. Pulls open the doors, yelling like a madman. Goes inside, reappears. He stares out at the surrounding bush, cocks his head to one side. Then he lurches around the yard firing shots randomly off into the bush. The shots crack and echo in the stillness. I crawl deeper into the scrub, away from the road. I lie flat in a shallow donga behind a clump of trees. A bullet hits an ant heap twenty metres away, sending up a puff of red dust. Another clips a branch from one of the trees behind me. He fires again and again. Then silence. He stands, teetering against a gatepost, peering open-mouthed out at the bush. Everything is still; everything quiet, save my pounding heart. Brak grabs a handful of bullets from his pocket and reloads, stooping unsteadily to pick up some rounds he has dropped on the ground. He cocks the rifle and leans against the gatepost, scanning the countryside. His eyes swing towards the trees behind me. For a

230

moment he seems to be looking straight at me. I return his gaze, mesmerised. I think of that wounded man he hunted and killed, how when their eyes locked, the man's fate was sealed. Hunting is intuition, Brak said. I pray that he is too drunk to follow any intuition now. I only breathe when Brak turns away and looks down the road. He yells something, then lifts the rifle, aims and fires two shots, before staggering back towards the house. At the veranda steps he stops and stares, perplexed, as Gator approaches him. He looks back towards the gate once more, then goes inside.

I wait. When Brak doesn't emerge from the house again, I get up and start limping towards the main road.

At the crest of a low rise a kilometre from the main road, I see Reggie's car heading towards me, a plume of brown dust billowing behind. It accelerates up the rise and skids to a halt next to me. Through the whirling slipstream dust I see Clara is with Reggie; hazily I register the horrified expression on her face. It occurs to me that I must look less than spruce: standing there in my underpants, my vomit-stained shirt torn and bloody. I can barely see through my puffed up eyes; my upper lip is split and swollen.

They get out. I'm light-headed, nauseous; I seem to be swaying. Clara grabs my arm, steadying me.

'Frank . . . Jesus, what happened, Frank?' she says.

I just look at her, struggling to focus, my mind blank.

Reggie peers into my face and gently touches the gash between my eyes. She feels around my scalp, locating two big lumps on the back of my head. 'Probably concussed,' she says to Clara. She looks into my eyes. 'Frank, can you see me properly?'

I nod.

'Where's Brak, Frank?'

I point back down the road.

'At the house? Is he still drunk?'

I nod. 'He's got a gun. He's crazy. Don't go there, Reggie.'

Reggie looks down the road. 'He won't hurt me. Let's go.'

'Shouldn't we be getting Frank to a hospital?' Clara says.

Reggie inspects the gash between my eyes again. 'Ja, you can take my car but drop me off at the house first.'

'Don't go there,' I say. 'He's crazy.'

'I have to, Frank. I'm more worried about him than you right now.'

'No, Brak caused this,' Clara argues. 'He can bloody well wait.'

Reggie looks at her, resolute. 'All I'm asking you to do is drop me off at the house. A few kilometres won't make any difference.'

'Don't go back there, Reggie,' I plead. 'He's not . . .'

What I was going to say slips my mind.

Reggie smiles. 'I know what I'm doing. Brak needs me now. Just drop me off at the house.'

'Don't go, Reggie,' Clara says. 'Look at Frank. Fuck Brak! You're mad to go anywhere near him.'

Reggie turns towards the car. 'Are you going to drive, or must I?'

Clara turns to me and slaps her hands on her thighs helplessly. I struggle to make sense of the situation, yet something in Reggie's assuredness calms me. The morning sun beats down on us.

'Make up your minds,' Reggie says, getting into the driver's seat.

I climb into the back.

'This is crazy,' Clara says, getting in next to Reggie.

No one speaks as we drive. The car rattles loudly along the road. The sight of the house triggers a sudden panic in me, though I struggle to remember this morning's incident in sequence or detail. My memory seems able only to conjure up Brak's mad face and his drunken braying. Reggie stops at the gate. For a while we just sit there looking at the house. Cracker runs up, wagging his tail, cautiously followed by Gator. Reggie heaves a long sigh and gets out. She pats Cracker and allows Gator to sniff her legs. Gator gives a long trilling howl.

Reggie leans in the window. 'I'll pick up the car from your place sometime, okay?'

232

Clara nods.

'We can't leave you here,' I say.

'Don't worry about me. I'll be okay.'

'We'll wait awhile, just in case.'

Reggie's eyes scan my face. 'You need to get yourself seen to.'

'We'll wait. Let us know if everything's okay.'

We watch her walk up the driveway and enter the house.

'What happened, Frank?' Clara asks.

I shake my head. 'Not now, Clara.'

We sit in silence, waiting. No sound from the house.

Then Clara says: 'In case you're wondering how I happen to be here, Reggie came banging on the door last night after midnight. Wanted to know if Vic was there – she thought Vic could maybe talk some sense into Brak. But Vic and my mother decided on the spur of the moment yesterday to go to Victoria Falls for a break. Reggie spent the rest of the night talking to me about Brak's problems. I'm sure she didn't think it would come to this, though.'

'I wasn't wondering,' I reply.

'Why did you get so drunk? Reggie told me she'd warned you about Brak's drinking.'

I shrug.

Clara shakes her head and turns away, staring out the window. A wave of tiredness overwhelms me. I struggle to keep my eyes open. I try to inspect my thorn-ravaged feet but can't seem to focus properly. Then Reggie emerges from the house and comes down the drive, my trousers and shoes bundled up under her arm. She hands them to me.

'He's asleep. Passed out on the floor. Take Frank to the Mater, Clara. I'm sorry about this, Frank. He can be a monster when he drinks.'

'Are you okay staying here?' I ask.

Reggie nods, her face strained. 'I know him, Frank. The only person he's likely to harm when he sobers up is himself.'

'Do you want me to talk to Jervis?'

'No, we'll cross that bridge when we come to it. It's not the first time we've been in this situation.'

Clara shifts across to the driver's seat. Reggie straightens up and stands back from the car.

'I know it's a big ask, Frank,' she says. 'But try not to hold it against him.'

She waves tiredly as we drive off.

XI

My travel insurance covers my medical expenses at Bulawayo's private Mater Dei Hospital. My injuries are 'superficial' according to the doctor who examines me: slight concussion; a gash between the eyes requiring six stitches; a broken nose that will heal on its own and look no worse than it already does; a stiff neck; some bleeding beneath the scalp at the back of my head; and other minor cuts, swellings (two black eyes and a thick lip) and abrasions. This along with a king-sized hangover. The doctor prescribes a few days bed rest.

Since Hazel and Vic are away for the rest of the week, Clara insists that I stay at the house in Hillside (a relief, since I'd be mortified for the Ogilvy household, including Rosie and Geldof, to see me in this state). 'You can recuperate in peace,' she says. 'The maid and gardener have been given the week off, so we have the place to ourselves.' She installs me in the main bedroom and equips me with a pair of Vic's pyjama shorts. I shower and get into bed, feeling distinctly uncomfortable about invading Vic and Hazel's inner sanctum, yet too exhausted to object. From where I lie, half-paralysed by painkillers, I can't escape a large painting on the wall of a charging buffalo, its eyes glinting and horns silhouetted against a setting sun – the same painting that once graced the lounge in Vic's farmstead long ago. Also in my line of vision is Hazel's chaotic dressing table with its unbelievable clutter – magazines, hairdryer, cosmetics, lotions and potions. How much make-up does it take for a woman to look so unadorned? A small galaxy of photographs stuck to the mirror. Much like my mother's dressing table used to be. I sleep for hours. When I wake in the late afternoon my clothes have been washed and are neatly folded on a table next to the bed. The vomit gone from my shirt, the bloodstains not entirely. Clara tells me she has explained the situation to Milton. She has organised for him to pick up my car from Prospect Autos and drop it off later this evening.

I feel sufficiently recovered to get up for a light meal of toast and soup, my first meal in almost two days. Clara and I sit in the lounge eating off our laps. I try to explain what happened but the precise details are increasingly elusive; I can only manage a sketchy summary. I even try to joke about it, but inside I'm shaken, empty. I struggle to make sense of anything. Nothing is solid, dependable.

Milton arrives in the Nissan just as we finish eating. He lugs my suitcase inside and sits in the lounge; he chats briefly, cheerfully, something about Vernon having made his school's First Cricket Team – exceptional for someone so young. The lights go out; Milton doesn't miss a beat, continuing his banter while Clara goes around lighting candles. He says that Geoffrey Dlamini was dismayed to hear of Chombo's deceit and wishes to assure me that he will renew his own efforts to track Lettah down. This reminder of my original purpose here is like salt in my wounds. A woozy anger rises. I feel like sending word back to Geoffrey to stop playing games. There'll be no more money for fruitless searches. Or if his dismay is genuine then for God's sake wise up. There's no need to atone for anything. Not in this place where the only rules are those of tooth and claw.

But I just nod dumbly. At one point Milton looks at my swollen face and seems about to say something but doesn't – I think my expression tells him the subject of Brak is out of bounds. He gets up to go. I awkwardly shake his hand for no particular reason. My voice quavers as I thank him.

While Clara drives Milton home I try to phone Brak. The line is dead. I don't know why I tried. Perhaps, bizarrely, I seek his love like a child who has been chastised. For am I not also to blame? Reggie's warnings about Brak's drinking; the smashing of the guitar – why didn't I heed the signs? Brak's drinking makes my own occasional excesses seem like child's play. I know nothing about the frightening realms in which a man becomes something else through drink. A beast set loose.

I take a sleeping pill and am out like a light before Clara returns.

When I wake there is a ceaseless singing in my head, like distant cicadas. Even when I block my ears it continues undiminished. I lie in the darkness trying to ignore the sound, mercifully drifting off again. Somewhere in the night I feel Clara climb into the bed next to me. She nestles her head on my chest. Her hair smells sweetly of shampoo.

'Are you awake?' she asks.

'Yes.'

'Do you mind?'

Clumsily I kiss the top of her head. 'No.'

She kisses my neck and runs her hand over my chest. 'I like flawed men.'

I don't know what to say.

She laughs quietly. We lie there without talking, just a sheet covering us. I run my hand up along her bare thigh. She kisses me softly again and sinks back against the pillow. She starts to snore gently. Far-off, a dog barks. I feel the blood coursing through my veins, more aware of it than ever before.

I think of that insane look of intent on Brak's face as he pounded my head on the floor, as though by destroying me he would destroy his demons, as though *he*, not I, were the one fighting for his life. This is all I can remember now from the incident and I cower from the thought of it. I thank God that I had the simple good luck not to have fought a war that could not be won, and to suffer the consequence – the futility of being on the losing side. How do men like Brak heal? I think of what he said about the cathartic value of military parades and ceremonies. With victory come the spoils of catharsis and redemption. With defeat comes the long fall inside.

For days I drift in and out of sleep. In my conscious moments I'm plagued by headaches, dizziness and nausea, constantly drowsy and confused. The singing in my head persists. I visit the doctor again: it seems my concussion is worse than first thought. The doctor arranges a CT scan. There is only one local facility available, in Mpilo Hospital in the townships. I wait an entire day in this chaotic place before being attended to. The scan clears me of any bleeding in the brain; there is, however, a small fracture at the base of my skull. Nothing serious, the doctor says (an inveterate optimist); it will heal on its own but headaches and other symptoms may persist for weeks, even months. In the meantime I must take it easy. Clara tells me Reggie has phoned three times. Brak is apparently so depressed he won't leave the house. Reggie has talked things over with Jervis who responded with admirable compassion, assuring Reggie the job is Brak's to come back to when he is ready. She's been trying to get Brak to come and see me. I'm relieved to be spared the encounter.

Hazel phones frequently to find out if Clara is managing at the shop. She and Vic are staying in a self-catering holiday chalet in a bush resort a few kilometres from the town of Victoria Falls. It was Vic's idea to give Hazel a break from the stress of closing down the shop. Hazel complains that the resort is empty – the only people around are the manager and a handful of staff who knock off in the afternoons, and a solitary night watchman who spends his work hours busily snoring on a spare mattress in the storeroom. She says she is bored out of her mind. Victoria Falls appears to be a shabby shadow of its former self, having virtually ground to a halt as a tourist destination. The people who throng the streets now are mostly destitute locals; crime is rife. Clara tells her mother not to worry about the shop and implores her to relax and enjoy herself.

238

Clara mans Zambezi Pride each day, until noon when Vera takes over. She returns after lunch with awful tales of the terror and intimidation that is erupting across the country now that electioneering has started in earnest. Somehow Tsvangirai continues to traverse the country in a big red bus, attending rallies, despite constant harassment by the police. She tells me there has been havoc in the city. Crowds of looters, following the example of the police and army, have rampaged through stores, helping themselves to what little was left on the shelves. Shopkeepers who protested have been assaulted. Fortunately, Zambezi Pride has not been affected, African craft being way down on the looters' shopping lists.

We catch a news bulletin on TV where some fat apparatchik foists blame for the economic chaos on the business community. 'Let me take this opportunity,' he wheezes with straight-faced candour, 'to warn these economic saboteurs that time is up for them to mend their wayward behaviour by curbing their unbridled greed, corruption and self-enrichment at the expense of the majority of our people.'

Clara scoffs dryly. 'How wonderful to hear such succinct self-analysis!'

There is little about any of this that I find amusing. I'm plagued by black bouts of paranoia. Everything in this mad place is falling apart. A crazy president mouthing threats at every turn, exhorting his followers to violence. Inflation running at over a million percent. Store shelves bare of essentials. It's common now to have power cuts of twelve hours duration each day. Petrol stations have closed, due to sporadic supply. Since there is no fuel, there are no buses or trains. No shortage, though, for the Chinese warplanes that swoop low over the city. A sign of what to expect if things don't go Mugabe's way.

I can't wait to escape this unrecognisable land of my birth; it's just the tender ministrations of Clara that make it tolerable. I ponder how deeply she feels for me; I try to envisage a future together but can't. My flight back to Australia is still two weeks away; I must see about bringing my departure forward. Better still, perhaps a short stay in South Africa will make this journey worthwhile – perhaps I can entice Clara to come with me. When I put this to her, she surprises me by her immediate enthusiasm. We make plans: we will fly to Johannesburg and hire a car. Drive down to Pietermaritzburg where I'll show her my old stamping ground, and then continue down the coast to Cape Town . . .

But then I start to fret about whether we will be able to leave under the present circumstances. Will the airport be operating? Will there be fuel if we wished to leave by road? I feel trapped, claustrophobic. For the first time I understand what it means to be trapped in a fucked-up country. Clara laughs at my fears, doubling up when I put forward the worst-case option of hitchhiking to the South African border. 'I wish my mother was around to hear you,' she says, wiping tears away.

Yes, tribulation's perverse humour. A form of sustenance for Zimbabwe's stoic sufferers. Their mainstay. Joking while the country burns. Dancing in the grave.

At night she sleeps with me. We try to make love once but I can't perform, incapacitated by a splitting headache. Again, Clara is amused. An actual, genuine headache, she says. One for the history books.

The weekend looms. Hazel and Vic will return on Sunday afternoon and I'll need to move out. Back to Milton's.

Better not to think too far ahead.

Saturday – where has the week gone? I wake feeling somewhat better; the headaches and nausea have abated. Another hot, dry day beckons. We go for an early swim and have breakfast – mielie meal porridge with a lump of butter – outside on the veranda next to the pool. As far as food goes, it seems the Kent household will take a while before it feels the pinch; Hazel and Vic have stockpiled a sizeable hoard of mielie meal, flour and other basics in the pantry. The birds in the trees seem louder than usual; I wonder if it's a prelude to rain. As we eat, Clara suddenly puts her hand to her mouth, stifling laughter. She swallows and giggles helplessly.

'What's so funny?' I ask.

She shakes her head. 'Sorry. I just remembered how Reggie and I found you. Standing there in your underpants, looking like you didn't have the faintest clue what you were doing. Imagine if we hadn't come along – imagine if you'd had to hitch a ride back to Bulawayo looking like that!'

She dissolves into laughter again.

'You're a real font of sympathy, aren't you?' I say.

We swim again. To keep the stitches on my nose dry, I'm confined to wallowing about at the shallow end. I catch Clara staring at the big bruises on my abdomen and self-consciously cover myself with a t-shirt when we return to the veranda. We are drinking tea and perusing some South African road maps when Brak's Cruiser appears at the gate. Reggie opens the gate, then drives up and parks beside her Datsun under the flamboyant trees next to the house. Brak is slumped in the passenger seat. For a long while they sit in the vehicle; Reggie talks animatedly, Brak just stares downwards. The levity I felt earlier evaporates like water on a hot stone. Reggie gets out, sees us on the veranda and comes over. Her jeans and cotton blouse look grubby; her hair is a mess. Face drawn, haggard.

'Hi. Thought I'd better come and pick up my car.'

'Pity,' Clara says. 'I was getting quite fond of it as a garden feature.'

Reggie smiles grimly. Her eyes scan my face.

'Howzit, Frank? You're looking better than when I last saw you. The swelling's gone down, hey?'

'I'm okay, thanks,' I say.

Clara offers her some tea. Reggie shakes her head. Sighs miserably. 'No thanks. This isn't exactly a social call.' She glances over at Brak in the Cruiser. 'That bloody idiot . . . He won't even get out of the car. Like a scared kid. It's so bloody pathetic.'

'Guys like him should never drink,' Clara says.

Reggie looks at her sharply, a flash of anger in her eyes. 'You think

I don't know that? You think he doesn't know that? It's easier said than done, Clara. It's more than just the drink.'

'He needs help,' Clara says.

'I know. That's also why I'm here. Will you talk to him, Frank?'

'Talk to him?'

'Please, man. He's sorry about what happened . . .'

Her voice falters and she starts crying. Clara gets up and helps her to a chair. 'Reggie . . . come on, girl. Sit down and have a nice cup of tea. Come on.'

Reggie blinks back angry tears. 'Help him, Frank. He's your friend.'

I look at her, bewildered. 'He needs proper help, Reggie . . . professional help.'

'He'll listen to you, Frank. He needs your forgiveness.'

'He has my forgiveness.'

'*You* tell him that.'

'I don't know, Reggie —'

'Please talk to him. He'll listen to you.'

A short silence. Reggie and Clara stare at me.

'Talk to him, Frank,' Clara says. 'You don't want to leave Zim with this hanging over your head, do you?'

I shrug helplessly. 'Reggie . . .'

'Please, Frank,' she says. 'Just talk to him, man.'

I feel their eyes on me as I drag myself down the veranda steps and across the driveway to the Cruiser. I stop a few paces from the Cruiser, wary of the wounded animal inside. Brak sits facing away from me, looking down at his hands. As I come forward, he glances up at my face; he appears startled by what he sees and looks down again. The glimpse I get of the haunted torment in his eyes confounds me — it's as though another man sits there in Brak's skin. I stand at the window, angry yet still fearful of him, unable to find words. He just sits slumped forward, staring down at his swollen, scabbed hands, big and burly as ever — that battered wildebeest head, the huge chest and arms — yet diminished so completely that it dispels my anger and fills me with pity.

Words come, finally: 'Next time you want to party, remind me to bring a bodyguard along.'

He looks at me, shamefaced.

'Ja, I'm talking to you, you big bloody ape.'

The flicker of a desolate smile. He shakes his head. 'Won't be a next time.'

'Of course there will.'

'I'm never drinking again. Ever.'

'I'd love a dollar for every time you've said that.'

The same desolate smile. 'I can't go on like this, man.'

'Ah, the dawning of enlightenment —'

'Please, china, don't joke. I'm serious.'

'What can I say? No point in me shitting on you, is there?'

Brak puts his head in his hands. 'Shit on me all you like. I'm sorry, man. I can't believe the things I do . . .' He looks up, tears streaming down his face. 'I swear, it's like someone else takes over. I got no control . . .'

I open the door and climb in next to him. Awkwardly, I put my hand on his shoulder.

'Don't be sorry. Just get on top of it, man.'

'I *am* sorry! Fucking sorry.'

'It's okay, Brak. No hard feelings.'

'It's not okay. I always wreck everything. I destroy everything — every friendship, everything good in my life. This is it, Frank. I'll never drink again. I'll blow my brains out if I do. I swear to God!'

'That might be technically impossible.'

A short burst of laughter. 'Fuck off, Cole. I'm serious. It's over.'

There's a long silence. I glance over my shoulder. Reggie and Clara are watching us.

'Come on, let's go and sit with the girls. Both of us could do with some intelligent conversation.'

It's as if he hasn't heard me. He looks down at his hands again. 'I don't remember any of it. It's no excuse, I know, but I don't even remember getting back to my place.' He spreads his fingers, palms

243

downwards. 'Woke up with my hands all fucked up and the house looking like a war zone — didn't have a clue what happened. Reggie told me what I'd done to you. I just couldn't believe it. I turn into someone else when I drink, china. Believe me. The person you see sitting here would never hurt a friend.'

He puts his head in his hands again. Groans loudly. 'God, God, God...'

I flounder for words. 'Don't punish yourself. Just get on top of it, man.'

He sobs. 'I just wanna live a normal life. That's all I want.'

I put an arm around his shoulders. 'I'd be lying if I told you I wasn't pissed off. But I'm also to blame. I shouldn't have let things get out of hand. Reggie warned me about you. But what's done is done. From my side, it's over, okay? No hard feelings. There're much bigger things than me that you need to deal with. Just do what you have to do, man. You'll get on top of this — I know you will. You've got Reggie behind you all the way. That woman's something special. If I can help, just tell me how.'

He stares downwards. I reach out my hand. 'Come on, shake hands. Time to look ahead.'

Sheepishly, he sticks out his swollen paw. I clasp it hard. He gasps. I laugh. 'Ha! Gotcha!'

Brak laughs and wipes his face with his sleeve.

'Come on,' I say. 'Let's have some tea and talk to the ladies.'

Brak nods grimly. 'Ja, time to learn some fucking manners, hey.'

They stay the rest of the morning. We talk about good times, good things. Some lost ground is regained. The old Reggie emerges; she chaffs Brak in her blunt slang; she laughs and conjures up bright possibilities for the future. Some of the old Brak emerges too, though he can't quite dispel that doomed look, and lurking behind the up-beat banter is the indelible knowledge that things are not what they were.

They leave around noon. Exhausted, I go to the bedroom and fall asleep, my mind free at last of the angst that has plagued me since the assault, though I can't quite rid myself of the perverse notion that *I* am the one forgiven, not Brak — the psychiatric fraternity will have a name for this condition. I wake in the late afternoon. Clara and I swim and braai some chicken outside next to the pool, while the weaverbirds noisily roost in the nearby trees. We eat and discuss our travel plans. On Monday we'll organise flights to South Africa. Tomorrow, Hazel and Vic return; we savour our last evening together.

An inevitable power cut awaits us when we go inside. We shower in the dark and go to bed early. We make love by candlelight; Clara is in a playful mood — I am frequently referred to as 'Father Time' or 'Old Man River'. Something Márquez wrote about young women and old men floats into my consciousness. *Among the charms of old age are the provocations our young female friends permit themselves because they think we are out of commission.* Be warned, Clara! In the shadow of la grande mort, the little death grows ever sweeter.

Afterwards, we lie there, spent. The flickering candlelight on the walls of the room seems not of this century. Clara asks me if I believe in eternity, in the hereafter. I confess my scepticism. 'I do,' she says. 'I believe we're each the fulcrum of our own eternity.'

I imagine my mother peering down, shaking her head.

We talk for hours, it seems, before I drift off. I'm awoken by the telephone ringing. Clara groans and gets up to answer it. The slap of her feet on the parquet floor as she runs. The power is back on; there are lights shining down the passage and the faint mumble of the TV we forgot to switch off. Her voice saying cheerily: 'Hi, Mom, how's everything going with you two lovebirds?' A long silence. Then: 'You didn't tell me you were coming back tonight . . . Okay, just stay where you are. We won't be long.'

I switch on the bedside lamp. Clara appears at the door.

'That was my mother. They were on their way home and ran out of petrol. Just as well. Imagine if they'd come back to this.'

'What? To this *Cosmo* centrefold in their bed?'

245

Clara laughs and gestures at our things strewn about the room. 'Jesus, Vic would've had a fit.'

'What possessed them to drive back at this time of night?'

'A spur of the moment thing. Mom said they just couldn't bear another night at that crappy resort. Come on, we'd better get cracking. Are you okay to drive?'

'I'm fine.'

A quick change of sheets and pillowslips. Clara tidies the room while I pack my suitcase and load it in the Nissan, along with a jerry can of petrol and a funnel. We set off through the city and out along the Victoria Falls Road. Beyond the city lights the void of night closes around us, its darkness seemingly absolute but for the grass and trees rushing past, eerily illuminated. Shabby signs, one announcing: *No Petrol for 160 km.* Optimistic, one would think, in today's Zimbabwe. A strange sensation that we are plunging, our motion downward, not forward. Just a lonely flickering light every so often out in the blackness. We encounter no other vehicles. The headlights catch the occasional glint of eyes in the bush up ahead; I slow around each bend and over every rise, my recent brush with Zimbabwe's livestock still a raw memory.

Clara chats away, dispensing a limitless store of irrelevancies, only one of which is of passing interest – the origin of her name. Apparently, Hazel named her after a prehistoric site called Clara Cairns near the battlefield of Culloden, which she and Clara's father visited while honeymooning in Scotland. The picture of a young violet-eyed Hazel wandering about the Highlands, deciding to name a daughter after an ancient burial site, seems strange, given her avowed love of Africa. I'm surprised she didn't give Clara an African name.

Our lights pick up the VW almost an hour out of town, next to a sign pointing to St Luke's Mission. It seems Hazel and Vic have whiled away the wait constructively. They are seated in deck chairs around a folding table next to the car. Before them, an array of bottles and the remains of a picnic dinner. They raise glasses to us as we pull up next to the VW, grinning like two elderly meerkats around some roadkill.

Vic is positively festive. 'Hallelujah!' he booms. 'What took you so long? Cars are equipped with more than one gear, you know.'

'And I believe they require petrol to move,' I retort, climbing out. 'I thought motoring stuff-ups were my specialty, Vic.'

A big cheesy smirk. He turns to Hazel. 'Did you hear that, woman? That boy's developing a sense of humour at last!'

Hazel giggles tipsily and gets up from her chair and kisses Clara and me lavishly. 'What a magnificent, *shpectacular* night,' she slurs, waving at the stars.

'Mom, you're drunk!' Clara exclaims. 'Both of you!'

'Oh, don't talk rubbish. My generation does not get drunk. Young people today are *so* boring!' She catches a glimpse of my face in the reflected light. 'Except Frank, of course. Goodness me! What on earth have you been up to?'

'What's he done now?' Vic says, getting unsteadily to his feet.

'Frank here looks like he's been on the wrong end of a mule kick.'

Vic hobbles up and inspects my face, breath reeking of beer. 'Jesus H. Christ. And I suppose your friend Malan had nothing to do with it, hey?'

'Leave him be,' Clara says. 'Come on, it's late. How are either of you going to drive home in your condition?'

'Condition?' Vic booms. 'What condition? I'm perfectly bloody capable of driving, young lady.'

'No, you're not. Neither of you.'

'It'll be a cold day in hell before you tell me when I can drive, girl.'

Clara slaps her thighs, exasperated. 'God sakes! Are there any sober people left in this damn country?'

'Come on,' I say. 'Let's pack up and go.'

While I decant the petrol into the VW, Vic and Hazel pack up the table and chairs, amid much juvenile laughter and effusive exclamations. Clara attempts again to dissuade Vic from driving; Vic responds by plonking himself down in the VW's driver's seat, sniggering like a schoolboy. Clara implores her mother to travel back with us, to no avail. Hazel brushes her aside and gets in beside Vic.

Fishing in his pockets for the car keys, Vic sings raucously: 'Never mind the weather, as long as we're together – we're off to see the Wild West Show-oh-oh!'

A hoot of laughter from Hazel. Vic tries to start the engine and floods it. What I had smugly thought to be a reversal of favour in the auto-gaffe stakes ends ignominiously when Clara and I are called upon to push start the VW. After a few failed attempts, the engine finally splutters into life and off they go, wheels spinning on the road-side gravel, sounding like an old sewing machine missing the odd stitch.

We climb in the Nissan and follow. I floor the accelerator for a few kilometres trying to catch up, but Vic is going like the clappers. 'Slow down,' Clara says. 'You're just egging him on, trying to keep up. My God, they've both regressed to adolescents!'

I drop back; we watch the VW's tail-lights disappear into the darkness ahead.

'I've never seen my mother like that,' Clara says. 'I hope she's okay.'

I laugh. 'Of course she's okay. It's good to see her let go. All this stuff with the shop . . . it's cathartic.'

'Maybe. I hope so.'

Clara puts a hand on my leg and rests her head on my shoulder. We drive on in silence. I'm exhausted; the exertion of pushing the VW has given me a headache. After a while, Clara starts to snore gently. Her head slides off my shoulder; she jerks upright and yawns. 'How much longer?' she asks.

'Not far,' I reply.

We reach the city and drive through to Hillside. It's just after two; the roads are deserted but for a few stray dogs. The street lights in the suburbs are off, the houses are shrouded in darkness. Turning into Sable Avenue, Clara sighs with relief at the sight of the VW at Hazel's gate, lights shining, up at the end of the street. 'At least they're home in one piece,' she says.

As we drive up the road a man suddenly bursts into vision; I brake as he runs past the car, arms flailing, and disappears behind us into the night. Just the flash of eyes and teeth. A dirty torn shirt. 'Jesus . . . what was that?' Clara blurts out, looking back out the rear window. I drive on and turn into the driveway behind the VW. The VW is still running, its doors open. We emerge to a terrible theatre. Lit by the VW's lights, Hazel is lying up against the gate, her arms around Vic. Vic is on his back, his striped polo shirt gleaming darkly with blood. A red froth around his mouth, an edge of his loosened dentures protruding. His eyes have rolled back, white and sightless. Hazel is keening like a frightened child.

XII

A day of policemen and forensic procedure. We go through it in a daze. Hazel summons enough composure to walk detectives around the crime scene. She signs a statement written out laboriously by one of the detectives, an enormous bald-headed man called Mkonto. Because Clara and I witnessed the fleeing assailant, we too must answer questions and sign statements. The policemen go but Mkonto returns with a thick folder of mugshots which we peruse without success. It was all a blur to Hazel, the killer just a black shape against the glare of the VW's headlights. All Clara and I can recall is the white flash of eyes and teeth. The flapping of his unbuttoned shirt as he ran past. Finally, Mkonto leaves. Clara makes tea and we sit, exhausted, around the dining room table, the silence deafening. Hazel seems calm and collected; she volunteers some small talk about the old Ndebele woman who wove the small round mats on the table – something about her having been born with just a thumb and finger on both hands. But then she sees Vic's suitcase standing in the hallway. Her eyes glaze and she slips back into shock.

I return to Kumalo in the evening. Ruby and Vernon are shocked by my grisly appearance but nothing is said. Rosie and Geldof stare at my still-swollen nose and puffed eyes, open-mouthed; Precious emits a long 'Mayibabo!'

I take refuge in the cottage, like a beast in its hole. I collapse on the bed and fall into a deep sleep, filled with bad dreams. I wake sweating in the darkness, seeing Vic's sightless eyes, still tasting his blood in my mouth after trying vainly to resuscitate him. Hazel's eerie keening . . .

I imagine her getting out of the car to open the gate. I see the man leap out of the darkness into the glare of the headlights. So suddenly, she barely has time to utter a cry of alarm before he grabs the handbag slung over her arm. Instinctively, she hangs on to the bag's strap. A tug-of-war ensues. Struck dumb with terror, yet still holding onto her bag, Hazel stumbles about until she loses her footing and falls heavily against the gate. The man looms over her, a knife in his hand. Perhaps he intends to kill her; perhaps he intends merely to threaten her or to cut the bag free. Whatever lurks in his thoughts in this instant remains mercifully inert — Vic's final moment has come. It has taken a few seconds for Vic's addled brain to compute what has been happening in the glare of the lights. Now, realising the mortal danger Hazel is in, he erupts from the car, roaring as only Vic can roar. His eruption from the car, it's fair to assume, is slow and ponderous, given his age and inebriation. However, there is nothing slow and ponderous about his vocal chords — a deep-throated barrage of abuse flies thick and fast. Unnerved by the crazed, white-haired old man bearing down on him, brandishing his walking stick, the robber panics and turns to flee. But Vic is already upon him, managing to mete out a couple of solid clouts with his stick. The robber lashes out, stabbing Vic twice — in the stomach and heart — before running away. Vic gives a sharp cry before collapsing onto Hazel. And she knows by his limpness that he is already dead.

Hazel shuts herself up in the house in Hillside and won't see anyone but her doctor, Clara and the maid, Daphne. The doctor prescribes a course of tranquillisers which Clara struggles to get her mother to take, resorting to crushing the pills and mixing them in cups of tea. She drops in at Milton's from time to time to let me know how things are. I ask if there is anything I can do, knowing the answer. Time – she just needs time, Clara says. Needless to say, there is no further talk about travelling to South Africa.

I try to phone my father but can't get through.

Speaking of phone calls, Geoffrey Dlamini calls to give me updates on his renewed search for Lettah. He lists several charity organisations and church websites he has consulted. When he calls a second time I can barely contain my exasperation.

'Look, Geoffrey,' I say, 'I don't believe Lettah Ndlovu can be found. There's no need for you to persist –'

'Don't misunderstand me, sir. I don't want more money. I want to show you that we are not all like Chombo. The world must know that among Zimbabweans there are still many people of honour.'

'Of course there are. But –'

'I am a man of faith, Mr Cole. I believe in the premise: seek and ye shall find. I called today to say that I have placed a notice on my church email newsletter. It goes to people all over the world.'

'Thank you, Geoffrey. You've done more than enough.'

After putting the phone down, I lean my head against the wall. Fuck. Why these small mockeries . . .

My attempt to present a façade of composure to the Ogilvy household proves futile. So I confine myself mostly to the cottage, emerging only for an occasional dip in the pool or to join the family at mealtimes. I count the days until my departure, the spectre of Vic haunting my thoughts.

One evening, there's a knock on my door. Milton enters, clasping an old Olivetti typewriter to his chest, a ream of paper balanced on top.

'Thought you might find a use for this old beast,' he says.

He puts the typewriter and paper down on the table and sits on a chair. He looks at me, prone on the bed, with a wry smile. 'You might as well grow a beard and change your name to Van Winkle,' he says.

'I guess so.'

'We live in interesting times, boyo. No time to waste sleeping.'

'Interesting?'

A long silence. Milton drums his fingers on the table. 'You know, when I first met Vic I thought he was the biggest fool on the planet. That big mouth. Strutting around like he owned the world. I remember when we took on his case, him bellowing: "You bloody lazy shysters better get those kaffirs off my land, or else!"' Milton laughs and shakes his head. 'I felt like asking him: Or else what? The old bigot never seemed to twig that he was powerless. He seemed blissfully ignorant that when Rhodesia changed to Zimbabwe power also shifted from whites to blacks. Ja, Franco, I thought a lot of things about Vic Baldwin, and most of it negative. But then he does the knight in shining armour caper. He comes to the rescue of his damsel, Hazel. His courage is tested and he's not found wanting. It kind of redeems him, don't you think? Makes us realise that there's more to people than we think.'

I shake my head. 'Hazel should've just given her bag to that thief. He would've run away. There was no need for any heroics.'

'But she didn't. And Vic did his duty as a man. If that isn't worth writing about, I don't know what is. Can't you see what I'm getting at? It's time to get your arse into gear. Get to work, boyo. It's been handed to you on a plate.'

I look at him dumbly, chastened.

Milton gets up. 'Come on, Ruby says dinner's just about done.'

Tiring of persistent enquiries as to her health, Hazel decides to have a few friends around for evening drinks. I arrive at the house at dusk and park behind a dozen or so cars in the driveway. Clara opens the door when I knock; she administers a cool, aunt-like peck on the cheek and shows me inside. Hazel's guests, mostly elderly couples, are gathered in the lounge – the only one I recognise is Vera Ndube. Daphne shuffles around with a tray of savoury nibbles, her eyes red from weeping.

I'm shocked by Hazel's appearance. She sits in her chair like a shrivelled bird, smoking with a trembling hand. A glass of sherry stands untouched on the table beside her. I'd never looked on her as old before, now she seems ancient, skeletal. I'm relieved that my own appearance is considerably improved, attracting only a few inquisitive glances: the swelling on my face has subsided, the stitches have been removed. I kiss Hazel on the cheek. She looks at me with a slightly glazed expression, smiles and nods. Clara points me to a chair in the corner, asks me if I'd like a drink and leaves me to my own devices when I decline. I watch uncomfortably as Hazel's friends chat quietly. Soothing tones. Offers of support; gentle reminiscences. I shake my head when Daphne also offers me a drink. Across the room, Clara is deep in conversation with Vera, her back to me.

Hazel stares blankly ahead; now and then she attempts to take part in the conversations, but her sentences dissipate into nothing. The effect of the tranquillisers, I suspect. Then her eyes focus on me; she beckons me closer. I crouch next to her chair.

'Clara told me what happened with Brak,' she whispers. 'Are you all right?'

'I'm fine.'

She stares at me and smiles. 'Have you phoned your father? Does he know about Vic?'

I shake my head. 'I've tried but can't get through.'

'Try my phone. Go on, Errol would want to know.'

I glance at my watch: it would be around midnight in Perth. A bit late to be calling, but a good excuse to escape. I go to the phone in the passageway. The fickle gods of Zimbabwe's telephone service are with me tonight: after only two attempts, Errol answers. I explain what happened. After a long silence, he says: 'My God, that's terrible news. How is Hazel managing?'

'She's taken it hard. Still in a state of shock, I think.'

Another silence.

'Has there been any mention of the funeral?'

'Not as far as I know.'

'Make sure you attend. It's important. Your mother and Hazel were very close. Give her my condolences. Tell her I'll phone, okay? Tomorrow.'

'Okay, Dad.'

'I suppose you're looking forward to coming home.'

'You suppose correctly.'

Back in the lounge, Hazel's friends are clustered around her and Clara is still yakking away with Vera. I can't bear the scene any longer.

'Dad sends his condolences,' I tell Hazel. 'He'll phone tomorrow.'

'Thanks, Frank. I'm glad you got through.'

I lean close. 'Hazel, I . . . I'm terribly sorry about what happened. I'm sorry about the things I said about Vic. If there's anything I can do . . .'

Hazel smiles soporifically and nods. 'Thank you, Frank. Don't fret.'

Clara follows me outside. We stand in the darkness next to my car. Crickets singing. She takes my hand and kisses me. 'My mother's been a full-time −'

'You don't have to explain anything, Clara. I understand.'

'She needs me, Frank.'

'Of course she does.'

She embraces me. Though we kiss long and tenderly, I feel we make a ludicrous spectacle.

A door closes and another opens. Each day I rise early and take my place in front of Milton's typewriter. I write until lunch, surprised at how quickly the initial trickle of words becomes a steady stream. There is no grand message in what I write; I seek merely to make some sense of my journey. I write about my search for Lettah, undaunted by the shadow of failure. And I begin to understand that the gift I was entrusted to give has bestowed another upon me.

A succession of cloudy, humid days. Hawks fixed on prey flutter high against brooding, heavy skies; there are distant rumbles of thunder but nothing comes of it. Still, the parched countryside seems to take heart in the promise of rain. In the shadows of clouds, the shrivelled bush acquires a faint blush of green. You get the impression that what has survived so far in this place of drought will prosper, given the smallest chance.

I exist in a strange, suspended state. On the one hand, a sense of failure. My search for Lettah farcical in its naiveté. My reunion with Brak a debacle, to say the least, and now Vic . . . On the other hand, there are these pages piling up next to Milton's typewriter. I well know the folly of overstating creativity's restorative powers, but that tired old sense of futility that has wreaked my own drought for so many years seems to have loosened its grip. Something long dormant has germinated, the words I write its pale shoots.

Clara has told me, unequivocally, that our travel plans to South Africa are out of the question. She is too preoccupied with looking after Hazel and winding things up at Zambezi Pride, which has now been placed largely on her shoulders. That and a dozen other things. All completely understandable, except that her strategies of extrication are plain to me, being a master of them myself. Perhaps, in the wake of Vic's death, she has gained objectivity and sees our brief affair as a minor virus to which she's now become immune. Still, it's by no means a complete volte-face. She vacillates between stand-offishness and sporadic bouts of affection. She drops in at the cottage from time to time, but never stays long. We have dinner twice at the Selbourne Hotel in town. On both occasions she is warm and cheerful — even festive, after a few drinks. She gives me some copies of the photographs she took at Brak's place. The one of Brak and me in front of the dead donkey on the car rather horrifies me, but I pretend good humour. She laughs at my banal witticisms; she expresses seemingly genuine disappointment that our travel plans have come to nought, yet adds that she's keen to visit Australia. She kisses me passionately, though briefly, in the car when I drop her off at the house in Hillside. And the next day — aloof, distant. I gird myself for the inevitable. In moments of cold reason I too begin to see our relationship for what it is — a passing encounter, a fling — though I'd hoped it was something more. I'm forced to acknowledge that I have met my match in Clara. Our aversion to commitment makes us soul mates of a sort. C'est la vie, as she would say. The only way to retain any dignity is to keep my composure.

I've postponed my departure a few days so I can attend Vic's funeral. My bags stand beside the cottage door, half-packed. My health is much-improved; the headaches are few and far between, the nausea and dizziness all but gone. Each afternoon I visit Hazel, never staying too long. She is looking much better, more her bright and cheerful self. I spend the late afternoons ambling through the kopjes near the Hillside Dams, searching in vain for those San paintings I saw as a boy. In the evenings I have long chats with Milton. About writing. About life. It pleases us both to know that our friendship has grown in strength. We pledge not to let so much time elapse before we meet again. Milton has his car back. Prospect Autos has done an excellent job; the old Cortina looks brand spanking new. Milton is delighted with the metallic-blue finish. It warms my heart to see Rosie and Geldof lording it off to school, noses in the air, in what Geldof now calls the 'spensive car'.

Bulawayo's dwindling white community feels the deaths of its members keenly; consequently there is a respectable turnout at Vic's funeral at the Anglican chapel in Hillside. I kill time outside the chapel before the service, standing in the shade of a drooping frangipani tree, just about melting in my tweed jacket. I watch the mourners turn up, sweating in their formal wear. Hazel and Clara arrive with Vic's sons, Hugo and Cecil, who have been staying with them since arriving yesterday. Hazel in a plain grey frock and a thin black shawl around her shoulders; she appears serene, composed. Clara wears a snug-fitting black dress, showing perhaps too much cleavage for this occasion. They smile and wave at friends and go into the chapel.

257

Hugo and Cecil have flown in from Manchester and Toronto respectively — Vic's other sons, now living in America, couldn't make it. Fat, bald businessmen in black pinstripe suits, the two tarry outside the chapel entrance, smoking nervously. I only know who they are because they arrived with Hazel and Clara — had they walked past me in the street, I'd never have recognised them. When I introduce myself they greet me with back-slapping gusto. I notice Cecil still has the lisp that afflicted him as a boy; he has learned to avert attention to it by choosing his words carefully, unlike Hugo who gabbles on like a parrot. They pull the same genial show when Brak pitches up, arm in arm with Reggie. Brak is amused by the Baldwins' hale-hearty greetings. No doubt, they remember him from their Que Que Junior School days. He never took kindly to their bullying. After he planted a fist on Hugo's nose and made him cry, they gave him a wide berth.

When Hugo asks about the few residual bruises on my face, I say that I whacked my head on the diving board at the municipal swimming pool. Brak sighs audibly as the Baldwins commiserate and just smiles stonily when they ask if he's been practising his diving too.

Hazel emerges from the chapel and hurries over. 'My dear, I'm such a scatterbrain!' she exclaims, putting a hand on my arm. 'I meant to ask you earlier. We need two more pallbearers. There seems a dearth of able-bodied young men around. Would you and . . . ?' She glances at Brak. 'Good gracious, I don't believe it! Brak Malan — is that really you?'

Brak smiles. 'Hello, Hazel.'

'My, my, now there's a surprise! Would you and Frank be so kind?'

'I'd be honoured,' Brak says.

She stands on tiptoe and kisses him on the cheek. 'My, how you've grown . . .'

Brak, bursting out of his old grey suit, blushes crimson.

We go inside. Hazel greets Daphne and the gardener, Jeremiah, sitting patiently in their Sunday best in the back pew. I sit next to Brak and Reggie, two rows behind Hazel and Clara and the Baldwins in the front pew. The chapel entrance and altar are ablaze with flowers, the air filled with the fragrances of roses, chrysanthemums and strelitzias.

The congregation waits quietly for the service to begin. Milton and Barry Braithwaite arrive last and quietly take a seat at the back next to Daphne and Jeremiah. Fans hanging from the rafters whirr loudly. A wrinkled old lady with tightly coiffed white hair and tortoise-shell spectacles plays a succession of sombre tunes on the organ. I listen, my eyes fixed on the stained-glass windows above the altar depicting the Resurrection. In the middle of a ponderous version of 'How Great Thou Art', there's a power cut. The organ dies, emitting a sad, falling note; the fans above rattle to a stop. The organist gives the congregation a philosophical smile, removes her glasses and gazes heavenwards. The sweating congregation titters.

We wait. Vic's coffin is positioned in front of the altar, bedecked with a bouquet of white chrysanthemums. My eyes stray to Clara. Her auburn hair has been done up in a simple bun, exposing the freckled whiteness of her neck. I stare at the graceful forward tilt of her neck, swanlike beneath the sharp square line of her jaw. She reminds me, obscurely, of a fifteenth-century marble bust of Isabella of Aragon that once caught my eye in a book – poised, winsome; a strange, ethereal demeanour haunted by a pious inwardness. Strange how we construct from opposites.

Clara reaches back and rubs the nape of her neck. I avert my gaze.

The service is conducted by Reverend Buchanan, a grey-haired priest with the tall, gaunt build of a long-distance runner. He enters in his white robes and stands at the pulpit. We start with a hymn, 'Praise, my Soul, the King of Heaven', led by an impromptu choir comprising five earnest though not entirely harmonious octogenarians, taking up position next to the defunct organ. Beside me, Brak and Reggie sing with zeal.

After the hymn, Reverend Buchanan blesses the congregation in a pronounced Geordie brogue: 'May grace and peace from the Lord be with you. Those who die in Christ share eternal life with him.

259

Therefore, in faith and hope we turn to you, dear God, who created us and sustains us all. Let us reflect upon the life of Victor Baldwin, the dear departed soul before us . . .'

I lose track of the service trying to get my head around the notion of Vic dying in Christ. I think of his booming blasphemous tirades; the way he ridiculed Brak's conversion, raising his hands above his head and clapping. How did he earn the respect of these people? How did he earn my father's respect? How did he win Hazel's heart? Why was Brak 'honoured' to be his pallbearer? What have I missed in this man who now lies in a box before me? The image of Vic lying with Hazel against the gate in the car's headlights assails me suddenly. Those blind white eyes bulging from their sockets; the bloodied dentures poking out of his mouth . . . I shiver.

Reverend Buchanan speaks of the terrible cost of Zimbabwe's descent into anarchy:

'. . . the madness and cruelty that afflicts the hearts of those who govern this land has consequences far beyond the more obvious spectacles of political oppression. It is easy to witness the sight of protesters being beaten, of homes being bulldozed, of farmers being chased off their land by thugs – it is easy to witness such evil and put two and two together. But when a desperate thief, stealing so that he might live, takes the life of an innocent man, the arithmetic becomes more complex. The true quotient is much more difficult to calculate. But, dearly beloved, if we are honest and accurate in our calculations we will see that it adds up to exactly the same thing. This is the true tragedy of Zimbabwe, that out of desperation ordinary men become complicit in the bigger crime committed by those in power. So I ask you all, as God's children, to harbour no malice towards the one whose tragic actions have brought upon us this sorrow. Ours is not to pass judgement. Do not harden your hearts with hatred and bitterness. God awaits us all. Trust in Him and you shall receive the Kingdom of Heaven . . .'

Hugo delivers a eulogy that starts as a confident, humorous series of anecdotes, but ends in choked whispers. He paints a picture of a larger-than-life father, a man of the soil, strict but fair, a stalwart Rhodesian. He tells of an idyllic life growing up on the ranch, of the joys of returning home from boarding school and how he never dreamed then that their piece of Africa would soon be gone. Vic emerges a saint, always with the best interests of his family at heart. Hugo glances at the coffin below the pulpit and fights back tears. As he struggles on, Hazel pulls her shawl close around her shoulders.

Brak and I join Hugo and Cecil and two other men in carrying the coffin out to the waiting hearse. The coffin seems extraordinarily light; I remember how emaciated Vic had been, the folds of skin hanging like furled sails off his arms and the flap under his chin looking like a bull's dewlap. We load the coffin into the hearse. Hazel puts her hand on it for a few seconds. She closes her eyes and mouths a few silent words. Then the undertakers close the hearse doors and depart for the crematorium. Hugo and Cecil watch the hearse go, their faces grim.

Brak and Reggie offer their condolences to Hazel and the Baldwins and depart immediately – Brak must get back to work at Prospect Autos; Reggie, I learn, has just started part-time work as a manicurist at a friend's beauty parlour – it seems odd to me that such things as beauty parlours still exist in Zimbabwe. Milton and Barry Braithwaite also have pressing engagements at the office. A few others, including Daphne and Jeremiah, depart too. The rest of the congregation assembles in the adjoining hall for tea and cakes. I find myself stuck in an endless exchange with Hugo and Cecil. We reminisce on what fun we had as kids in the good old days when life was perfect. When Rhodesia was God's own country. I'm puzzled by my compliance in a camaraderie that has no real basis. I nod with assurance when Hugo suggests that I visit him in Manchester. Hazel sidles up, cup and saucer in hand. She informs me that they – she, Hugo and Cecil – will be driving up to Kwekwe to spread Vic's ashes on the old property. To my dismay, she puts me on the spot by asking me to accompany them.

'Oh, I don't know, Hazel. I've still got a few things to tie up.'

Hazel laughs. 'Nonsense. It'll take just a day.'

With no way out, I agree. Hugo slaps me on the back.

'It'll be mush to visit the old joint,' he says.

Mush? Ah, yes, another quaint expression of yesteryear. I glance at Clara who has managed to avoid me again by talking with Vera. Yes, it will be mush to get away from Bulawayo for a while. Even with old enemies.

As soon as the Baldwins' attention is diverted by a passing tray of scones, I make my escape, only to be intercepted by Reverend Buchanan who has stepped outside the hall for a quick fag. He offers me a smoke and soon I find myself deep in conversation. The old cleric has a way of teasing out information from the unwary. In no time at all, I've divulged the story of Lydia's will and my futile search for Lettah. Taking long drags on his cigarette, Reverend Buchanan listens, smoke streaming from his nostrils, asking a probing question now and then. He talks of his own experiences during the Gukurahundi terror of the eighties; how he gave refugees from the countryside shelter in this hall – the churches, he says, were often the only sanctuary for the persecuted. Stubbing his cigarette out with his heel, he rummages around in his robes for a notebook and pen. He writes down Lettah's name and promises to keep an ear to the ground. You never know, he says.

XIII

I become increasingly light-hearted and sociable as my departure, which I now look upon as my 'release date', draws near. I enjoy a succession of pleasant evening outings with Milton and Ruby to various friends' houses and a perfectly civilised alcohol-free dinner with Brak and Reggie at the Churchill Hotel — so civilised, in fact, as to be agreeably dull.

And I look forward (almost guiltily — pleasure seeming an improper indulgence at such a time) to the hours I spend each day at the type-writer. Perhaps this rekindled passion lies in the noble though tenuous thought that the world might conform to purpose through words and sentences; perhaps I merely seek refuge in the long silences as time slow-marches by . . . still, a strange assuredness has taken hold of me. In my mind, Australia has assumed an almost transcendental status. My impatience to return lies not so much in resuming my life there but in the firm conviction that a *new* life awaits.

Clara has continued in her flighty way. To say that I'm unaffected by her behaviour would be a lie, but I'm not exactly moping around either. Last night there was an unexpected visit. Passionate and brief. Almost what we briefly had, yet an ending too.

I was lying awake when she arrived at the cottage in the early hours. A shuffle of footsteps outside; a knock on the window. I pulled the curtains aside, then got up and let her in. Smiling, she extracted a flask of brandy from her jacket pocket and waved it in front of my face. Without speaking, she rummaged around the cupboard for two glasses and poured us each a stiff drink. We sat at the table in the darkness, staring at each other, taking swigs of fire. Her strangeness too much to question. She glanced at the typewriter and the stack of pages next to it and nodded to herself. Hardly a word had passed our lips when suddenly we burst into laughter. Relieved laughter, as though a great weight had been lifted from our shoulders. Then we fell silent again and drank. Clara kept topping up our glasses until the brandy was finished. Then she undressed and lay on the bed. Serenaded by crickets and the barking of distant dogs, we made love in the darkness with a melancholy intensity. My hands committed her body to memory; her breasts, the softness of her stomach, her smooth flanks, all stored for future reminiscences of loss. We kissed as she heaved under me. She climaxed and rolled on top of me and rested her head on my chest, squeezing her thighs as I huffed and puffed my way across the line of the masters event. She bit my skin gently, her panting slowly subsiding. I ran my hands down her sweating back, lingering on the Promised Land.

She laughed softly. 'I think you have a bottom fetish.'

'Tell me about it.'

'Mmm, what would you boys be without your wee perversions?'

She sighed and rubbed her hand over my chest. The shampoo in her hair smelled oddly like raspberry cordial is meant to taste.

'Do you think I'd like Australia?'

A little flame flickered.

'I think God made Australia for people like you.'

'Why?'

'Maybe he thought the world needs a home for the uncommitted and irresolute. People like me and you.'

'And Perth? Do you think I'd like Perth?'

'Like Perth? I promise, when God built Perth he had you in mind. He said, right, how can I build a beautiful city next to the Indian Ocean that would make a beautiful, irresolute red-haired girl happy?

A girl with the name of a prehistoric site in Scotland and a perfect bum. And, voilà! Perth was born. Just for you.'

She laughed. 'Liar!'

We lay there listening to the night sounds.

'You know it's not going to happen,' she said.

'What?'

'Me going to Australia.'

'Why not? What else are you going to do?'

'Stay here. With my mother.'

'Jesus, you and your mother. Living proof of genetic insanity.'

She giggled. 'I'm being serious, dammit! Now that Vic's gone, I can't leave my mom alone. Not at her age. I've given it a lot of thought, Frank. With my overseas income I could afford to take over Zambezi Pride. It'll be tight, but I could keep it going for a few years at least.'

'And what happens if it all falls through? What then?'

'I'll face that when it comes. But I have faith in the future. Mugabe can't live forever. When he goes things will turn around.'

'You're crazy, Clara.'

'Maybe. But it's a chance for me to do something. Something real.' She kisses me. 'You could always stay too.'

'And do what?'

'This country was once the most literate in Africa – you could help make it that way again. There're thousands of kids here just dying to be taught. I don't know, Frank. Do what you have to do. I've made my choice.'

Then she got up and started dressing. I watched her in the darkness. She finished and sat on the bed next to me.

'Frank, I won't be at the airport when you go. I hate soppy goodbyes.'

I got up and embraced her. We kissed for a long time. Her cheeks were wet. The last thing she said was: 'The real Perth is Scotland's ancient capital, by the way. Just up the road from Edinburgh. I have relatives there, on my father's side. A bonny place.'

*

265

Hazel and the Baldwins pick me up just after seven. We set off to Kwekwe in the Baldwins' hire car, a Peugeot sedan with a broken air conditioner; Hugo and Cecil up front with Hugo driving, Hazel and me in the back with the urn containing Vic's ashes between us. It soon becomes hot and uncomfortable, even with all the windows wound down. Only Hazel seems unperturbed by the heat. A sheen of sweat covers the faces of Hugo and Cecil, now both clad in short trousers and safari-style shirts. Thongs on their chubby white feet. Hugo appears to believe in the necessity of non-stop conversation; he talks and talks, about politics — the war in Iraq, Islamic fundamentalism (dropping a 'nucular' bomb on northern Pakistan is his answer to finding Osama Bin Laden); and social issues — pornography and the internet, bad role models (the solution to the likes of Britney Spears and Paris Hilton, he says, is to recommission the pillory and shoot the paparazzi). Vic unplugged. Cecil is more circumspect. A man of few words. I remember how mercilessly Hugo and his brothers used to tease him about his lisp, their singsong incantations: My name ith Thethil. My mommy thays I'm thpethal. Thpethal Thethil. Thpethal 'cauth I'm Thethil . . . on and on they'd go until Cecil erupted and fists started flying and Vic would have to go hunting for a stick.

Still, Hugo's garrulousness spares the rest of us from any major contributions to solving the world's problems. Hazel seems her old self, laughing at the odd hybrid accents of us three 'boys' — a curious mishmash indeed. 'Isn't it fascinating?' she says. 'All these funny half-Rhodesian accents. What strange mongrels you are!'

Hugo and Cecil opt for a quick stop at a butchery in Gweru for some biltong. The best on the planet, Hugo claims. Or it used to be. Hazel and I wait in the car while they lumber inside like two bulls, the sweaty seats of their trousers plastered against their fat backsides.

Hazel huffs. 'My goodness, just look at the size of those boys! They've just had breakfast and all they can think about is stuffing their bellies! They must spend half their lives on the loo.'

Perish the thought. We wait, watching the throngs of people in the shade of shop awnings. 'Nothing else to do but stand around waiting for better days,' Hazel says. 'Dear me, such a waste. Such a waste . . .'

She lights a cigarette and takes a few drags, blowing the smoke out the window. 'I was hoping I'd get a chance to talk to you alone. I'm sorry about Clara. I'd so hoped you two might make a future together. You seemed so suited.'

'We are suited, perhaps for not the best of reasons.'

Hazel smiles. 'She exasperates me, that girl. All of her relationships have been the same. I thought it might be different with you.'

I laugh. 'What? Did you think our allergies to commitment would cancel each other out? Maybe it's for the best.'

'I'm fond of you, Frank. I'm sorry it's like this. I wish it was different. For Clara's sake, I wish it was different.'

'I'm sorry too, but she's done a good thing.'

Hazel nods. 'Yes, I can't look a gift horse in the mouth.'

The Baldwins return to the car. Hugo plonks a huge brown paper bag full of sliced biltong between the seats. 'Help yourselves,' he says. Hazel declines. As we proceed on our journey, Hugo and Cecil tuck into the biltong with unseemly zeal. It keeps Hugo's jaws occupied for a while, at least. I manage to salvage a few pieces; the biltong is, as Hugo claimed, superb.

As we cross the Kwekwe River, ten kilometres from the town, I recall my earlier visit to Sunnyside – the people occupying my old home, the two men and the women watching me from the veranda while I took photographs, the kids begging for money. The sense of unease. It seems a lifetime ago. I think of the derelict house and wonder about the power of place, about the deep pull of nostalgia. What are places of origin, other than fonts of loss and longing? Why is it our human lot to yearn for the past, when such yearning is surely futile?

Coelum non animam mutant qui trans mare currunt. Those who cross the sea change the sky above them, but not their souls. Of all the Latin that was drummed into my head at school, this imperial dictum by the Roman poet Horace is all that remains. English-speaking whites in Africa will always be British was the implication. But a broader implication – that the place, the home, from which the soul emanates also remains unchanged – strikes me now as sadly delusional. Those who travel away from home seldom realise that while their souls may remain unchanged, their home, like everything else, transforms with time. There are no souls so lost as those chained to the past. To the memory of home. Like me, they return to find their home inhabited by strangers. Only its shell recognisable.

At Kwekwe's outskirts a faded blue Standard Bank sign greets us with the confident slogan: *Inspired. Motivated. Involved.* Hugo pipes up: 'Anyone need a pit-stop in Kwekwe?'

'I'm fine,' Hazel replies. 'Do you want to go past your old house, Frank?'

'No thanks.'

'Are you sure? It's no trouble.'

'I'm sure.'

It takes only a couple of minutes to drive through Kwekwe, along the avenue of jacaranda trees with their white-painted trunks, past the high school and post office, down through the shabby heart of the town. I'm engulfed again by that strange déjà vu I experienced during my first visit. Everything so familiar, yet another place entirely. Hazel points out the old shop she owned, now, like many others, empty and boarded up. We pass a mosque with an emerald green dome on the northern outskirts, the only building in good nick, and emerge again into the shimmering countryside.

A few kilometres beyond the Sebakwe River we turn off the Harare road and head east along a rough dirt road towards Dutchman's Pool. Horizons dance behind heatwaves. The roadside scrub is coated with fine brown dust lifted by passing vehicles. We turn off again onto a road heading north-east towards a range of hills called the Great Dyke. Granite sandveld, dry, mostly infertile; cattle country, though now the land appears devoid of stock. Dense msasa woodlands peter into patchy acacia bush and open grassland vleis. Some lowveld trees, mopani and baobab. Hugo ceases his gabbling; the brothers gaze pensively at the familiar countryside, pointing out a landmark here and there. I wonder what their memories hold. In what esteem do they hold this place that was once their home? We've passed several squatter camps flanking the road; mud huts and makeshift shanties surrounded by meagre plots of brown, withered maize. People emerge languidly from these dwellings to watch us pass by, heedless of the dust swept up by the car. The only animals we see are a few dogs scavenging around the settlements, starving wretches with tails between their legs.

We cross the Great Dyke and come within sight of the ranch. A mood of unease permeates the car. The Baldwins become increasingly jittery. 'Hope it's okay driving around these parts,' Hugo says. 'Maybe we should've checked with the authorities.'

Hazel scoffs at the notion. 'Authorities? What authorities?' She remains calm, gazing ahead serenely, as though every problem of the world has some divine purpose. She is adamant that we go on, insisting it was Vic's wish to have his ashes spread next to a spring near the Baldwins' old homestead, a place he remembered as being always lush and green and loud with birdsong. 'It took the thought of dying to bring out the poet in him,' she ruminates. Without her, I suspect Hugo and Cecil might have dumped Vic's ashes on the side of the road and beat a hasty retreat back to the safety of the main road.

At last Hugo pulls up at the entrance to the ranch. He is surprised to see the old sign – a half-log, grey with age, with the name Thorn Drift carved into it – still hanging by two chains from the bough of a dead gum tree next to the gatepost, which once boasted a gate. He and Cecil gaze apprehensively up the old road that used to wind for a couple of kilometres through thick bush before you came to the homestead. Now it runs only as far as a dozen or so huts a few hundred metres from the entrance.

Hugo shakes his head. 'No way we can drive on that road. Remember how sandy it was, Cess? We had to put gravel on it every year. I bet it's never been maintained since Dad got kicked off. What d'you reckon, Cess?'

Cecil shakes his head too. 'No way.'

'Park here,' Hazel says. 'We can walk.'

Hugo and Cecil look at her as though she is touched.

'What?' Cecil says, pointing at the squatter camp. 'Walk through there? You've got to be kidding, Hathel. No way!'

'Oh, for heaven's sake! You boys are frightened of your own shadows. Have you ever heard of *diplomacy*?'

Hugo grunts and looks back up the road. 'If you want to take a stroll through that happy little hamlet, be my guest, Hazel.'

A woman tending a fire in front of one of the huts spies us. She shouts out something; people emerge from the huts. Soon a mob of about twenty stands there watching us. A buzz of talk. Some men begin to walk towards the car.

'Drive in,' Hazel says. 'The road looks fine to me.'

'Bullshit,' Hugo replies. 'They've got axes and knobkerries.'

Hazel rolls her eyes. 'Axes and knobkerries are like socks and shoes in this country. It doesn't mean they're hostile.'

Hugo is gripping the steering wheel, his knuckles white. 'I'm not taking this car onto that bloody road. Look at it! A bloody sand trap. If we get stuck, then we're really stuffed.'

'Dear me! You young fellows! So quick to fear the worst, hey?'

In this matter I find myself squarely in the Baldwins' camp. 'We shouldn't be taking unnecessary risks, Hazel,' I say.

Hazel sighs, exasperated. 'We're just throwing some ash on the ground, for heaven's sake. It'll be fine if we just explain.'

With the car running, we wait for the group of men, six or so, to approach. The man leading the procession is old and wizened with a white goatee. His tattered khaki overalls look as if a grenade exploded in them. As he comes closer, Cecil exclaims: 'Well, I'll be buggered, Hugo! Geth who that ith?'

'Holy Moly!' Hugo says, the realisation hitting him. He turns to Hazel and laughs. 'That's our cookboy – old Bobo!'

'Bobo? I wouldn't be calling a dignified old African man a baboon in modern Zimbabwe,' Hazel says. 'However endearing you may think it is.'

Hugo looks stricken. 'Oh, for Chrissake! What was his real name, Cess?'

'Thit, I dunno.'

Hugo almost yells: 'Shilling! That's it — Shilling!'

'Thank Chritht!' Cecil sighs.

Hazel chuckles. 'You mean he had a demeaning nickname before you gave him another one.'

Hugo switches off the engine. 'Shilling was a good munt, hey Cess? He won't cause any crap with us.'

He and Cecil climb out of the car and walk towards the approaching men, their thongs making *thok thok* sounds. Both sweat profusely in the midday sun, their skin pale, anaemic. As they meet with Shilling and the other men, Hugo affects his now familiar show of heartiness. He jaws away, shaking Shilling's hand enthusiastically, African-style, all smiles and laughter. Cecil does likewise, shaking the other men's hands too. Shilling does not appear to reciprocate with any pleasantries. His face is like stone. No smiles, no laughter from the men flanking him either. They just watch the fawning white men impassively. Hugo babbles on, gesticulating towards the car, pointing in all directions.

'What's he saying?' I say.

'I don't know,' Hazel replies. 'I don't speak Shona.'

'Doesn't look as though he's making much headway.'

Hazel raises her eyebrows and nods. The sun burns down with a fierce intensity. We open the back doors to let the air through.

'I'm not sure if this was the brightest of ideas,' I say.

'I didn't think anyone would object to us just throwing some ash on the ground.'

Now Shilling is talking, loud and angry. He points his knobkerrie emphatically at the car. Go, the gesture says. You and your brother, go! Hugo begins to argue, his voice plaintive. Shilling shakes his head briskly and points the knobkerrie again. When Hugo continues to argue, Shilling switches the knobkerrie around in his grip, so that the ball is in his hand, and, without further ado, whacks Hugo hard across the side of the head with the other end. He clouts him again across the shoulders. The other men raise their knobkerries and axes and feint at Cecil who stumbles backwards in fright. Hugo stands there dumbly holding his head, apparently in shock. Another clout across the head from Shilling elicits a short, high-pitched yelp. Needing no further indication as to the status of their welcome, the Baldwins turn and walk smartly back towards the car. When Shilling and the men begin to follow, waving their weapons in the air, Hugo and Cecil bolt like spooked cattle. The pent-up breath in me escapes like a slow puncture. Oh Christ, I think, what have we got ourselves into here? Hazel, usually so calm and composed, grips my arm tightly. It occurs to me to jump into the driver's seat and prepare for a quick getaway but the keys, I notice with dismay, are not in the ignition.

'Christ, Hazel. We're completely bloody helpless!'

Hazel doesn't reply. She just watches Hugo and Cecil stampeding towards us, knees pumping, her nails digging into my arm. The Baldwins pile into the car. Cecil has lost a thong. In a wild panic Hugo fumbles for the keys in his pocket; he starts the engine and stalls while attempting to reverse out of the entrance. Suddenly Shilling and his men are around us, brandishing their weapons. Eyes wide, teeth bared, shouting and taunting. One of them strikes the bonnet with an axe; the blade breaks through the metal and remains lodged. A deafening banging as they pound the roof with knobkerries. Cecil yells in terror. Hugo starts the engine again and wheelspins backwards, away from the men. Back on the road, he slams the car into gear and roars off in the direction we came. His ear is bleeding; blood is soaking the collar of his shirt. 'Fucking bastards!' he curses. He and Cecil are streaming with sweat; they pant, open-mouthed, like dogs. I look back: Shilling is clowning around, dancing in small circles, waving his knobkerrie surmounted by Cecil's lost thong. The men around him laugh and cheer.

Hazel takes some tissues from her bag and dabs at Hugo's ear. He winces.

'Here, hold this until the bleeding stops,' she says.

Hugo holds the tissue against his ear with his left hand. He is driving, one-handed, like a maniac; the car careens around bends, the axe embedded in the bonnet swinging from side to side. Shilling and his mob have long since disappeared from view; still, Hugo guns along. Hazel reaches over the seat and taps his shoulder. 'Slow down, Hugo,' she says.

'That bloody old kaffir!'

'Stop the car, Hugo,' Hazel says. 'Come on, calm down.'

'We shouldn't have come here in the first place! I'm sick of this bloody country! These idiots can have it for all I care!'

'You're forgetting something, aren't you?'

'Bugger the ashes, Hazel!'

'Please stop the car, Hugo.'

'Hazel, I am not —'

Cecil almost shouts: 'Lithen to her, Hugo! Pull over, man!'

Hugo heaves a long, loud sigh, jams on the brakes and skids to a halt in the middle of the road. Just the distant chortling of a dove filters through the seething silence.

'Now, let's think about this, boys,' Hazel says. 'We've got a job to do here.'

Hugo puts the car into neutral and applies the handbrake. We get out and inspect the damage. Cecil wrenches the axe out of the bonnet and flings it angrily into the bush. Hugo runs his hand over the roof of the car, peppered with small round dents. He wipes the sweat from his forehead with his sleeve. 'Christ almighty!' he curses. 'Who's going to fix this, hey?'

Jervis's saturnine visage looms. 'I can recommend someone,' I say.

Hazel asks: 'Where's the boundary of your property, boys?'

'Back a bit,' Cecil replies.

Hugo says, 'That bloody spring is out of the question, if that's what you're thinking.'

'We'll just have to compromise, then, won't we?' Hazel argues. 'I suppose it doesn't matter where precisely we spread the ashes.'

'Yeah,' Cecil agrees. 'Anywhere on the farm will do.'

We drive back to where the boundary of the farm begins, near a derelict cattle-loading ramp. From this point we can see at least a kilometre in all directions; there's no sign of life anywhere, no huts, no people. We clamber through the barbed-wire fence near the ramp. Hugo and Cecil glance around nervously, trespassers on their own land. We walk towards a windmill near a baobab tree, some fifty metres from the fence. Cecil steps gingerly on his one bare foot. Hazel carries the urn with both hands against her breast. The windmill's pump shaft is broken and the rusted blades spin futilely in the fickle breeze. We stop and stand together. The heat is like a weight on our shoulders. The bushes around us aloud with insects. The windmill squeaks and rattles as it turns.

Hazel hands the urn to Hugo. 'This is for you boys to do.'

Hugo nods and takes the urn. With sudden tears gushing down his face, he opens the urn and shakes some of the ashes onto the ground. It lies almost invisible on the powdery earth. He hands the urn to Cecil who spreads some more. Then Cecil gives the urn to Hazel; she empties it.

They stand silently. The windmill squeaks and rattles. Insects sing. Hugo puts his hand on Cecil's shoulder and says in a choked voice: 'I've already said my piece at the funeral. Hope you're satisfied, old man. But I can just imagine you looking down at us, bitching like hell because we didn't do exactly what you wanted. Anyway, now you're back on your land – back home again. Rest in peace, you old tyrant. Say howzit to Mom for us.'

Cecil bows his head, staring grimly at the ground. Sweat drips from his nose. The words in him seem to burst like the sounds from a drowning man's mouth. 'Well, Dad, here we are. Hope you're happy back where you belong. Back on your land. Too bad how it all ended. I got only one thing to thay: Demanded love ith not love. God be with you, old man.'

Hazel looks at him, baffled by this last-minute insubordination. She clears her throat. 'I suppose your father was a difficult man, but he did the best he could in this world.' She pauses, eyes closed. In a thin voice, she recites:

> When that this body did contain a spirit,
> A kingdom for it was too small a bound;
> But now two paces of the vilest earth
> Is room enough: this earth, that bears thee dead,
> Bears not alive so stout a gentleman.

I feel my chest gradually tighten. I struggle to breathe, smothered and confused by conflicting emotions. Unexpected tears well into my eyes, not just for Vic and his sons, or Hazel, but for my parents too, one gone, the other old and frail. I yearn for both, am thankful for both.

'Okay, that's it,' Hugo says abruptly.

He turns and starts walking back to the car. I follow, my head averted from the others.

Demanded love is not love. Everything I harbour against those who use brute force to make others bow before them is somehow summed up in that one unoriginal statement. A statement all the world's tyrants might reflect upon. How did Cecil – dull Cecil with his terrible lisp – manage to hit the nail on the head? Perhaps it was just the way it was said, the naive honesty of it, or the bitter inflection he gave to each word. It makes everything else that was said in the wake of Vic's death burn away like mist.

I'm busy in the cottage wrapping some gifts – books, chocolates and a Wallabies rugby jersey for Milton, Ruby and Vernon; some US dollars in an envelope for Precious, Rosie and Geldof – when Milton shouts from the house: 'Frank – telephone!'

I hurry across to the house. It's Geoffrey Dlamini.

'From what your friend Milton tells me, I've caught you just in time,' he says. 'I'm very happy to report that I've had some luck in locating your Lettah Ndlovu. Remember the notice I put on my church's email newsletter?'

'You did mention something . . .'

'Eh-ja. Well, a priest from South Africa has emailed me to say a Zimbabwean woman answering to that name is at his mission in Zululand. A place called Hlabisa.'

I'm stunned. 'Are you certain?'

'All I can say is that a woman answering to that name and approximate age is at this mission. But I cannot be completely sure if it's the same Lettah Ndlovu. Better you talk with this priest. His name is Reverend Gabriel Mkhondo.'

'I don't know what to say, Geoffrey. Look, can I pay you —'

A dry chuckle. 'I'm not Chombo, sir. You have already paid me for this result. I'm happy that you can have trust in me. Now, do you have a pen? I have the details here.'

I scribble down the priest's name and telephone number and thank him profusely before putting the phone down. I stand there for a while, dumbfounded by this last-minute turn of events. Is this how life must always be? Unpredictable — coming in surprises? I can hear Ruby and Precious chatting in the kitchen. They have been busy all afternoon, preparing what they ominously call my 'last supper'.

Milton looks up from his newspaper when I go through to the lounge. He nods slowly as I share this unexpected news.

'Amazing how these things pan out,' he says.

'To be honest, I'd put Lettah out of my head completely.'

Milton puts his newspaper down. 'So how does this affect your travel plans?'

I sit on the couch next to him. 'Not much. I was planning to spend a week in South Africa anyway. I'm not banking on anything. It's not certain this *is* Lettah.'

'Can't be that many Lettah Ndlovus in the world. Will you be passing through our old crime scene en route?'

I nod. 'I'll have a beer at the Imperial Hotel for you.'

'Ah, the good old Imp . . .' Milton's eyes widen with alarm. 'That doesn't mean you'll be hiring any more cars, does it? I understand that yet another car underwent a violent transformation up in Kwekwe –'

'You can't pin that on me.'

'On the contrary, Franco. We lawyers are trained to spot the links between things. Now if you take a number of recent vehicle mishaps, including one involving the sad demise of an innocent beast of burden, what would you say is the common factor?'

'Get stuffed.'

Milton laughs. 'We're going to miss you, boyo. Zimbabwe's automotive repair industry will too, I'm sure. Jervis should be here to present you with a gold watch or something.' He stabs a finger at the newspaper's front-page photograph of Mugabe embracing Iran's President Ahmadinejad. 'Once you're gone it'll be back to Zim's Goon Show re-runs, starring Comrade Bob.'

'You're always welcome in Perth if the comedy gets too rough.'

'Who knows? Maybe some day.'

We sit in silence for a while. There is the clattering of dishes in the kitchen. Precious cries out: 'Aibo! Kuyatshisa!'

'Ja, I told you it's hot,' Ruby says. 'But you don't listen!'

Precious laughs: 'He-hehh!'

'I suppose you'll be glad to get back to Oz,' Milton says.

I nod. 'I'm afraid this little school of hard knocks is a bit much for me. I'll leave Africa for romantics like you.'

Milton smiles. 'Romantic? Me? The only romantics are you bastards overseas who know bugger-all about Africa.'

'I don't know how you live with it, Milton. How can you stay here, knowing it's never going to change?'

'Franco, Franco . . . who said it's never going to change? You have to have faith, man. There are more good folks out there than bad.'

'The trouble is the good folks never get to call the shots here.'

'They will. One day.'

I get up. 'I'd better get back to my packing. Thanks, Milton.'

Milton waves his hand dismissively. 'Why don't you give that Mkhondo fellow a call. I'm sure you're dying to talk to him. Give your old man a ring too.'

'I think I'll leave my father out of it for the time being. I'm scared it'll be another dead end.'

'Have faith, Franco. Have faith.'

I try Reverend Mkhondo's number a few times. I get through but it just rings. I look at my watch: six-thirty. Must be his work number.

A curious logic has guided the reconstruction of Bulawayo's Joshua Mqabuko Nkomo International Airport. In a country where three-quarters of the population live below the poverty line, where life expectancy hovers at just over thirty, it was decided to build an enormous state-of-the-art airport. To cope with what? A massive increase in air traffic? All those tourists and foreign business folk flocking to Bulawayo? As it is, South African Airways has downgraded its service to Bulawayo from Boeing jets to small Fokker turboprops. The old airport, which faithfully served Bulawayo since colonial times, has been demolished and scaffolding for the new airport stands proudly in its place, devoid of any signs of activity. As an 'interim' measure, domestic and international arrivals and departures are processed in a large oven-like hangar.

My luggage is checked in. There's an hour to go before take-off; the customs officials have not yet arrived. I sit at a table in a makeshift lounge sipping a Coke. Comrade Bob stares at me from his portrait on the wall. I'm now heartily sick of that wretched gaze. I think of how some, very few, still manage a semblance of normality in their lives here despite the havoc he has wreaked. Like the Ogilvys. The fine meal we had last night. A roast leg of lamb and vegetables followed by an old-fashioned gooseberry pie. Precious, Rosie and Geldof joining in the occasion. Milton topping up our glasses of soft drink with as much panache as a waiter dispensing good wine. Rosie and Geldof flanking Vernon at the end of the table, chattering away with their mouths full, eyes gleaming. Vernon leaning over and helping Geldof cut his meat, laughing when Geldof abandoned cutlery altogether, much to Rosie's disdain. Geldof raising his plastic mug aloft like a torch of freedom when Milton proposed a toast to better days. Yes, sweet moments of normality . . .

I can't help overhearing the talk at a table close by. A family leaving the country. Talk of who will be there to meet them in New Zealand. Last-minute calls on their cell phones.

The stifling heat drives me outside. In the shade of a jacaranda tree near the car park, I smoke my last cigarette – to mark the occasion of leaving Zimbabwe, I've vowed to quit. A lazy trickle of traffic comes and goes. I take a last drag and stub the butt out with my heel. With an air of grim finality, I scrunch up the empty cigarette pack and throw it into a bin.

Inside, the customs officials have still not appeared. I sit down at a table again, exhausted. I hardly slept last night. I close my eyes, trying to think of what lies ahead.

'Howzit, china.'

I open my eyes. Brak is standing there in his overalls.

'Thought I'd drop in and say cheers.'

I pull out a chair. 'Hey, Brak!'

He sits down and looks around at the other travellers. 'Suppose they're all gapping it.'

'I suppose so.'

'Ja, well, good luck to them. Can't be easy making the move overseas.'

'A bit easier than staying here, I'd guess.'

Brak smiles and nods slowly. He eyes Mugabe's portrait on the wall. 'Hey, Bob, what d'you reckon? When you gonna croak, you bastard?'

We shoot the breeze. Brak tells me his landlord overseas has virtually scrapped the rent, to entice him to stay on. Now that he and Reggie are both working, things are looking up. No talk of them leaving. People like them kind of deserve Zimbabwe, he says. Not for the faint-hearted. Best wait and see what happens with the elections. If

Mugabe goes everything could turn around, just like that. He tells me the two dogs, Cracker and Gator, are now the best of mates. He jokes about the day to day dramas at Prospect Autos. Yet all the while he seems ill at ease, drumming his greasy fingers on the table, glancing around. Three customs officials, thin as scarecrows, stroll in through the main doors with a collective air of importance. We watch as they take up their position in their cubicles. The people around us hurry to join the queue.

'Suppose it's time to say adios,' Brak says.

'That queue will take a while to get moving.'

Brak drums his fingers again. Then he leans forward.

'China . . . look I don't know how to say it, man. I'm sorry about what happened. I just hope there're no hard feelings . . .'

His voice tails off; he smiles cheerlessly.

'You don't need to say anything, Brak.'

'Ja, but I hope it's not an issue.'

'It's not an issue. Forget it.'

But it is an issue. I know it. He knows it. And it has nothing to do with forgiveness. Looking at him across the table, huge, hulking, so troubled, I feel closer to him than my own brother. Yet I fear him too. The other Brak.

'You know, it's strange,' he says. 'There were only two times in my life when I really felt I was doing something right. That I was of some purpose to the world. The first was in the army. The second was when Reggie and I were up at Kariba.' He nods to himself. 'Ja, purpose . . . funny how it can be two completely different things. I suppose it's all about belief, hey? Belief gives you purpose.'

'I suppose it does,' I say.

The queue is starting to move.

'No hard feelings, Brak. Just look after yourself.'

'Keep in touch, china.'

We stand and shake hands. Brak pats my shoulder awkwardly. 'Come again when this hellhole decides to join the civilised world.' He laughs. 'That may be never. Come again, anyway.'

'You bet,' I say.

Brak smiles, and in his eyes I see something of the kid I used to know. I join the end of the queue. Brak waits until I have gone through customs. He waves as I go through security.

As the plane gains altitude, I can see, far below, the vast wilderness of Matobo. I catch a glimpse of the cross on the bald dome of Nungu glinting in the sun. How small that rock colossus seems now. I watch it vanish into the distance behind the plane. And I think of the time I looked up from down there and saw the vapour trail of another plane. I think of how different I am now.

XIV

During the flight, it seemed Lydia and Lettah were perched on my shoulders. A long-forgotten incident from Que Que kept bobbing to the surface of my thoughts. I was walking on my own through the bush near Sunnyside. It was late winter and the bush had recently been burned off in anticipation of the spring rains. I came across a wide donga filled with ash. The ash was white and pure like I imagined snow to be. Too much to resist, I waded into it. The ash was wonderful, exquisite, softer than powder. When I was waist deep I raised my arms and keeled over headlong into it, not expecting the bed of still-smouldering coals lying beneath – young boys and common sense are mostly birds of a different feather. The pain was instant, terrible. I reared (dare I say ashen) from the donga, my hands, forearms and legs covered in big red burns, and limped home to Lydia.

My mother was a stickler for old-fashioned remedies. If the old folk believed that burns were best treated with hot water who was she to argue? I howled as she submerged me in a steaming bath. A glimpse of Lettah at the bathroom door, an expression of distress on her face. Cupping her hands over her ears. After virtually parboiling me, Lydia put me to bed, then drove off to get some salve at the chemist. I heard someone running more bathwater. Lettah appeared at the bedroom door. 'Woza, nkosana,' she said. 'Come, I will make you better.'

I shrank away in terror.

'It's cold water,' she said. 'I promise it won't hurt you.'

She led me back to the bathroom and helped me into the bath. I lay in the cool water. What wonderful, immediate relief! The relentless pain was gone in an instant.

'Stay in the water,' she said. 'When your mother comes back let her see that the cold water works better. But don't tell her it was me who showed you.'

I hire a car at the airport in Johannesburg and drive down to Pietermaritzburg. It would, of course, be easier to catch a connecting flight to Durban, but I reasoned the six-hour drive would give me time to get things into perspective. Lost in thought, I traverse forgotten landscapes: the bare bleakness of the highveld; the epic vistas of the Drakensberg; the rolling meadows and forest plantations of Mooi River and Nottingham Road. There have been good rains in South Africa, especially in KwaZulu-Natal; the dams are full, the countryside is green, cattle and crops are abundant — nothing could contrast more starkly to drought-ravaged Zimbabwe. Thoughts of Zimbabwe, now my terrible yardstick, trigger conflicting emotions: I'm relieved — grateful — to be away, yet cannot escape an unexpected sense of loss, of bereavement. I thought I wasn't one to pine for a mother country. Something has changed. I'm glad to be away from Zimbabwe's depressing hopelessness, yet as I revel in the verdant landscapes of South Africa, I can't escape a simple irony. Zimbabwe has blown life into my dank, shallow lungs.

Memories of the past weeks are mostly too raw to dwell on, though. I still must shield my mind's eye from Vic lying dead, or Brak's drunken rage. It will take time to come to terms with these things. Clara, too. Hindsight offers little comfort when it comes to her. Each time I reach out to close the door she left half-shut I see a classroom full of expectant African children waiting for me to enter. Ah, Clara . . . what is shared when voids intersect? Yet, strangely, this prospect – me returning to Africa to teach – doesn't seem entirely implausible. There are options open to me. Many things are possible. Right now, though, it's best that I banish her from my thoughts. Let me finish this journey first.

I reach Hilton, on the outskirts of Pietermaritzburg, at dusk and book into a hotel for the night. I phone Reverend Mkhondo from my room – the first time I've been able to speak to him. We talk briefly; I am lucky to have reached him in his office at that hour, he says. He gives me directions to find the mission hospital near Hlabisa. He is adamant the Sister Lettah Ndlovu employed at the hospital is the one I'm seeking. He begins telling me something about a speech impediment – he uses some technical terms I assume are de rigueur among speech pathologists – and promises to explain when I get there. We agree to meet two days hence.

After breakfast I drive down the Sweetwaters road into Pietermaritzburg and spend the day slowly cruising about. The city still has its old Victorian charm, yet seems to wear its colonial history like an exfoliating skin. No longer the English oasis I knew. White faces are scarce among the dense crowds in the city centre; most whites appear to have retreated to the suburbs, barricading them-selves in homes that have become small fortresses. Our old house in Scottsville is almost unrecognisable, having undergone major exten-sions, including an electrified security fence; a bull mastiff watches me from behind a tall iron gate as I drive past. Judging by the signs affixed to virtually every suburban property, armed-response burglar alarm systems are obligatory. All so different. Still, there are moments of déjà vu: Alexandra Park along the Dusi River with its swathes of plane trees, just beginning to lose their summer greenness; Maritzburg College with its red-brick buildings and terraced sports fields, like something out of Kipling. I pass the Imperial Hotel, but don't stop to have that beer for Milton in the Emmeline Pankhurst Bar. I'm sure he wouldn't object.

I park in the shade of some trees in Alexandra Park next to the Dusi, a spot where my family often used to picnic. Watching the murky brown river flow by, I tuck into a greasy meat pie and a can of ginger beer for lunch. There is a strong compulsion to have a cigarette, but quitting smoking has become something of a test of fibre for me, as my mother might have put it. With all this driving around visiting old haunts Lydia is much in my thoughts. Everything seems to remind me of her – strange, in that I've never associated Pietermaritzburg with her before in any significant way. I find myself in silent conversations with her and remember how happy she had been here, how that brooding expression in her eyes seemed to lighten with contentment. Pietermaritzburg suited her. A nice, easy town. Not too big, not too small. A plain little house in Scottsville that she transformed into a home. A happy family and a good circle of friends. Had Max and I not left for Australia, and had illness spared her, I can quite imagine she and my father would still be here.

Under the trees next to the Dusi, I'm suddenly glad to be on my own in the place that had made Lydia happy. Alone with her presence.

In the evening I drive down to Durban and book into a hotel on the beachfront along the Golden Mile, as it was formerly known. The concierge warns me not to venture on foot outside the hotel after dark as the chances are I'll get mugged. My room is on the thirteenth floor. I keep my windows wide open all night, letting in the sea breezes. I sleep restlessly, waking often. I lie there, sweating in the humid air, listening to the traffic down below and breathing in the dank, fetid smell of the sea.

There is the same dank smell as I drive north towards Zululand. The Indian Ocean's warm amniotic breath. A ceiling of low cloud slowly burns away, leaving the air hot and humid. It's a three-hour journey; a dual carriageway as far as Mtunzini, and good roads, I'm told, thereafter up to St Lucia and on to Hlabisa, near the Swaziland border.

The greenness everywhere is a sight for sore eyes. Vegetation seems to explode from the ground. Through patches of coastal forest and endless fields of sugar cane, I think of the multitude of chance encounters that have led me here. The almost total extent to which our lives are shaped by others has never occurred to me so profoundly before. People use the term *spitting image* to denote likeness. Hazel said that I'm the spitting image of my father. To me, this had always been a nonsensical term until I learned that it's a corruption of *spit and image*. The notion that we can be the very substance and likeness of others presents a tantalising contradiction. We are unique because of all of those who comprise us. All of those whose lives have intersected randomly, coincidentally, with ours. We are all made of others.

A quaint thought, but will Lettah — if this person at Hlabisa *is* Lettah — harbour such fancies? Or will she have cut out that part of us that exists in her, like a surgeon cuts away a tumour? Perhaps the violence that eclipsed her life has been so great that it routed everything that came before.

Near St Lucia I branch off inland. Away from the coast, the land opens up into vast valleys ringed with distant blue krantzes. The vegetation thins into acacia bushveld, strewn with eerie green fever trees and aloes on the rocky ridges. The road to Hlabisa cuts through the Hluhluwe-Umfolozi Park. Glimpses of game: giraffe, impala, zebra; a rhinoceros browsing alongside the road. These sights lift my spirits. Perhaps on the way back I might take a more leisurely drive through the park. Perhaps even stay a night in one of the lodges.

Beyond the park, the road rises up over a great range of hills. Long blue wreaths of smoke from Zulu kraals dotted along the slopes hang in the valleys below. I overtake buses and taxis filled to overflowing with human cargo. I zoom past herd boys waving on the side of the road, tiny against the surrounding vastness.

Hlabisa is typical of the small neglected towns of South Africa's old Bantustans: a dusty huddle of buildings straddling the road north to Swaziland. Shops with security grates. Pep Stores, Spar, KFC. Billboards with smiling kids eating porridge or sporting shiny school shoes. Roadside vendors selling vegetables under bright umbrellas.

A cell phone dealer operating from a shipping container. Lined-up minibuses with flamboyant names: Baby Cakes, Lover Boy, Tequila Sunrise. People wandering about, congregating in the shade of trees. Litter. Stray dogs foraging around overflowing bins. A heifer nibbles at tufts of grass at the base of a telephone pole.

Following Reverend Mkhondo's directions, I drive through the town along the Nongoma Road. A few kilometres further on, Hlabisa Mission appears on the left across a small valley, against a south-facing hillside. From a distance the mission is dominated by a church steeple, a double-storey hospital complex and a reservoir on the hill above. A high security fence glinting with razor wire runs around the perimeter of the complex – South Africa's crime epidemic affects even missions, it seems. I negotiate a winding dirt road across the valley, passing processions of people heading to or coming from the mission. I stop at a boom gate; a security guard hands me a clipboard with a form on which I enter my name, the vehicle's registration number and time of arrival – 10.55 a.m. I ask the whereabouts of Reverend Mkhondo. The guard points towards a building fronted by a long veranda adjacent to the church. The office at the end, he says.

The gravel road crunches loudly under the tyres as I drive slowly towards the building. I park outside the office, climb a flight of steps to the veranda and knock on the door.

Reverend Gabriel Mkhondo is a stocky man of indeterminate age. When he opens the door, I assume he's in his mid-thirties, but soon realise he's older – somewhere around my own age, perhaps. He greets me warmly with a handshake and a broad smile display-ing widely spaced teeth. His head is shaved completely, enhancing his youthful appearance. Black-rimmed glasses. A slight nervous tic beneath his left eye. Despite the heat he wears a full-length black cassock.

I'm ushered inside and accept his offer of tea. He pulls up a chair for me next to his desk, switches on a kettle standing beside a small sink next to the window and busies himself making tea. The office is cluttered. A computer hums on the desk. The walls are painted with pale institution-green enamel, bare except for a whiteboard with what appears to be a roster scrawled untidily on it, its metal frame festooned with notices. A crucifix on the wall above the desk carries the legend: *God Will Guide You*. Filing cabinets line two walls. Folders are balanced in teetering piles on the desk and all over the grey-carpeted floor.

'Excuse the state of my office,' he says, tapping the contents of a sachet of dried milk into the steaming cups of tea. 'As you can see, we are struggling to cope.' He removes the tea bags from the cups. 'This used to be a general hospital. TB, measles, kwashiorkor. Now it's a different story. Now everything is AIDS.'

Whistling tunelessly, he hands me one cup and sits behind the desk. He pushes aside a pile of folders and puts his cup down in front of him.

'Eh-ja,' he says. 'We are like a small island in a rising ocean, Mr Cole. The situation is not good. But that is another matter. You must be wondering why Sister Lettah is not here to meet you. She has been on night shift and will only be ready to see you at lunchtime.'

'And you are certain she's the person I am looking for?'

'Oh, yes. There's no doubt. Sister Lettah herself has confirmed it and has been preparing herself for this meeting.'

Preparing herself? The spectre of Chombo looms, then vanishes – another scam seems unimaginable. We sip our tea. Reverend Mkhondo loosens his priest's collar and fans himself with one of the folders.

He goes on: 'It's not a straightforward situation, Mr Cole. Sister Lettah has been afflicted with a very serious disfigurement. The result of terrible brutality. Through the grace of God she has managed to live with this problem, but you should prepare yourself. She has great difficulty speaking. Your meeting will not be easy.' He reaches for a sheaf of papers next to the computer. 'I've taken the liberty of consulting her original pathology report just to put you in the picture – she agreed that I should do this . . .'

The tea scalds my lips; I sip tentatively, sweating, as he reads certain sections of the report. He describes how the injury was inflicted. The information is objective, disengaged, dispassionate. It needs to be. I recoil from putting it all together – I seem capable of only registering isolated bits. A blunt bayonet. Pliers. There are terms I've never heard before: labiodental fricatives, bilabial sonorants and plosives . . .

Outside, I can hear children singing.

Finally Reverend Mkhondo puts the report down. Bizarrely, he has a stab at humour: 'So, to cut a long story short, Sister Lettah will not be whistling any tunes.'

'Tell me, Reverend, with this . . . this impediment, how has she coped?'

'Sister Lettah is a woman of extraordinary fibre. If I were in her shoes, I might have lost the will to live. We take so much for granted. Thanks be to God that we were able to provide a place of refuge for her. In the beginning it was very hard for her to come to terms with her injury. But she responded to our acceptance of her and found true faith in God. Fortunately, she is an Ndebele. As you know, the Ndebeles were originally Zulus, so she at least understands the language and customs of people here. She became very determined to overcome her injury. Because we are a largely autonomous mission, we allowed her to train as a nurse. She has since gone on to do a degree in theology by correspondence. She even became our CPN, our chief professional nurse, for many years. Now she is of retirement age but refuses to give up working.' Reverend Mkhondo shakes his head. 'Through the grace of God, she has overcome all obstacles. Truly, she is an example to us all.'

'How long has she been here?'

'Let me see . . . Nearly twenty years.'

'And how did she get here? It seems incredible that she managed to find her way to this place.'

'In 1988 my predecessor, Reverend Arthur Jones, who has since passed away, travelled up to Zimbabwe and witnessed first-hand the aftermath of the Gukurahundi atrocities in Matabeleland. He came across Lettah who had found temporary refuge in a mission in the small town of Gwanda. When he was told her story, he took pity on her. It was he who persuaded her to come to Hlabisa. He organised her passport and brought her with him when he returned. Reverend Jones was blessed with an abundant heart. When he died seven years ago, Lettah was inconsolable. He was her saviour.'

'It's hard for me to imagine what she has been through.'

'There are reasons why God places limits on our imagination.'

'I'm very anxious to see her.'

'I'm sure you are, Mr Cole. All in good time. Meanwhile, let's finish our tea and I'll show you around the mission. Have you ever been to a mission before?'

I shake my head.

He laughs. 'The blind come to us in many forms. I think you will find it instructive.'

I'm relieved to escape the stifling office, although marching out into the blazing midday sun offers no sound alternative. I sweat profusely; the back of my shirt clings to my skin as we tour the mission. First, I'm shown the small church, with its thatched roof and whitewashed stone walls, built a century ago – now a national monument. Reverend Mkhondo gestures proudly at a blaze of brightly coloured friezes covering the walls. Biblical scenes culminating in the Crucifixion and Resurrection in the apse. All the central characters, including Christ, are black. Reverend Mkhondo tells me these friezes were painted by a patient with tuberculosis back in the sixties. I'm transfixed. While the characters, with their awkward postures and big staring eyes, appear naive, the sophisticated layout and idiomatic leaps of the imagination (the Nativity scene in a traditional beehive hut) are extraordinary. Apparently, attempts were made to force the mission to remove them during the apartheid era – Black Christs have an unfortunate tendency to upset ideological apple carts, Reverend Mkhondo remarks dryly.

Emerging again into the sun, we walk up to a vantage point on the hillside above the mission where Reverend Mkhondo points out the U-shaped hospital, the antenatal clinic, the nurses' hostel, the kitchen and laundry, the maintenance workshops, vegetable gardens, an orchard of avocado trees — all of it, he explains, running on an increasingly limited budget. He stands there for a while, cowed, it seems, by the scope of his responsibilities. Then he leads me down a path towards the hospital. Again, the sound of children singing wafts across. Reverend Mkhondo cups a hand to his ear. 'Ah, the voices of angels,' he says, pointing towards a small modern building abutted by half a dozen prefabs against the security fence. 'That is our orphanage. Sister Lettah will want to show you the children.'

An incongruous sign forbidding firearms catches my eye as we enter the main entrance of the hospital. On the ground floor there are waiting rooms filled with silent people, mostly women, mesmerised by a game show blaring from television sets mounted on the walls. All waiting to receive antiretroviral drugs, Reverend Mkhondo explains. We walk along corridors past long queues outside the counselling and testing units. Safe-sex posters on the walls. Schematic diagrams depicting the causal stages from initial HIV infection to the onset of AIDS. Other posters, ranging from bilharzia symptoms to skin and eye diseases, seem an ironic reminder that this hospital once contended with less fearsome maladies.

Upstairs we pass through wards filled to overflowing. The windows are wide open, letting in a harsh white light. Electric fans spin overhead. A smell of antiseptic soap, soiled sheets, wasting bodies. Gaunt men and women stare at us with haunted eyes as we pass by. Reverend Mkhondo unleashes a barrage of statistics that elsewhere might have been meaningless to me. Of every hundred people they test, seventy-five to eighty will be HIV positive — the tip of the iceberg, he says, since so many avoid being tested in fear of being stigmatised. The HIV prevalence among women attending the antenatal clinic is forty percent. There are at least five million people currently living with HIV in South Africa. Over one thousand AIDS deaths each day. Parts of rural Zululand have been

291

devastated by the epidemic. Families and communities decimated. A situation not helped by an obdurate president who refuses to accept any link between HIV and AIDS, and a health minister who insists a good dose of beetroot, not antiretroviral drugs, is the way to treat HIV. Reverend Mkhondo shakes his head angrily; he suspects the cost of supplying antiretroviral drugs lies behind much of this sort of hocus-pocus. And now the horse has bolted. Too late have they agreed to make drugs available. Too late have they made the drug Nevirapine available to pregnant women to stop mother-to-child transmission of HIV.

As we move from bed to bed, I feel increasingly sapped of strength. Witnessing these withered, haunted souls is torrid, overwhelming. Their looks of hopeless resignation . . . and these are the lucky ones, Reverend Mkhondo reiterates. At least they have someone to care for them and a Christian burial when they die. In other places they are just thrown into mass graves. Forgotten people. He stops at the bed of a young woman who looks wizened, ancient. She lies on her back staring at us, her hands folded limply on her chest.

'Kunjani, tombi?' Reverend Mkhondo asks.

The woman stares back emptily; just her mouth moves as she voices a silent reply.

Reverend Mkhondo turns to me and whispers: 'She has not got long to go. Just one of thousands infected by their husbands returning from the mines. They get drunk and consort with prostitutes, then come home to Zululand and infect their wives and mistresses – that's why there're more women infected than men. This woman's whole family has been wiped out. Her husband is already dead. No brothers, no sisters. Two of her children infected, the others cared for by distant relatives. I tell you, this disease will make this whole country an orphanage.' He turns back to the woman. 'God be with you, tombi.'

We come to the children's wards. What confronts me here is almost too heavy to bear. All I can do is traipse wordlessly beside Reverend Mkhondo. One after another, the shrivelled bodies, the veined skulls, the same gaunt stares. To those who are awake, Reverend Mkhondo delivers a gentle, cheerful greeting. Sakubona, Gibson – did you finish your breakfast this morning? Kunjani, Selina – how are you, sweetie? When these kids look at me something flickers in their eyes. Hope? The fleeting thought that this stranger might possess a miracle cure? I find it hard to breathe. I wasn't expecting to have my heart torn in this way.

'Just the tip of the iceberg, Mr Cole,' Reverend Mkhondo says. 'These are the ones who could have been saved by Nevirapine. Between the bastardry of the government and the hideous superstitions of the people we face an uphill battle.'

'Superstitions?'

'There is a belief among African men that having sex with a virgin will cure AIDS. This has led to young girls – even babies – being raped. Some of the girls in these wards are here because of this obscene practice. That is just one example.'

I suppress the urge to gasp with relief as we emerge from the hospital. But there's more. Reverend Mkhondo points to a large prefab building adjoining the hospital. In it are approximately a dozen beds. A glimpse of a skeletal patient staring into space with glazed eyes, mouth open, just the flicker of a hand denoting life.

'That,' he says, 'is where the conveyor belt ends. That is what we call Ifelekhaya – the house for dying. This is where we put those who are in the very last stage of their sickness.'

'My God,' I say.

He puts a hand on my shoulder. 'I'm sorry to put you through this, Mr Cole. I can see you are shaken by the experience. But it's important for outsiders to know the facts. If only our government ministers would visit more often.' He glances at his watch. 'Ah, it's lunchtime. Can I interest you in a quick bite to eat before we see Sister Lettah?'

'No thanks.'

He laughs. 'Not hungry? Not to worry, I'm sure Sister Lettah will at least have some tea to offer you.'

*

We cross to the nurses' hostel, a long sandstone Victorian building with a green corrugated iron roof, partially obscured behind a row of plane trees. The building is cool inside; we tramp down an echoing passageway past the dormitories, offering glimpses of two or four tidy beds per room, metal lockers with photographs stuck to the doors. Our footsteps echo in the silence; light from clerestory windows above the passage flecks the walls and red polished floor. Reverend Mkhondo explains that because of her long time at the mission Lettah has been allocated single quarters. At the end of the passageway we reach a closed door. Reverend Mkhondo pauses, then knocks. 'Uvukile, Sister?' he calls. 'Good morning. Are you awake?'

Silence, then a muffled voice.

He opens the door and enters. I hesitate at the door, taking in her quarters at a glance: a bedroom, a bathroom and a small kitchen. Above her bed, a framed picture of Christ holding a lamb. The blanket on her neatly made bed is grey with three black stripes across one end. The kitchen has a hot plate, a kettle and a fridge. A crucifix hangs on the wall above a simple wooden table. A smell of soap and tomato soup.

'Kunjani, Sister — how are you?' Reverend Mkhondo says cheerily.

She is sitting at the table, facing us. In front of her is an enamel mug with a plastic spout and a pile of books, including a Bible and a dictionary, and a writing pad on which some neat paragraphs are written. A walking stick with a worn handle leans against the table. She wears a nurse's uniform: a white folded cap pinned to her grey hair; a knee-length purple dress and white blouse with epaulettes; a crucifix and a watch hang over her breast. She has a veil which covers half her face, from the bridge of her nose down, held in place by a cord looped over her ears. The veil is damp over the mouth. When she breathes it billows slightly away from her face. She is stout and very old. The joints of her hands, clasped together on the table, are swollen with arthritis.

'I have brought a visitor,' Reverend Mkhondo says. 'All the way from Australia.' He turns to me. 'Come in, sir. Come closer.'

She stares at me as I come forward. Despite her veil, I recognise her at once – her eyes, though lined and bleary with age, are unmistakeable. Those beautiful almond eyes, like an Egyptian queen. I know without a shadow of doubt that it's her. Lettah. I stand mute, returning her stare.

Reverend Mkhondo laughs. 'Heh–hehh! What a commotion! You mustn't get too excited!'

I find my voice. 'Lettah, I've found you at last. Do you remember me? I'm Frank. Frank Cole. Errol and Lydia's son.'

Lettah nods, a smile in her eyes. From beneath the veil comes a garbled sound: 'Hhrank. Hhrank.'

'As you can see, Sister Lettah cannot pronounce her words properly,' Reverend Mkhondo says. 'Those who are used to it understand her. Strangers have difficulty.'

Lettah gets slowly to her feet and extends both her hands. 'Sahhona, Hhrank.'

I take her dry raspy hands in mine. To my astonishment, my eyes brim with tears, my throat aches. I choke as I embrace her. She stands still in my arms, her face buried in my shoulder.

Reverend Mkhondo shifts his feet uncomfortably. 'I'll leave you alone. Call me if you need me.'

He leaves the room, closing the door quietly behind him.

I regain my composure and loosen my grip on her. She stands back. Her eyes downcast, she speaks slowly, flicking her tongue around syllables: 'Like sunn tea?'

She points at the kettle.

'Tea?' I repeat. 'Yes, please. I'd love some tea.'

Lettah takes her walking stick and shuffles across to the kitchen counter and switches the kettle on. She spoons tea leaves into an aluminium teapot, then watches the kettle intently as it heats up, as though the process demands rapt attention.

Wiping my eyes on my shirt sleeve, I say: 'Reverend Mkhondo has explained what happened to you. He explained the physical nature of your injury. I'm so sorry such a terrible thing happened,

Lettah. The world is a cruel place. What men do to others is beyond comprehension. Please don't feel that you must talk, if it's difficult. I'm just very happy to have found you. I'm just happy to be in your company.'

Lettah glances at me and returns her attention to the kettle. An admonishing glance? I realise immediately that I have been speaking very slowly and loudly, as though she were hard of hearing, or retarded. I wait in silence as the kettle boils and she makes the tea. She opens a cupboard and takes down a cup and saucer and some Marie biscuits. She pours my tea through a strainer and points to a bowl of sugar on the counter. I shake my head. 'No sugar, thank you,' I say. She shuffles across and puts the tea and the biscuits in front of me. Then she takes her enamel mug to the counter, removes the plastic spout and pours herself some tea and replaces the spout. She returns to her chair.

I sip my tea and nibble at one of the biscuits, which is slightly stale. Lettah pushes the spout under the veil, tilts her head back slightly and swallows loudly. It occurs to me that she would have no ability to sip. When I begin to talk, she holds up her hand, gesturing for me to wait. She pushes the writing pad across the table and points to the words she has written. I read the first paragraph out loud:

This is how I communicate with those who cannot understand my speech. You can speak, I write. My heart was glad when I was told that you will be visiting me. I remember you and your family well and have often longed for that time. How are your parents, Errol and Lydia? How is Maxwell?

I look up. 'Max is very well. He is happily married with children. He lives overseas in Australia — in Perth, where I live, where Errol lives. My father is old, but well. He said if I find you to pass on his best wishes. My mother, Lydia, passed away a short while ago. She was very ill. She's the reason I'm here.'

I continue to read:

Reverend Mkhondo said he would explain to you my disfigurement. It is some-
thing I do not like to think about. But for you I will explain. When the soldiers
did this to me I wanted to die. I wanted to die with all my heart. I wished they
had burned me with my family. They called me uMahleka — she who always
laughs. For years I hid because of shame. I covered my mouth with a rag. I
drifted from one place to another in Zimbabwe, an outcast. I lived on the streets,
begging, always wishing I was dead. Then God saved me. He sent Reverend
Jones to save me. To bring me here. It was Reverend Jones who found me and
gave me refuge and purpose. I am no longer ashamed of my disfigurement. I
wear this veil only because it keeps my mouth damp and because it saves others
from discomfort. The children I tend to would be frightened if I did not wear it.
Are you frightened of my disfigurement?

I look at her, astonished at how she anticipated my reactions.

'I'm frightened, Lettah. But I'm prepared for it.'

Lettah returns my stare. She reaches up and releases the veil from around her ears. She folds it neatly and places it on the table in front of her. She keeps looking at me.

I'm not prepared for it. I've been told by Reverend Mkhondo what to expect, but nothing could have prepared me for this. The awfulness defies words. She has no lips. They have been hacked away, crudely, along with the muscle and skin up to her nose and as far down as her chin, leaving only a scarred ridge that makes a ragged grey circle around her teeth and gums, bared in a perpetual grin. I can't help myself. The horror of it makes me close my eyes. In the blackness of my vision, I can see her lips as they used to be. The small scar on the upper lip. Laughing. Always laughing. I force myself to open my eyes, to look at her. I think of the life she has had to lead.

'Hleka,' Lettah says, her tongue flicking behind her teeth, the remnants of muscle around her gums quivering futilely. She points to the word uMahleka on her pad. The name given to her by devils.

Hleka — laugh. One word she can pronounce without difficulty. How is it possible to forgive this? How is such evil possible? What sort of men are capable of this? Men who revel in the terror and suffering of their victims. Capable of herding a whole family into a hut and setting it alight. Listening to the shrieks of the dying, then turning on the family's only survivor, raping her and committing this wickedness. Is this strength? Does strength come down to harming the weak and defenceless without qualm or mercy? How do you combat such strength? By committing the same acts? Must we become evil to fight evil? Must we fight fire with fire?

I'm filled with hatred for the men who maimed her. I wish the same horror could be inflicted on them. Yet Lettah's eyes hold no anger. She watches me undergo my revulsions with a serene patience. She lifts her tea, tilts her head back and drinks. I glimpse her tongue squeezing the spout up against the roof of her mouth.

Bewildered, I shake my head. I reach across and put my hand on hers. 'It's impossible for me to comprehend what you've been through. There are no words for this. I lose faith in everything when I think of the men who committed this evil.'

Lettah frowns. She says something completely unintelligible. I shake my head. She pulls her hand from under mine and reaches across for the pad. She takes a ballpoint pen from the pocket over her breast; slowly, she writes something and pushes the pad back across to me: *No. It is what brings faith. Tell me about Lydia please.*

I explain the circumstances of Lydia's sickness and death. Lettah listens with that expression of serene patience. She shakes her head when she hears of Lydia's suffering; she quietly utters: 'Ah! Ah! Ah!' I explain the details of Lydia's will. At the mention of the money Lettah displays no emotion. She just listens and nods. As I speak, I'm conscious that my eyes are darting about, unable to find a place to land on her face. Sensing my discomfort, Lettah retrieves her veil and fastens it back over her face.

She nods when I finish. 'Thankku,' she says, taking the pad again.

It is sad about your mother. I loved her very much. I am sure she is in heaven. What about you, Frank? Tell me about yourself. Where do you live? Do you have a wife? Do you have children?

Lettah listens as I talk, sucking on her tea every so often. Her eyes linger for a few seconds on my broken nose. I reach a point where telling the story of my life no longer seems to matter. All my little worries, my petty paranoias . . . what are they in the face of Lettah's life? My voice fades to silence.

Outside, the church bell rings.

'I had so much to tell you, Lettah, but it's become so little,' I say.

Lettah's eyes smile. She writes: *Come, let me show you my children.*

We walk down the gravel road towards the hospital. Progress is slow. Lettah shuffles along, aided by her walking stick. It's obvious that her arthritis is not confined to her hands. As she walks, her writing pad, hanging on a chord around her neck, sways from side to side. She hums a tune – hnnn nah, hnn nah nah – and pauses at a tap at the roadside. She leans down and splashes water onto her veil.

'Dry,' she says, pointing at her mouth.

As we walk, I get down to business. 'The money my mother has left for you is waiting in Australia. I can get my father to send over the documents. Once all the paperwork is done the money can be transferred into a bank account here.'

Lettah appears not to hear. She stops to listen to the raucous calls of a flock of hah-de-dahs flying overhead. She mimics them, 'Keh! Keeeh!' and laughs.

'What happened between you and my mother?' I ask. 'All these years I've wondered what happened.'

Lettah looks at me, surprised. Her eyes crease with humour. She gives a wave of her hand, as though dismissing my question.

We turn up a cement path that goes around the hospital and up the hillside to the small modern building and prefabs that Reverend Mkhondo had pointed out earlier. Lettah points her walking stick at the building. 'Ornage,' she says.

'Orphanage?' I say. 'Reverend Mkhondo said you would bring me here.'

There's a sign above the entrance: *Little Flower Children's Home*. We enter a reception office; a young nurse with intricately braided hair behind a computer greets Lettah cheerily: 'Hello, Mama. Kunjani. How are you today?' Lettah splutters a reply unintelligible to me to which the nurse laughs gaily. 'You are my mama. You are everyone's mama!' she says. Lettah introduces me by writing my name on her pad and holding it up for the nurse to see. 'Hello, Mr Cole,' the nurse responds. She points to a badge on her chest. 'My name is Sister Mary Ngobeni.' She briefly explains that she, Lettah and two other nurses run the orphanage. No mean task, apparently. This small team must cope with nearly seventy-five children on a shoestring budget. When she explains that Lettah has forgone her retirement to help keep the orphanage going, Lettah gives an impatient wave of her hand and ushers me out of the office.

I follow her along a corridor and enter a large hall, into a deafen-ing buzz of chatter. Children ranging from infants to early teenagers are crammed around tables, lustily shovelling food into their mouths and talking simultaneously. The walls of the hall are covered with brightly coloured paintings, crayon drawings and cardboard figures with papier-mâché heads. Fans whirr overhead. A strong smell of putu and boiled cabbage.

Lettah claps her hands. 'Hallah!' she calls.

The chatter ceases.

'Hallo, Mama!' the children sing back in chorus.

Lettah points at me. 'Say hallah.'

'Hallo!'

The chatter picks up again. I'm introduced to the other nurse on duty, Sister Dorothy Mvubu, who is busy spoon-feeding a toddler. A plump middle-aged woman, Sister Dorothy has a no-nonsense demeanour.

'What are you doing here, you naughty girl?' she demands of Lettah. 'This is my shift — you are supposed to be resting!'

Lettah laughs and Sister Dorothy's stern façade dissolves into a smile. She holds her hands out helplessly. 'What can we do with her, Mr Cole. All she wants to do is work, work, work!'

We watch while the children finish eating. They appear a happy, exuberant bunch, carrying on like kids anywhere. Boys goofing around, girls giggling. I'm reminded of Rosie and Geldof, of their bright, boundless enthusiasm. But there among the noisy horde, surreptitiously pointed out by Sister Dorothy, are the ones who remind me that these are not normal kids. The quiet ones with the blank stares and nervous gestures. The ones yet to realise that this boisterous mob is their only family now. Sister Dorothy explains the financial struggle to keep the orphanage going. 'We can only trust in God to provide,' she says.

When they are finished Sister Dorothy leads the infants off to some thin foam mattresses on the floor in an adjoining room for their afternoon siesta. Then with a booming voice she tells the rest to stack their bowls and cups on trolleys and go outside and play. While Sister Dorothy ensures the trolleys are properly stacked, Lettah rummages in a cupboard and produces two enamel mugs, one with an identical spout to that which she used in her room. She goes over to a stainless steel urn on a table against the wall and pours tea into the mugs and then leads me out to a long veranda where we sit at a table. She begins writing on her pad. A group of small boys approaches. One of them, carrying a battered soccer ball, asks Lettah a question in Zulu. Lettah laughs and writes: *They want you to play.*

I hesitate, complaining of the heat. Lettah frowns; the boys give a collective groan. Come on, you lazy old oxygen thief, their looks say. Hoisting a half-hearted smile, I step off the veranda into the blazing sun and follow them to a dusty, sloping playground nearby with makeshift goalposts at either end. I find myself in a team of five players; the opposing team numbers eight — I'm mildly flattered the boys deem this surfeit appropriate to even things up. The game commences. For a while I acquit myself reasonably well (one of my cross-kicks even results in a goal). Sadly, though, my inevitable transition from team asset to liability is embarrassingly emphatic and the boys quickly realise, as they begin to run rings around me, that their earlier adult-to-child calculation was seriously flawed. They laugh with delight at my clumsy attempts to control the ball, at my huffing and puffing. They convulse with mirth when one of them dribbles the ball straight through my legs. Every so often, I'm forced to rest, bent over, hands on my knees, sucking in air. I glance over at Lettah on the veranda, busy writing on her pad. A small girl interrupts her, leaning against her, laying her head on her lap. Lettah places her pen down and strokes the girl's head, then continues to write. She writes for a long time. Stoically, I play on, though my contribution now consists of ambling around issuing instructions (the memory of Hazel laughing at my pathetic attempts at soccer as a boy springs cruelly to mind). Each time I look over at Lettah, the little girl still has her head on her lap. Then Lettah lifts the girl's head gently and gets up. She beckons me.

I take leave of the boys and head back to the veranda. The boys stop the game and follow me, imploring me to continue playing. Lettah says something in contorted Zulu that seems to placate them. Sister Dorothy comes out onto the veranda, holding a cup of tea and fanning herself with a newspaper. Lettah points at me and says something to her.

'You are leaving us already!' Sister Dorothy says. She puts the tea and newspaper down on the table and bellows for the children to gather. They come running, surrounding us. Some of the smaller kids cling to Lettah's dress.

'Say goodbye to Sister Lettah and to Mr Cole!' Sister Dorothy booms.

'Goodbye, Mama! Goodbye, Mr Cole!'

Some of my soccer teammates give me high fives. That they could be so charitable gets me a bit choked up.

Lettah and I walk away from the hospital complex, past the church and along a path that leads to a padlocked gate in the security fence. Lettah takes a key from her belt and unlocks the gate. She ushers me through and locks the gate after us. We proceed along a ridge up the hill into the bush surrounding the mission. As the ridge winds around the hill, a valley suddenly opens up in front of us. We come to a wooden bench beneath a big spreading tree. Leaning on her stick, Lettah slowly lowers herself onto the bench; I sit beside her. In front of us the hazy scrub-freckled hills of Zululand stretch out forever.

Lettah cups a hand to her ear. 'Kiet – silence,' she says.

I nod. 'Yes, it's nice and peaceful.'

She gestures out at the vista. 'Nice.'

'Beautiful,' I reply.

She reaches down and picks up a bright red berry off the ground. She studies it closely, breaks it open with her thumbnail and lifts it to her nose, breathing in deeply. Then she flips over a few pages of her pad and writes quickly. When she is finished she hands the pad to me. I read:

> *You can find this same tree in Zimbabwe. Your father once told me the white man's name for it. The dog plum. My father invented his own name for it. The stop-shitting tree. Because its bark could be used to cure dysentery. I don't know why my father had to use such a rude name. But it reminds me of home. Of the good things. That is why I had them put this bench here for me to sit. Here I find peace.*

I hand the pad back to her. She points at the canopy above and says something unintelligible. Seeing my blank look, she shakes her head and waves her hand as though it is unimportant. She flips back the pages of her pad to what she must have been writing on the veranda at the orphanage. She hands the pad to me; I read:

> *I loved Lydia like my own sister. I thought of her as my sister. Deep down, I think Lydia felt the same, though it was not a conscious thing for her. I thought of you all as my family, but I knew I was only your servant. One day Lydia and I were no longer sisters. There was no argument or fight. No event that forced us apart. All there was was the history of the country we shared. It was this history that ensured that we could never be sisters. It was my decision to leave the family, for this very reason. When I heard you were going to South Africa, I made*

the decision then. For what was I to be in the long term? Forever your servant? Forever at the beck and call of my missus? Never sure of my place in this world? No, I decided to go back to the farm. To find a husband, to have children. I would be among family. I would have a father, a mother, my own children.

My decision made Lydia very angry. She saw it as a betrayal. I took her anger as a compliment, as a sign of love. I hoped that her anger would fade, but she could not overcome the upbringing that blinded her. Servants did not disobey. And it was this — Lydia's inability to understand that I just wanted the simple things she herself had in life — that made our lives together impossible. It made Lydia hard and unforgiving. She treated me poorly but I hold nothing against her. I still love the memory of her. The true sadness is that when I left I never married. My husband-to-be would not marry me after I miscarried his child. The sadness is I ended up with no husband, no children. And the history of my country followed me. The history of my country made cruel men violate me and take away my voice.

Please do not carry guilt. There is no guilt to be carried. Your mother was made by our country. It is time to move forward. This money of which you speak. Lydia's money. I am thankful that I was in Lydia's thoughts when she passed away. In this, she has in some way overcome the history that separated us. But I have no need of this money. If you wish to give it away then I ask you to give it to the children here. Then it will have a good purpose.

I look up and stare into the distance. So that was it, the simple answer: two women who might have been sisters, were it not for the history of their country. Just behaving the way their country behaved.

'The money is yours, Lettah,' I say. 'It's yours to do with as you like. If you want to give it to the children, that's your right.'

Lettah shakes her head. She takes the pad from me, scribbles something down and hands it back: *No. I want you — you, Frank — to give the money. You came all this way to find me. It can be your purpose.*

I stare at my feet for a long time, unable to find words, feeling the emptiness that comes with knowing I have not lived my life fully. Yet with this emptiness comes not despair nor desolation, but a pang of hunger for the fullness of what lies ahead. For a purpose that beckons.

'May I keep what you have written? My father would wish to see it.'

Lettah nods. I tear the pages from the pad and hand it back to her.

We sit together looking out over the hills. Lettah reaches across and puts her hand on top of mine. She sighs contentedly. And in this moment, I see the smile beneath her veil, as warm and beautiful as it used to be.

Author's Note

Sincere thanks are due to the following: Peter, Allen, Shaynne, Nabeel and Farida Lang for their invaluable knowledge and support; Kim Cheng Boey and Marika Osmotherly for advice and opinion; Anthony B-W for his patient expertise in IsiNdebele; Karen MacGregor for assisting my AIDS research in South Africa.

I am deeply indebted to Karen Colston of Australian Literary Management for her belief in this novel and tireless efforts to see it in print. Finally, my heartfelt appreciation goes to Madonna Duffy, Rebecca Roberts, Deonie Fiford and the UQP team for making this book a reality.

MORE *CRACKING* FICTION FROM UQP

GONE
Jennifer Mills

There can be no straight road home.

A young man is released from a Sydney prison, his hands empty, his identity gone. He catches a southbound train out of town, then hitchhikes west. He hasn't been home for fifteen years.

For days Frank rides the highway through an unforgiving landscape, surviving on what he finds and the kindness of strangers. As he edges closer to a home he struggles to remember, his boyhood looms. Out of the past, something is coming that will tear through his fragile hold.

Chilling, haunting, suspenseful, *Gone* is a journey through one man's splintered world.

> '*Gone* is a plaintive, intense, and staggering novel, and it sets the bar high for Australian fiction in 2011.'
>
> *Canberra Times*

> 'A chillingly atmospheric Australian mystery'
>
> *Age*

> 'Mills is clearly a talent.'
>
> *Australian Book Review*

ISBN 978 0 7022 3871 0

UQP

MEN OF BAD CHARACTER
Kathleen Stewart

Do you ever really know the man you love?

When Rose's eighteen-year relationship ends in the most shocking and unexpected way, she emerges from years of what she thought was a loving relationship and realises the extent to which she was being emotionally manipulated and controlled. While trying to pick up the threads of her shattered life, she meets a charming and elusive new man. He offers hope and possibilities for the future, but as Rose is drawn further into the labyrinth that is Gary's life, she starts to wonder if he is the man she thought he was.

Compelling and darkly humorous, *Men of Bad Character* is a novel about modern love and dangerous liaisons.

PRAISE FOR KATHLEEN STEWART

'Exquisite, haunting, gripping, intense'

Luke Davies on *The After Life*

'With her growing reputation as an intelligent and discomforting writer prepared to say things often left to lie untouched, Stewart is already a significant voice.'

Sydney Morning Herald

'Stewart writes with sensitivity, keenness and, at times, a hilarious comic touch.'

Canberra Times

ISBN 978 07022 3773 7

UQP

THE UMBRELLA CLUB
David Brooks

The breathtaking new novel from the Miles Franklin-shortlisted author of *The Fern Tattoo*

During World War I a friendship between two young Englishmen, Axel and Edward, is forged on the battlefields of France. There, inspired by barrage balloons, they develop a mutual fascination that will change the course of their lives. After the war, as his passion for flight and freedom consume him, Axel sets off to balloon across the highlands of New Albion, a largely unexplored island north of Australia. When he fails to return, Edward travels to the island to solve the mystery of his friend's disappearance and retrace his final journey. What he finds there will challenge his sanity and his faith.

The Umbrella Club is an adventure to the frontiers of colonial exploration and the depths of the human soul.

'Idea and shadow, substance and illusion play subtle roles in this intriguing mixture of philosophical fable and adventure yarn.'
Sydney Morning Herald

'A gripping and satisfying mystery'
Canberra Times

'A sense of deliberation and imaginative power imbues his work'
Age on The Fern Tattoo

ISBN 978 0 7022 3723 2

UQP

THE CHINA GARDEN
Kristina Olsson

Winner of the Barbara Jefferis Award 2010

Over two hot weeks one summer, cracks emerge in the veneer of a small coastal town.

When a newborn baby is found abandoned in a backyard, this dramatic event pierces the lives of three very different women. Laura has returned home for her mother's funeral after years in exile, only to discover her upbringing was based on a lie. Elderly Cress, who is the moral compass of the community, conceals her own vices, while young Abby walks the streets, her bruises wrapped in baggy clothes. But it is gentle Kieran, an unlikely guardian, who knows their secrets and watches over them.

As their lives collide, what is buried can no longer remain hidden. *The China Garden* is a captivating story about betrayal and its echoes across generations.

'Olsson is a gifted writer with considerable verbal flair . . . a vivid and dramatic novel of small-town secrets.'

Age

'*The China Garden* makes a lovely literary read, particularly for someone who has the time and inclination to set aside an afternoon or two to loll in the sunshine and really immerse themselves in the small town's secrets.'

Bookseller & Publisher

'Without feeling the need to resolve every absence or mystery, Olsson gently suggests that it is always possible to make new things out of the past, however fractured or painful.'

Barbara Jefferis Award judges' comments

ISBN 978 0 7022 3697 6

UQP